Kathy looked to her right. "Hurry, Anna."

They were in the long straight stretch. Anna Tyree jammed the accelerator to the floor just as the vehicle swerved toward her. The impact caught the rear right quarter panel. The front of the car took on a life of its own as Anna fought with the useless steering wheel. In her own headlights she saw the road vanish into an impossible curve.

Kathy saw it, too. "For God's sakes slow down!"

Anna tried. She stood on the brakes, but the car continued to roll forward toward the killer curve. "He's behind us. He's pushing us!"

Her headlights flashed back from the gleaming metal of the oncoming guard rails. The glare blinded her. Finally, her brakes began to squeal. And so did Anna and Kathy . . .

# A.K.A.

## Dave Pedneau

BALLANTINE BOOKS • NEW YORK

Library of Congress Catalog Card Number: 89-92930

ISBN 0-345-35719-1

Manufactured in the United States of America

First Edition: July 1990

FOR DIANE AND CHRIS

# PROLOGUE

UNFRIENDLY EYES watched from the balcony as the woman tucked her bulky purse under her arm and started toward the library's rear door. The woman, although well into middle age, was more attractive than the watcher had expected. A little younger, too. The full cheeks of her ass shifted beneath the tight sheath dress she wore, first to one side and then the other as she walked away from him. Did women practice that walk? Or was it the high heels that made them walk that way? Her dark hair, probably dyed, was trimmed tightly against her head, almost a man's haircut. The watcher savored the view. If the watcher delayed much longer, though, she would be out of the library.

Down on the main floor, assistant librarian Eloise Weldon reached the exit that led to an employee parking area in the rear of the building. She stopped and turned to make a final visual inspection before locking up for the night. She mentally cataloged the list of things that she should have already done. The computers were turned off in the student computer room on the balcony. The library's main computer system had been powered down. The basement doors should still be locked since she had never unlocked them for the brief Sunday shift. She hadn't overlooked anything important. The library was silent, not just people-quiet as it was always supposed to be but rather empty-quiet . . . closing-time quiet.

1

She reached for the main light switch and flipped it. The library went dark.

Upstairs, the watcher quickly kicked the bottom of a metal bookshelf. The boots he wore were black and heavy, and in the hushed gloom of the library the act produced a sound not unlike a gunshot. It echoed twice.

The startled librarian wheeled around and fumbled for the light switch. She clicked it back on.

"Who's up there?" she cried, glaring at the railings that circled the balcony wing of the Milbrook College Library. The student computer room was located on that part of the balcony floor just above her head. It wasn't unusual for kids to try to hide in the library at closing time so they could play computer games late into the night.

Eloise, her purse still clutched under her arm, backed up until she could see the door to the computer room. It was closed, just as she had left it moments before when she had made her final check of all three library floors.

"Stop playing games," she shouted. "Come down this instant."

The volume of her voice made her cringe. Eloise despised jarring sounds in the tranquillity of the library.

She listened for a response. When she received none, she said, "If you come down now, I won't report you to the dean of men." She didn't know why she assumed the after-hours trespassers were male, except for the fact that they always were.

"Damn," she muttered. There was a movie on cable at nine. Eloise had hoped to be home just a few short minutes after it started. Tossing her compact purse onto a nearby table, she started toward the other end of the library and the marble steps that ascended to the balcony floor. As she climbed, her heels clicked sharply on the stone surface. She made no effort to soften the sound, intending that it convey the angry frustration she felt. It hadn't even been her regular

night to work. The head librarian, Julia Pynchon, had asked
Eloise to substitute for her on the normally serene Sunday
night shift. Julia had had a dinner to attend with members of
one of the several garden clubs to which she belonged. Eloise
hadn't minded at all, except that she wanted to be home as
soon as possible because of the movie.

At the top of the steps she paused to listen. The library
was once again empty-quiet. She marched around the
balcony until she reached the door to the computer room.
She flung it open. The seats in front of the dozen ma-
chines were all empty, the screens black. She went to
each and touched the top of the terminal. None of them
was warm.

Perhaps the sound had been nothing more than a pipe
popping. In the cold Appalachian winter, the plumbing hammered and rattled with a distracting vengeance. The racket
was intolerable. How could one expect students to study or
research quietly when the building itself made its own din?
To her credit, Julia Pynchon twice had sent notes to the college maintenance department. Both times the head of the
department had returned a memo saying that nothing could
be done short of installing a new heating system. That wasn't
likely to happen anytime soon. Still, an uncharacteristic
warmth had settled over the central Appalachians that spring,
and the heat had not been on for at least a week. As much
as she wanted to believe that the sound came from the pipes,
Eloise knew better.

She exited the computer room and started into the rows of
bookcases. The shelves in the balcony level housed the library's collection on science and technology. She peered
down each aisle and saw nothing in the shadows thrown by
the high stacks of books. As she searched, she worked her
way back toward the steps.

She said nothing else until she reached them. "If you're
here, you had best come out now. If I have to call secu-

rity—'' She left the threat unspoken. In truth, there was little more she could do than report the offender to the dean of men. If the Dean ran true to form, he would let the student off with a stern father-to-son talk, especially since it was so close to the end of the year.

She peered over the railing at the table-cluttered main floor of the library. Nothing stirred. Eloise shrugged to herself and started back down the steps. She was halfway down, her heels this time making hardly any noise as she descended on the balls of her feet, when a book sailed down from the balcony. It smacked flat and loud on one of the highly polished tables. The sharp crack made Eloise yelp.

She heard footsteps, certainly not her own, and glanced back over her shoulder. Out of the corner of her eye, she thought she saw the silhouette of a human form vanish into one of the aisles between the bookshelves. For the first time, she felt apprehensive, perhaps even a little afraid.

''That's not funny!'' she shouted. ''I'm calling security.''

She trotted down to the bottom of the steps and was heading for the main desk and its telephone when the shower of books started. The first exploded on the floor just in front of her, its yellowed pages ripping free from its aged binding. She stopped. The second book struck a glancing blow to her thigh.

Anxiety blossomed into fear. ''Stop it,'' she cried, this time her tone of command displaced by the whining of a plea.

But the books didn't stop. They pelted down on the floor all around her. She started moving backward. A small volume collided with the back of her neck. She lifted her hands to cover her head.

''For God's sakes, please stop,'' she cried. Tears, produced as much by her fear as her pain, rolled down her cheeks.

An exhaustive study on organic chemistry, fully two inches thick, crashed against the left side of her clavicle. The pain, intense and immediate, paralyzed her upper torso. Her hands dropped down from her head, and she collapsed to the floor, her hips writhing against the agony. Another book, this one on gas chromatography, struck spine first on her nose. Blood splattered the floor around her. On her back as she was, the gush of crimson fluid poured into her eyes, blinding her.

"Oh, God, please," she wailed. In her pain-clouded mind she realized that she might actually die. Fear ballooned into a muscle-tightening terror.

Then the storm of books stopped.

With her right hand she tried to wipe the blood from her eyes. Her face itself was numbed by the sudden shock of agony.

This really isn't happening, she thought. I'm going to wake up, she told herself. Find out this is just a bad, bad dream.

That's when she heard the heavy feet on the marble steps. She turned her head to the side so that she could see. Bone grated against bone. She squealed in pain.

The dark figure, his head round with a shiny mirrored face, towered above her. She tried to blink away the blood—tried to see what this strange and terrible creature was.

"Sorry, Mrs. Pynchon."

She squinted upward. The black, melon-headed intruder blocked out much of the light. "But I'm not—"

Before she finished her sentence, she saw a flash of silver and felt the initial brain-rocking concussion as something metal-heavy impacted against the side of her head. Several more blows softened the left side of her skull. They didn't matter, though. With that very first whipping blow, her eyes had opened wide. Her dilated pupils had locked into position. It had ended for her then—the fear and the pain. The rush of blood from her ruptured skull diminished to an ominous dribble as her heart stopped pumping. She drifted down into the comforting clutch of forever.

# ONE

MONDAY MORNINGS were no worse than any other workday for Whit Pynchon. He felt just as trapped on Fridays as he did at the beginning of a work week. At least it was a warm and sunny Monday. That was more than a little consolation. His job at the prosecuting attorney's office could wait. The morning was just too summer-like. He was tempted not to show up for work at all, but there were a few things he had to do. Those official chores, however, could wait until a little later in the morning.

With acid fertilizer in hand, he went out into his backyard and prepared to feed the towering rhododendrons lining the rear of his property. The swollen buds were just beginning to show tiny slits of purple color. Whit considered himself something of an expert on the shrubs, and he always fed them as soon as he noticed the first hints of color. Several years before he had applied the water and fertilizer mixture much earlier in the spring. The blooms had been sparse and underdeveloped that year. The plants had used the extra strength to produce new growth rather than large, sprawling blooms.

Even after completing that task, which only took about fifteen minutes, he didn't feel any compulsion to rush to the office. Instead, he returned to the kitchen and poured himself a cup of coffee, which he carried out to the wide deck that graced the back of his small house. The wind was almost calm, and the temperature hovered in the low sixties. Not quite as warm as Whit preferred his mornings, but it was about the best one could expect for early May in southern West Virginia, especially since the region was still due—at least historically—for one more killing frost. In one corner of his yard, the fronds of his pale green ferns swayed sensuously in the gentle morning breeze. A fat bumblebee buzzed about the large rhododendron, just as anxious as Whit for the gravid buds to burst open.

He was just finishing the coffee when Anna Tyree, her eyes still heavy from sleep, padded out to join him. A turquoise velour robe covered her shapely body. Balancing her cup of coffee, she settled into a deck chair beside him and started to sneeze.

"Bless you," Whit said.

"This pollen's about to kill me."

"It's probably a cold," Whit said.

She shook her head. "It's an allergy, dammit. Aren't you going to be late for work?"

He shrugged. "What's Tony gonna do? Fire me?"

Tony Danton was the prosecuting attorney of Raven County. He had held the position for nearly twenty years. For more than three-fourths of those years, Whit had served as the office's special investigator.

"You shouldn't take advantage of Tony's friendship," she said.

He chuckled. "Who's taking advantage of who?"

She sneezed again.

"There's some antihistamine in the medicine cabinet."

She pulled a tissue from the pocket of her robe and blew her nose. "It makes me sleepy," she said.

"Things are kinda quiet right now," he said, staring up at the deep azure sky. "Why don't we head down to Myrtle Beach for a few days? They've gone through their pollen season already, and the salty air will cleanse your system."

She shook her head. "The election's less than two weeks away."

"So what? I'm not running for anything. Neither are you."

"But Gil Dickerson is. Or have you forgotten?"

"How can I? It's become your current crusade. Besides, we can get back in time for the election."

"I want to be here until the election—just in case the other side tries to pull something."

"Jesus, Anna. Gil's either gonna win or lose, and there's not much that you're gonna do to change that."

She looked at him, shocked by his suggestion. "We're going to endorse him."

Anna Tyree was editor of the *Milbrook Daily Journal*. When she had first met Whit, she had been a reporter for the paper. The two had clashed immediately. Whit Pynchon had made it clear that, in his estimation, reporters were one step below pond scum on the scale of evolution. Anna, who was then burdened with the horrendous byline of Annie Tyson-Tyree, hadn't cared much for cops. In spite of their mutual dislike for each other's occupation, the two had somehow fallen in love. She had moved into Whit's home during the winter.

"So, you can write the endorsement now. You already know what you're going to say. Kathy can see that it gets in the paper. After all, she is the publisher, and her interest in Gil is probably stronger than yours."

But Anna continued to shake her head. "I don't intend to miss this election. I can't wait to see Jake Brimm's face when Gil whips his ass."

"Aw, c'mon, Anna. If we wait much longer, the damned kids will take over the beach. You know I always go down in the spring."

Anna finished her coffee. "Go on down then. I'm staying here, at least until the election is over."

"What if Gil loses?"

"No way," Anna snapped.

"Brimm's a master of Raven County politics, Anna. Half the damned officeholders in the county can thank him for their jobs."

She stifled another sneeze, then said, "All except Tony Danton, and he's on Gil's side."

Whit had to grant her that, but he said, "Sure, but Tony got elected before Brimm became so powerful."

Anna rose to get another cup of coffee. "Well, I'll tell you this. If Gil loses by one vote, then he oughta kick your narrow-minded ass all over this county."

"Don't start that again, Anna. I've been registered as an independent for years. I can't help it if this crummy state refuses to allow us to vote in their primaries."

"You just like to be a horse's ass, Whit. You of all people should want to keep Brimm out of office. You're the one that says he'd make such a lousy sheriff."

Whit rolled his eyes. "He killed a man, Anna. Murdered him in cold blood when he was sheriff before."

"Which," Anna said quickly, "you couldn't prove."

"He's guilty just the same."

"But you won't lift a finger to see that he doesn't get back into office."

"I won't change my registration."

"It's too late now anyway. The deadline's past." She vanished into the kitchen. He rose and flung the dregs from his coffee cup out into the thick stand of grass below the deck. From inside the house he heard the ringing of the phone.

"I'm already gone," he shouted to Anna.

Too late, though. She handed the cordless phone out the back door. "It's Tony," she said.

"Gee, thanks." He accepted it. "Morning, boss."

"I didn't realize today was a holiday," Tony Danton said. Whit glanced at his watch and saw that it was almost nine-fifteen. As a rule he was in the office by eight-thirty. "I was enjoying this beautiful morning."

"Well, enough of that," the prosecutor said. "Don't bother coming by the office."

Whit smiled. "Are you firing me, I hope?"

"Not today. You've got a crime scene to visit. Pronto!"

"A crime scene?"

"Yeah, hotshot. A homicide. And you're gonna love the circumstances."

The smile was gone from Whit's face. "Why do I get the feeling that you are just about to shove one up my ass?"

"Because I am, pal. One of the assistant librarians at Milbrook College was murdered sometime last night. Your ex-wife discovered the body when she came in for work this morning."

"Sweet Jesus, no!"

"Yeah, and right now the campus security force is securing the scene. Need I say more?"

"I'm on my way," Whit said.

"Step on it. They called in the complaint about eight-twenty. I kept waiting, thinking that you would honor us with your presence. The president of the college just called back. They'd like to remove the body from the middle of their library."

"I said I was on my way—just as soon as you stop yapping at me."

"Bye." The prosecutor hung up.

Whit carried the phone back into the kitchen.

"What's going on?" Anna asked.

After living with the woman for several months, Whit had learned the futility of trying to withhold such things as homicides. He still kept a lot to himself, but only when it was necessary. "There was a murder at the college library last night. Julia—of all people—found the body."

"A student?"

"No, one of the assistant librarians."

"Who would wanna kill a librarian?"

"As soon as I know, you'll know." Whit had gone to his closet and was pulling down the small .357 that he carried. He slipped the holster inside his belt. In deference to the warmth, he selected a lightweight tan sports coat instead of the tan corduroy that he usually wore.

"Can I tag along?" Anna asked.

Whit glared at her. "No way."

"I can be ready in five minutes." That was true. Anna Tyree woke up beautiful. Blessed with skin that appeared to always sport a tan, she used hardly any makeup. Her eyelashes and eyebrows were a shade darker than her auburn hair. "All I have to do is dress. I can do the rest in the car."

"I'm out of here," Whit said, not giving her a chance to say anything.

"You son of a—"

He slammed the door on her epithet.

Norman Meeks was mad. As captain of Milbrook College's five-man security force, he figured he could handle a homicide case as well as the next cop. After all, college security officers had the same authority on campus as a deputy sheriff. Like most police officers in the state, he had attended the West Virginia State Police Academy near Charleston. None of that, though, had made the slightest impression on the sniveling wimp who served as president of the college. The guy had called the sheriff's department anyway. They in turn had called the prosecuting attorney, who was sending out some special investigator.

The body remained on the floor, the books scattered around it. A plastic trash bag covered her upper torso. The president had ordered that, too. Meeks sat on a library table with Bill Conners, one of the county deputies who had stopped by to see if the college officers needed any help.

"Who is this guy, anyway?" Meeks asked.

"Pynchon?"

"Yeah—if that's his name."

Conners, one of the veteran county officers, smiled. "If you ain't met Whit Pynchon, then I feel sorry for you."

"Our head librarian is named Pynchon."

"She's his ex, I hear."

"No shittin'," Meeks said. "Talk about a tight-assed bitch. What's the story on him?"

"Not for me to say, Norm."

"Why?"

"Just best I don't say much," Conners said.

An ambulance crew waited beside a stretcher. They had already unrolled a coal-black body bag.

"C'mon, Bill, what's the deal? If that bastard of a president didn't want me handling this, what was wrong with you guys doing it?"

Conners shook his head. "Don't ask me. Pynchon investigates all homicides in the county. That's the way the prosecutor wants it, and what the prosecutor wants he gets."

"Sounds like a lotta bullshit to me."

The deputy glanced around to be certain no one was within hearing distance. "Pynchon's the prosecutor's fair-haired boy. He also likes giving us regular cops a hard time."

"The prosecutor?" Meeks asked.

"I meant Pynchon. If somebody claims we roughed them up, or if someone accuses us of something wrong, Pynchon handles the investigation. He's got no love for us guys in uniform. I haven't had much contact with him myself, but I hear he's a real bastard. Fact is, several years ago he tried to pin a murder rap on the guy who was sheriff then. Most of the guys at the department hate his guts."

"Which sheriff?"

"Jake Brimm."

"Oh yeah, the one running for sheriff."

"We gotta watch what we say because Dickerson, the newly appointed sheriff, and Pynchon are asshole buddies."

"Sounds like I oughta vote for Brimm," Meeks said.

Bill Conners smiled. "Yeah, you sure oughta."

Meeks shoved his hefty body off the library table and pulled the Sam Browne belt up around his ample midriff. "Well, if this Pynchon thinks he's gonna come marching in here and give us a hard way to go, he's got another think comin'. I'm state civil service, and I don't hafta take crap off nobody."

A tall, stately man, dressed in a light gray pin-stripe suit, stuck his head out of the office of the head librarian.

"That's Hardison," Meeks whispered.

Conners squinted at the approaching figure. "Who?"

"The college president," Meeks said quickly.

Willard Hardison made a wide circle to avoid the body. He kept his eyes averted from it as he walked up to the head of his security department. "Has Investigator Pynchon arrived yet?"

Meeks, still very much irritated, just shook his head.

"Where on earth can he be? I've called twice. We need to get . . . uh, to put things back in some semblance of order. It's exam time, and students require access to the library."

The county deputy, who was still seated on the library table, eased himself off and offered his hand to the college president. "I'm Deputy Conners."

Hardison, his own hand trembling, weakly grasped the deputy's. "Thank you for coming."

"From what I know about Pynchon, I suspect your library will be tied up most of the day."

The president had thick wavy gray hair and bushy gray eyebrows, the latter so long that they tended to curl up toward his low forehead. When he knitted them, as he was doing at that moment, the ends almost reached his hairline. "I can't understand what's keeping him."

"Pynchon operates on his own schedule," the deputy said.

Hardison nodded back toward the office of the librarian. "Mrs. Pynchon was just telling me the same thing. Perhaps I erred in phoning the sheriff's department, Captain."

"I told you we could take care of it."

Hardison kept glancing toward the front door. "Please understand, Captain. I'm not accustomed to dealing with . . . with—" He was waving his hand at the body.

"We've been trained by the state, sir. Me and the boys coulda handled it."

The president glanced at the Rolex on his wrist. "Perhaps I should phone the prosecutor's office and advise them that I do wish this to be handled in-house, so to speak."

The deputy sheriff laughed. "Don't mean to butt in, sir, but you'd be wastin' your time. The prosecutor'll want Pynchon to take charge of the investigation. That's his policy."

"Then he should be here!" the president snapped. He wheeled and marched back toward the library office.

"Kinda tense, ain't he?" Conners said.

Meeks glared at the back of the official. "He's a spineless son of a bitch," he whispered.

Conners grinned. "I get the idea you don't like the guy."

"Bastard," Meeks said, still under his breath. He waited for the president to vanish into Mrs. Pynchon's office. "Last year, a bunch of students showed their asses."

The deputy nodded. "I remember, something to do with some building the college was gonna tear down."

"Yeah, the old dorm. Hell, they stopped usin' that building when these kids were still pissin' in their diapers. Nothing but a gawdamned eyesore, so the state decided to take it down. Well, you remember—the students started raising hell. They gave my guys fits, but Mr. Wimp there—the president?"

Conners was nodding that he knew who Mr. Wimp was.

"Well, he tells us just to let the little bastards get it outta their system. The dean of men ain't no better. He sided with Hardison.''

"What did you wanna do, Norm?''

"I thought we oughta busted heads. Kicked ass and took names. You know what I mean. You guys do it all the time.''

"Shit!'' Conners pulled a pouch of chewing tobacco from his hip pocket. With practiced ease he gathered a plug in his fingers and jammed it into his mouth.

"What's that mean?''

"It means shit, Norm. We don't do that kinda stuff no more. Haven't for eight years. Not since Jake Brimm was sheriff.'' The wad of tobacco formed a knot on one side of his face. "Those days are over. All we do is serve civil papers and play like taxi drivers for the damned courts. Hell, the state boy don't do much head knocking anymore. Even if Jake does get elected, and he's gonna, we still won't be doing that stuff anymore.''

One of the members of the ambulance crew moved over to the captain. "Cripes, Meeks, we don't move her soon she's gonna start to smell. What's the holdup?''

Conners beat Meeks to the answer. "Waiting on Pynchon.''

The kid beamed and wheeled back to his buddy. "Told ya, didn't I? It is Pynchon.''

"So you know him, too,'' Meeks said.

The kid turned and nodded. "He reamed my ass one time for trying to revive a murder victim.''

Meeks's mouth dropped. "You're shittin' me?''

The ambulance attendant held up his right hand. "Swear to God. Said I was fuckin' up his evidence.''

"Was the guy dead?'' Conners asked.

The question appeared to stun the kid. "Hell, yes. What does that have to do with it? We're s'posed to try. Leastways we *were* s'posed to. Nowadays, we just stand back when we answer somethin' like this. Makes us look pretty damned sorry, too, but none of us wanna put up with Pynchon's crap."

The door to the librarian's office opened once again, and Hardison stepped out. He didn't bother crossing the thirty feet to the head of his security. Instead, he simply motioned for Meeks.

"Gawdamn it to hell," the captain muttered. But he moved quickly toward his boss.

Conners glanced to the ambulance attendant. "I got a five-spot that says he and Pynchon are into it five minutes after the asshole gets here."

But the kid knew better. "No thanks. I bet it won't be five minutes."

The captain rejoined them. "Pynchon's on his way. The wimp called the prosecutor again. Just like you said, he in-sisted that Pynchon do it."

At that moment the front door to the library opened. For a second time, Meeks hoisted the gun belt up over his belly. "That him?"

They all knew it had to be someone official. Two of Meeks's officers were stationed outside the front door to keep out sightseers.

"Yep," Conners said.

The ambulance attendant said, "I'm gettin' out of his way."

The man stopped just inside the door. He studied the scene. "Don't look like such hot shit to me," Meeks said.

In fact, to the captain of the Milbrook College Security Force, Whit Pynchon looked the part of a wacko college professor. He wore a tan sports coat over jeans. He stood maybe an inch or so taller than Meeks. That would make him six-two or six-three. His hair was gray, still streaked with a few wedges of darker color. His face was tan, like maybe he didn't have so much to do and he could sit out in the sun when other guys had to work.

"What's he doin' just standin' there?" Meeks asked.

"Knowin' Pynchon, lookin' for somebody's ass to rag."

Whit didn't know what to expect at the crime scene. The security officers outside were college employees. Whit hadn't known either of them. At first they had blocked his way, but he flashed his I.D. "Who's in charge?" he'd asked.

The older of the two college cops had nodded toward the door into the library. "He's in there."

"Who?" Whit had asked.

"Captain Meeks."

Once inside, Whit had paused to get an idea of the layout. From the corner of his eye, he had noticed the pear-shaped figure standing near the body. Since he was the only one dressed in the same dark brown uniform as the guards outside, Whit figured him for Meeks. Deputy Bill Conners stood with him.

He moved toward the man. "You Meeks?"

The captain nodded. "Yes, sir . . . in charge of campus security."

Whit glanced down at the body, its face concealed by glistening black plastic. "What's her name?"

"Weldon," Meeks said. "Eloise Weldon."

"She married? Got a family?"

Meeks shrugged. "Damned if I know."

"If you don't, who does?"

"The lady in there," the captain said, nodding toward Julia Pynchon's office.

Whit didn't even allow himself to blink. "What time was she found?"

"A little before eight."

"How come the sheriff's department wasn't called until eight-twenty?"

"We were discussing how we should handle it—and trying to calm Mrs. Pynchon down. Hardison didn't get here until eight-fifteen. He took one look at the body and dashed into Mrs. Pynchon's office. Next thing I knew he'd called you guys. To tell you the truth, Pynchon, we coulda handled this. I've been trained at the academy.''

Whit had been staring down at the body. He allowed his eyes to roll up at the college cop. "Obviously, the president doesn't share your opinion. Where can I find him?''

Meeks felt his face warm up. "Still in there.'' He was nodding back toward Julia Pynchon's office.

Whit knelt down and lifted the trash bag. He grimaced, both as a result of the sight and the smell. She didn't reek of corruption yet. Not enough time for that, but the odor of the dried blood, going rapidly sour, was pungent. Her nose wasn't there anymore. It had been splattered back against the face. Her eyes gazed upward, milky and dry. Dark brown clots of blood matted her short hair. Whit leaned closer to her, his experienced eyes noting the long dark slash on the left side of her head. The wound was nearly concealed by her hair and the sticky crust of blood.

"Anybody touch her?'' he asked, not looking up.

"We know better,'' Meeks said. "Kinda ironic, huh?''

Whit glanced up at the security officer. "What's that?''

"A librarian killed by books.''

"Why do you think that?''

" 'Cause I got two eyes,'' Meeks said.

"So does a monkey.'' Whit turned his attention back to the victim.

"What the hell does that mean?'' Meeks asked.

"It means, Captain, that a good cop shouldn't judge a book by its cover—if you'll pardon the pun.''

Meeks looked over at the deputy sheriff. "What the hell's he talking about?''

"Got me,'' Conners said.

Whit ignored the comment. "Deputy?''

Conners knelt down by Whit, who was fishing in his pocket. "Yes, sir."

"Would you go out to my car?" he asked, handing the officer his keys. "In the trunk there's a package of paper bags and some string. Bring them in here."

Conners frowned. "What for?"

"Just do it, please."

Conners shrugged. "If you say so."

The college president once again emerged from the library's private office. He sagged with relief when he saw the man dressed in plainclothes bending down with the body.

"Are you Investigator Pynchon?" he asked as he approached.

"I am," Whit said. "You must be Hardison."

"President Hardison," the man said. "Mrs. Pynchon would like to see you."

"All in good time."

"She's very upset, Mr. Pynchon."

Whit had permitted the plastic bag to fall back over the woman's face. With a flourish he pulled it away. Hardison flinched and turned away.

"This lady comes first, Hardison. I'll talk to Julia when I'm finished with her."

The president's jaw tensed. "Which will be soon, I hope. Miss Weldon has lain there quite long enough."

"Has anyone arranged for a photographer?" Whit asked.

Hardison shook his head. "Not that I know of."

Whit was looking at Meeks. "Does your department have a camera?"

"I guess so. Maybe somewhere."

"It might be nice to have some crime-scene photos," Whit said. "Juries like to see that kind of thing if we ever end up going to trial in this case."

"Go see if you can find it," Hardison said. "If you can't, I'm certain someone around this campus has one."

"Black and white," Whit said as Meeks started off.

The campus cop turned. "Black and white?"

"Color, too, Captain. But definitely black and white. I thought maybe they had taught you that at the academy."

"Look here, Pynchon—"

But Hardison, too, was puzzled. "No one uses black and white these days, Mr. Pynchon."

"Professional police departments do, Hardison. The courts don't like showing color photos to juries. They say it tends to inflame jurors and undermine their impartiality."

"That's ludicrous."

"Be that as it may," Whit said, "I do require black-and-white photos."

Conners was returning with the items Whit had requested.

"Do you happen to have a camera with you and some black-and-white film?" Whit asked.

The deputy handed Whit the paper bags and small ball of string. "Not with me. We got one back at the department."

"How about asking them to bring it over here?"

Conners glanced at Meeks. "Don't they have one?"

"They're still debating the point," Whit said. "I'd say we'll all be out of here a little faster if your department can provide one."

"Ten four." Conners looked at Hardison. "Got a phone I can use?"

"It's located at the main desk," Hardison said.

Whit had knelt back down beside the body. He took two paper bags from the pack.

"Of what use are those?" Hardison asked.

"They go over the hands," Whit said, breaking off two short lengths of string. "Just in case there's evidence adhering to the hands."

"Evidence?" the president said.

Whit carefully lifted one of the hands. The muscles were rigid with rigor mortis. "Maybe she scratched her attacker and has bits of his flesh or blood beneath her fingernails. Whatever's there should be preserved for the M.E.''

The college president made a face. ''You have an unpleasant job, Mr. Pynchon.''

Whit smiled. ''Yeah, tell me about it.''

''You took your sweet time, Whitley.''

He recognized the voice at once. When he glanced up, Julia Pynchon was standing beside Hardison. Her eyes were swollen and red, her face gray and strained.

''Got here as soon as I could, Julia. I'm told you found her.''

''Can we talk back in the office?'' she asked.

''Just as soon as I'm finished here.'' He secured the bag to the woman's marble-cold wrist with one of the pieces of the string.

''I need to talk to you now!'' she snapped.

The sharp edge to her voice startled Hardison. ''Mrs. Pynchon—''

''Can't you understand?'' she said, her voice trembling. ''It was supposed to be me. That's who he meant to kill.''

# Two

DEPUTY MARSHA VIA wanted to scream. She was on the phone with the judge's secretary, who was telling her that one of the jail's inmates was late for an appointment with a local psychiatrist. She had another line on hold—a call from Conners who was at the scene of a homicide. Two other lines were ringing.

"Damn," she said aloud.

"What on earth's wrong?" the judge's secretary asked.

"This place is crazy. Why in the hell do they put four lines into this place and then only have one person to answer them?"

The secretary chuckled. "I'll hold if you wanna grab the calls. The judge is down in the probation department."

"Thanks. I won't be a second."

She jabbed the hold button and switched to one of the flashing lines. "Sheriff's department."

"It's me, Marsha."

"Oh, Bill." She had meant to key into one of the incoming calls.

"I need—"

"Please hold, Bill . . . just a few more moments."

She punched the hold button again and then jabbed a second flashing line. "Sheriff's department."

"Can I speak to the sheriff?"

"Hold please," Marsha said.

23

"But this is an emergency!"

The woman caught Marsha just before she was placed on hold.

"What's the nature of the emergency?"

"There's a spaceman prowling—"

"Please hold," Marsha said. *A spaceman!* That caller would be last on her list.

The fourth line stopped ringing.

Marsha sighed with relief and quickly tried to remember which button connected her with the judge's secretary. She picked the middle one. "Linda?"

"It's Bill, Marsha. Dammit, don't put me on hold again."

"Sorry, Bill . . . just a few more minutes."

"Marsha!"

She heard him, but she still put him back on hold—for the third time. Christ, she hoped she didn't get the nut case this time, the one with the spaceman. Timidly she keyed into another line. "Linda?"

"This is Judge O'Brien, Deputy Via."

"Oh, good morning, Your Honor."

"It's a busy morning, Marsha. My secretary hasn't time to be left on hold."

"I'm sorry, sir, but—"

"No 'buts.' Please tell me why that prisoner hasn't been delivered to Dr. Punjabi's office."

"My units are tied up, sir. We have a wreck just outside of town . . . a murder—"

"A murder?" the judge said.

"Yes, sir. At the college."

"Who's the victim?"

"An employee of the library from what I understand. I don't have her name yet."

"Well, I'm sorry to hear that, but the inmate still needs to be at the psychiatrist's office at once. I need that report before your people can move him to the penitentiary. I'm certain the sheriff wants him on his way as soon as possible."

*I'm sure the sheriff doesn't give a shit.* That was what Marsha thought. She said, "I'll ask the chief to take him."

"You *tell* the chief to take him," the judge said. "If he doesn't, I'll want to know why."

"Yes, sir."

The phone went dead.

Marsha quickly jumped over to the line on which Conners waited. "Sorry, Bill, but it's been a madhouse here."

"Jesus, Marsha. We've got a corpse here. Do you know how long you've kept me waiting?"

"Screw you, too," she snapped. "I just got reamed by the judge for keeping him waiting. I'm not gonna take any crap off you. What do you want?"

"Don't get your blood pressure up."

"Me?" she said. "It's you—"

"Okay . . . okay. Look, just send someone out with the department's camera."

"Who?"

"Whaddaya mean?"

"I mean, everyone's tied up. If you want it anytime soon, you'd best come after it."

"What about the chief?"

"He doesn't know it yet, but the judge just gave him a medical transport."

"Where the hell is everyone?"

"There's a wreck on Tabernacle Mountain Road. The other two guys are out there."

"Why two?" Conners asked.

"Because it's a bad wreck, dammit. Traffic's snarled."

"Forget it," Conners said.

"Are you coming in?"

The deputy laughed. "Not too soon, Marsha. I'm gonna stay here where it's reasonably quiet."

"You bastard."

This time, he hung up on her.

One button continued to blink. The woman calling about the spaceman was still on the line. For a moment she considered forgetting about it. After all, she did need to track down the chief deputy.

But she decided against that, took a deep breath, and jabbed the button. "Sheriff's department . . . sorry to keep you waiting."

"I could be dead by now," the woman shouted.

"I'm sorry, ma'am, but—"

"I demand to talk to the sheriff."

"He's out," Marsha said. "Can I help you?"

"I need a policeman."

"I'm a deputy sheriff," Marsha countered.

"I mean a real deputy."

"I am a *real* deputy. Listen, if you have a complaint to file, I'll take it. Otherwise, I'm going to hang up."

"You mean I complain about you to you?"

"Lady, why did you call?"

Marsha heard a sharp intake of breath. "I told you! Before you cut me off!"

"I put you on hold."

"Same difference."

"Ma'am, you mentioned something about a spaceman?"

"He's been prowling on my property."

Marsha didn't even have a standard complaint form in front of her, and she doubted this would be one worth writing up anyway. She made notes on the desk pad. "How do you know he's from space?"

"He's got one of those space suits on. It's all black and shiny. The face mask is like a mirror."

"Can you describe him?"

"I just did."

"I mean, height . . . weight—"

"Heaven help us! I could barely see him sneakin' across the yard just outside my house. He went into the woods."

"We'll send a deputy just as soon as we can, ma'am. Please stay inside. It might be a little while before he can get there."

"What if he tries something?"

"Just stay inside," Marsha said. "I'm sure you'll be safe."

"My husband's due home any minute."

"Well, just stay inside until your husband arrives. A deputy will be there as soon as he can."

"Hold on a minute," the woman said. There was a hint of panic in her voice.

"Is something happening right now?" Marsha asked.

"No, it's . . . well, you didn't even ask me my name or where I live."

"Just try to calm down," Whit said to his former wife. They were seated in her office with the college president.

"Calm down? You might be accustomed to dead bodies. I'm not, especially when it's a friend and fellow worker. That was intended to be me, Whitley."

Whit looked at the college president. Hardison looked off to the side, staring down at the floor. He obviously planned to remain neutral on that issue.

"Julia, it certainly could have been you," Whit said. "—if you had been working. You weren't."

"I said it was intended to be me. That's what I meant."

"How can you be certain?"

"I feel it," she said.

"Well, I don't. Now, please try to cooperate with me, Julia. I know this is difficult."

"I have been cooperating," she countered.

"Tell me about the victim."

"Eloise Weldon. She does have a name, Whitley."

Whit sighed. "Yes, Julia. I know. What do you know about her?"

"Volumes, Whitley. Precisely what do you want to know?"

"Jesus, Julia—"

"I mean it, Whitley. I know a great deal about her. It would take a long time to relate it all to you. Please ask me specific questions."

Whit clinched his teeth. "If that's how you want it, Julia, that's fine by me. Was she married?"

"Divorced."

"And where can I find her former husband?"

"He isn't a suspect," Julia said.

"How the hell do you know?" Whit asked, piqued by her response.

"No need for your crassness. I know because her former husband is deceased. He died of a stroke several years ago."

"Any children?" Whit asked, trying to keep their discussion as professional as was possible.

"Two, both of whom live in Florida. Who will notify them?"

Whit glanced up at her. "If her friends don't want to, then I'll ask the sheriff's department to pass a message through channels."

"That's cold-blooded," she said.

Whit smiled at her. "Hey, feel free to call them yourself."

"I'll call," the president said. Those were the first words he had spoken since the three of them had entered the office.

"Thank you," Whit said. "Now, Julia, can you think of anyone who might have had something against the victim?"

"Eloise," Julia said. "Her name is—"

"I'm sorry. Eloise then."

"I told you that I feel I was the intended victim."

Whit nodded. "Yeah, you've told me, and I'll certainly

consider that angle. But do it my way, Julia. I'm the investigator. Do you know of anyone—''

"No," she snapped.

"Think about it, Julia. Don't just react because you're mad at me. This is serious."

"I found her! I know how serious it is! It took you half the morning to get here."

Whit flipped his notebook closed. "Hardison, would you excuse us for a minute?"

The president looked to Julia. "Do you want me to remain?"

She glared at Whit. "No, sir. I can assure you that I can handle the investigator."

"I really think I should stay, Investigator Pynchon."

Whit just pointed toward the door.

"I am the president of this college, and—"

"I appreciate that," Whit said, "and you'll still be president on the other side of that door."

Hardison shrugged and hurried from the office. Whit stood and started to pace. "Julia, I'm sorry that I'm the one who has to investigate this. It would be easier for us both if there was someone else, but there's not."

"What's the point, Whitley? What I said was true. It did take you forever to get here."

"That doesn't mean I'm not taking this homicide seriously. I need some information from you. I need it quickly and succinctly, unflavored—if you will—by your dislike for me."

For the first time she seemed to relax. "I don't dislike you, Whitley."

He laughed. "Christ, you coulda fooled me. Hell, you have fooled me—for many years."

"I'm just upset. It really was supposed to have been me." This time there was no defiance in her voice. In fact, when Whit looked at her, he saw the shimmer of moisture in her eyes. The last time he had witnessed such an event had been many, many years ago on the day they had decided to get a divorce.

"And this coming on top of the mess with Tressa?"

Tressa was their daughter. She lived with her mother but spent a lot of her time with Whit. In a few weeks she was to graduate from high school. "What about Tressa?" Whit asked.

"That man she's seeing."

"Give it time, Julia. It's an infatuation. It'll wear off."

"You keep saying that, and she keeps seeing him. He's not right for her. I tried to talk to her this morning, but she walked out on me. She gets that aspect of her personality from you."

"They're not engaged yet or anything like that, Julia."

"It's coming. I feel it. He's much too old for her."

"He's three years older than she is." Whit settled down on the desk in front of his former wife. "I don't want her making any mistakes either, but I have faith in her. If we try to make her stop seeing him, we'll just make it worse. She got that from me, too."

"Don't remind me," Julia said.

"Let's get back to what happened here."

She looked up at him. "Will you talk to her, Whit? To Tressa, I mean. Try to talk some sense into her."

*Whit?* She hadn't called him that for years either. "What makes you think she'll listen to me?"

"She always listens to you. I had to raise her. I always had to be the ogre, the one to tell her no. You were the one who always spoiled her."

"No, I did not, Julia. I—" Whit stopped. "Let's talk about this later. I need to get this crime scene wrapped up."

"So go wrap it up. I'll be okay."

"I have some questions, Julia. I need to know about the vic . . . about Mrs. Weldon."

She nodded. "I know. But I can't think of anything that would really help you. She worked here, and she went home. That was her life—except in the summer when she went down to stay with her two kids. She never wanted to work during the summer sessions. She spent half the summer with one and half with the other. She was already making plans for this year."

"Did she ever date?"

Julia seemed stunned by the question. "Eloise?"

"From what I could tell, she wasn't that old."

"Forty-five."

"And she was attractive."

But Julia was shaking her head. "Yes, she was. She never dated."

"Maybe she just didn't talk about it at work."

"Whitley, I do not think she dated. I cannot prove it beyond a reasonable doubt if that's what you want."

"What about her work here? Any enemies?"

"For God's sakes, Whitley, who makes enemies working in a library? College students don't commit murder because of fines for overdue books."

"Why then do you think someone wanted to kill you?"

Julia slowly shook her head. "I'm certain I have no idea, but I just have this sense that I was supposed to have been the victim."

Whit, who was mentally toying with a theory, ignored her suggestion. "Libraries are quiet places. They have lots of dark corners, nooks, and crannies. Are you aware of any suspicious activity going on in here?"

His former wife was frowning. "I don't understand your meaning."

"Well, I was thinking—"

A knock on the door interrupted him. Bill Conners, the Raven County deputy, eased open the door.

"What is it?" Whit asked, annoyed by the disturbance.

"I got a problem getting a camera."

Whit tensed. "I want crime-scene photos."

"Well, there's a photographer outside," Conners said.

"Outside?"

Conners nodded. "Yeah . . . from the newspaper. He said he'd make photos for us."

"No damned way," Whit said. "Let me guess. Anna's with him."

"Sure is," Conners said. "She wants to see you."

"Jesus Christ."

"Is this Anna Tyree?" Julia asked.

"I'll take care of it," Whit said.

"But surely the newspaper wouldn't publish a photo of Eloise? Not like she is."

Whit was heading toward the door. "I said I'd handle it."

"Just one minute, Whitley Pynchon." Julia's voice was sharp enough that Whit stopped.

"What were you going to ask me about suspicious activity?"

"Drugs, Julia. I was wondering if students might have been using the library as a safe place to exchange or even sell drugs."

The suggestion stunned Julia. "I've never thought about it. I don't think so. I've certainly never noticed any indication of—"

"Think about it," Whit said. "I'm going out to talk to Anna."

Once out of the office, Conners stopped Whit. "Looks to me like it solves the problem if we let that newspaper guy shoot the photos."

"What about your department's equipment?" Whit asked as he marched toward the front door of the library.

"There's no one to bring it here."

"And you can't go get it?"

"Damn, Pynchon. There's a photographer right here. He's better at it than me."

"But he's also with the fuckin' press, Conners."

"So what? They ain't gonna run no body shots."

The size of the crowd gathered outside the library building infuriated Whit. "Look at 'em," he said to the deputy as they stepped out into the warm morning air. "They're ghouls! They all want to see some blood and guts."

"That's the public we serve, Whit."

"Friggin' ghouls," Whit said again. He saw Anna standing down at the bottom of the steps that led up to the library. She was talking with Hardison, the college president, but was looking up at Whit. A young man with a small 35-mm camera around his neck and a bag of equipment in his hand stood with her.

"The crowd's gettin' bigger," Conners said. "I don't wanna tell you your business, but I'd say you best get the body out of there as soon as you can."

"Where the hell are the college security people?"

Conners pointed back at the library. "In there. Norm Meeks and the other guys are all that's working today."

"Go back in there and tell them to get out and start dispersing this crowd."

"What about the photos? If you want me to go after the department camera, I'd best be on the way."

"Just go back in there and get Meeks and his buddies."

Conners shrugged. "Ten four."

Whit motioned to Anna. She detached herself from her conversation with Hardison and climbed the steps. The photographer followed her. To Whit, he didn't look as old as most of the students who milled about the lawn in front of the library.

"Didn't you think I'd tell you about it?" he said.

She smiled. "I figured you'd tell me what you wanted me to know."

"Can this guy—" Whit nodded toward the photographer, "—take some crime-scene shots for us?"

Anna's eyes widened. "You're kidding me?"

"Dammit, Anna—"

"Okay . . . okay. I'm just shocked that you would even consider the idea."

"I'm backed into a corner. We need to move the victim as soon as we can."

Anna glanced back at the photographer. "How about it?"

The young man's jaws worked furiously on a piece of gum. "Whatever you say, boss lady."

Whit rolled his eyes. "Boss lady?"

"Bugs you, huh?" Anna winked at him.

"Look, Anna, I need some photos—"

"I know what you need," she said. "What about what we need—a shot or two for the paper."

"Not of the body."

Anna made a face. "C'mon, Whit, you know we're not going to run any splatter and gore in a family paper. I thought maybe we could get a shot of you bending over the victim, assuming the body's covered, of course."

"No damned way," Whit said. "There are some college security guys in there and a deputy. Take pictures of them. They'll love it."

"I want one of you. I don't think we've ever published a photo of you before."

"And you won't this time either."

Anna shrugged. "Suit yourself. We'll just wait out here for the ambulance crew to come out with the body."

The muscles in Whit's jaws flexed. "You're blackmailing me, Anna."

She wheeled on him. "No, I'm not. You're the chief investigator in this case. I want a picture of you investigating. That's all."

Whit looked to the photographer. "Can you do both color and black-and-white?"

The photog patted the bulging case. "You bet."

Whit turned to Anna. "Just one shot of me."

But the editor of the *Journal* wasn't ready to yield. "We always take several, Whit. Just in case we get back to the office and discover that something fouled up. It's policy."

The anger on Whit's face faded into a look of submission. "Whatever . . . let's just get it over with so we can load up the poor woman."

They started into the library.

"Is Julia in there?" Anna asked.

"Yeah, and she's pretty upset."

"In other words, I'm in for a hard time from her, too."

"Not at all," Whit said. "For once she's too shaken to practice the black art of bitchcraft."

They were at the door. Anna stopped. "What did you say?"

It caught Whit by surprise. "Whaddaya mean?"

"Did you say bitchcraft?"

Whit was holding the door open. The photographer headed on inside. "Yeah, that's what I said."

"Bitchcraft?"

"I made up the word," Whit said, "right after I met you."

Maude Mann glanced at the old pendulum clock atop the mantel. It was 10:05 A.M. and still the law had not arrived. She had called them over forty-five minutes ago. Archie, her husband, was late, too. Usually, it just took him an hour to drive in to the post office in Milbrook, pick up the social security check, and deposit it in the bank. Unless he had to stop for medicine at the drugstore, he was always back by nine-thirty at the latest.

She started to reach for the phone to call the law, but a sharp thrust of pain in her shoulder made her wince.

"Lord, give me strength," she said aloud.

With each passing day, her arthritis worsened. If only they'd let her keep taking the cortisone. After one or two doses of the small white pills, the agony in her aging joints eased. Her doctor, though, had refused to renew her last prescription.

"It has side effects, Mrs. Mann. Cortisone produces physical dependency, and it can increase your chances of developing leukemia," the young Indian physician had said.

So what, Maude had thought. At least the stuff made the pain tolerable. At her age what difference did those other things make? On the way home from his office, her husband had said that the doctor was just afraid of getting sued. Maybe she ought to sue him for not giving her the medicine. That would show him.

A muted thump from outside jarred the old woman back to the dilemma of the present. She had been hobbling in from the kitchen an hour or so earlier when she had seen it through the front window. The figure, all dressed in sleek black and unrecognizable because of the round mask, had moved right across her front yard.

Her heart had fluttered at the sight as the oddly dressed trespasser had vanished into the thick woods on the eastern side of the yard. She had moved as quickly as her condition permitted to the phone and had called the sheriff's office.

For what good that did, she thought, glancing again at the mantel clock.

"C'mon, Archie. Get your butt home." The old fool, he was probably chewing the fat with some other retired miner there at the post office.

She thought about pushing herself to her feet and going to the front window again. She was steeling herself against the pain when she heard the throaty rumble. The force of the noise rattled the windows of the small log cabin.

"Dear God," she prayed.

The sound intensified. It reminded her of an old tractor that Archie had owned back when he was able to farm their place, except that this was much louder. Maude tried to get up. Her gnarled hand reach for the aluminum walker that she used for support. Somehow, though, in her frightened state she misjudged the distance she had to reach and struck the metal contraption with her red, swollen wrist. The immediate shock of the pain brought tears to her eyes. For that short instant she forgot about the loud racket from outside. By the time the pain subsided, the noise had stopped.

# THREE

GIL DICKERSON HAD been sheriff of Raven County only for a few short months, and already he was wondering if he had made a mistake in accepting the appointment. As he drove the black Oldsmobile furnished to him by the county down Milbrook's main street toward the offices of the newspaper, he reflected on the events that had landed him in the job. At the time he had been flabbergasted that the Raven County Commission had even given him any consideration. Sure, he had wanted the job, but he wasn't a politician. He was a cop. At least he had been a cop until a year or so before when a bullet shattered his knee. After the surgery and his slow recovery he had retained his title as lieutenant with the sheriff's department, but the chief deputy had assigned him to a desk job. Following the untimely death of Ted Early, the incumbent sheriff, it had been Tony Danton, the Raven County prosecutor, who had come to Gil to see if he was interested.

"You gotta be kiddin'," Gil had said.

But Danton hadn't been kidding. Nor did he pull any punches with Gil. "I wanted Whit Pynchon to accept the appointment," Tony had told him, "but you know Pynchon."

Gil had laughed. Yeah, he knew Whit, and he found it hilarious that the prosecutor would have even broached the subject with his cantankerous investigator.

But Tony had more to tell Gil. "If the commission gives

you the appointment, it will be because they think you'll make a weak candidate in the primary. That way, Jake Brimm can have a better shot at the nomination."

Gil knew Brimm. In fact, Brimm had hired Gil as a deputy some ten years before. More than that, Gil knew just how potent Brimm was in Raven County political circles.

Gil had been puzzled. "So why don't they just appoint Brimm?"

Tony had smiled. "That's the rest of the bad news. There's only a few months left of Early's term. If you take the appointment, it means you can only serve one full term as sheriff—if you get elected."

Gil hadn't tried to conceal his ignorance. "I don't understand. Why not?"

"In West Virginia a sheriff can only serve two consecutive terms. Then he has to step down, at least for one full term, after which he's eligible to run again."

"I know that," Gil said.

"Well, any part of a partial term counts as one of those two terms."

"I see. And Brimm wants to have two full terms—again."

Tony had nodded. "And he thinks that you, a political virgin, will be easy pickings."

Gil had agreed to accept the appointment, and he had agreed to run for the office even if he could only serve one term. At the time it had represented a preferable alternative to filling out crime statistic reports and filing warrants all day long.

Now, however, with a mere two weeks before the election, it appeared as if his term as sheriff was going to come to a premature end. By all assessments Brimm was probably going to whip Gil's political ass. Most of the county's political types were supporting the former sheriff. They had no choice. They owed Brimm.

On Gil's side of the slate, he had the help of Tony Danton and the *Milbrook Daily Journal*. In fact, he was heading to the newspaper so that they could take his photo. Anna Tyree intended to run it beside a front-page editorial endorsing his candidacy.

Driving was one of the normally routine aspects of daily life that gave Gil the most trouble. His knee remained quite stiff and painful. In the cramped quarters of the car, it throbbed almost constantly. He sighed with relief as he braked to a stop in front of the *Journal*'s office. Usually he wore a sports coat and tie to work, but on this day he had donned the uniform of the sheriff. He glanced in the rearview mirror and straightened the black tie. The gold trim of the uniform glittered in the bright spring sunlight.

When he stepped out of the car, he saw Katherine Binder, the owner and publisher of the newspaper, standing behind the front door. She was smiling at him. She wore a dress with a heavy floral pattern and a low waist that appeared to add a few pounds to her thin figure. With her light blond hair and flawless but pale complexion, she reminded Gil of a teenage girl on the verge of womanhood. He hiked the gun belt up around his waist and started inside. In the glass of the door he could see his own crippled reflection. It made him cringe. He looked young enough, his hair still a rich dark brown and his face free of wrinkles. However, the trim figure of which he had always been so proud was a memory. Not that he was fat. He just wasn't trim anymore. His waist was as big as his chest. It came from a lack of exercise—that plus the fact that in the past year he just hadn't cared much. That attitude had changed, though, and he now paid weekly visits to a physical therapist who had designed a series of exercises that didn't stress his patched-up knee.

The publisher opened the door for him. "You were primping," she said, smiling.

"Just checking my tie."

"I hope you can wait a few minutes," she said as she escorted him through the front offices.

"Sure, but where's Anna? I thought she was going to meet me." He followed the publisher toward her private office.

"She's at the scene of a murder."

Gil stopped. "A murder? The one at the college library?" Marsha Via, the dayside's dispatcher, had told him about it.

Kathy had stopped, too. "Yes, and I'd say she and Whit are already at each other's throats."

"She was just going to have my picture made. I guess we could go on and do that."

Kathy was shaking her head. "Sorry, she took the photographer with her. You'll just have to come in my office and have a cup of coffee."

At that moment the publisher's secretary—as if on cue—appeared with two steaming ceramic mugs. She offered one to Gil. "Two sugars, Sheriff. Isn't that right?"

Gil accepted it. "That's right."

Kathy was holding the door open to her office. "C'mon inside."

Gil balanced the hot coffee carefully as he stepped into the ornately decorated inner sanctum. He waited for her to close the door. "Your office decor still reminds me of a New Orleans whorehouse."

Kathy took the coffee and set it down on a table in front of a couch. She set her own beside it and then turned back to him. "And just how many New Orleans whorehouses have you visited?"

The sheriff smiled. "Well, since you put it that way, maybe I should say the place looks like your typical sleazy lawyer's office."

She laughed. "You sound like Whit Pynchon."

"I've been accused of worse." Gil stepped close to her, leaned over, and pressed his lips against hers. His hands remained down at his side. They kissed that way—with just their lips touching—for a long time before Kathy finally wrapped her arms around the back of his neck.

"Some photographer you got there," Whit said as he and Anna waited beside the body of Eloise Weldon.

"For chrissakes, Whit, most folks aren't as jaded as you. He got sick. He couldn't help it."

Bill Conners was grinning. "I thought for a moment that he was gonna puke all over the corpse. Hell, she ain't that bad. She hasn't even started to smell yet."

Whit looked at his watch. "If we don't get things movin' along here, she's gonna start to do just that."

The color in Anna's face heightened. She was glancing around the library. The only other people in the library were the college security men and the ambulance crew. They stood at the front door and could not hear the conversation.

"That's what I like about cops," she then said. "You all have so much compassion."

"What's that supposed to mean?" Whit said.

"Jesus, Whit. The poor woman's dead. Someone beat her to death with books. To hear you two talk, she's nothing more than a hunk of meat."

"That's all she is now," Conners said.

Anna whipped out her notebook. "You want me to quote you on that, Deputy?"

It was Conners's turn to fly mad. "Hell, no! Look, lady—Miss Tyree—you're the one that wanted in here so damned bad."

Whit stepped between them. "Easy, Bill. Go down to the bathroom and check on the kid."

"Yeah, maybe I'd better before I say somethin' I'll regret."

Once he was out of sight, Whit said to Anna, "You were

out of bounds. Cops have to develop some form of defense to the things they see.''

"But you're both so cold-blooded. I mean it, Whit. How can you stand over this woman and joke about her?''

"Do you think she can hear?''

Anna jabbed a finger at him. "*That* is just what I'm talking about.''

"Well, do you? Do you think she can hear?''

"I could hear,'' Anna said.

"We didn't force you to listen, or even to be here for that matter.''

Conners reappeared with the young photographer in tow. The kid's face remained a pasty green, and he was wiping it with a wet handkerchief.

"He's still pretty shaky,'' Conners said, not quite repressing his smile.

"I can handle it,'' the photographer responded.

"Good,'' Whit said. "As I told you before, I want both black and white and color.''

"Gotcha.'' The kid lifted the camera to his eye to frame the shot. "What's those paper bags on her hands—''

Anna interrupted. "Before you start taking his photos, how about taking ours? Just get a shot of Whit and the deputy looking down. Don't get her in the shot.''

Whit was smiling.

"What's so funny?'' she asked.

"Now who's cold-blooded?''

"I've got a job to do.''

"Exactly, and so do I. If you care as much for the dead lady's dignity as you say you do, then you'll let us get our shots and get her out of here before the flies start to gather.''

"What are those bags for?'' the young photographer asked again.

Before anyone could say anything else, Hardison and Julia

Pynchon exited Julia's office. Whit moved to meet them half-way.

"We'll be done in a few minutes," he told them.

A slight twitch had developed above the college president's right eye. "Does it always take this long?"

"Sometimes," Whit said, suppressing a more caustic reply.

"Mrs. Pynchon and I were wondering about something. Will it be necessary to draw one of those chalk body outlines on the floor?"

Whit laughed. He couldn't help himself.

"What's so amusing?" Julia asked.

"I've never really understood what purpose that serves," Whit said. "I think we can avoid defacing your floor."

"It's not that," Hardison said. "It's just . . . well, exam time is approaching, and the students need access to the library. It could be distracting."

"What about fingerprints?" Julia asked.

This time, Whit withheld his amusement. Instead, he just shook his head. "If we did that, then every student who used the library this semester would end up as a suspect. There are some public crime scenes where fingerprinting is totally useless."

A flash went off behind them.

Julia moaned. "Eloise would just die if she—" She stopped. "I mean—"

"The crime itself aside, that's one of the real horrors about murder," Whit said. "We'd all like to die gracefully. Maintain our dignity. A killer robs us of that one final hope."

Julia blinked. Hardison seemed surprised. "You're something of a philosopher, Mr. Pynchon."

"Yeah, it's one of my many flaws."

Norm Meeks, the captain of the college security force,

joined the group. "Mrs. Pynchon, there's a young lady outside who says she's your daughter."

"Tressa?"

Whit and his former wife traded concerned glances.

Meeks continued. "She heard that someone here was killed, and she was worried—"

"The small town grapevine," Whit said. "I'll go talk to her."

"Just let her in," Julia said.

Whit glanced toward the body. "You want her to see that?"

"Cover her, Whitley."

"Christ, Julia, the guy's still taking pictures."

But it was too late. Anna was leading the Pynchons' daughter around the side of the library out of direct view of the remains. When the young girl saw her mother, she trotted to her and hugged her. "I thought it was you," she said, holding tightly to Julia Pynchon. "Someone told me it was the college's librarian."

Startled by her daughter's concern, Julia returned the pressure of her embrace. "An assistant librarian. It was Eloise."

Tressa, who visited the library often, moaned. "Not Mrs. Weldon?"

"I'm afraid so."

Whit put a hand on his daughter's shoulder. "Why don't you take your mother into her office? She's had a rough morning."

Tressa eased away from her mother. "Who did it, Daddy?"

"We don't know."

Tears streaked Tressa's face. "She was a nice lady. No one would want—"

At that moment another flash went off. It drew Tressa's attention to the center of the library. She stared.

Julia took her arm. "Come, dear, let's go to my office."

The young girl didn't resist.

Anna stood with Whit. "When I went outside, she was beside herself with worry. That's why I brought her in."

"It's okay," Whit said.

The photographer approached. "All done," he said. "Sorry I got . . . well, I've just never seen a murder victim before. I saw my grandpa die, but he just sorta drifted off to sleep."

"Forget it," Whit said.

"Did you get a shot or two for us?" Anna asked.

The kid smiled and nodded back toward Meeks, who stood with the ambulance crew. "Yeah, the campus cop there was dyin' to have his picture made."

Anna glared at Whit. "You've managed to escape this time, but I won't forget that you obtained our help by false pretenses."

"You've got a photo for the paper."

"But not of you."

"What are the bags for?" the photog asked for the third time.

"To preserve any trace evidence on her hands," Whit said.

The kid nodded. "Neat."

"So, where do you go from here?" Anna asked.

Whit didn't answer. He was motioning to the ambulance crew. "Go on and transport her. I want her sent to the state medical examiner's office."

"Did you hear me?" Anna asked.

"Is this for publication?"

She shook her head. "I'm just curious."

"Right now I'm heading to the office," Whit said.

"I was talking about the investigation."

The photographer hurried toward the front door. He planned to snap a few photos of the crowd and the body being loaded. Whit and Anna were walking more slowly.

Whit stopped. "Well, to be honest, I haven't had a chance to give it much thought. The only thing we know is the identity of the victim. I'll start there. More than likely, the key to the crime deals with her."

"But what if it doesn't?"

Whit shrugged. "Then things get a lot more difficult."

Anna glanced back toward Julia Pynchon's office. "Do you want me to take Tressa?"

"No, I think her mother needs her right now."

"Are you leaving now?"

"I was about to, but I have to go back. Julia was going to give me the victim's address. Besides, I'd best check on Tress."

"Is she still seeing that college student?"

"Yeah," Whit said, "and Julia isn't happy about it. She wants me to talk to her about it. I think it's a mistake to try to make her give him up."

"She hasn't had a lot of experience with boys, Whit. I think Julia's right. She might be getting in over her head."

"So you talk to her."

"Are you serious?"

Whit nodded. "Damn right I am. She looks upon you more as a friend. I think she'd listen to you without feeling coerced."

"What's Julia going to say about that?"

"If you can slow down this romance, I suspect she'll be forever grateful."

Anna's face reflected her uncertainty. "I don't know about that. Julia really resents me for some reason."

"It's because Tressa talks so much about you. Tell you what . . . I'll sound Julia out about it first."

The ambulance crew had the body loaded onto the stretcher and was rolling it toward the front door. Whit headed them off. "Remember, tell the pathologist at the hospital that I want her sent to Charleston at once."

"They'll probably just send us on up with her," one of the crewmen said.

"I'm leaving now," Anna said, anxious to get out ahead of the body. "Oh, I guess this means your beach trip is history."

"We'll see," Whit said. He watched Anna hurry from the library and then moved back to the area from which the body had been removed. He made a close inspection of the floor and even noted the titles of several of the larger books, just in case the photos didn't show them. That's when he realized that he had a final question to ask his former wife.

Both Julia and Tressa were dabbing at their eyes as Whit entered the office.

"Is she gone?" Julia asked.

Whit nodded. "You might want to call your custodial crew. They can start to clean things up. There is one more thing I need to know."

Julia nodded. "I do want to help."

"Did the victim—Mrs. Weldon—did she carry a purse?"

Julia's eyes widened. "Yes, but I haven't seen it."

"Where would she have kept it while she was working?"

Julia was already on her feet. "Under the front counter."

The two of them exited the office. Tressa followed. Julia made a thorough search of the front counter area. "It's not here."

Whit sighed. "So maybe we know why someone kills a librarian."

"To rob her?" Julia said.

Whit nodded.

"But she hardly ever carried any money."

"The killer probably didn't know that until after he had the purse."


After leaving the campus, Whit made a stop at the prosecuting attorney's office. Tony Danton, the Raven County prosecutor, was just coming down the steps from the courtroom on the third floor. He carried a handful of files.

"I thought you didn't have any cases today," Whit said.

"The city boys arrested a couple of Milbrook's finest on fugitive warrants from Virginia," Tony said, falling in step with Whit as they headed toward the prosecutor's suite of offices.

"Did they waive extradition?"

"Hell, no. O'Brien appointed Charlie Ayers to represent them. You know Charlie. He's made his reputation being an asshole about everything."

"What were they charged with?"

"A.D.W.," Tony said. In police reports, it was a common abbreviation for assault with a deadly weapon. "They cut a couple of guys up with a mowing scythe."

Whit grimaced. "Jesus Christ."

"According to them, it was self-defense."

Whit laughed. "Who are they?"

"Ike Todd and Billy Jim Henderson."

The two men entered the suite of offices assigned to the prosecutor's staff. "Todd I know," Whit said. "He pulled hard time on a felony assault before."

"If Virginia doesn't put Henderson away, you'll get to know him, too. He just turned eighteen. He was the one that did all the damage with the scythe. I gather Todd was more of an onlooker or a lookout."

They had stopped in front of the secretary's desk. She handed each of them several phone messages. "Not that you'll return any of them," she said. "I don't know why I bother."

Whit showed a couple of them to Tony. "From the news hounds in Charleston. It doesn't take long for word to spread."

They headed back toward Tony's office. "What's the story on it?" Tony asked, referring to the homicide.

Whit shook his head. "Right now, I've got nothing. It looks like a robbery, but that's a little too pat. From what Julia told me, the woman didn't date. She's divorced, but her ex-husband died a few years ago. No motive—other than robbery. No suspects."

Tony settled into the high-back chair behind his desk. "Any theories?"

Whit sat on the desk's corner. "Well, given the library schedule, we have to assume she was killed around nine last night. That's closing time, and she would have been gone not long after that. The condition of her body indicates that she's been dead for maybe twelve hours. I'm wondering if she discovered some students conducting a drug deal."

Tony blinked. "Where did you come up with that?"

"Thin air," Whit said. "I'm just trying to figure out why someone would want to kill a matronly librarian. Her purse was missing."

"So why so skeptical about the robbery?"

"The fact that the woman was killed, and the way she was killed. I dunno. It just looks too violent to have been simple robbery." He explained about the books.

"Drug-related robberies tend to be violent," Tony said.

"Yeah, but this guy took some time. I'm just not ready to put it down to a robbery."

"What does Julia say?"

Whit eased himself off the desk. "She thinks she was supposed to be the victim."

Tony sat straight up. "She what?"

"She was supposed to work last night. It's just a guilt trip, Tony."

"Why didn't she work?"

"She had some garden club affair to attend. Eloise Weldon—that's the victim—worked in her place."

"It's an angle to check," Tony said, toying with a pen he had pulled from his pocket.

"Right now I'm going over to the victim's apartment. Maybe I can turn up something there."

"She live alone?"

"So Julia says. She knew the woman pretty well. I might have to force a door or break a window to get in."

Tony tossed the pen on the table. "Do what you have to do. God, I hate these kinda murders."

"Well, gimme a chance to check her apartment. Maybe I'll turn up something. We might discover that Julia didn't know Eloise Weldon as well as she thought she did."

Tressa sat on the short flight of concrete steps that led up to the front door of Rob Fernandez's one-room flat. She had looked for him at the campus student union and even in the administration building, but he was nowhere to be found. Not that she had really expected to find him. On Monday, Wednesday, and Friday, his classes didn't meet until one and two. His heaviest schedule came on Tuesday and Thursday.

She checked her watch and saw that it was a little after noon. If he didn't return to his apartment, she planned to drive back to the campus to try to catch him before he went into his first class.

His flat was one of several in the old building, all of them occupied by Milbrook College students. One, a sophomore whom she knew only as Dale, pulled a battered old Volkswagen beetle into the parking place in front of his unit.

"Have you seen Rob?" she asked.

Dale smiled at her. "He left out around eight this morning. If you need a man, think I might do?"

If he hadn't said it so jovially, Tressa might have been offended. As it was, she just laughed. "I need to see Rob."

Dale managed to look crestfallen. "Rejected again." But his face had quickly brightened. "Hey, I guess you heard about the murder at the library."

"I heard," Tressa said.

Dale snapped his fingers. "I forgot. Your mother's the head of the library."

Tressa nodded.

"Tough, huh?" Dale said.

"I knew Mrs. Weldon. She was a nice lady."

Dale appeared pensive. "I've been tryin' to place her, but I don't spend any more time in that place than I have to. I'll probably spend less now."

Tressa frowned and started to speak, but a powder blue Ford Colt turned into view on the street.

"There's Rob," Dale said. "I'd best get inside and change. We've got a softball game lined up this afternoon."

"See ya," Tressa said.

She knew the car very well. She sighed in relief as it wheeled into the place assigned to it, and a tall thin figure emerged.

"Tressa, what are you doing here?"

She ran to him and threw her arms around him. "It's terrible, Rob."

He hugged her. "What's terrible?"

"Haven't you heard?"

He eased her back to look down into her china-doll face. "Heard what?"

"A lady Mother works with was murdered last night?"

Rob's face went slack. "A woman she worked with?"

"Mrs. Weldon, one of the assistant librarians."

"God, that's terrible. Who did it?"

"They don't know. Daddy's handling the case."

"Let's go inside," he said.

"I thought you had class. I don't wanna make you late."

"The hell with class. It's business law, and I've a solid A average. I can miss one day. It's no big deal."

He wrapped his arm around her, and they headed into the apartment.

"She was beaten to death with books."

The young man still had his keys in his hand, and he quickly unlocked the door. "It kinda makes you wonder, doesn't it? You'd think that nothing like that happens in a place like Milbrook."

The interior of the building was cool and comfortable. Tressa went to a worn couch that sat next to a small refrigerator and settled down on it.

"How about a cold drink?" he said.

"A Diet Coke if you have one."

"Coming up." He opened the refrigerator and extracted two cans.

"Where were you?" Tressa asked as he opened the drinks.

"Job hunting."

Her eyes brightened. "You mean you're going to stay through the summer."

He settled down on the couch beside her. "Well, I'm going to work at that fast-food seafood house downtown, so I guess I'd better stay."

Tears filled her eyes. "I'm so happy. I was sure you were going back to Georgia."

He slipped an arm over her shoulder. "It's too hot in Georgia in the summertime. Besides, I'd miss you too much."

"I'd love for you to meet my mother and father," Tressa said.

He gave her a disbelieving look. "C'mon, girl, I know how your mother feels about me. I can tell when she answers the phone."

"That's because she doesn't know you. She just thinks you're a little too old for me. That's all."

"What about your father? What does he think?"

"He doesn't say much one way or the other. You know how fathers are, though. But he's one of a kind in a lot of ways. You'd really like him."

"Sometime I'll have to meet them."

"Soon?"

"Yeah, we'll try to work it out."

# FOUR

ELOISE WELDON LIVED in a small four-room apartment three blocks east of Milbrook College. The building sat on the left rear corner of a lot primarily occupied by a sprawling two-story turn-of-the-century brick. As Whit pulled his car down the narrow driveway toward the compact apartment, he studied the larger structure to his left. It appeared to have been diced up into smaller apartments. Huge houses such as the one on the front of the property were relics from a bygone age. They had become too expensive to heat, and few couples were now interested in having families large enough to demand such houses. As a result, many of the old two-stories in Milbrook's central residential area had suffered the same fate as the one he eased by.

He pulled his car to a stop on the spacious asphalt lot behind the brick building. A breeze tussled his graying hair as he stepped from the car. It smelled of rain, just as the weathermen had promised, and already the blue skies of morning were now milky with haze. The region needed it desperately, and so did Whit's rhododendron.

The size of the parking lot confirmed his suspicion about the fate of the primary residence on the property. The Milbrook City Council did little to restrict landlords, but along the residential streets of the small city they had required landlords to provide off-street parking for tenants of the converted homes. In this case the ordinance had consumed what had

55

been the backyard of the house as well as the front yard of Eloise Weldon's apartment. Not that she was in any position to care any longer.

Whit went to the back door of the larger house and knocked. No one answered. He turned back and briefly eyed the lower half of the garage apartment before heading for the steps to the second floor. Based on the rickety white hand-made doors over the two vehicle entrances, it appeared to be nothing more than a garage. He climbed the steps. Dark brown wasps bumped against the scaling white paint of the small second-story porch.

A single solid-wood door, topped by what appeared to be a handmade screen door, provided entry to the tiny apartment. The screen was unlocked. Whit tested the interior door and found it secured by a sturdy dead bolt that had been installed—very recently, it appeared. He made a mental note of it, wondering if the woman had developed some recent fear that prompted the new lock installation.

The upper half of the door was decorated with panels of glass. Whit peered through and saw a key inserted into the other side of the lock. He shook his head. A lot of folks did the same thing, not realizing that the presence of the key defeated the purpose of the dead bolt. He stepped back and with a quick hitch of his elbow shattered the pane. Then he reached inside and twisted the key. The stagnant heat rolled out to greet him as he opened the door.

He swatted back a wasp that tried to gain entry behind him and quickly slammed the screen. He found himself standing in a stuffy and modestly furnished living room. The furniture appeared to be new but rather cheap, the kind of stuff one bought at those places that advertised no credit checks and made good on the promise. Given the interest rates they charged, they could afford the write-offs on those items they couldn't reasonably repo. A worn rug, six inches short on all four sides of being wall-to-wall, covered the floors. The boards creaked beneath Whit's bulk as he slowly circled the room. An old television, enhanced by a cable box, sat on a small stand. A pair of glasses rested on a table beside the sofa as did a phone and a small address book. He picked up the address book and then turned his attention to a small bookshelf. A row of pictures sat on the top.

"Jesus," he mumbled.

Whit hated to prowl through the belongings of a murder victim. He cherished his own privacy and detested the thought of invading the privacy of others. Still, his job demanded it, so he moved toward the photos. Family photos obviously . . . of the woman's children. Actually there were four shots of two separate families. Whit didn't remember what Julia had told him about the children, so he didn't know which ones were offspring or in-laws. It didn't matter. All of the adults in the photo were attractive. Had that college president already made the phone calls to them? The thought made Whit shake his head. How in the hell did people handle the news that a close member of the family had been brutally murdered? It was an experience Whit hadn't suffered. He hoped he never would.

He abandoned the bookcase for the moment and drifted toward a hallway. It led to the building's other three rooms. The kitchen and living room occupied the front of the apartment. A bathroom was located off the hall. Down the hallway, Whit saw, were two bedrooms. He went first to the kitchen.

It was spotless. No dirty dishes in the sink. Nothing at all on the small kitchen table. No clutter on the countertops. So he at once noticed the small green chalkboard attached to the side of the refrigerator. Two word's had been printed on the small surface.

WILLIE'S BIRTHDAY.

"Who the hell is Willie?" Whit asked aloud.

He pulled out a ragged notebook and wrote the message

down. He also made a note to check on the recently installed lock.

That's when he heard the noisy creaking of the apartment's floor.


Anna brought the still damp photos of Gil Dickerson into Kathy's office. The publisher was scanning that day's edition of the *Charleston Gazette*.

"I thought you might like to see these," Anna said, balancing the moist prints.

Kathy wrinkled up her nose. "God, I hate that darkroom smell."

Then she saw the photos themselves. A smile crept over her face. "Isn't he handsome?"

Anna laughed as she placed the three photos on the newspaper spread out on Kathy's desk. "Don't tell me you're one of those women with a uniform fetish."

"Only if the uniform has him in it."

"You sound like a teenager."

Kathy winked at Anna. "For the first time in years I feel like one."

"Oh, God. The woman's in love."

"Let's just say I'm smitten."

"Smitten?" Anna laughed at the word. "Bitten is more appropriate. However, I do think Gil shares your feelings, and he is a nice guy . . . for a cop-type."

"Look who's talking. You're involved with Dr. Jekyll and Mr. Hyde. The trouble is, Whit prefers being Hyde."

Anna studied the face of her friend and employer. She was actually overjoyed at the budding romance between the two. Both of them were widowed, and both had lost their spouses under the most tragic of circumstances. Kathy's husband— the former publisher of the *Journal*—had been the true re-incarnation of Jekyll-Hyde. The side of his personality that was displayed at the paper and even to his wife had been pleasant and intelligent. But there were times when some deep demon, perhaps a by-product of his years in Vietnam, possessed the man. He had been unfaithful to Kathy, and, when faced with the possibility of discovery, he had committed multiple homicides to protect his reputation and position. William Binder had died in a shoot-out with the police, one of whom had been Whit.

Kathy had taken over the stewardship of the newspaper and had drowned her guilt in a frantic frenzy of work. She had also lifted Anna from the position of reporter and placed her in the editor's office. Slowly Katherine Binder was putting the horror out of her mind. Kathy managed the business operations of the *Milbrook Daily Journal*, while Anna handled the news gathering and editorial side.

Gil's wife, on the other hand, had been the victim of a cop gone both bad and mad. It had been Gil, then a deputy with the sheriff's department, who had discovered her mutilated body while answering a complaint. That killer, too, had died, but not before a bullet from his gun had forever crippled Gil Dickerson.

In spite of Whit's skepticism, Anna had invited them both to dinner several months earlier. The attraction had been immediate, but both, still recovering from their losses, had not allowed themselves to recognize it. Anna had continued to work as a catalyst. She liked the two of them and felt that they could help each other to work through some of the private miseries that haunted them both.

"You're way out of line," Whit had said on more than one occasion.

Surprisingly Kathy had been the more resistant to allowing a relationship to develop, perhaps because her loss had been the more recent and perhaps because of the senseless guilt she still felt over her husband's infidelity and the orgy of mayhem to which he had resorted to cover it up. Gil Dickerson had asked her to dinner twice before she had accepted—and only then because of Anna's urging. After the second date, the romance had taken root. Now it was ready to blossom.

"I like this one," Kathy said, pointing to the center photo of Gil.

"He looks awfully stern there," Anna said. It wasn't her favorite. She preferred the shot in which Gil was smiling. The man had a charming smile, a sort of half smile that was made bittersweet by his personal history.

"But in this one he looks like a sheriff."

Anna chuckled. "Well, I guess we should let the man himself make the choice."

"Is the editorial written endorsing him?"

Anna shook her head. "I'm still working on it. I really want it to be a powerful statement about him."

Kathy was silent for a moment, lost in some obviously distracting thought. When she spoke, it was to ask Anna a question. "Does he have a chance?"

The question had been floating between them for weeks. Certainly they had discussed it right before Gil's appointment and immediately thereafter. After Gil took the oath of office, and as the campaign moved into high gear, it became something they didn't talk about, a kind of taboo when they were all together.

Anna took a moment to frame her answer. "I'd like to think so. I mean, look at the two candidates. You have Jake Brimm, a former sheriff and an old-time political operative. Tony Danton says he's the next thing to a crook, and you know what Whit says about him. Then there's Gil—young, intelligent, a very good cop. I wouldn't think there was any question."

"But," Kathy said.

Anna smiled. "Yeah, always a 'but.' Tony tells Whit that Brimm has to be the favorite to win. Brimm knows the people in the precincts. He's got money. Most of the officeholders in the county feel he was instrumental in their election."

"It's not right," Kathy said, anger in her voice.

"And it's not over. We've still got a couple of weeks. Gil's television and radio spots start this week. Brimm hasn't even purchased any television spots. From what I was told up at the TV station, there aren't many good time slots left because of all the statewide campaigns."

"What does Whit say?"

"What does Whit know?" Anna countered.

Kathy shrugged.

"I meant," Anna said, "what does he know about politics?"

"So he doesn't think Gil can win?"

"Kathy, Whit's a cynic. More than that, he doesn't want Gil to get his hopes up. In his way, he's preparing Gil to lose. Maybe that's a valuable function."

"God, Anna, he's got to win."

Anna saw the emotion in Kathy's face. If Gil did lose, and most people expected him to, she would take it worse than the candidate himself. "So what if he loses, Kathy? The world won't stop turning. You two will still like each other."

"But he needs to win, Anna, to bolster his self-image."

"I think Gil's got things well in hand, and—"

The phone rang.

Kathy punched the intercom line. "What is it?"

"You have a call on line one."

"Who is it?" the publisher asked.

"A man, but he wouldn't say. I asked his name, and he just told me to tell you that it was a 'serious personal matter,' his words exactly."

"You'd better take it," Anna said.

Kathy clicked off the intercom and picked up the phone. "Katherine Binder."

Anna saw a sudden look of annoyance sweep over her friend's face.

"Who are you?" Kathy was asking.

Anna tensed and sat forward in her chair.

"I don't deal with anonymous callers."

"What is it?" Anna whispered.

"Repeat that," Kathy said. She made a note on the margin of the *Gazette* she had been reading. Then she hung up the phone.

"Who was that?" Anna asked.

Kathy seemed stunned. "A man. He refused to identify himself. He said that if I wanted Gil to win the election, I needed to be at the overlook on Tabernacle Mountain at nine tonight."

"What?"

"That's what he said."

Anna was shaking her head. "It sounds fishy to me."

"Me, too, but I have to go."

"Alone?"

The publisher shook her head. "He didn't say alone. Will you go with me?"

"Try and stop me."


Whit whirled just as a woman peeked around the corner.

The woman screamed. The piercing sound startled Whit more than her presence did.

"Jesus Christ!" he snapped.

"Who are you? What are you doing here?"

The woman, well into her sixties if Whit was any judge, still just peeked around the corner.

"You tell me first," Whit said, reaching into his coat for his badge.

"Oh dear God, don't kill me!" she wailed, vanishing around the corner.

"I'm a cop!" Whit shouted as he heard her trying to shuffle out the front door.

The sound of her movements stopped.

With his badge on display, he eased around the corner. She was standing just at the door amid the shards of shattered glass, holding the screen door open. She was short and bent, very willowy in stature.

She eyed his face and then the badge.

"You're letting the bees in," Whit said, pointing to one of the wasps which now bumped against the textured surface of the ceiling.

Still she kept the door open. Anxious confusion clouded her face. "What . . . what are you doing here?"

Whit eased toward her. "Listen, lady, I'm an investigator with the prosecuting attorney's office. I need to know why you are here."

She straightened up just a little as she said, "I own this building."

"I see. Do you own the brick house in front?"

"I live there."

"I knocked but no one answered."

"I was in the bathroom. I don't move as fast as I used to. Did you break in here?"

"I had to. That's why I knocked at your house, but I figured it was occupied by renters, too. It looked to me as if it had been split into apartments."

She started to frown. "It has. My husband—God rest his soul—did it just 'fore he died. I live in one and rent t'other. Now just what are you doing here? Why did you break in? I think maybe I still oughta call the city police."

"Has Mrs. Weldon rented from you long?"

"Is she in some kind of trouble?"

"Please, ma'am . . . answer my questions."

She let the screen door close. "Not till you answer mine, mister. I ain't afraid of you."

"She's dead," Whit said. He had discovered long ago that there wasn't any easy or better way to say it.

The old woman gasped. She started to stagger but caught herself, just as Whit reached her. He put a hand under her arm.

"I'm okay," the woman said, clutching the door facing.

"Sit down on the couch," Whit said.

He helped her to it.

When she was down, she looked up at him through her tarnished metal glasses. Her eyes were yellow with age, but the irises remained a clear, ice-cold blue. At that moment they glistened with emotion.

"What happened to her?"

"She was murdered."

The woman's wrinkled hand went to her mouth. "Oh, dear God in heaven, no. Not Ellie."

"Ellie? Is that what you called her?"

The woman nodded and started to weep.

"You were close to her?"

Again just a nod.

"I'd like to ask you some more questions, ma'am, but we can wait a few minutes." Whit didn't know what else to do. He didn't have a handkerchief to offer her. It was one of those things that most people carried—except Whit. He went to the dead woman's bathroom and found a box of tissues, which he brought into the living room.

She was waiting for him. "Have her children been notified?"

"Yes, the college officials are taking care of it."

"Oh, the dear things. They'll be destroyed. They loved her so."

A bitter anger replaced the shock on the woman's face. "Who did it?"

"We don't know, Mrs.—"

"Worley. Alice Worley."

"At the moment, Mrs. Worley, we have no suspects. That's one reason I'd like to ask you a few questions."

Mrs. Worley blanched. "Me! You don't think I know anything—"

"No . . . no!" Whit said quickly. "We just don't know that much about Mrs. Weldon. The head librarian provided—"

"That shrew!" the lady landlord said.

Whit gaped. He couldn't help himself. "You know her?"

"I just know what Ellie told me."

"She didn't like her?"

The woman shrugged. "Well, Ellie liked her, I presume, even if she was always being taken advantage of by her."

"How so?"

"Making her work all hours. Why, sometimes she worked as long as sixteen hours!"

"Really?"

"Yes, sir. That's the gospel."

"Wasn't she usually home by nine or so?" Whit asked.

"Nine? Why, the poor thing was lucky if she was home by midnight sometimes."

"But the library closes at nine."

"Yes, but the head librarian made her work late very, very often. Too often if you ask me. I told Ellie that there were other people who oughta be asked to work late, but Ellie was the type that let folks run all over her."

"So you weren't concerned when she didn't return last night?"

The old woman shrugged. "Actually I didn't know that she hadn't. I go to bed early. Always have—and always get up before dawn."

"But you didn't notice she hadn't come home."

"How would I notice?"

"What about her car?"

"Oh, she didn't have one. She had a thing about driving."

"So how did she get back and forth to work?" Whit asked.

"Usually she walked. On bad days, the bus . . . sometimes a taxi . . . and sometimes someone from the college drove her."

Whit cocked his head at her. "You're a brave woman, confronting me like you did."

"What the deuce have I got to lose? I'm eighty-four."

Whit studied her. "Eighty-four?"

"Turned it last week."

Whit wouldn't have thought her more than sixty-five. "Well, you coulda fooled me. In fact, you did fool me."

"You smoke?" she asked.

Whit nodded. "I'm afraid so."

"You won't make eighty-four then."

Whit had to laugh.

"I mean it," she said, offended by his reaction.

"Well, I'm not so sure that I want to make eighty-four," Whit answered. "I don't mean to offend you by saying that."

For the first time she smiled, and Whit saw a very white brace of what had to be false teeth.

"Actually, mister, you're right. Nothing worse than seeing all your family and friends die 'fore you. A long life can be a curse on you."

"Can I ask you a few more questions?"

She set the box of tissues on the table. "Yes, sir. If it'll help catch whoever did this. How did they do it anyway?"

"It appears she was beaten to death."

Whatever good humor had been on her face vanished. "The bastard," she said.

Whit liked Alice Worley. "Tell me," he said. "Did she socialize . . . I mean, did she date any men?"

Whit braced himself, expecting the old woman to come to her dead tenant's defense. Instead, Mrs. Worley managed a wry smile again. "Well, to tell ya the truth, I think she was seeing somebody. She never talked about him, but I kin tell when a woman's got herself a man. You can see in their eyes, smell in the way they start wearing perfume, even the way they dress. She didn't use to wear her hair short like that either. She always wore it up in a bun till a few months ago.''

"Who's the man?''

The woman shrugged. "Search me. Like I told ya, she didn't never mention him to me. I just suspicioned it.''

"You never saw him here?''

"Lordy, no! Never did. I gotta admit I was kinda watching some for him, too. Old folks get nosy, ya know. We done lived out all our excitement, so I guess we try to steal some from those younger'n us.''

Whit had settled beside her on the couch. "What about other women friends?''

"That head librarian—the Pynchon lady—if you could call her a friend. And there was Chris Bradford.''

"Man or woman?'' Whit asked, ready to make a note.

"A woman. An old schoolmate of Ellie's. I guess Chris was what you might call her best friend.''

"Where does she live?''

"Charleston. I reckon somebody might oughta call her.''

"The kids will probably notify her.''

The woman was shaking her head. "Not likely. I'd wager they're in their cars on their way here if they've been told.''

"Did she know anybody called Willie?'' Whit asked, remembering the name on the kitchen chalkboard.

Mrs. Worley thought. "Not that I know of, but like I said—''

"I understand,'' Whit said.

He opened the small address book he had retrieved earlier and turned to the B's. Christine Bradford was the first name on the page. There was a work number and a home number.

"What does Christine Bradford do?'' Whit asked.

"She's a nurse of some kind.''

A distant grumble of thunder prompted Whit to check the

time. The afternoon was quickly getting away from him. "If you don't object, Mrs. Worley, I'm going to search Ellie's things. Maybe I can get some clue as to who killed her."

The woman appeared shocked. "You don't mean that whoever killed her mighta knew her."

"That's usually the way it works, ma'am."

"Well, not with Ellie. She was as nice as the day is long. I'd bet one of them college kids, all high on drugs, did it."

"Well, that's a theory, but I still need to take a look through her things. I'll try not to disturb anything."

The woman pushed herself up from the sofa. "Don't reckon it matters any. I still can't believe it."

"How long has she rented from you?"

The woman paused to think. "Seem's like a coon's age, but I guess it's been about five years. She came here after her divorce. Her youngest was still with her then, but she got married not long after Ellie moved in."

"Where did she live before that?"

"Somewhere outside of Milbrook . . . on a farm, I think." The thunder grew louder.

"I best get back over to the house 'fore the storm gets here. I don't move as fast as I used to, Mr.—"

"Pynchon," Whit said.

The woman frowned. "That's the name of—"

Whit was smiling. "She's my ex-wife."

The woman's eyes narrowed. "Did you say ex-wife?"

"Yes, ma'am."

Alice Worley smiled. "That makes you a pretty smart man in my book, Mr. Pynchon."

# FIVE

By 3:00 P.M., the chaos in the sheriff department's control room had subsided. It usually happened that way. The day shift had already started to close out its work, and the second-shift officers hadn't come on duty yet. Marsha Via was enjoying the relative peace and quiet as she filled in the blanks on her daily activity sheet.

The field deputies had transported a total of four inmates, one of which was a mental health patient who had been committed to Huntington State Hospital. She entered four transports in the appropriate space on the form. She then turned to the radio.

"County to unit four."

A brief burst of static was followed by a tired male voice. "Unit four, county . . . go ahead."

"How many papers have you served today?"

"Stand by."

"Shit," she said . . . not with the mike keyed. They knew she was going to be asking the same questions at this time every day. No reason they couldn't have the information ready.

"Unit four to county."

"Go ahead," she said.

"Twenty," the voice said.

"Ten four." She made a note of his response.

She followed the same procedure with the other two units

still in the field and was just about to total up the results when the phone rang.

"Sheriff's department."

"Marsha, it's Jake."

She froze. "Why are you calling me here?"

"Because that's where you are," Jake Brimm said.

"These calls are taped."

"I thought you said nobody listened to them."

Marsha was watching the door that opened into the courthouse. "Usually they don't."

"So stop fretting."

"What do you want?" she asked.

"I need to see you tonight. Will you be home? It'll have to be late, maybe ten-thirty."

"Where else would I be at that time?"

"If you can, take those time sheets you were telling me about home with you today."

"I can't do that," Marsha said. "They're department documents. What if I get caught?"

"Can you make a copy of them?"

"Jake, you're gonna get me in a world of trouble. I can't afford to get fired."

"C'mon, hon, take it easy. Dickerson's too damn dumb to know what's going on. I'd like to see those time sheets."

Marsha felt a queasiness in the pit of her stomach. "You can't tell that much from the time sheets for one pay period."

"I've got a friend with the Department of Labor in Charleston, Marsha. He wants to take a look at some of the time sheets. He owes me."

"I dunno."

"C'mon, hon. You trust me, don't you? You're gonna be my chief deputy when I take office."

Brimm had been telling her that for the past four or five months, usually when they were in bed together. She wasn't

sure she wanted to be chief deputy. What she needed was
more money, not more work.

"I'll see," she said.

"Don't see, dammit. Do it."

"I said I'd try."

A buzzer sounded, and Marsha yelped.

"What is it?" Jake wanted to know.

"Someone's buzzing to get in. It scared me. I gotta go."
She pushed a button that allowed the door into the courthouse
to open.

"I do need those time sheets—"

She cringed as the current sheriff himself walked through
the door.

"Gotta go. See you tonight."

She replaced the phone just as Gil Dickerson stepped into
the control room. With his limp, he reminded her of the
Dennis Weaver character from "Gunsmoke." Dickerson
usually wore civilian clothes, and she was a little surprised
to see him in the uniform.

"You look good," she said, smiling.

Gil returned her smile. "Thank you. I feel good in this.
Maybe I should wear it more often."

He did wear the uniform well. The longer she was around
him, the less she noticed the pronounced limp. In a way she
wished it was Dickerson with whom she had become involved. Unlike Jake Brimm, the sheriff didn't have a wife to
complicate things. God knows he was better looking than
Brimm, too. On the other hand, everyone in Raven County
knew he was going to lose to the former sheriff.

"You look frazzled," Gil said.

She shook her head. "Just a typical Monday."

He was studying the immense wallboard that displayed the
current list of inmates. "I see we've added one since yesterday."

"Yes, sir. A female, too. One of the magistrates put her in for bad checks."

"For bad checks?"

"Yes, sir. She had about eight warrants on her."

"Any chance she can post bond?" Gil asked.

"We let her make a couple of calls. No luck yet."

"Damn," Gil said. "Let her make more if she thinks it will help."

One of the problems he had inherited was an overcrowded jail, at least according to a federal judge who had heard a recent class action brought by a group of inmates. Gil had taken his oath of office the day before the hearing in Beckley's federal court building. He had traveled to the hearing with Tony Danton who had told the judge that the lack of facilities in the jail was a prime concern of the new sheriff. The judge had suggested that the county work out some plan for alleviating the crowded conditions. Gil, through Tony, had assured him that he would. The judge had continued the hearing for six months to give them an opportunity to solve the problem.

The sheriff continued to study the board. "She's the only female in here, I see."

Marsha nodded. "Yes, sir. So we have to give her a cell all by her lonesome."

"Damn." Gil wheeled on his stiff leg and started out the door.

"Any word on pay raises for next year?" she asked, trying to sound interested but offhanded.

The sheriff stopped. "No, Marsha. The county commission has discussed it, but I don't look for a decision before the end of June. They want to see how things stand at the end of the fiscal year. Frankly, I wouldn't count on one. Things are tight."

Marsha shrugged. "I know, but it's been two years since we've had a raise. You know what deputies make."

Gil nodded. "Yeah, and I promise to do my best to work out a raise, but I'm not very hopeful. Are you having problems?"

The female officer glanced up at him. "Isn't everyone? My daughter needs braces, and I haven't got any support payments from my ex-old man for four months."

"So take him back to court."

There was no humor in her laugh. "I gotta find him first. Last I heard he was crewing on some cruise ship outa Florida."

"He's a sailor?"

"God, no. He's a womanizer. He probably cleans toilets or clears tables."

Gil looked at the clock and then pondered something for a moment. He came back toward her desk. "Actually, Marsha, I've been wanting to talk with you about something."

He settled into a chair by the desk.

"Have I done something wrong?" Marsha asked.

"Oh, no. Not at all. I'd like to talk to you about a new role here."

"A new role?"

"Yes, we're getting more and more cases of alleged sexual assault, both of women and children, and also more cases of child abuse. We need an officer trained in dealing with the victims of those sort of offenses. Frankly, it should be a female."

"I can see that," Marsha said.

"Rape victims are understandably uncomfortable talking to male cops. Besides, some of our guys aren't the most sensitive fellas."

"That's the truth," she said.

"The kids who are victims seem to relate better to a female, too. One of the things I wanna do with the department is to beef up our efforts at criminal investigation. I don't know that it would mean more money, but would you be interested in a job in the C.I.D. division?''

"Yes, sir. Anything but dispatching, and that sounds interesting.''

"Well, no sense in doing anything until after the election, but once it's finished, and assuming things work out all right, then we'll talk more.''

"I hope you win,'' she said as he rose to leave. It bothered her that she really meant it.

Whit had returned from his search of Eloise Weldon's apartment and was about to examine the victim's personal effects with special attention to her address book when the medical examiner's office called.

"Great,'' Whit told the prosecutor's secretary. "Put him through.''

"It's not Barucha,'' she said. "It's some foreign guy. I didn't even get his name.''

Whit winced. "Okay, you've warned me.''

He waited for the line to come alive. When it did, he said, "Pynchon here.''

"This is Dr. Swa—'' Whit understood no more of the man's name.

"Where's Barucha?'' Whit asked, referring to the state of West Virginia's chief medical examiner.

"He's attending conference. I autopsy the lady.''

Whit bit his lip, trying not to lose control. "When will Barucha return?''

"Not for while. After de conference, he goes to vacation. I have report on dis lady for you.''

"You'll have to speak slowly, Doctor. Your accent is rather heavy.''

"You understand me. No problem.''

No problem, thought Whit. Like hell. He had talked to this guy before.

"She died of blow to left side of skull, inflicted, I think, by—"

Whit managed to understand him up to that point. "Slow down, dammit! What was the blow inflicted by?"

"Excuse me?"

The bastard didn't understand him! "When the fuck are you gonna learn to speak English?" Whit snapped.

"Pardon, I speak English."

"Not so anyone would notice," Whit countered. "What kind of weapon was used?"

"Unspecific," the doctor said. "Not really blunt, but heavy . . . very heavy."

"A book?" Whit asked.

"Pardon?"

"Was the woman killed by a book?"

"No . . . no . . . no . . . no book. Probably metal with—"

Again Whit lost the words. "Please repeat. Metal with what?"

"Sharp edge."

"A knife."

"No . . . no . . . no . . . not cut. Pardon, I mean not sliced."

"Jesus," Whit muttered.

"Cwavakal was broken."

"What did you say?"

"Cwa-va-kal. It was frac-tured."

"What the hell is a cwa-va-kal?"

"Collarbone," the doctor said with remarkable clarity. "Broken by heavy blunt object. Book maybe."

"Anything else?"

"Yes, please. Victim suffered many blows to head, but first—"

"Doc, you're speeding up on me again. The first was what?"

"The first was kil-ling blow. Others pro-ba-bly post-mor-tem."

Whit had to smile. At least he had the guy trying to make himself understood.

"When can I expect the written report?"

"Next week . . . maybe. But there is anudder ting."

"What?"

"Sum'ting else."

Whit braced himself. "Okay, but speak slowly."

"De victim, she had sex wid'in day of death."

Whit wondered if he had heard the man right.

"Did you say that she had sex?"

"Wid'in day of death."

"For chrissakes, was the woman raped?"

"No, do not think so."

"How do you know about sex?" Whit shook his head, shocked that he had started talking in Pidgin English.

"Found sperm in va-gi-na . . . still mo-bile."

"But no sign of molestation."

"No . . . no . . . no infestation."

"Mo-les-ta-tion, dammit! Not in-fes-ta-tion."

Tony Danton stuck his head into the office. Whit motioned for him to come in.

"No . . . no . . . no mo-les-ta-tion. Va-gi-na is normal."

"Anything else, Doc."

"No." The pathologist hung up.

Whit slammed the phone down. "Damn . . . damn . . . damn."

Tony settled into one of the chairs. "What the hell was that all about?"

"That was an assistant medical examiner. The one that can't speak English. Remember him?"

"Like I remember a toothache," Tony said.

"Well, he autopsied Eloise Weldon."

Tony rolled his eyes. "Where was Merrill?"

"At some fucking conference. Anyway, the foreign guy just muddied the water a little."

"How so?"

"Eloise Weldon. Our somewhat prim-and-proper widow? She was screwed the night before she died."

Tony raised his eyebrows. "Did he rule out sexual assault?"

"I think so. He found mobile sperm in her vagina."

"Sperm can remain mobile for up to forty-eight hours."

"Yeah, but she was dead for twelve or so. The cooling of the body would restrict the mobility factor, I guess. He didn't tell me. At least if he did, I didn't understand him. Besides, it was warm in the library, so her body temp didn't drop too quickly."

"What was the cause of death?"

Whit shook his head. "Well, she died from a blow to the side of the head, inflicted by a sharp object."

"A sharp object?"

"Probably a heavy metal object, and she had a broken cwa-va-kal."

"A what?"

"Clavicle . . . a collarbone. Christ, I wish Barucha had posted her."

"Yeah, let's hope we don't find ourselves having to depend on any autopsy evidence from what's-his-name."

"Swannie Mahannie or something like that. Is there any chance we could get them to put the remains in cold storage until Barucha gets back?"

"No way," Tony said. "I've already heard from one of her kids, actually her son. Both daughter and son are driving up from Florida. He phoned from somewhere down in South Carolina to ask for an appointment tomorrow morning. I talked with him briefly. I get the impression that the family wants to take an active interest."

"Well, they have a right," Whit said.

Victim's rights—and in this case the rights of a victim's survivors. It had become a political football in recent years. In the past prosecutors could guide their cases through the maze of the courts without the slightest consideration for a victim or a victim's family. Most prosecutors chose to involve the families. A few did not. As a result of those few, the legislature had adopted a set of laws requiring the prosecution to keep victims and their families apprised of the investigation and the subsequent judicial proceedings. Even at the sentencing of a convicted criminal, the victims were given the right to make statements to the court.

"Just warning you," Tony said.

Julia Pynchon stared in feigned amazement as her daughter stepped through the front door. "It's just after seven. I can't believe you're home so early."

"Oh, Mother, don't be sarcastic. Rob had to study for an exam tomorrow."

Her mother was watching "Jeopardy" on the television. She always prided herself on knowing so many of the answers. "I'm glad someone's concerned about their studies. You've been letting yours go now ever since you started seeing that man."

Tressa settled down into one of the living room chairs. "You know my grades are fine. Besides, I graduate in a few weeks. Everything's under control."

"Except this infatuation that afflicts you."

"Oh, Mother." Tressa got to her feet, preparing to escape to her room.

"Your father called," Julia Pynchon said, knowing that would stop her.

"When?"

"Earlier this evening. He's coming by in a few minutes to ask me some more questions about Eloise. We're also going to discuss this situation with you."

"The situation with me?"

"I just don't think you understand what you might be getting yourself into."

Tressa decided to ignore her and headed up the steps to her room. She considered it a sign of her developing maturity that she could now overlook her mother's snide manner. She was an expert at it compared to Whit Pynchon, her father, who had divorced Julia more than a decade earlier. They were so diametrically opposed—her father and mother. Whit was almost pure emotion and instinct, which made Tressa smile when she thought about Tony and Anna trying to get him to run for sheriff. Jesus, he'd spent most of his life collecting enemies. Not that he was a bad person, just the opposite in fact. In many ways he was much too good of a person. He didn't tell lies, not big ones anyway. Sure, he had told his daughter twenty times that he had stopped smoking when he really hadn't and had no real intentions of even trying. But that was just to make her feel good.

A person knew where she stood with Whit Pynchon. He was a good cop who almost always got his man, and Tressa was very proud of him. Her mother was something else altogether. She enjoyed the garden clubs and what passed for culture in backwoods Milbrook. Because of her position at the college, she got to hobnob with the kind of people she enjoyed—the Daughters of the American Revolution, the United Daughters of the Confederacy, the members of her three garden clubs. Not that Tressa saw anything all that wrong with any of those groups. It was just that Julia Pynchon was so vastly different from the man she had once decided to marry so many years ago. It had been a doomed romance from the start.

A year or so ago, when Whit and Anna Tyree had met each other in the line of their respective duties, it had been a combination of both love and hate at first sight. Love had emerged the victor. They were crazy about each other, thanks—Tressa liked to think—to her own efforts as a sort of referee and Cupid. But they still made each other crazy at times. Tressa found it a cute relationship. That Whit's relationship with Anna piqued Julia Pynchon was just something of an unanticipated side benefit.

Tressa knew all about love now, thanks to Rob. Her mother claimed he was too old for her. It wouldn't have mattered how old he had been. Her mother still wouldn't have liked him, just as she didn't approve of Whit or of Anna or of Tressa's friends. Her friends' parents weren't members of the small self-declared social elite of Milbrook.

The phone rang. Tressa had an extension beside her bed. She snatched it up quickly.

"Hi hon." It was Rob.

"You studying?" she asked.

"You bet."

Tressa heard the distinct telltale click that indicated her mother had picked up the line.

"It's for me, Mother."

There was a moment's pause before her mother said, "Don't tie up the line very long. I'm expecting several calls tonight. Eloise's family are coming in tonight, and they might need to call me."

"But we have call waiting, Mother. If you get a call, I'll answer it and let you know."

Still, her mother didn't hang up right away.

Tressa's patience wore thin. "Mother, the call *is* for me."

There was a sharp click.

"Is she off?" Rob asked.

"Who knows?" Tressa said, frowning.

"I just called to tell you I love you," Rob said, "but I can't talk long. I have to get back to the books."

The frown slipped from Tressa's face. "I love you, too. Can I see you tomorrow?"

"How about right after school?"

"Great."

"I'll pick you up."

"Mother's on my case about you."

He sighed. "She's never even met me. How can she not like me?"

"It's not you. It's the idea of you. Dad's coming over in a few minutes. I know she's going to bring it up."

"What will he say?"

"He'll be cool. He's always cool. I want you to meet him . . . and Mother, too. Maybe then—"

"We'll see," he said.

"You can't keep putting it off."

"Well, I best get back to the books. I hate economics."

"So, why did you take it?"

"It's required for a degree in business administration."

"Poor Rob, I wish I could come help you study."

He snickered. "We wouldn't get much studying done."

"Yes, we would. I'm very disciplined. That's what the guidance counselor at school tells me. When there's work to be done, I jump to it, just like my father."

"I'll see you tomorrow."

"Right after school," Tressa said.

There was an ominous click on the phone.

"Mother? Are you on the line?"

"I need to make a call, Tressa."

" 'Night," Rob said. He hung up.

Tressa's face glowed red. "Mother, sometimes you make me so mad." She slammed the phone down.

"I think we're being followed," Anna said, watching a pair of distant headlights in her rearview mirror.

"Now who's jumpy?" Kathy asked.

"The car's been behind us all the way through town."

"So, maybe he—or she—needs to get to the other side of town just like we do."

"Maybe," Anna said, paying more attention to what was behind her than where she was going.

"You just missed the turnoff over to Tabernacle Mountain Road," Kathy said.

"Shit!" Anna slammed on the brakes.

Kathy had to laugh. "For goodness sakes, Anna, what's the matter with you?"

Anna stopped the car. "I just have a bad feeling about this late-night rendezvous. I think it's probably just some political dirty trick. And you took the bait—hook, line, and sinker."

"You didn't have to come along."

Anna's attention was focused on her side mirror now. The vehicle that had been behind them was rapidly approaching.

"Here he comes," Anna said. Her eyes widened as she saw the car's blinker come on. It veered to the right. "Ohmigod, he's pulling in behind us."

Kathy turned her head to look through the back window. Again, she started to laugh. "It's a police cruiser, Anna. Maybe Whit sent someone after us."

Anna squinted in the rearview mirror. Now, finally, she could make out the silhouette of the bubble gum machine on top of the car. "It's one of the city boys. What'd I do?"

Kathy looked in disbelief at her friend. "You missed the turnoff, slammed on your brakes, and whipped over to the side. I'd say that might have looked a little suspicious from his vantage point."

"He probably just noticed two women in a car and decided to try out his charm. You know cops."

Kathy shook her head. "Not as well as you."

"Here he comes," Anna said, "walking with that typical macho swagger."

She rolled down her window when he reached her door. "Good evening, officer."

The cop bent down. "Oh, Miss Tyree."

Anna smiled. "Yep, it's me."

"Is everything all right?" he asked.

She saw his nose twitching, as if he were trying to detect that catch phrase bit of probable cause—*the odor of an alcoholic beverage.*

"Everything's fine. I was chatting away with Mrs. Binder and missed the turnoff."

The cop, who Anna recognized from her days on the police beat, smiled. "I thought your maneuver was a little erratic. Just doing my job."

"I understand," Anna said.

"You ladies have a nice evening. Give my regards to Whit."

"The bastard!" Ann said once her window was back up.

"What's wrong? I thought he was very courteous."

"That damned crack about Whit. Everyone's always saying something like that. I'm not Anna Tyree. I'm Whit Pynchon's live-in lover."

"So get him to marry you."

Anna waited for the cop to pull away. Then she slammed the car in reverse and backed down the street.

"If I did that," she said as she scowled over her right shoulder, "then I would just be Whit Pynchon's wife."

Kathy's smile had turned into a frown. "Do I detect a hint of dissatisfaction?"

"Not really. I'm just out of sorts. I always get the impression that Whit and I are some sort of public joke—"

"An anomaly," Kathy said, "but not a joke."

Anna made the turn. "Oh, thanks. That's a damned big help."

"Well, you are. It's like that old gospel song, the one where the lamb lays down beside the lion."

"And I guess I'm the lamb, Kathy."

"No, sometimes you're the lion, and he's the lamb. You two have this amazing ability to shift roles. Someday you should write a book about this relationship."

She turned the car onto the highway that would carry them toward the double summit of Tabernacle Mountain.

"Wouldn't that thrill Whit? A book about us."

"Have you two even discussed the issue of marriage?"

Anna knitted her naturally thick brows. "Why?"

"You know it's going to remain an issue in a town as small as this."

"We've discussed it, but certainly not in that context. I don't intend to let that kind of provincialism influence a decision as important as that."

"Now you sound like don't-give-a-damn Whit."

"Well, in some ways he's right."

"Sorry to butt in," Kathy said, turning her attention to the increasingly steep road.

"Besides," Anna said, "he's never asked."

"What?"

"He's never asked me to marry him, the son of a bitch."

Kathy laughed. "So, why don't you propose?"

"Like hell I will."

"It gets dark once you get away from town," Kathy said, deciding to change the subject.

The lights of the roadside beer joints and used-car lots were behind them, and Kathy was right. It was dark that night—so dark that neither of them saw the old brown truck parked on a dirt road that turned off the main highway. With headlights off, it pulled onto the highway behind them.

# Six

"JULIA, YOUR FRIEND engaged in sexual intercourse the night before she died." Whit braced himself for her response.

She blinked. Then she blushed. Sex, in any form, had never been something Julia Pynchon could discuss easily. "How on earth do you know?" she asked.

"The pathologist has his ways of telling."

They sat in her kitchen. She had actually offered him a cup of coffee when he arrived. He had asked if Tressa was out again.

"No, she's upstairs."

Once in the kitchen, Julia had wanted to talk about Tressa, but Whit had stopped her. He hadn't wasted any time telling her about the medical examiner's discovery.

"I really don't believe it, Whitley. Maybe she was raped by the person who killed her."

"The M.E. pretty much ruled that out. It was actually obvious from our observations that her clothing remained intact. Rapists don't usually redress their victims."

She was sincerely shocked. "I will not believe it."

"I went to her apartment this afternoon and searched it."

She made a face. "As I said this afternoon, you have a miserable job."

"I agree. I met her landlady."

"Mrs. Worley," Julia said.

"She's not one of your admirers."

"My heavens! What have I ever done to her?"

Whit shrugged. "Well, she says you made the vic . . . I mean, Mrs. Weldon work too much overtime."

His former wife's mouth dropped. "Overtime! She never worked overtime. We don't have the money in the budget for it. Besides, we don't have all that much need to work over-time."

"According to Mrs. Worley, Mrs. Weldon often did not get home until midnight."

"That's not true, Whit. I can prove it. You can go look at the payroll records. Why, I never—"

Whit held up his hand to stop her. "I believe you, Julia."

"Then why, for heaven's sake, would the woman lie about such a thing?"

Whit took a sip of the coffee. As she always had, she brewed it so weak that it tasted like flavored water. "I don't think Mrs. Worley was lying, but I do think Eloise Weldon was coming home late very often. I don't think she was at work. I think she was involved in an affair, probably with a married man since she seemed to have been so clandestine about it."

Julia pushed herself to her feet. "Is that how you're going to handle this? Besmirch her reputation? Make her out to be the criminal?"

"Damn, Julia, don't get your bowels in an uproar."

"I knew this would happen. Isn't that how you police always do it? By the time you're finished, it's the poor victim who becomes the villain."

"Look at the evidence, Julia."

"What evidence?"

"The medical evidence for chrissakes! The woman's hab-its. Her misleading statements to her landlady. In her apart-ment I found a note about Willie's birthday. Do you know a Willie?"

"Willie might be one of her grandkids."

"Maybe. Be assured I'll check that out. Any other Willies come to mind, Julia? It's a young person's name. Could she have been involved with a student at—"

"Whitley Pynchon!"

"Come off it, Julia. I'm just doing my job. Don't you want the person who did this caught?"

"Of course, but—"

"Right now, the individual with whom she had sex Saturday night is our best suspect. I've got to find him."

"I just think it's revolting—"

"Sex has always been revolting to you. I know that, and I'm sorry that I'm the one that has to talk to you about it. Now, can you think of anyone called Willie?"

She considered his question. "No, no one."

"You're sure?"

"Of course I'm sure."

Whit finished his coffee and stood up. "I'd appreciate it if you could keep your eyes and ears open. By the way, I'll also be talking to the rest of the folks who work with you at the library. I'll stop by tomorrow and pick up a list of them."

She was still on her feet. "Are you leaving?"

"Yeah, I'm beat."

"What about Tressa?"

"I was going to give her a shout on my way out."

Julia's face tightened. "I thought we might discuss this man she's seeing with her."

"Not tonight, Julia."

She came around the table at him. "Oh, too busy for your daughter, is that it?"

Whit dropped his head in frustration. "Actually, Anna is going to talk to her."

"Anna?"

"She and Tressa are friends. It won't seem to Tressa as if you and I are ordering her not to see him, which we really can't do anyway. You might like to know that Anna agrees with you about this guy.''

Julia threw up her hands. Her face was crimson with anger. "Fantastic! Your live-in whore agrees with me about the moral dilemma of my daughter.''

Whit froze. He resisted the overwhelming urge to backhand her. It was difficult, but he managed. "You damned bitch," he said. "Where do you get off—''

"Daddy?" It was Tressa. She was coming down the steps.

Whit turned from his ex-wife and went into the hall. "Hi, Tressa.''

She danced down the steps and hugged him. "How's the case coming?''

"Slow.''

She saw the trembling of his lower lip, and she looked down the hall toward her mother, who avoided her eye contact. "You two have been arguing again.''

"I gotta go, hon." He leaned down and kissed her cheek. "You take care.''

He headed for the door.

"Stay a few minutes, Daddy.''

But he was out the door.

She wheeled to face her mother. "What did you say to him?''

Julia had stepped into the hall. Tressa was shocked to see a hint of dampness in her mother's eyes.

"Something I shouldn't have, Tressa.''


"Now I'm beginning to wonder if this was wise," Kathy said.

Anna didn't respond at once. She was fighting with the steering wheel as she guided the car around one of the meet-your-ass curves that gave the two-lane highway to the mountain's double summit its treacherous reputation.

Once they were through the curve, Anna said, "What did you say?"

"Is this wise, Anna? Coming up here in the middle of the night like this in response to some unknown caller."

"Probably not, but you know what they say about curiosity. You're sure he didn't say for you to come alone?"

Kathy shook her head. "I don't think so. I can't remember that much about the conversation now. It happened so quickly, and I always react with so much resentment toward anonymous callers. Are we almost there?"

"Almost," Anna said.

Kathy grimaced as Anna guided the car into another vicious curve. As the editor gunned her car out of it, her headlights revealed a reasonably long stretch of straight road. She was nearly through it when the headlights glared into her rearview mirror.

"There's a car behind us," she said.

Kathy looked back. "Do you think that's him? The fellow who phoned."

"Who knows? I have no idea how much traffic there is on this road at this time of night."

"It seems like we've been climbing for a long time."

"I guess I forgot how far up we had to go to reach the overlook," Anna said, squinting ahead at the nearly obliterated double yellow lines that bisected the highway all the way from the foot of the mountain to the top. The car behind her was maintaining its distance. In fact, with the twisting curves, Anna hadn't seen its headlights since she completed the straightaway.

The night itself was warm but cloudy. In spite of the afternoon thunder, the storm had not materialized. That had happened often during the dry spring. Behind them the lights of Milbrook filled the broad plateau that provided a base for Tabernacle Mountain. The new spring foliage had already started to appear on most of the trees in Milbrook itself, but up on the mountain, which towered to a height of four thousand feet at the highest of its two summits, the branches of the trees remained barren.

"We haven't passed a single car coming down," Kathy said.

"Most travelers use the interstate now," Anna said.

"I can understand why. This road could make a sailor carsick."

"I think it's just around the next turn."

"If it's not, we're going to start down the other side pretty soon."

Anna glided into the turn and accelerated as the car went through it.

"Jesus," Kathy said, her stomach beginning to rebel against the constant shifting motion.

"I told you," Anna said.

The headlights of her vehicle illuminated the overlook. Sure enough, there was a dark-colored car parked there. Anna eased her vehicle into the gravel-covered pull-off. As she did, her headlights illuminated the interior of the other car.

"What on earth?" Kathy said.

Anna gaped. Two heads were visible, momentarily pressed together before the sudden assault of lights shocked them apart. A girl and boy stared back insolently into Anna's headlights.

"They were making out!" Anna said.

The young boy fired up the engine of his car and sprayed Anna's vehicle with gravel as he squealed away from the overlook.

"Bastard!" Anna shouted.

"I guess we spoiled their night," Kathy said. "I don't believe that was who we came to see."

In the rearview mirror the taillights from the car vanished from view. The headlights from the vehicle that had been following them flashed into view.

"Sit tight. This may just be our date."

But the vehicle, an old battered farm truck, drove right on past them and on toward the summit of the mountain.

"So what now?" Kathy asked.

Anna pulled the car up to the guardrail. Below, Milbrook's lights twinkled in the night air. In the distance, to the west of Milbrook, lightning continued to tease the drought-stricken region.

"We wait," Anna said, "for a little while anyway."

Benny Johnston staggered across the unpaved parking lot outside of The Grasshopper. He'd been chasing shots of Jack Daniels with beer since six-thirty that night, so he didn't notice that his truck was gone until he reached the place where he remembered parking it.

"Shee-it," he mumbled, slowly turning . . . stumbling . . . looking around the parking area. There were maybe a half dozen cars outside the beer joint. At least beer was all The Grasshopper was supposed to sell, but the tavern's owner saw no harm in dispensing hard liquor when he knew the crowd.

"Double shee-it," Benny said.

His truck was flat-ass gone.

He stumbled back toward The Grasshopper's front door. Just as he reached for the knob, the door flew open. The sudden sense of forward motion pulled Benny face first down into the door opening.

"Fuck, Benny. You on your ass, ol' man. You gonna drive like that?"

Benny rolled over on his back. "Not gonna drive—"

"Least let me get my ass home 'fore you get out on the road."

The man above Benny was Ike Fraley. They'd gone to school together a lot of years before.

"Shum motherfucka shtole my truck."

Ike bent down.

"Whatcha saying?"

"My truck!" Benny screamed. "Motherfucka shtole it."

Ike looked out at the lot. "You sure? You kinda shit-faced, boy."

"Fuckin' A I'm shure."

Ike looked back into the bar. "Hey, Mikie, somebody stole ol' Benny's car."

"Did him a gawdamn favor," someone shouted from inside the bar.

Ike laughed. "Yeah, he'd have to tie a five-dollar bill to that piece of shit before he could give it away."

"Shtole my fuckin' truck," Benny was mumbling as he turned over on his stomach and tried to get up.

Ike reached down and helped him.

"C'mon over here."

Mikie Post, the owner of the beer joint, came to help. "Jest don't get sick, Benny. I don't like pukin' in my place."

"Motherfuckas. Shtealing my truck."

They wrestled him into a booth. Benny collapsed back into it, his back resting against the wall.

Mikie leaned down toward him. "You ain't gonna puke, are you?"

"I just want my truck!" Benny screamed.

"Want I should call the cops?" Mikie said, his mind cataloging all the things he would need to do before they arrived—like clear the table of liquor glasses, check the ashtrays for roaches, get the tip board that was laying on the bar.

Benny tried to pull himself up. "Fuck the copsh . . . no copsh . . ."

"Maybe I'd better," Mikie said. "I don't need no hassles with 'em."

"Gawdamn motherfuckas," Benny said, falling back into the booth.

"Call the cops," Ike said. "Maybe they'll take the

drunkin' asshole home. Otherwise you gonna be stuck with his sorry ass all night.''

Mikie hadn't thought about that. ''What if they take him to jail for being drunk?''

Ike chuckled. ''Probably save his ass. He goes home like that, his ol' lady gonna bust his balls.''

''I'll go call 'em,'' Mikie said.

Benny Johnston tried to pull himself up again. ''I'm gonna pu—''

But he didn't get to say it. He just did it. The contents of his stomach, nothing but beer and booze and belly juice, sprayed over the table.

''Jesus, boy.'' Ike backed away.

Mikie, who was on the phone, started shouting, ''Haul the asshole outta here.''

No one volunteered to do so.

By the time Mikie finished his conversation with the sheriff's department, Benny was laying facedown on the table, gurgling in his own vomit. ''I oughta kill the son of a bitch,'' the joint's owner said.

''What about the cops?'' Ike asked.

''Useless jerkoffs. They said they'd take a complaint. Claimed a fuckin' dee-tective would be out tomorrow.''

Ike shook his head. ''Didn't they ask for no description of the truck?''

''They asked. I told 'em. I ain't gonna clean that shittin' puke up. Not me, not this time.''

''They want a license number?''

''Yeah, but I told him the owner was on his ass drunk. They just said fine . . . see ya in the morning.''

''That's it? That's all they said?''

''No, the cocksucker told me not to let him drive home drunk—like what the hell's he gonna drive. Dumb cocksuckers.'' The stench from the table was beginning to nauseate Mikie.

Ike was still shaking his head. "Friggin' cops, they just ain't what they used to be."

The two women weren't saying much as Anna guided the car back down the mountain. They were both angry, mad that they had been hoodwinked by some practical joker. The silence was tense. It made the sudden violence of the jolt all the more startling.

Kathy screamed. Anna lurched forward, her chin striking the steering wheel.

"God, what was it?" Anna said.

It happened again, but this time they were braced for it.

"Behind us," Kathy cried. "I think someone's behind us."

Anna, her chin streaming blood, didn't dare put on the brake. The car squealed through a tight curve before she risked a quick glance in the rearview mirror. At first she saw nothing. Certainly no headlights. Then, in the red glow of her taillights, she saw a glimmer that formed into a smiling sort of grill.

"I see it," she said just as the impact almost drove her right over the side of the mountain.

"Jesus, Anna. They're trying to kill us."

"Hold on." Anna's fists were wrapped around the steering wheel. She didn't even realize that blood was running down her throat and between her breasts.

"ASSHOLE!" Anna shrieked, mindless with panic. She leaned forward, trying to see better. The blood from the cut in her chin started to drip into her lap and on the plastic surface of the steering wheel.

Headlights flashed on. The beams flooded the interior of Anna's car, momentarily blinding her.

"Look out," Kathy shrieked.

Anna hissed when she saw the guardrail in front of her. The steering wheel was slick now with blood, but she managed to wrench it to the right. The front left corner of the bumper wailed as it nicked the metal. Sparks flew.

"Oh God, we're going to die," Kathy said.

Anna was too busy regaining control of the car to worry about dying. The light that had invaded the car faded.

"He's dropping back," Kathy said.

But her friend knew better. "He's coming up beside us. Hang on tight."

Kathy looked to her right. "Hurry, Anna."

They were in the long straight stretch. Anna jammed the accelerator to the floor just as the vehicle swerved toward her. The impact caught the rear right quarter panel. The front of the car took on a life of its own as Anna fought with the useless steering wheel. In her own headlights she saw the road vanish into an impossible curve.

Kathy saw it, too. "For god's sake slow down!"

Anna tried. She stood on the brakes, but the car continued to roll forward toward the killer curve. "He's behind us. He's pushing us!"

Her headlights flashed back from the gleaming metal of the oncoming guardrails. The glare blinded her. Finally her brakes began to squeal. And so did Anna and Kathy.


Marsha Via wondered if Jake Brimm would be so brazen about his visits if she lived in Milbrook. She didn't, of course. She lived on a small five-acre farm south of Milbrook. It had been her parents' place, and it was all that they had left her. Donna, her eight-year-old daughter, was up in her bedroom asleep when Marsha heard the smooth purring of the Cadillac's engine. She sat in a chair in the small living room, still fully dressed, watching some silly mystery movie on network TV. One day, when she had the money, she wanted a satellite dish. Of course, there were many things she wanted, only a few of which she actually needed.

Her visitor didn't knock. He just opened the door and

stepped into the living room. Jake Brimm wasn't a bad-looking man for his age, not that Marsha really knew his age. He wouldn't tell her. So she guessed he was around fifty-seven. He had something of a paunch, but then so did she. His short gray hair was starting to recede a little. His face was always a little too red. At first, she suspected him of drinking, but she soon discovered that he never touched alcohol. He had a case of high blood pressure.

He was smiling. "The little one in bed?"

Marsha nodded. "She was awfully tired tonight. To be honest, I am, too."

He plopped down on the couch. "Me, too. I had a hard day of campaigning. I spent the afternoon down around Tipple Town. That place is depressing."

She just nodded.

"Didcha get the time sheets?"

She knew the question was coming. "No, the secretary had carried them upstairs before I had a chance."

"Dammit to hell, woman—"

"I'm sorry, Jake. And don't shout. You'll wake Donna."

"I need those time sheets. I need them now."

"Look, there wasn't anything I could do. Besides, Jake, I think you're getting a bum steer about the overtime."

"Who gives a shit? I can throw some smoke with it. Nobody really knows much about the wage-and-hour stuff anyway."

"I can't afford to lose my job."

He climbed to his feet. "Look, you wanna be my chief deputy, you're gonna have to do something for it."

She glared up at him. "I have been doing *something* for it."

He was the one who had initiated their relationship even before the death of the prior sheriff. That far in advance of the election he had still planned to run. He wanted someone on the inside, someone who would be well rewarded when he took office. Everyone assumed, of course, that Brimm would win. He hadn't lost an election yet. Not a single one, neither on his own behalf or on behalf of someone else.

The sex had come a few months later. Marsha hadn't minded it. He was a good lover at first, but the longer it went the more things changed. He asked her to get him things from the department that put her at risk, and in bed he only seemed to respond to her when she gave him head.

"Look, Marsha." His tone mellowed. "Some of the other guys have come to me. They think Dickerson's screwing them on their overtime."

"He's not."

"I hear it different."

"I can't get this week's time sheets. Maybe next week's."

"The election is getting near. Next week may be too late."

"It'll have to do," she said.

"Don't let me down now, Marsha. You've got as much riding on this election as I do."

She heard her daughter cry out. "I've got to go up to her."

She rose and started toward the steps. He reached and grasped her arm. "I'd like to stay awhile."

That meant he wanted a blow job.

"Not tonight."

His face clouded. "What's with you?"

"I told you. I'm tired."

"Mommy!"

"I've got to go up. I'll probably sleep with her tonight." She started up the steps.

"One more thing, Marsha."

She stopped and sighed. "What is it?" she asked without turning around.

"My boy got a ticket last week from one of your hot-shots."

"Jamey?"

Jake nodded. "Think you can do anything about it?"

"What was he doing?"

"Aw, some chickenshit crap . . . just riding his motorcycle without a helmet. No big deal."

"I'll handle it," Marsha said. "G'nite."

Kathy willed her eyes open. For a moment she had no idea where she was—no idea why such hideous pain was coming from her leg. She tasted something. It was salty, coppery. She groaned.

Slowly her vision started to focus. She was looking out the car windshield, looking through a spiderweb.

A spiderweb?

The windshield had been cracked all over. It was the windshield itself that she saw, shot through by a thousand small interlocking cracks. A smear darkened it right in front of her . . . a wet splatter of—

"Oh, God," she wailed as she remembered. "Anna?"

She looked over. Her friend was slumped against the steering wheel. "Anna?"

She reached over to shake her.

That's when the car shifted.

Kathy yelped and sat motionless. The vehicle was pointing forward at a frightening angle. They had smashed through the guardrail and gone over the mountainside. The thick forest, though, had obstructed their progress and had eventually stopped the vehicle.

"Anna?" This time she whispered and was reaching over to touch her friend when she heard the noise.

*Footsteps!*

"Dear God, please help us."

She was so cold, her stomach so nauseous. She tried to see out her window, but her view was blocked by the bough of a huge pine that was pressed against the glass.

"Please! We're in here!"

The maker of the footsteps moved around the front of the

car—into Kathy's narrow line of vision. Her eyes widened as she saw the odd round shape of the head.

"Help us!" she shouted.

The figure was on Anna's side now.

That's when Anna coughed.

"Oh, thank God, you're alive."

The next thing she saw was a flash of silver coming from Anna's side of the car, and the windshield exploded in her face.

# SEVEN

"DID YOU HEAR THAT, Archie?" Maude Mann was rigid, her arthritic back held as straight as the spine-jarring pain allowed.

Archie listened. He heard several things. The ominous hum of their rickety refrigerator. It didn't sound as if it was going to last the rest of their waning lives. He heard the gurgling of a commode that needed a new set of insides, just like he and his wife. There was the distant grumbling of a storm. But he heard nothing to prompt any real worry.

"You've been hearing spooks since we've lived in this house, woman." Archie pushed himself out of the battered, off-center recliner that sat in front of the small stone fireplace. "After twenty gawdamn years, you oughta be used to this place."

Maudie Mann remained tense. "Weren't no spook, and I wasn't seeing things this morning neither. The law never did come."

"Good thing, too," Archie said. "They wouldn't have found anything. Embarrassed you and me both if they hadda come."

"I saw what I saw, and I just heard what I heard. It sounded like a motor. Just go see."

"A motor?"

"Please go see, Archie."

"I'm going, dammit. Just as fast as I can." In Archie's

circumstances, that wasn't too swiftly. The drop in barometric pressure that foreshadowed the storm aggravated his own milder case of arthritis. Not that Archie minded the storm. God knows they needed the rain. He lifted his cane off the back of his recliner.

For the first few years, whenever his wife had been aroused by some disturbance, either real or imagined, Archie had snatched the small single-shot .410 from its place above the stone fireplace. After so many false alarms, he'd ceased to bother. Now, it would have been awkward anyway, trying to carry the small shotgun in one hand and the aluminum cane in the other.

"You be careful," she warned as he hobbled across the plank floor toward the front door.

He just glanced back at her, his disgust evident.

"I swear to God, Archie. I heard something."

Archie threw up the hand that wasn't full of cane. "For chrissakes, woman, ain't been nobody within a mile of this place all day long."

"You weren't here. There *was* someone prowling around this morning."

"Sure there was. A spaceman, right? No wonder the damned cops didn't come, but I'll go take a look-see. Just like I always have—for the past gawdamn twenty years . . . just to keep you happy."

The same scene played frequently at the Manns' cabin, usually two or three times in a single week. Occasionally, about once every six months or so, Archie managed to discover an explanation for the threatening sounds his wife heard. Twice, he'd discovered a raccoon digging down into the thirty-gallon metal drum that Archie used to burn trash. Once, about three months after they had bought the remote mountain home, he had actually found a small black bear sitting on the wooden door covering the potato cellar that was dug in the yard. Attracted by the aroma from the apples that Archie had stored inside, the bear hadn't offered to move when Archie had come around the side of the house. He'd gone back inside in a hurry. Several minutes later, the bear had snorted his frustration at not being able to get to the source of the fruity scent and had lumbered off into the woods.

There were things to be heard when you lived in as remote a hollow as the Manns did. Their small log cabin sat at the very end of a graveled private right-of-way that branched off the old, now-abandoned two-lane road a mile or so down the hollow. Several folks lived in mobile homes down at the mouth, but once past those small homes, and for the next mile, the rugged right-of-way snaked its way through the thick oak forest covering the slopes of the two ridges that formed the hollow. Archie, a retired mine foreman, had fallen in love with the little cabin and its seclusion. Sure, it had something of a sullied past, but then so did Archie.

In a lot of ways, he enjoyed the sense of self-sufficiency, especially back when he was able to keep his garden. The house's main source of water came from a two-hundred-foot deep well that never seemed to run dry. When the power failed, as it sometimes did during the winter, he had the old surface well in front of the house from which he could draw water. He had his fireplace to keep him warm and a generous supply of potatoes and apples in the cellar outside, which he now was forced to stock from grocery store purchases.

For most of the twenty years, he had been able to work in the mines and manage a small farm. Now he did neither— wasn't able to—but he still appreciated the isolation. At least he could step out his back door and fart without offending any neighbors. He could even pop off a few gunshots at a tin can without disturbing anyone but Maudie.

He had to lean the cane against the wall in order to open the door. It took two hands to manage the dead bolt that his wife had insisted he install—one hand to twist the knob and the other to put pressure against the door so the metal bar would slip free of the slot. Archie had installed it himself, and as usual his measurements hadn't been as precise as the hardware required.

"There!" his wife snapped, as if vindicated. "You heard that, didn't you?"

Archie glanced back. "Didn't hear shit, woman. Keerist, you got a case of the jumpies tonight."

"You're getting hard of hearing, old man. It was a thud—"

"There's a storm coming. That's what you heard, the thunder clap echoing."

"Nosiree, Archie."

"Okay . . . okay. I'm checkin' it out."

"Please . . . please be careful."

He retrieved the cane and opened the door.

"Be back in a second."

Whit hadn't expected Anna to be home when he returned from Julia's, and she wasn't. Usually she stayed at the *Journal* until the next day's edition was "put to bed," as she liked to say. Still, after his unsettling encounter with his former wife, he decided to call Anna, needing the comfort he often received from hearing her voice. Not that he was going to tell her that . . . exactly.

In the small kitchen he mixed himself a strong bourbon and Coke and returned to the living room where he settled down in a chair near the phone. The throaty grumble of distant thunder penetrated the walls of the house. After taking a few sips from the drink, he reached for the handset. Just as his hand touched the cool plastic, the phone rang. Whit actually jumped—and then cursed, as much at himself as at the phone. He glanced at the clock and saw that it was almost eleven.

"Pynchon here," he said, fully expecting—even hoping—to hear Anna's voice at that time of the evening.

"Mr. Pynchon?" It was a male voice.

"Yeah," Whit said, now irritated by the call.

"This is Ken . . . Ken Burns. I work down at the *Journal*."

"So?"

"I was calling to see if Ms. Tyree was there."

Whit frowned. "No, she's not. Isn't she there?"

"No, sir. She and Mrs. Binder left around nine P.M. and said they'd be back in an hour or so. They're not back, and we need Ms. Tyree to approve the front page before we send it down to be shot."

"To be shot?" Whit said.

"By the press camera. She said she'd be back in time."

"Oh . . . well, Anna's not here. Did you try Mrs. Binder's residence?"

"Her machine answered," the young man said.

"They probably got to talking somewhere and let time slip on them."

The caller paused. "We really need to find her. We're getting desperate. The assistant editor is out of town, and there's no one with authority to check out the page."

"I'm sorry about that," Whit said, "but I don't know where she is."

"It isn't like her not to be here, Mr. Pynchon. Frankly, I'm a little worried."

So was Whit, but he wasn't about to admit it. "Well, if she comes home or calls, I'll tell her that you need to talk to her."

"She knows that, sir. That's what worries me."

"Did they say where they were going?"

"Nope. I've checked with everyone. They went in Ms. Tyree's car. Mrs. Binder's vehicle is still out in the lot."

"When she gets there," Whit said, "have her call me."

He hung up and immediately dialed the number for the sheriff's department.

"This is Pynchon," he said. "Have you all had any wrecks reported tonight?"

"Earlier," a male deputy said. "Over beyond Tipple Town. A bunch of kids wrapped a car around a power pole."

"Who's out in the field tonight?"

The dispatcher listed three officers.

Whit then asked him to notify his units to keep an eye out for Anna's vehicle. He provided them with a description.

"What if they see her?" the deputy asked.

"Tell her to get in touch with me."

"Ten four."

Whit hung up and started to pace. Where the hell was she? She should know better. His first strong reaction was that of anger.

A sharp crack of thunder rattled the house. It started to pour outside. Whit went to the front door and opened it. A gust of wind whipped a shower of cold raindrops into Whit's face.

Outside the Manns' house, a storm-cooled wind whispered through the leaves on the few trees that had started to produce their spring growth. The towering oaks still clutched many of their weathered brown leaves from the prior season. They rustled, too, and continued to fall. A few, though, would not drop until the new buds pried their tenacious death hold from the gnarled limbs. To Archie, the oak was something special. Its fiber was hard and tough. Its roots snaked deep into the rocky ground of the mountains and held it firm against the worst winter winds and gusting spring storms. It was the last to lose its leaves, clinging to them even when they were dry and crunchy. In every aspect, the oak resisted the worst that Mother Nature could hurl at it. For many years Archie had thought of himself as a sort of oak, and he was still resisting, but he was resigned to the fact that his beloved oaks would outlast him.

A flash of bright light illuminated the ridges that surrounded his little patch of homestead. It was only seconds later that he heard the rumbling. The storm was fast approaching. More than likely, it would move along the higher mountain ridges to the south of his hollow. Another bolt flashed over the ridge to his left. Milbrook was probably catching hell. Archie hoped the storm came his way. The prior season's desiccated leaves that littered the forest floors were little more than firebox tinder just waiting for a lightning strike or a carelessly tossed cigarette. Three times in the last twenty years, his cabin had been threatened by forest fires, and at those times the woods hadn't been nearly as dry as they were now.

He eased himself down the steps. Once at the bottom, he used the cane to brace himself as he lowered his bony hips down on the second step. The air was warm, the temperature still in the high fifties. The wind was refreshing. It smelled of spring, Archie's favorite season. How many more would God grant him? Two or three? He hoped so. Their only daughter lived down in Wytheville. Just two months ago she'd given birth to their first grandchild, a little girl, and he at least wanted to live long enough to be called Gramps. Surely that wasn't asking too much. At that moment his daughter and infant granddaughter were on some crazy jaunt to South America of all places, carried off by that nutty husband of hers. Some goddamn stupid thing to do with a baby, but then he hadn't been consulted when they were planning the trip.

A twig snapped off to his left. It momentarily reminded the old man of a miniature crack of lightning. This time, though, Archie tensed. His head riveted around, and his eyes, still sharp, peered into the thick woods that came up to the driveway that ran along that side of the house. He heard nothing for a few moments, not even the wind that had died down for the moment. Then he heard the shuffling. Something was moving through the crinkly blanket of leaves that covered the forest floor.

Archie eased himself to his feet. The mountains around his home were well-stocked with all kinds of critters—raccoon, possum, squirrel, still an occasional bear—but the foot noises he was hearing were suspiciously unique. Whatever was making the noise, it moved on two feet. The swishing crunchy sounds, each distinctively spaced, told him that much. This was one time he wished that he had brought along the gun. In his younger days, either armed or unarmed, he would have confronted the trespasser. Over the years, though, as his own life came closer to its end, he became more respectful of risk. He moved one step at a time back up to the porch.

Once there, he stopped and squinted down the gravel road, his eyes searching for a car. Surely, no one would have walked up to his cabin. If they had, then it had to mean their intentions weren't honorable. He saw no car. He turned to go into the house.

A sound stopped him . . . a low moaning.

It came from his right.

Lightning flashed again, and Archie saw it, a body stretched out on his porch. "Sweet Jesus," he mumbled and started toward the figure.

It moaned again as he reached it. Archie knelt down. The storm accommodated, unleashing a barrage of flickering light by which Archie saw that it was a woman—a red-haired woman whose face was covered with blood.

"Hey there, missy?" He reached down to shake her.

When he heard the board creak behind him, it was too late. He didn't even get to look around before something whacked against the side of his head.

\* \* \*

Maudie had been waiting but not so patiently. She was fidgeting in her chair, still listening, when she heard the commotion.

"Archie!"

He didn't answer. She lurched to her feet and limped toward the front door. "Archie! Answer me!"

But he didn't—or couldn't.

She reached the door and leaned against it so that she could slide the dead bolt into its chiseled-out slot. Only after it was secure did she dare to pull aside the muslin curtain that covered the window. Her heart was racing, and she was wheezing down deep in her chest.

Peering out into the darkness she could see absolutely nothing. Then the lightning flashed, still very far away, but in that single burst of white brightness she caught a glimpse of the cane. It rested on the front porch.

"Archie!" She wailed his name and was at once petrified that the cry would bring whatever was outside in on her. She glanced over to the phone.

*The police!*

She hobbled toward the small telephone stand as fast as her decaying hips would allow. She didn't even think about how long it would take the law to reach her—thirty or forty minutes at least . . . and that was assuming that someone would respond to the call at once, which itself was almost unthinkable. She considered none of that, and it wouldn't have mattered anyway. When she lifted the receiver, the line was dead.

"Oh, dear God!" She pounded on the switch hook with a forefinger twisted and swollen with arthritis.

Just as she dropped the useless hunk of black plastic to the floor, the front window shattered. A shower of twinkling shards of glass crashed into her. A rock exploded against her side, almost knocking her to the floor. She staggered toward the center of the room, her hand going to a place on her forehead where there was a stinging, burning pain. The hand came away covered with deep red blood.

"Oh, Jesus," she prayed.

Maudie Mann had thought she had been frightened many times before. Suddenly she knew better. Maybe she had been edgy, apprehensive, but never before had she ever been truly scared—not until that night. Inside her frail chest, her aging heart felt as if it were doing flip-flops. Her bladder, none too retentive at the best of times, was out of control. She could feel the warm dribbles down the inside of her thigh. The blood from the ragged slice on her forehead poured down her face . . . into her eyes where it blinded her . . . into her mouth where she tasted it, warm and pungent, like over-brewed coffee.

The pounding started then as if someone was using a sledgehammer on the door. She peeked up at it and saw the panels splintering under the withering blows.

Maudie sunk to her knees. As her weight settled upon the swollen joints, she whimpered in pain. Her curved spine actually creaked as she rocked forward to bury her bloody head in her hands.

"Now I lay me down to sleep—" It was a silly prayer, but at the moment it was the only one she could think of—the one she had taught her daughter to say each night as she went to bed.

"I pray the Lord my soul to take. If—"

The door flew open.

"You're in my house," a voice cried.

But Maudie didn't look up. She never even saw the face of the person that killed her with a single roundhouse swing of a shiny, oversized metal sprocket chain.

# EIGHT

GIL DICKERSON GRIMACED as he tested the coffee in the white Styrofoam cup. "I should know better than to try to drink this stuff at this time of the morning. It's been cooking all night."

Whit was on his feet, pacing the small confines of the sheriff's office. "Your coffee always tastes like swill to me. Damn, I wish to hell I knew where those two were."

"There's some logical explanation," Gil said.

"If they're out there chasing down some harebrained story—" Whit didn't bother to finish the balance of the sentence.

Just before midnight Whit had phoned Gil at his home to tell him that both Kathy and Anna were missing. The recently appointed sheriff of the county had called the sheriff's office at once to order the full second shift to go on overtime. With the incoming third shift, five officers were patrolling the county in search of the two women.

Gil and Whit had met at the jail at 12:30 A.M. It was now 1:00 A.M. "Did anyone notify the city boys?" Whit asked.

"I'll check." Gil phoned down to the control room. "Did any of you notify the city department?"

The look on Gil's face told Whit that they had not. "Forget it," Gil was saying. "I'll call them."

He hung up the phone. "Jesus, Whit. None of these guys can take any initiative."

110

"You want me to call the city?" Whit asked.

But Gil had already picked up the phone again. "No, I'll do it."

Whit headed into the sheriff's private bathroom while Gil made the call. When he returned, he saw that the sheriff had something to tell him.

"What is it?"

"The guy on the desk was working over from the evening shift. While he was patrolling earlier, he stopped Anna and another woman—Kathy, I assume—around nine this evening."

"Where?"

"Over on Wallace Street. He said that Anna was driving rather erratically, but she seemed okay."

"Where were they going?"

"They didn't tell him."

"Christ Almighty, Gil. I'll be honest. I'm really worried."

"You wanna go out in the car? Take a look for ourselves?"

"Anything," Whit said. "Otherwise I'm gonna start chewing on my nails."

The temperature had dropped into the high forties following the thunderstorm. It had moved through quickly, dropping a mere quarter inch of rain on Milbrook before moving toward the northeast. In its wake it left a mass of damp air over Raven County that foreshadowed thick early-morning fog. Gil used his wipers to clear the moisture from his windshield. "Coolest night we've had in a while," he said, trying to make conversation. "I think maybe our warm spell is over."

Whit remained silent, his eyes fixed on the road ahead.

"She's probably fine, Whit. You know those two. They're totally unpredictable."

"Not when it comes to getting out the paper, Gil. Anna knew she was supposed to be back to check the front page.

Something's happened. Otherwise she would have been there at the *Journal*. She's obsessive about that damned paper.''

"So where do we go?" the sheriff asked.

"Let's drive over to Kathy's house and check it out.''

"They've already called there," Gil said.

"I know, but let's go look it over. It's the only place I know to start. I just left my house, and there was certainly nothing there.''

They were almost to the publisher's home when the radio came alive. "County to Unit One.''

Gil snatched the mike from its position on the dash. "Go ahead, county.''

"I have an employee from the newspaper here who may have some information for you.''

Gil glanced at Whit, then said, "Can you relay it?"

There was a moment's pause before the dispatcher said, "Negative. This individual wishes to speak with Investigator Pynchon in person.''

"Probably bullshit," Whit said.

"I guess we'd better go back and check it out.''

"I guess," Whit said.

Gil keyed the mike. "Advise the subject to meet us outside the jail in five minutes.''

Anna tried to open her eyes, but it didn't help. She still couldn't see a thing. All she remembered was the wild ride down the mountain . . . the car behind her . . . the guardrail coming straight at her . . .

"Oh, God," she said, her voice hoarse and hardly audible even to herself.

She tried to move, but she couldn't. Not her arms. Or her legs. Her chin was on fire, and her head throbbed. She slipped in and out of a crazy, foggy kind of consciousness. It was a mental roller coaster ride that made her head seem as if it were spinning.

"Kathy?" she whispered.

No answer.

"Kathy?" She called out her friend's name.

Still no answer.

Her mouth tasted of blood. She wet her lips and once again tried to open her eyes. They were open, she decided. She just couldn't see anything. She was blind.

She again willed her arms to move, then her feet. She felt the coarse fibers cut into her wrists and ankles. At that moment, as her mind finally slipped into gear, she realized that she wasn't blind—she was blinded. A piece of material covered her eyes. Nor was she paralyzed. Rather, she was bound by ropes.

"What the hell—"

She started to struggle against the rope.

A man laughed, and Anna froze. "Where am I? Who are you?"

Footsteps approached her. She detected a gentle movement in the air, and then she smelled something, the odor of grease mixed with gasoline. A leathery hand touched her cheek. She tried to wrench away, but it was useless. The ropes lashed her tightly to the chair.

"Damn you," she screamed.

"Take it easy," a male voice said in a harsh whisper. Again his clammy hand caressed her cheek. "You've got a nasty bruise on your head and a bad cut on your chin."

He touched her temple, and she cried out in pain.

"See," he said. "Maybe even a concussion."

"Where's Kathy?"

"The woman who was with you? She's probably still in the car. Maybe dead for all I know or care."

"You son of a bitch."

Blindfolded, she didn't see the blow coming. In a way, that was probably for the best. She didn't know to tense, so her face simply moved in the same direction as the impact.

"Don't call me that!" the man hissed. "Don't ever call me that!"

"You son of a bitch!" she shrieked again, infuriated.

This time, she braced herself for the blow. It didn't come. Instead, fingers touched her breasts. She stiffened as he found the nipple of her left breast beneath the fabric of blouse and bra.

"What are you doing?"

The fingers squeezed. She cried out in pain.

"I said, don't call me that. You understand?"

The man kept pinching.

"Oh dear God, yes!"

He released her, and she took a deep breath. "What do you want from me?"

"From you? Nothing. Not a damned thing." He was still whispering as if trying to conceal the true sound of his voice.

"I don't understand," Anna said. "Was it you that ran us off the road?"

"Yeah."

"But you don't want anything?"

Anna had already suspected the fact that she was probably going to be raped. What then? Killed?

"I didn't say that. You asked what I wanted from you. I told you—nothing. I didn't even have an idea I'd get you, not tonight anyway. Nice surprise when I saw your car instead of the other woman's. You can make it easier on yourself if you behave, but it doesn't make any fucking difference to me one way or the other."

Anna's dizziness was returning. Her stomach was queasy. "What is it you do want?" she managed to ask.

This time he didn't answer. She could hear him moving around on the wooden floor.

"I asked you a question."

Still he did not answer, but she sensed that he had moved very close to her again. She could smell that same aromatic stench—oil and gasoline. She felt a sudden movement of air and a piece of cloth was pulled tightly over her mouth. She tried to scream, but when she opened her mouth the material snapped tighter, squelching her sound.

"No more talking," he said, tying the gag tightly behind her head.


"I'm Burns," the young man said. "From down at the *Journal*. I'm the city editor. I called you earlier."

Whit and Gil were still in the sheriff's Olds. The newspaper employee stood by the passenger-side door, leaning down so that he could see Whit.

"What's so important?" Whit asked.

Burns shoved a newspaper through the open window. "This is today's *Charleston Gazette*. I found it on Mrs. Binder's desk. There's a note on it."

Gil reached up and flipped on the dome light. Burns pointed to the right-hand margin. "There."

"Tabernacle Mountain Overlook . . . 9:00 P.M.," Whit read.

"I thought maybe it might be important," the city editor said.

Whit was studying the newspaper's date. "Well, it had to be written today. That's for certain."

Gil was leaning over, looking at the large precise handwriting. "No doubt but what Kathy wrote it. And that's about the time that city cop saw them out."

"Thanks, kid," Whit said. "We'll check it out."

"We're all worried," Burns said.

"Yeah, so are we. If you come up with anything else, let us know."

The newspaper employee hesitated. "One thing, Mr. Pynchon."

Whit glanced up at the young man. "What's that?"

"Don't tell Mrs. Binder I was messing around in her office."

The two men stood on the gravel surface of the Tabernacle
Mountain Overlook. The sheriff's cruiser was parked behind
them, its lights shooting directly into the bright aluminum
guardrails that separated the narrow pull-off from the precip-
itous drop down the steep slope.

Whit used the illumination to examine the ground itself.
Gil was looking out over Raven County, its rugged terrain
hidden by the dark shroud of the moonless night and the haze
that would mature into ground fog by morning. "Why the
hell would they be coming up here?"

Whit gave up his investigation of the surface of the overlook itself. "With those two, who the hell knows? Usually,
when you make a note like that on a newspaper, it's because
you're on the phone. Maybe somebody called them."

"But why?"

Whit shrugged. "God only knows."

Gil checked his watch. "Jesus, it's almost two A.M. I wish
to hell something would give. I can't stand this . . . this
silence."

Whit had wondered how long Gil could maintain the dis-
passionate attitude he was displaying. "They're both probably fine—probably off on one of their wild-goose chases."
Funny, an hour earlier Gil had been trying to calm Whit.
That's how it had gone, each one wavering between a false
confidence and out-and-out apprehension.

The sheriff moved back to his cruiser and slumped down
against the front grill. Insects, drawn from the forests by the
bright headlights, swarmed around him. "I don't know if I
could take something like last time. I'm in love with Kathy,
almost as much as I was with—" His words trailed off.

Whit swatted at a large moth as he moved to assume a

position beside the sheriff. "Let's not bury them yet. There's no reason to think anything like that's happened."

"Then where the hell are they?"

"I wish I knew."

Gil, his eyes glistening with moisture, glanced up at the night sky. "Scary, isn't it, Whit? Just how damned quickly you can get involved with someone. After DeeDee's death, I told myself that I wouldn't ever love anyone that much again. I said to myself, 'Gil, dammit, if you don't let it happen again, you can't get hurt like that again.' I promised I'd never let it happen."

He paused for a moment and then laughed. "That's surely what I told myself, Whit. Now look at me."

The sheriff brushed a tear from his cheek.

Whit hung his head. "You're talking to the wrong guy. After my first marriage, I managed to stay clear of any entanglements for—" He paused to think. "Hell, for more than fifteen years. Now look at me."

Gil was looking at him. "You're worried, too—more than you're letting on now. You couldn't sit still back at the jail."

Whit chuckled. "I'm scared, Gil. I'm just flat-out scared. I know I should be trying to offer some words of comfort, but I know Anna too well. That newspaper means a hell of a lot to her; God knows why. Something musta happened to keep her from getting back on time."

Gil looked back out over the mountainside. "Christ, I hope they're okay. I feel so fuckin' helpless."

Whit had turned and was glancing up at the twin summits of the mountain. "The clouds are starting to lower. Think we oughta go on to the top before that pea soup swallows it up?"

Gil looked back. Even in the darkness, he could see the cottony mass of the clouds clustering around the double peaks. "Naw, let's head back down."

As soon as they climbed back into the car, Gil grabbed the mike and radioed his dispatcher. "Any word?" he asked.

"Negative, Sheriff. The units are still on the lookout."

They started back down the mountain.

"Have you and Anna ever talked about marriage?" Gil asked as he navigated the tight curves.

Whit was keeping his eye on the left side of the road. "Not really. I guess I'm being an asshole, but the thought of marriage gives me butterflies. Frankly, Gil, I just wonder how long she can put up with me. I'm no great catch. I can be a real jerk, and I know it. I can't even claim that I want to change. I'm . . . well, I'm just how I am. I don't know if anyone could put up with a lifetime of living with me."

Gil managed to laugh. "Yeah, you're a real hard case sometimes."

"How about you and Kathy?"

Gil's laughter mellowed into a smile. "Well, we haven't really been seeing each other all that long. With all this damned electioneering I've been doing, we really haven't got to spend much time together, not the kind of time people need. After the election, I dunno . . . we'll see then."

"She's a first-class lady—and to make it even better she's no pauper."

Gil nodded, slowing down as they entered a small pocket of foggy mist. "Yeah, I know both of those things. I don't give a damn about the money. She doesn't either, not really. That's what I like about her. I mean, she likes clothes, but what woman doesn't? It's just that she isn't a . . . well, a snob. She doesn't fool around much with that country club type of stuff."

"Just a common rich person, huh?"

Gil was starting to laugh when he saw the pale shadow. "What the hell's that?"

Whit squinted ahead into the panoramic glow created by

the headlight beams as they cut through the thickening haze. "It looks like a person."

Gil applied the brakes and started to slow the vehicle. The figure was staggering down the left side of the road, walking away from them.

The sheriff slowed the car even more. "Jesus, Whit—"

"I can see," Whit said. "It's a woman."

"Christ, it's Kathy."

He eased the car over behind her, but she just kept walking. In the beams of the headlights, they could see the dark stains on the back of the light-covered long coat she was wearing.

"Oh, dear God," Gil said. He tapped the horn.

She kept walking.

Whit didn't even wait for the cruiser to come to a complete stop. He threw open the door and hopped out. "Kathy!"

At the sound of her name, she finally turned. By that time Gil was out of the car. The front of her coat was soaked in blood.

"Kathy!" he cried, hurrying toward her.

She stumbled to meet him.

They hugged.

"Oh, Gil. It was terrible."

Whit was beside them. "Anna, where's Anna?"

The woman looked at him. A wide gash just beneath her blond hairline still seeped blood. "She's gone, Whit."

He braced himself as his head started to spin. "You mean dead, Kathy."

She shook her head. "No, I mean 'gone.' Not in the car. Just gone."

Anna's car rested some thirty feet down from the tortured length of guardrail through which it had plunged. The thick trunk of an oak had stopped its downward journey. The highway above it was cluttered with police vehicles and a tow truck. The crew from the truck stood waiting while officers rushed to search the steep slope around the vehicle for Anna Tyree before the congealing fog made their task impossible.

Both Whit and Gil had returned to the wrecked vehicle. "Kathy insisted she wasn't thrown from the vehicle," Gil was saying. "She remembered Anna being in the car with her."

Whit used his flashlight to scour the leafy ground around the car. "Maybe Anna got out after Kathy blacked out?"

"She said someone else was here, the person who forced them off the road."

Whit didn't want to believe the implication. "C'mon, Gil. Kathy got a pretty solid whack on the head, and—"

"Which she says happened after the accident, Whit. She says she was assaulted."

Whit slumped back against the car. "So you think Anna was abducted?"

Gil nodded.

"This doesn't make any sense," Whit said.

The sheriff took the flashlight from Whit. "Look right there, that dark paint." The circle of light settled on the dark streaks on the rear quarter panel of Anna's white car. "Someone forced them over the side of the gawdamn mountain. They got them up here and tried to kill them . . . or kidnap them."

The full import of Gil's words finally reached Whit. He lurched away from the vehicle. "I don't wanna mess up any evidence."

"You know how useless paint comparisons usually are."

"Sure, but who knows? Maybe the bastard left a print on the door handle. Why don't you head on up and go to the hospital? Maybe Kathy can tell us some more."

Gil didn't seem optimistic. "She blacked out again as they were loading her into the ambulance, but I think I will head on back so I can be with her. You wanna go?"

Whit shook his head. "I'm staying here until they get the car up the bank. I want to try to secure it as much as possible—just in case there is something. How about calling the state CID? Ask 'em if they'll print this car, every inch of it. They can take a stab at paint analysis while they've got it up there."

Gil glanced at the glistening damp metal. "It's probably a waste of time."

"So humor me, Gil."


The near silence tortured Anna. She could hear things. The creaking of the structure in which she was being held. The distant and feeble operation of some small motor, probably a refrigerator. A faint water drip.

After opening a window, he had left. She had heard him walk from the room and close the door. A second door had closed seconds later, probably an outside door. Then a motor had fired up. It seemed as if it had taken an eternity for the motor sound to stop. Perhaps that had been her imagination. Surely it couldn't have taken as long as it had seemed.

Worst of all, she heard the sound of her own pain, a loud intermittent throbbing behind her left eye—a bass drum that came alive every minute or so to keep her on a tormented edge. In between the attacks of pain, she listened to the sounds beyond herself—the few that there were. Cool air flowed through the open window, and so, too, did a few noises. The chirping of a night bird. The sound of the wind whispering through tree leaves. She detected no traffic noise, no distant voices . . . nothing but the sounds that come from an empty, lonely place.

Once, when he had still been there and moving around, her nose had picked up on two odd scents. The first had been the fragrant aroma of a woman's cheap bath powder. The other, oddly enough, had been a pungent wisp of odor that she had not immediately placed—oddly familiar and medicinal . . . of that she was certain. Then she remembered. It smelled like Absorbine, Jr. When she had been a child and had visited the home of her grandmother, that same smell had always been present. The old woman had rubbed it on her knees three times a day.

She tried to rock the chair in which she sat. It refused to budge. She struggled with the ropes. They merely cut more painfully into her wrists in retribution to her efforts.

What the hell was she supposed to do if she had to use the bathroom?

She ached to cry.

She couldn't even do that. *Damn the bastard!*

*The son of a bitch!*

# NINE

DETECTIVE FRANK CARDWELL rubbed the grit from his eyes. He wasn't a morning person, and on that morning they had called him out at 4:00 A.M. It was 7:30 A.M., and he hadn't accomplished a gawdamn thing. Not a single friggin' thing. What would he get for the useless inconvenience? Time off? It made him so mad he could—

"Shit," he said.

Deputy Gerald Branford—"Cowboy" to his fellow officers—was finishing up the accident report for the sheriff. When any of the officers had paperwork, they commandeered the extra desk in Cardwell's office. It was located just off the jail's control room.

Cowboy looked up when Cardwell spoke. "What's wrong?"

"What the fuck am I doing here?"

Cowboy grinned. "You're s'posed to be investigating an assault and kidnapping."

"If it'd been anybody but the sheriff's girlfriend, and that gawdamn Pynchon's girlfriend, we wouldn't be here."

Cowboy shrugged. "That's how it goes. 'Sides, it was pretty serious."

"Sure, but why the hell did they need me? I come in at 4:45 this mornin'. Why, gawdammit? Just so Danton and Pynchon could brief me? Hellfire, man, they coulda done that at eight." He took a sip of the coffee. At least it was fresh.

"You oughta be proud. We figgered they'd called the state boys to handle it."

Cardwell shook his head. "No way. Pynchon and the sheriff are asshole buddies."

"Maybe the state lab can come up with something off the car."

Cardwell laughed. "Are you kiddin' me? It'll probably get hauled to the far end of the evidence lot. They'll get around to it maybe before Christmas."

"The sheriff talked to somebody. They were s'posed to go to work on it first thing this morning."

Cardwell shook his head. "That ain't right either. I got some forged checks up there I been waiting on for a couple of months. They're playin' favorites."

Cowboy returned his attention to the accident report. "You just wanna bitch, Frank."

"Damn right I do."

At that moment Marsha Via, who had come in at seven to assume the dispatching duties, ambled into the office. "What are you bitchin' about?" she asked, having heard the tail end of the conversation.

"This whole damned thing," Cardwell said. "I don't like working for nothin'."

The female deputy had a sheet of paper in her hand. "What do you mean?"

"I mean, they called me out at four o'clock this morning on this shit, and they'll probably give me friggin' comp time. I'm gettin' tired of this cheap-ass place. If they're gonna make me lose sleep, I at least oughta receive cold cash, not time off."

Marsha had worked with male cops long enough to take their language in stride. In fact, if she wasn't careful, she found herself talking the same way. "You can leave anytime, Frank. I hear the city's got an opening."

Frank glowered at her. "Last time I heard you were bitchin' about the comp time, too."

"That was before Sheriff Dickerson took over—when they were givin' it to us weeks after the fact or not at all."

"Don't make a damn bit of difference. I'm entitled to overtime, not comp time. I talked to a lawyer, and that's what he said."

Marsha placed the paper on the desk. "Then you had better find you a lawyer who knows what he's talking about, Frank."

"What's that?" he asked, staring down at the paper she had delivered to him.

"A complaint, Frank. It came in last night. A stolen car. Well, a truck, actually."

"Well, shit." He snatched it up.

Marsha headed out of the office.

The form was handwritten, and the detective was squinting at it. "What was the color of paint ya'll found on that car?"

Cowboy was busy trying to draw a diagram of the accident scene. It was a waste of time, but the forms provided by the state required it. He didn't hear the detective's question.

"Gawdammit, Cowboy!"

The deputy looked up. "What, Frank?"

"I asked what color was the paint on the car."

"You mean the smears?"

"Of course I mean the smears, the ones left by the other car."

"They looked dark brown, but I didn't see them in the light. Somebody said they were brown."

Cardwell glided the paper across the room to the deputy. "Don't that say 'brown truck'? If you can read the friggin' handwriting?"

The report hit the floor, and Cowboy bent down to retrieve it. He skimmed through the scrawled handwriting. "That's what it looks like to me."

"Not too damned many brown vehicles out there."

Cowboy was still reading the report. "Stolen from a beer joint, huh? Some drunk probably ran it off the highway somewhere and just abandoned it. Didn't want to get busted for drunk driving. Figgered he'd report it stolen to cover his ass." He stood and handed the report back to the detective.

"Maybe," Cardwell was saying as he accepted it, "but I guess I'd best go over to the prosecutor's office and tell them about it. At least I come up with something."

Cowboy grinned. "Shit, you mean it fell in your lap."

Cardwell was already on his feet. "You take what you get."


"I'm not going to school," Tressa said to her father. He was on the phone, telling her about Anna.

"Of course you are," he said. "What's to be gained by you staying home?"

"I can come keep you company."

"Christ, hon. I'm gonna be working."

"I thought you said the sheriff's department was going to be handling it."

"The department's detective will be chief investigator. That doesn't mean I won't be involved."

"Oh." Tressa still didn't understand. "I still won't be able to concentrate at school."

"Go on to school," Whit said. He glanced at the clock. It was almost eight. "And you'd better hurry. You'll be late."

"I'm going to try to call Rob. He'll want to know."

*Rob?* Whit had to stop to think. "Well, just don't be late for school."

"Mother wants to talk to you."

Whit cringed, but he said, "Put her on."

He rolled his eyes at Tony Danton, who was sitting in his office, and mouthed the word "Julia."

Tony stood and left the office.

"Whitley, what have you found out about Eloise?"

"Nothing yet. We're working on it."

"So what's this about Ms. Tyree?"

"Anna, Julia. You can call her Anna."

"I'll call her what I want, Whitley."

"She's apparently been abducted."

There was a moment of stunned silence. When his former wife spoke, all she said was, "Abducted?"

"Kidnapped, Julia. She and Katherine Binder, the newspaper publisher, were ambushed up on Tabernacle Mountain. Someone forced their car over the mountainside. Kathy's in surgery right now, and Anna's no place to be found."

"Well, I'm sorry. I hope things work out." For Julia, that was quite a lot to say.

"I appreciate it," Whit said.

"I hope this won't influence the investigation into Eloise's death."

Whit's jaw clinched. "Dammit, Julia—"

"I didn't mean that quite as it sounded," she said.

Whit sighed. "I know that, Julia. You can't help but be yourself."

"What precisely does that mean?"

"Nothing, Julia. I'll be in touch." He hung up.

Tony, accompanied by Detective Frank Cardwell, came back into Whit's office. "Cardwell has something," he said.

Whit tensed. "What is it?"

The stocky detective, dressed in an old suit coat, a plaid shirt, and a worn pair of blue jeans, offered Whit a sheet of paper. "It's a complaint about a stolen brown truck last night."

Whit grabbed it. "Was this investigated last night?"

Tony and Cardwell settled down on the chairs in front of Whit's desk. "Hell, no. We don't work that way."

"Just how do you work?" Whit asked.

Cardwell's face reddened. "Uh, actually, I came over to show it to the sheriff. Is he here?"

Tony shook his head.

"I was told he was here," the detective said.

"He's at the hospital," Whit explained. "Mrs. Binder's in surgery."

"That bad?" Cardwell said, surprised.

Tony nodded. "About four they decided she had a subdural hematoma, and—"

"A what?" Cardwell said.

"She's bleeding inside her head, Detective. They have to operate."

Cardwell shook his head. "Jesus, I just thought she had a concussion or something."

"So why wasn't this checked on last night?" Whit asked.

"It tells you on there."

Whit read the brief report a second time. "Like hell it does."

"The gawdamn owner was drunk outta his mind. The beer joint owner made the complaint. It didn't seem like no big thing. If it had, the dispatcher woulda sent a deputy to do a preliminary investigation. Then I woulda got the complaint plus the preliminary this morning. I guess the guys were all tied up on the accident."

Whit's gaze rested on the time of the complaint. "This came in before we found Anna's car. It may have been reported even before we started looking."

"Christ, Pynchon. I dunno why they didn't check it out. I guess they decided it was a crock of some kinda shit, like maybe the drunk drove his car into a pole somewhere and just didn't wanna face a drunk driving rap. So he claims it was stolen. Happens all the time. We might still find the damned thing smashed up somewhere.''

Whit was looking for the address of the owner. ''There's a place for the victim's address. It's not filled in.''

''Like I said, he was shit-faced. He didn't even place the call.''

''How the hell are we supposed to find him? This report doesn't even have a license tag number?''

''We can run his name on the teletype.''

Whit read the name. ''Benny Johnston? The computer will probably kick back several of those.''

''So—''

Whit shoved the report back at the detective. ''Make me a copy of this, and then put out a B.O.L.O. for the truck . . . now!''

Cardwell grabbed it. ''I thought I was heading this investigation.''

''Just for appearance sake,'' the prosecutor said. ''Put out the B.O.L.O.''

''Ten four,'' Cardwell said, suppressing his fury. ''I'll go track down the owner.''

''Forget it,'' Whit said. ''I'll handle that.''


As soon as Cardwell had left his office, Marsha Via had pulled a small piece of pink paper from the center drawer of the dispatcher's desk. She hurried back to the detective bureau. Cowboy Branford was still working on the diagram.

''You remember this one?'' she said, placing the pink copy of a traffic citation in front of him.

Cowboy studied it. ''Oh yeah! He was a little smart-mouthed punk.''

''Would you consider making it a warning?''

Cowboy looked up at her. ''You know him?''

''I know his daddy, and so do you.''

"His father?" He read the name of the kid aloud. "Jamey Christian. I don't know anybody by that name."

"His stepfather is Jake Brimm."

The deputy made a face. "The kid didn't tell me that, but it don't really make no difference, Marsha. The little asshole was hot-rodding that cycle around without a helmet. I think he'd been drinking some, too. Not enough to make him blow, but I smelt it on his breath."

Marsha shrugged. "Do what you want, Cowboy, but there's a better than even chance that Brimm is gonna be the next sheriff around here."

Cowboy Branford looked at the pink slip of paper again. "Hell," he said, tearing it in half, "just tell Jake to have the kid wear his helmet."

"Thanks," Marsha said. She turned to leave.

"Hey," Cowboy said, "you know Jake Brimm that well?"

"We've met," she said, turning to explain.

"Did he hire you?"

Marsha shook her head. "I came after he left."

"You helping him in the election?"

Marsha smiled. "You know we're not supposed to get involved in politics."

Cowboy smiled back. "Yeah, that's what they say. Put a good word in for me with him. I'd say you're right. He's gonna be the next sheriff."

Whit's first stop after leaving the prosecutor's office was Milbrook Hospital. He went straight to the small waiting room reserved for families who had someone in surgery. The room was crowded, but he didn't see Gil Dickerson. He saw a green-uniformed nurse exit the surgical wing of the small hospital.

"Nurse, I'm looking for Sheriff Dickerson."

She nodded. "You'll find him in the Doctor's Lounge. The

hospital administrator felt he would be more comfortable there.''

Whit thanked her and asked for directions. She provided them, saying that the door had the number ''10'' on it. As he headed down the hallway, he recalled a conversation he had had with Gil a few days before.

''It's a crime,'' Gil had said. ''People treat you differently when you become sheriff. Suddenly you're important. You're somebody. Someday, maybe, you can do something important for them, so you get the red carpet treatment.''

''Nice, huh?'' Whit had said.

Gil had shook his head. ''It sucks. It's wrong.''

The way the hospital had to show the sheriff that special treatment was to offer him the sanctuary of the Doctor's Lounge. At least Gil hadn't been too proud to accept the perquisite.

Whit found a door with the number ''10'' on it and pushed it open. Several faces turned to see who was entering, doctors, Whit assumed—since most of them were obviously foreign. They frowned when they didn't recognize the trespasser.

''Whit!'' Gil had been seated on a comfortable sofa in a far corner. He moved to greet him. That seemed to satisfy the doctors.

''Any word?'' Whit asked.

Gil shook his head as he led him back to the couch. ''She never regained consciousness before they took her in.''

''How long's she been in there?''

''A couple of hours.''

Whit could see Gil's hand trembling. ''Did the doctor give you any details?''

The sheriff nodded. ''More than I gawdamn wanted.''

Whit waited for his friend to gather his thoughts.

''It's up in here,'' Gil said, rubbing his temple and forehead. ''She's bleeding. They think it's just some small damage since she was conscious when we found her, but there's a chance—''

He paused to take a deep breath. ''A chance that she can be a vegetable, Whit. How can that be, I asked. I mean, she was talking to us last night afterward.''

Whit put a hand on Gil's shoulder. ''They always tell you the worse. Tony said it was something called a subdural hematoma.''

Gil shook his head. ''I dunno. Not exactly. They did a brain scan. What they called it after that was brain hemorrhaging.''

Whit patted Gil. ''Just take it easy.''

A tear trickled down Gil's face. ''What if I lose her, too? It's not fair, Whit.''

''I know.''

Gil wiped away the drop of water. ''Anything to go on about Anna?''

''You remember the note on the newspaper?''

Gil nodded that he did.

''Well, Kathy did receive an anonymous call yesterday afternoon. Her secretary phoned in to tell us that just before I left to come here.''

''Did her secretary know anything about it?''

''Nope. Kathy just took the call. She didn't say anything else to her secretary about it.'' Whit went on to tell him about the stolen truck.

''So what are you doing here?'' Gil asked. ''Get your ass outta here and try to find it.''

''I'll stay,'' Whit said, ''just for a little while.''

''I'm fine,'' said Gil. ''Go find Anna.''

A doctor, clad in surgical greens, entered the lounge.

''That's him,'' Gil said, springing to his feet.

The doctor had a slight smile. ''She came through the surgery fine. We found a small hematoma and hopefully dissolved it.''

"So she's okay?"

"Whoa!" the doctor said. "She survived the surgery. We don't think there will be any residual impairment, but we won't know until she regains consciousness. I'm optimistic, but we're not out of the woods. She received a nasty blow to the head. By the way, it wasn't consistent with the trauma produced by collision with a windshield or dashboard."

Whit was standing close to them. "What do you mean?"

The neurosurgeon looked at Whit. "Who are you?"

"Oh," Gil said, "sorry, Doc. This is Whit Pynchon. He's investigator for the prosecutor's office and a close friend of mine. He's also very close to the woman who vanished in the incident."

The physician nodded to him. "My sympathies. I mean, the wound that caused the hematoma appears to have been caused by a blow from an instrument capable of producing an elongated wound."

"A sharp instrument?" Whit asked.

"Well, not sharp enough to cut the skin cleanly, but it definitely had an edge of some sort."

The doctor's words struck a familiar chord with Whit. It sounded like the description of the murder weapon in the Weldon case. He attributed it to coincidence.

"How long before she will regain consciousness?" Whit asked.

The doctor shook his head. "Hard to say with brain injuries. Besides, once we establish consciousness, we'll want to keep her sedated. She might have quite a bit of pain."

"It would help to talk with her," Whit said.

"In cases such as this it's difficult for us to predict how soon she could communicate. I wouldn't count on talking to her too soon."

Anna had wet herself. It happened during the night. She didn't know when—sometime before dawn. For the first few hours, she had tried to restrain herself, thinking that maybe the man would come back. Maybe he knew that some things a person just had to do. Everyone knew that. But as the long lonely hours passed, with the discomfort from her bladder slowly becoming so bad that it displaced the pain in her head, she realized that he wouldn't be coming back. Then, it had almost been reflexive. The warm fluid had simply started to flow, and she had cried, humiliated and frightened.

With the window open, the room had cooled through the night, and by dawn—what she perceived to be dawn—Anna was shivering. The lower half of her body was chilled by the dampness, but she trembled all over. Her feet, still clad in her flats, actually ached from the cold. The birds had announced the arrival of the new day. Just a single warbling at first, then another and another, until she heard a chorus of birds beyond the walls of the house. Anna didn't even remember dozing at all. She just remembered her aching muscles, the throbbing inside her head, the burning pain of her chin, the discomfort of the dampness, the loneliness, most of all the fear.

The room itself had started to warm some, and the sound of the birds had actually lessened when she heard the motor sound again—a low hum at first, then becoming deep and throaty . . . the same motor she had heard vanishing the night before.

*He's back . . . Dear God, he's back.*

The realization filled her with both anticipation and dread. Maybe he'd come to his senses and was going to release her? Maybe he was going to kill her?

The engine shut off.

Even beneath the blindfold she squinched her eyes shut as she heard a door open. The urge to urinate returned with a sudden pressure, as if the fear inside her body had turned into a little imp that was bouncing up and down on her bladder.

The door to the room in which she was being held opened. "Morning," a male voice rasped.

Anna sat still as his feet crossed the floor to her.

He laughed. "I see you pissed all over yourself. Sorry 'bout that, but I wasn't actually prepared for you. I didn't expect you to be tagging along. I had other plans for you."

He walked around her chair. "But I've brought some stuff that oughta make you more comfortable."

"Mmmmmmmm . . . mmmmmmmm." It was all Anna could say.

A cool hand touched her face. "Got something to say?"

"Mmmm . . . Mmmm!"

His fingers undid the knot in the gag. It dropped away.

"Da—" Anna didn't even get her first word out before she started to cough.

"Better wait a few minutes before you start screaming at me, Ms. Tyree."

When Anna did speak, her voice was hoarse and soft. "Please, please let me go."

He had moved away from her.

"I'm gonna fix it so you can use a portable toilet seat for pissin' and the other." He still whispered. "You've given me a real challenge. Trying to come up with ways to keep you secure but still givin' you enough freedom to eat and piss and shit."

She realized that she wasn't going to be freed. Her stomach started to rebel as he spoke, and she tried to swallow the hot bile that was rising in her throat.

"So I've decided to chain you to the floor, and—"

"I'm going to be sick."

"—give you enough slack to use the potty seat—"

"I said I was going to throw up."

He laughed. "If it makes you feel better."

She did, but it didn't.

# TEN

WHIT WAS ON HIS WAY out of the hospital when someone tapped him from behind. He turned.

"Hi Daddy."

"Tressa! What are you doing here?"

"I couldn't help it. I came to see about Mrs. Binder. I called your office before I came. They told me you were going to stop here."

Whit noticed the wiry figure lurking behind his daughter.

Tressa saw his father make eye contact. "Oh, Dad, this is Rob . . . Rob Fernandez."

The man offered Whit his hand. Whit shook it. "Tressa's told me a lot about you." To Whit, he did look much older than Tressa. He was tall and carried himself with the lanky looseness of a basketball player.

"All good, I hope." He eased back, his shyness obvious.

"Too good to be true sometimes."

"Oh, Daddy."

He turned his attention back to his daughter. "How come you aren't in school?"

"It's my study period. I checked with the teacher. She said it was okay. And Rob agreed to give me a lift over here. He picked me up at the school. I just couldn't stand it, Daddy—not knowing what's going on."

Whit tried to be irritated with her, but he couldn't. Actu-

136

ally he was glad to see her. "Can I buy you two a cup of coffee? If the damned snack bar isn't too crowded?"

"Sure," Rob said.

Tressa walked beside her father as they headed back into the hospital. Rob followed.

"What about Anna?" Tressa asked.

"Not a clue," Whit said. "You'd like to think that people don't vanish from the face of the earth. Trouble is, sometimes they do."

"But who would do something like this?"

They had reached the door to the snack bar. Whit eased it open and peeked inside. "Not too bad," he said, seeing several available tables. He opened the door for the two young people. After getting their coffee, Whit guided them toward a table in an empty corner of the small room.

"You didn't answer me," Tressa said once they were seated. "Who would do such a thing?"

Whit shook his head. "Who knows? We think Kathy was lured up to the mountain by the anonymous call she received earlier in the afternoon."

"What call?" Tressa asked.

Whit realized that he hadn't really told his daughter anything. Rob Fernandez was in the dark, too, so Whit told them both about it.

"They were after Kathy?" Tressa said when he was finished.

Whit shrugged. "Who the hell knows? Gil's still got two deputies up on the mountain, just in case Anna somehow wandered off. Kathy swears, though, that there was a third person at the scene."

"And what about Kathy?" Tressa asked.

"She's out of surgery. According to the doctor, it went all right. Now it's just a matter of waiting, seeing how she is when—and if—she regains consciousness."

Tressa reached across the table and took her father's hand. "How are you?"

"Holding up," Whit said. "We've got a couple of leads. As soon as I leave here, I'm going to check them out."

"Not being nosy, Mr. Pynchon, but what kind of leads?" Rob asked. As if to explain, the young man quickly added, "I know this is going to sound—I don't know—silly, but I'm a fan of mysteries, especially police-oriented books. Sometimes I think maybe I should have been a cop."

Whit eyed the young man. "Should have been? You're not so old that you can't now, although it's not a career I recommend."

Rob smiled. "Well, I guess I'm sorta committed to a degree in business administration. Then maybe I'd like to get an M.B.A."

"Smart fellow," Whit said. "As for the leads, nothing world-shaking. We have reason to believe that a brown vehicle pushed Anna's car off the road. This morning, we discovered a report on a stolen brown truck. I'll check that out first. We're having Anna's car checked out by the state lab up in Charleston. Then there was the anonymous call to Kathy, but there's no way to check that out. For right now, that's it."

"Slim, huh?" Rob said.

"It's somewhere to start. So tell me, Rob, how do you like Milbrook?"

"It's a nice town. I like small towns."

"Tressa tells me you came from somewhere in the South."

"Georgia," the young man said.

Whit nodded. "Nice state. Did you live near the coast?"

"Naw, just outside of Atlanta."

"Too bad," Whit said.

"Daddy loves the beach," Tressa explained. "When he grows up, he wants to become a beach bum."

"Who wants to grow up?" Whit said.

Rob laughed.

Whit turned to his daughter. "When do you have to be back to school? It's almost noon."

Tressa glanced at the clock in the snack bar. "I guess I'd better be getting back."

"And I'd better start checking on leads."

They finished their coffee and headed out toward the parking lot, the three of them walking together.

Once they were outside, Whit said to the young man, "How did you end up at Milbrook College of all places?"

"It's a small college with a great business program. And the tuition was within my budget."

"Good reason," Whit said. They had reached his car.

"Rob had to park on down the way," Tressa said.

"Then I'll see you later," Whit said. "Nice to finally meet you, Rob."

The boy smiled. "Likewise."

Tressa threw her arms around her father. "I know how you must be worrying. I love you."

"Love you, too, kid. Take care."

The dampness in Whit's eyes surprised even himself. He tried to blink it back and offered a hand to the young man. "Once this is over, Rob, maybe you can stop by the office. I can tell you some old war stories."

"I'd really like that," the young man said. "Like I said, police stuff fascinates me. I hope everything works out all right."

Whit nodded. "Me, too, kid. Me too."


Marsha Via was almost hoarse from talking on the radio. The sheriff had phoned from the hospital very early that morning and had ordered that a double shift of men work that day. Two of her officers had just completed a search of the rocky mountainside near the scene of last night's accident. The other units were patrolling the county, searching for the brown truck that had been reported stolen. So far, no one had found it, but with so many units in the field the radio had remained constantly busy with chatter. The phone hadn't relented either, and she was the only one working in the control room.

It was lunchtime, though, and most of her units were taking their breaks. They were out of their cars at various small restaurants around the county. Marsha was just finishing a peanut butter sandwich made by one of the cooks in the jail's kitchen. She had a bite in her mouth when the phone rang.

"Dammit," she said, hurriedly swallowing the gooey combination of mayo and peanut butter.

"Sheriff's department," she mumbled.

"Marsha?"

She tensed at the sound of Jake Brimm's voice.

"Hi," she said. "I wish you wouldn't call me here."

"I got a call from one of your guys down there. He says half the department's out working today. What's going on?"

Quickly Marsha explained to him.

"Sounds like Dickerson's using the department for a sort of personal thing."

"Jesus, Jake. The publisher of the newspaper is in critical condition in the hospital, and Anna Tyree is missing. I think it's justified."

"The fella I talked to didn't seem to think so. Besides, he was griping because he won't get overtime, just comp time."

*Frank Cardwell.* That's who he had been talking to. Marsha knew it just as surely as if she had been eavesdropping.

"I really need this week's time sheets, so you make plans to get them for me. Got it, Marsha?"

"Please, Jake, I don't wanna do that."

"Don't get cold feet on me now."

"I'll try," she said, knowing in her own mind that she was going to find some way to avoid complying with Jake's request.

"Do better than that," he said, a hint of menace in his voice.

"I talked with the officer who gave your son the citation. You can forget it. It's taken care of. But, please, get the boy to wear a helmet."

"He always wears his helmet. This was just one of those things."

"The officer—his name is Branford—was happy to take care of it for you."

"Well, you tell Branford that my boy says he was a real hot dog—that he had a lot more mouth than he did sense when he wrote my kid up. I don't tolerate that kind of thing. Folks know they'll be treated with some respect when I'm sheriff."

"Christ, Jake, he's gonna drop the ticket. Let it go."

"I don't like smart-asses, and Branford sounds like one. Don't forget that I need copies of those time sheets. The *Daily Journal* won't give me any publicity, but I've got the TV station from over in Bluefield interested. They always like that kinda stuff."

"Yes," Marsha said, "they're not happy unless they're after someone."

"They got a good news department. Said they'd give me some time on the six o'clock news if I had some documentation. So get it for me, girl. You understand?"

The radio came alive.

"I have to go, Jake."

"Don't forget—"

She hung up the phone.

Whit waited until after lunch to drive out to The Grasshopper. Even then, he was surprised to find it open. The interior was dark and cool, and already several customers stood at the bar talking as they guzzled frosty mugs of beer. As Whit approached the bar, a short man with a sprawling paunch and greasy hair swept over a bald spot asked what he would have. Whit flashed his badge. The man's eyes narrowed. "What's up?" he asked.

"A report about a stolen truck was phoned in from here last night."

The bartender's face brightened. "Oh yeah. I made the call. The name's Mikie . . . Mikie Post. I didn't figger nobody was coming about it. The sheriff I talked to acted like he didn't give a shi . . . I mean, a crap."

"Do you know any more than what you told the sheriff's department?"

Post shook his head. "Not really. Ol' Benny—Benny Johnston, the owner?"

"What about him?"

"Well, he musta been chasing his beer with some hard stuff. Don't know where he got it."

"Sure," Whit said.

"Hey, man! What's that supposed to mean?"

"Just tell me about Benny."

"Well, he was pretty well gone . . . drunk, ya know. So's he goes wandering on out to leave—"

"You were going to let him drive away drunk?"

The suspicion returned to the owner's eyes. "Look, man, I tried once or twice to stop some slob from driving off drunk. All I ever got for my trouble was just that . . . more trouble. One guy rabbit-punched me. Another tore my place up. I figger if'n they gonna drive off and kill somebody, that's 'tween them and you."

"I hope you have a good lawyer."

"A lawyer? What do I need a lawyer for?"

"Forget it. What happened when he went outside last night?"

"Maybe I just best keep my mouth shut," Post said, glancing down at the other men lined up to the bar. They seemed pleased with what he had just said.

"And maybe I oughta come back some night with a search warrant, looking for tip boards or tip tickets, maybe even some illegal booze."

"That's harassment!"

"But it's legal," Whit said. "Just tell me about last night, pal. Then I can get the hell outta here and hopefully never set foot in here again."

Mikie Post had to think about that. "Okay, sure . . . I didn't do nothing wrong. Like I t'was sayin', Benny went outside. Ike—that's another guy that was here—he starts out the door and finds Benny spread-eagle on the stoop out there, screaming that somebody stole his truck. Ike helps Benny back inside. He's too drunk to call the cops, so I did it fer him. 'Fact, I don't think he even wanted me to."

"Did anybody go outside to be certain it was stolen?"

"I dunno. Somebody may have. I don't rightly remember. I just remember Ike telling me it was stolen. That's when I called the cops—for all the friggin' good that did."

"Did Benny leave?'

"Sure, he left when I tossed his pukin' ass out the door. I did that when he started barfing all over the place."

"Could someone who had been here earlier have stolen the truck?"

Post thought a minute. "Not too damned likely. Everyone I remember being here has trucks or cars better than that piece of shit Benny drives. I can't figger who in his right mind would wanna steal the thing anyway."

"Any new faces last night?"

"Shit," the man said. "You're the first new face in a week or two. We don't get many new faces. Just the same old farts." He said it loud enough for his other customers to hear. They laughed.

"You didn't provide an address for Johnston."

"Because I don't got one," Post said.

"Do you know where he lives?"

"Christ, now that I think about it I don't guess I do know."
Whit's eyes narrowed.

"I'm serious, man. I don't think I do. Somewhere out in the country 'cause he usually smells like pig shit."

Whit glared at the man. "Mikie, you aren't feeding me a load of pig shit, are you?"

The man held up his grimy hands in a gesture of innocence. "Hey, pal, not me. I honest-to-God don't know where the S.O.B. lives."

The bartender glanced down at his other patrons. "Anybody know where Benny Johnston lives? He ain't in no trouble. Leastways, I don't think so." Post looked to Whit for confirmation.

"No trouble," Whit said.

One of the men eased down a little closer. "I think he lives up on Canebrake Ridge. Least he used to. I bought a hog from him a lotta years back."

"Canebrake Ridge?" Whit said. He wasn't familiar with it.

"Some folks call it Windy Gap."

"Oh yeah," Whit said, cringing inwardly at the thought of a trip to that part of the county.

"You probably won't find him," the bartender said. "Not until later. He's probably in some ditch still soberin' up."

"One last question," Whit said. "Did he happen to say if he left the keys in the truck?"

Post laughed. "Keys? Hell, man, that's one of them old trucks that you start by pushing a button. You know the kind I mean?"

"And it still ran?" Whit asked.

"Once or twice a week," someone said.

The pain in her stomach would have doubled her over had she not been bound so stiffly to the chair. That morning, her captor had said he was going to solve those kinds of problems, and he had spent a very brief time hammering and drilling. Then, in a sudden fit of rage, he had started throwing things. Since Anna remained blindfolded, she didn't know what he was throwing.

"I'll be back later," he had said. "I forgot something."

"Don't leave me like this," Anna had pleaded. But he probably hadn't even heard her. The door slammed as she spoke the words.

The day passed slowly. She had nothing to do but think and try to control her bodily functions. Funny, the things that suddenly seemed important when a person was immobilized. She decided that she knew how quadriplegics felt— helpless to control themselves, to clean themselves. The pain in her head had eased somewhat. Long after he had left, she sensed those first faint stirrings in her gut. It sent a shock of dread through her.

Ignore it, she told herself. Hold back.

And she had managed for what seemed like hours. Now, though, the urge had turned into a series of cramps that were agonizing.

He had left the gag off. "Scream all you want," he had said. "No one will hear."

Right after he had left, she had shouted—and screamed and even cried. If anyone heard, no one responded.

Now she was moaning and talking to herself. "Please, God, let me wake up. Let this be some nightmare."

But it wasn't. She knew it was all very real. She had the grinding discomfort to remind her. On top of that, both her hands and her feet were ice-cold, afflicted constantly now with the sensation of millions of sharp pin pricks. If she wasn't freed soon, they would darken and rot and drop off.

God, the thoughts that haunted her.

Another wave of cramps seized her intestines. She grimaced and fought back.

Moments later, she heard the distant hum that gradually

increased in density and volume until it became a loud, throaty roar.

He was back.

Outside, the rider on the motorcycle pulled the vehicle right up to the front porch. The round, shiny-faced helmet remained in place as he gathered small packages from the saddlebags of the vehicle. Humming beneath the mirrored faceplate, he bounded into the small house and headed straight back to the bedroom in which the woman was being held. He eased open the door.

"Dear God," she cried. "Please let me loose. I have to go to the bathroom."

He laughed. "So go. I got a few things to do before I can do that."

"I promise," she said. "Keep my hands tied. Watch me. Whatever—just let me loose."

She heard the rattling of bags and the aroma of food drifted into her nostrils. At that moment she wasn't interested.

"Gotcha a hamburger from McDonald's," he said, his voice still raspy and soft. "Bet you're hungry. Didn't mean to take so long but I got hung up on something."

"I'm not hungry," she said.

"You will be. Now you keep quiet. Let me get to work."

Her fear and discomfort was suddenly replaced by a surge of fury. "You slimy bastard! Let me go! Now!"

Every muscle of her body coiled, and the energy actually allowed her to rock the heavy chair to which she was bound.

"God, you're strong," he said, surprised by her effort.

"I'm in misery," she said through clenched teeth.

"I know how you feel. I've been in misery all my life."

Anna allowed his words to sink in. "Who are you?"

"You'll know in good time. And so will Whit Pynchon."

"Is that what all this is about? Whit Pynchon?"

She heard chains rattling.

"He's gonna suffer like nobody has ever suffered before. He's gonna pay. He's gonna beg me to take him—beg me to leave everyone else alone."

"Why?" Anna asked.

"I gotta drill a hole in the floor. You best shut up, and let me get to work."

The sound of a drill filled the room. Whatever he was planning to do, he was going to a lot of trouble. If it meant that Anna was going to be allowed some freedom of movement, therefore some dignity, and ultimately perhaps a chance to escape, then she would do what he asked.

The drilling stopped. "I gotta go down under the house. Be right back."

She could hear him moving through the house and out the door. A fresh breeze surged through the room. Obviously, he had left the front door open as well as the door into the room in which she was being held. The breeze carried with it a new odor—the loamy smell of woods and rotten leaves. She sneezed. The damned allergy again.

Where the hell was she?

She could hear him under the floor, working with something. Hammering.

Minutes later he returned.

"I'm gonna remove the blindfold," he said.

Her captor stepped behind her. His fingers pulled her auburn hair as he worked to undo the knot. "You gotta understand," he was saying. "I'm just doing what I have to do."

She didn't respond. She was too anxious to be free.

The blindfold fell away. She kept her eyes closed, knowing that the light would sear them. He remained behind her, waiting.

Slowly she opened them. They teared as the light entered them. She flexed her whole face, trying to clear her vision.

"How's that?" he asked.

Things began to come into focus. She was in a small room,

its walls painted a light lavender. Opposite her was a double bed covered by an old-fashioned, handmade quilt.

He started to move around her. She turned her head toward him. The first thing she saw was black—black pants and a black jacket . . . shiny leather, it was. A wide band of silver circled the narrow waist. It was a belt made of metal, fastened by a garish buckle depicting a skull-and-crossbones.

"Like that?" he asked, slipping gloved fingers beneath it. "That's a sprocket chain off a big bike. A friend of mine put the buckle on it. Pretty neat, huh?"

When she didn't answer, he undid the buckle. The hefty chain fell away, but in an instant he had it in one hand, swinging it around his head. "You can smash a skull with this."

Her eyes, still full of burning tears, tilted upward, and she saw the helmet—all black, too, except for the metallic face-plate. Its color matched that of the deadly belt. Light glared off of it, making her squint.

"Who are you?" she demanded to know.

"The Black Knight," he said, replacing the belt around his waist.

He knelt in front of her as if he expected to be touched by a sword.

"What on earth are you doing?" she asked.

"Putting a chain around your ankles."

"Oh, Jesus," she said.

"That's so I can untie your hands, Anna, and then undress you."

# ELEVEN

WHIT SLOWLY GUIDED his car up the muddy, rutted driveway toward an aging mobile home. The exterior trim was rusting. Portions of the underpinning had fallen down. The front porch, added on later, sagged.

He wasn't at all surprised when a dog appeared from beneath the porch, an old hound that seemed hardly able to pull itself from its shady resting spot.

"Shit," Whit said, eyeing the animal as he brought the car to a stop.

The dog shook the dirt from its ragged auburn coat and stood there, staring at Whit's car with sleepy eyes that seemed deceitfully baleful. Whit clicked open his door. The dog tensed. Whit decided to take no chances. He pulled the door closed and started to honk the horn.

Moments later, the battered trailer door swung open, and a young woman stuck her head out. The head of a small towhaired boy appeared just beneath her ample bosom. Whit pointed to the dog. The woman, dressed in a grimy white sweater and torn jeans, stepped out onto the rickety porch. Whit rolled down his window.

"Whatcha want?" she shouted to him.

"I'm lookin' for Benny Johnston."

The dog settled back on its haunches.

The woman was shaking her head. "You ain't gonna find him here. He don't live here."

149

Whit smiled. "I didn't think he did. I was just hoping that you might be able to give me directions to his house."

"Just follow the stink of pig," she said.

Whit eased his head farther out the window. "What?"

"I said to follow the stink of pig."

Whit continued to smile. "Not much at tracking by scent, ma'am. Does your dog there bite?"

The woman shrugged. "If'n I want him to, he does."

Whit reached into the inside pocket of his jacket and pulled out his badge. He showed it to her. "Johnston's not in any trouble. I just need to talk to him."

The woman remained on the porch. The boy stood behind her, peeking around at it. "What kinda cop are ya?" she asked.

"I'm an investigator for the prosecuting attorney."

She finally moved down into the yard and kicked at the dog. "Scram, hound."

The animal hoisted itself to its feet and ambled back to the shade beneath the porch. Whit pushed his door open, keeping his eye on the spot where the dog had vanished.

"Like I said, ma'am, Benny's in no trouble. Somebody stole his truck last night, and I'm looking into it."

The woman faced Whit now. She was laughing, apparently amused by the theft of the man's vehicle. Whit noticed at once the unhealthy discoloration of her teeth. In another place, raised under other circumstances, she might have been a finalist in some beauty contest. It was that way with so many of the young women who lived in the hollows of central Appalachia. They lived in shacks and house trailers even worse than hers, the small rooms crammed full of children. They got together with a man early, became pregnant quickly, and all too often ended up raising the kids alone with the benefit of welfare.

"Frankly, mister, I don't really care none whether Benny's

in trouble or not." She nodded toward the west. "He lives on top of that ridge."

"Do I follow the main road up there?"

"For a ways. Then you turn left and go on up a dirt road." She glanced back at Whit's car. "I don't rightly know whether you'll make it up there in this or not. It's pretty rough. Say somebody stole that old piece of junk he drives, huh?"

"That's what I'm told."

"Say, you ain't heard nothin' 'bout my old man, have ya?"

The question caught Whit off guard. "I don't understand."

"You folks is lookin' for him."

"What for?"

The small boy had moved to the side of the porch and was jabbing at the dog with a stick he had picked up from the ground. "Jimmy Bob, you stop that!"

The child stuck his tongue out at her.

"Jimmy Bob, I'm gonna tan your hide!" She turned to Whit. "You gotta understand, mister. He's a little slow, just like his father."

"Is your husband wanted for something?"

"Yeah, for desertin' me'n the kid there. The welfare people got the warrants for him."

Whit understood then. Those types of cases had become a real sore point with Tony Danton. His office was required to prosecute husbands and unmarried fathers who deserted their families or otherwise refused to provide support. For years welfare agencies simply provided meager support to women, but in recent times the bureaucrats had become more aggressive, requiring women to cooperate in the prosecution of men who abandoned their families. If the women refused to cooperate, it cost them their benefits.

"I don't handle those cases," Whit said.

The woman shrugged. "No matter, I guess. I won't get

no more money if'n they do find him. Fact is, me'n the kid are better off without the bastard. He used to beat me and the kid. I hope they never find him.''

''Is that your only child?''

''Had one more, but it died a couple of days after it was born. That's when Cal—that's my old man—that's when he left. While I was still in the hospital. Believe that? Running off right after his kid died and his wife's still in the hospital?''

Whit shook his head and changed the subject back to Benny Johnston. ''So I just follow the main road and take the next turn to the left.''

The woman paused to think about what he had just said. ''I think it's the next turn. I'm not real sure. I ain't been up to Benny's for a while now. I used to go visit Sarah. That's Benny's wife. She's my old man's aunt. After Cal took off, me and Sarah kinda had a fallin' out. She got bent outta shape because the welfare took warrants for Benny. I told her that I didn't have nothin' to do with it—that they'd cut my check off if I didn't help them.''

The boy still had the stick in his hand, but he was no longer using it to torment the dog. Instead, he was poking under the trailer's underpinning. The dog's head came out from under the porch. Whit tensed, but the animal moved beside the boy and started to bark.

The woman saw Whit's reaction. ''Them two probably see a mouse under there.''

Whit opened his car door. ''Well, thanks for your help.''

''Shouldn't be no trouble findin' that old piece of junk,'' she said as Whit reentered his vehicle.

He closed the door and then asked through the still open window, ''Why's that?''

''He ain't had no muffler on the thing for years. You can hear it comin' for miles.''

Whit thanked her again and turned the car around in the yard. As he pulled away, easing back down the driveway, he glanced in the rearview mirror. The small boy was waving at him. Whit honked his horn in response.

"Kinda rank, huh?" Her captor, his face still concealed behind the helmet, was cutting away her clothes. They probably did smell, but she didn't notice. She was trembling, trying to fight back the tears. The stiletto blade zipped up the front of the blouse she wore. Buttons popped away and clicked as they dropped to the aging hardwood floor.

Her eyes remained riveted to the huge bolt that protruded from the center of the floor. A chain was attached to the circular eye of the device. It ran to her chair where it was attached by a large lock to another set of chains wrapped around her ankles.

*God, this can't be happening!* How many times had that same thought imposed itself on her mind since she had regained consciousness? A thousand?

"See, this way you can move around. There's even a potty seat over there for you to use." His voice remained a harsh whisper.

She glanced around the room and saw the device. "You thought of everything," she said.

He laughed. " 'Fraid not. The people who lived here already had it. If it had been up to me, I'd have just brought you a bucket."

The man pushed her forward and was slicing away at the shoulder seams so he could remove the blouse without releasing her hands.

"Where are they?" Anna asked.

"Who?" he asked.

"The people who lived here."

He didn't answer.

"Dead?" she guessed.

Still no answer. He jerked the left side of the blouse from

her body. She felt goose bumps erupt on her exposed skin.
He then went to work on the other shoulder.

"You must hate Whit an awful lot," she said.

"Yeah, I must. Now stop talking." He ripped away the
remaining shred of the blouse. "Now stand up."

"I don't think I can."

It was true. Even though the chains had replaced the tight
rope around her ankles, her feet still ached as the circulation
was gradually returning to them.

One of his gloved hands forced its way under her arm. He
lifted. "I said to get up."

She tried. The pain made her whimper. "Please," she
begged.

He held her up for a few minutes. "When I let go, you
best not sit back down. I gotta cut off those pants next."

She again fought back her tears, but there was nothing she
could do about her shaking. In many ways she could no longer
control her body. Fear had taken charge.

"I'll try," she said, her voice cracking.

He supported her for another few seconds, then eased his
hand away. She tottered a little, but she managed to stand.
He started at the back of the pants and sliced from the waist
all the way down the leg.

"They're still wet," he said.

For some reason, it embarrassed her. "I couldn't help it."

He turned to the second leg. As he worked the knife under
the material, the sharp point gouged into her skin.

Whit knew he had the right place. Even before he could
see the house, he smelled the odor of the pigs. The road itself
was a morass, the mud fresh from the previous night's storm.
It curved its way through a forest that was just beginning to
turn green. He rounded a blind curve and was shocked by
the devastated vision that greeted him. The land sloped upward to his left, but the greening trees and underbrush were

gone, replaced by a spacious plot of land that was tan and dark brown. He stopped his car to gape.

The ground was covered by rounded boulders, separated by narrow muddy ravines. As his eyes adjusted to the sight, one of the boulders moved. It wasn't a rock, though. It was a pig. Several of the masses that he had taken to be rocks were, in fact, bloated beige pigs. They lay sprawled among the boulders, soaking up the sun. Not a single green leaf was visible in the pen area. The only distinctive feature was a wooden lean-to located at the back of the square patch of barren soil.

The stench was overwhelming. He tore his eyes from the incredible emptiness of pigsty and shoved his car into gear. He lifted his eyes toward the road and was stunned to see a man pointing a huge shotgun at him.

Anna yelped and jumped.

"Stand still!" he commanded.

"You cut me!"

"Just a nick," he said as he started to slice through the material.

She tried to control her trembling, but the more she resisted the more intense it became.

"You cold?" he asked.

This time she didn't answer.

He let it go as he pulled away the material from her leg. "No panty hose?" he asked.

She just shook her head, wondering what she looked like, her hands still bound by ropes, her ankles chained almost together, dressed only in her bra and urine-damp panties.

He pulled off a glove and touched the swell of her buttocks.

She tensed. "Is this how you're going to get your fun?" she dared to say.

He stepped back from her. "You're an attractive lady, but

you're not my type. I was just checking to see how wet your panties were. I'll leave it up to you whether you want to leave them on or not.''

"Leave them on," she said, a little surprised.

"Try to walk. Remember, though. You'll have to shuffle.''

"You've got to be kidding.''

He shook his helmeted head. "Nope, you can do it. Trust me, I know from experience. You've got just about as much slack as I had when they shackled me in prison.''

It was one of the first things he had said about himself. Maybe it explained a lot. "I guess Whit put you there," she said. "That's why you're doing this.''

He snickered. "You're way off base. Pynchon had nothing to do with me going to prison, at least not directly. Now try to walk. I gotta get outta here. I got things to do.''

Anna moved her left foot forward first. She managed maybe six inches before the chain went taut.

"Now the other foot," he said.

She inched it forward.

"See, you can walk.''

"Can you loosen them some?" Anna said, extending her wrists. "There's hardly any circulation in my hands.''

He moved in front of her and took hold of her fingers. With his leather-covered fingers, he pushed on the skin on the back of her hand. "Yeah, they are a little tight. Actually I brought these.'' He produced a set of handcuffs from the back pocket of his leather pants.

With a quick move he snapped them on her wrists just behind the rope. Then he pulled out the knife and began cutting away the ropes. As soon as they fell away, he tightened up the cuffs.

"That better?" he said.

She nodded that it was.

"One thing," he said. "If you pull against those cuffs, they tighten up. They can get a lot tighter than that rope ever was. Trust me, I know about that, too. So don't get any cute ideas.''

"Can I use the bathroom now?''

"Sure,'' he said. "Just let me move it into your range.''

"Are you going to stay in the room?''

"I'm leaving,'' he said. "I'm about to suffocate in this helmet. When you get hungry, there's a burger there.''

He completed adjusting the furniture so that she had access to the toilet seat and the chair to which she had been bound. He moved the bag of food within her reach. "There's a drink in there, too, but I'd say the ice has probably melted. If you get sleepy, I guess you can just lay down on the floor.''

"Could you give me a blanket and a pillow from the bed?''

He reached over to the bed and yanked away the quilt and tossed it at her feet. He also gave her a pillow. "Wouldn't want you to be uncomfortable. I won't be back tonight.''

"What happens next?'' she said.

"By tomorrow morning Pynchon will know that some-one's out to make his life miserable.''

"What are you going to do?'' she asked.

He just laughed. "I dunno. It depends on how things work out.''

He started toward the door, but he stopped and turned. "By the way, your friend that was in the car with you?''

"What about her?''

"She died.'' He walked out of the room and closed the door.

Luckily Whit's badge case remained on the seat beside him. With his eyes on the barrel of the shotgun, he slowly lifted the gold piece of metal up so the man could see. The end of the gun was dropped.

Whit sighed and opened the door.

To his left a pig grunted, then charged toward the rickety rail fence that separated the pigpen from the road. Whit fell back into the car just as an explosion rocked the interior of the car.

"Christ!" Whit muttered, lifting himself from the seat.

The old man, wearing a baseball hat advertising tobacco and an old army coat stiff with grease, had moved around to the driver side. "Sorry 'bout that, mister. Lucifer there don't cotton to visitors. The sound of the gun stopped him, though."

The pig wasn't dead. In fact, he was at the fence, grunting, rubbing his nose against the coarse surface of the locust rail.

"Does that fence hold them?" Whit asked, pushing his door back open. He kept an eye on the massive animal as he eased out.

"Unless they get riled. Lucifer woulda knocked it down if I hadn't come along. Surprised he didn't do it when he saw yer car."

"I woke him up."

The man laughed. "He's gettin' a mite old. Guess I'll have to slaughter him 'fore long."

"Are you Benny Johnston?" Whit asked.

The man nodded an offered Whit a dirt-blackened hand. "Sure am. Who you be?"

Whit inwardly cringed, but he shook the hand. "Whit Pynchon. I'm an investigator for the prosecuting attorney. I understand you had a truck stolen last night."

The man nodded. "Thought that's what you might be here about. No sense makin' no fuss about the truck."

"Why's that?" Whit asked.

"Ain't worth that much."

"Can you give me the tag number?"

The man shook his head. "Nope, can't remember it."

"What about the title?"

"Got no title."

Whit frowned. "How did you get it licensed?"

Benny Johnston just shrugged. "You know how it is. Us poor folks make do as we can."

Yeah, Whit knew how it was. "In other words, Mr. Johnston, it's not licensed. Furthermore, you probably don't have any insurance."

"Weren't worth enough for insurance."

Whit shook his head. "That's not the kind of insurance I meant. The law requires you to have liability insurance."

Benny just laughed. "Yeah, well, I guess that's the guy's problem what stole it. I just used it for farm use. The law lets you do that without buying tags."

"Exactly what farm use was served at that beer joint, Mr. Johnston?"

The pig farmer lifted the greasy baseball cap from his brow and scratched at the scalp beneath. "I don't reckon I got much more to say to you, mister. Might be best if you just be on your way. Ol' Lucifer there is gettin' stirred up again."

The pig, however, was just looking at Whit.

"He looks calm enough to me, Mr. Johnston. Listen, I'm not interested in what you did with the truck or how legal it was . . . or is. However, whoever took it might have used it in a crime last night. I need some sort of information so we can locate it."

"You see it," Benny said, "you'll know it."


Whit returned to the courthouse late that afternoon. He didn't go straight to the prosecutor's office. Instead, he stopped by the sheriff's department. Marsha Via was on her way out the front door. They almost collided.

"Anybody found anything?" he asked.

"You mean the truck?"

"The truck? Anna? Anything?"

She shook her head. "I'm sorry."

"Have you heard from the sheriff?"

"He called just a few minutes ago. He's still at the hospital. Mrs. Binder hasn't regained consciousness yet, but the doctors said her vital signs were good."

"How is he . . . Gil, I mean?"

"Still upset. Mr. Danton's been looking for you. He called a few minutes ago to ask if we had seen you."

"I'll go on over to the office then."

He walked out of the jail's garage area with the female deputy. "Is Cardwell still working?"

She shook her head. "They sent him home at two this afternoon since he was called out so early."

Whit sighed. "Okay."

Whit turned to go into the main door of the courthouse. Marsha's car was located in the other direction. Before she parted company with him, she said, "I hope things work out for you and the sheriff."

He managed a smile. "So do I."

Tony was waiting to ambush him as he entered the office. "Where the hell have you been?"

Whit was startled. "Talking to the owner of that truck for what good it did. What's wrong?"

"I know you don't like the idea, but I wish you'd get a police radio in your car."

"No way," Whit said. "I've managed all these years without one. What's got you so riled?"

"I've got Eloise Weldon's family in my office. She has a son and a daughter, and the son's a horse's ass. I've been stalling them until you arrived."

Whit grimaced. "Jesus, Tony. I'm not up to that right now. Why don't you assign her case to the state police or to Frank Cardwell?"

They were talking in the outer lobby of the prosecutor's suite of offices. Tony pulled Whit to one of the room's corners. "The Weldon case may be over with. When the family came into the office, I was shaking hands with them, and the daughter managed to slip me a note. I didn't have a chance to read it until just a few seconds ago."

He handed Whit a small slip of white paper. The note was written in a small crisp hand. It read, "My mother was involved with a married man."

Whit read it a second time. "Does she know who it is?"

Tony shrugged. "How the hell do I know? Obviously, one of us needs to speak to her alone. I thought that maybe I'd keep the others company while you talked to her. I can send the secretary to get her."

"We can give it a try," Whit said, resigned to his fate.

"I know your mind is on Anna," his friend and employer said, "and just as soon as I can, I'll get the state police to take over this case."

Whit found himself about to break. "Christ, Tony, the past sixteen hours seems like a nightmare. I have this gawdamn awful feeling—" His voice trailed off.

Tony sent the secretary to his office to get Eloise Weldon's daughter. It didn't quite work out like Tony had hoped. When the secretary emerged, the daughter was following her, but so, too, was the dead woman's son.

The daughter looked helpless.

Tony made the introductions. "This is Investigator Pynchon of my office. He's handling the investigation into the case."

"Thomas Weldon," the son said, offering his hand. Whit shook it. "And this is Faye Morris, my sister."

"Actually," Whit said, "what I want to do, Mr. Weldon, is talk with each of you alone, and—"

"Why?" Weldon asked.

"It's the way I like to handle things, sir."

But Weldon was shaking his head. "Mr. Pynchon, that seems highly irregular to me. Obviously, we're not suspects, and—"

Eloise Weldon's daughter finally spoke. "It's all right, Mr. Danton. I guess Tommy ought to know, too."

Weldon cocked his head at his sister. "What are you talking about?"

She didn't answer him. When she spoke, it was again directed to Tony. "But I don't see any reason to discuss it in front of our spouses."

"What is this?" Weldon asked, his voice rising in tone.

Tony glanced to Whit, who said, "Let's go in my office. Tony, maybe you'd better come, too."

The prosecutor nodded. "This way," he said.

Weldon followed, still trying to ask his sister what she was talking about.

"I'll tell you in a minute," she snapped, irritated by his behavior.

She waited until they were all seated.

"Now what's this about, Faye?" It was her brother who asked the question.

Before she responded, she looked at Whit. "My mother really liked Mrs. Pynchon."

Whit was momentarily stunned. "Uhh . . . thank you, I think. You do know that Mrs. Pynchon and I are divorced."

"I know," the young woman said. "Mrs. Pynchon was just very good to Mother. I thought you should know that."

Whit didn't know what else to say, so he said nothing.

Weldon didn't seem to care one way or the other. He was fidgeting. "C'mon, Faye. What's all this about?"

"Mother was seeing a married man," she said.

Weldon's mouth dropped. "Faye! How can you say such a thing?"

"Because, Tommy, it's true. She's the one who told me. It was two weeks ago. We were talking on the phone. She needed to confide in someone."

Her brother's face had lost much of its color. "I can't believe this."

"Believe it," his sister said. "Mother wasn't an old woman, and she was very attractive. Frankly, I was hoping she would find someone. However, I certainly didn't want her to become involved in this kind of thing."

Whit had just listened. When he did speak, it was to ask, "Mrs. Morris, did she tell you who it was?"

The young woman had started to weep. She used a ragged tissue to wipe away the tears. "Yes, and I couldn't believe it."

Whit started to ask the next logical and unavoidable question when Tony interrupted. "Just a minute, Whit. Before we get too far along with this, I want to say a few things. First of all, Mr. Weldon, we already knew that your mother was involved with someone, and—"

"How?" Weldon asked.

"It's not important," the prosecutor responded.

But Weldon wasn't going to relent. "It is to me, dammit!"

"The autopsy," Whit said, hoping that the man would let it drop there.

It was Faye Morris, though, who reacted to his statement. "What about the autopsy?"

Whit made a slight face. "Mrs. Morris, you don't really want me to get too technical."

"Was she pregnant?" the young woman asked.

Weldon actually blushed. "For chrissakes, Faye. She was in her mid-forties."

"So what?" his sister snapped. "I want to know."

Whit shook his head. "No, she was not pregnant." At least Whit didn't think she was pregnant. He assumed that the medical examiner would have found such a thing.

"That's good," the woman said.

Tony said, "Why did you ask?"

"That's why Mother told me about the affair. She was concerned that . . . well, you understand."

Weldon was shaking his head. "I just can't believe this. If she was seeing someone, is this individual a suspect?"

Whit decided to level with them. "Yes, and right now he's our only one."

He looked back at the woman. "Who was she seeing, Mrs. Morris?"

The woman took a deep breath and looked at her brother as she revealed the information. "The president of the college."

Whit remembered the note on the small bulletin board. "I'll be damned," he said. "So that's Willie?"

Tony had lurched forward. "Willard Hardison?"

# TWELVE

TRESSA'S FORK WAS BUSY, pushing food around on her plate, but she wasn't eating. Her mother, sitting across the table, watched. "You have a long face," she said.

"I'm worried, Mother."

"About Anna Tyree, I assume."

Tressa lifted her eyes from the plate and glared at her mother. "Mrs. Binder, too. I guess you don't approve."

Julia Pynchon dropped her eyes. "No, dear. I mean—no, you're wrong. I understand. I really don't dislike Miss Tyree. In fact, I don't even know her. I think maybe I'm simply very jealous of her."

Tressa couldn't conceal her astonishment. "Jealous? You? I thought you hated Dad."

Julia placed her fork by her plate and stared out the dining room window. With daylight savings time, the sun remained high in the sky. "I've never really hated your father. I despise how he behaves, his crude ways, but I loved him when I married him, and in a way I still do."

Tressa's face reflected her confusion. "After so many years, you're telling me this? It would have helped to have heard you say this when I was nine or ten."

Julia's eyes were moist. "I know, dear. Your father can't help how he is, and you overlook his faults. I can't help how I feel about him. One reason I feel as I do, I think, is that you can tolerate his faults but not mine."

"But you're so . . . so intolerant of others—of the faults of others—"

Julia managed a weak smile. "And your father isn't?"

She had Tressa on that point. So Tressa changed the subject. "You said a moment ago that you were jealous. What do you mean?"

Julia was slowly shaking her head. "I don't honestly know, Tressa. When I married your father—heavens, so many years ago—I wanted it to work out. I had the same fairy-tale notions of life as every young woman. As your father said, I think I based my expectations on what I saw on television. I had the same notions that you have, I suspect. Even then, Whitley had so little patience with fairy tales. Oh, he wasn't as bad as he is now, but—"

"Mother! He's not bad."

"I didn't mean that, child. I meant to say he wasn't as cynical as he is now, but he has always been something of a maverick."

"You had to know that when you married him, didn't you?"

"One can't help with whom one falls in love. Sometimes, we need to simply resist our impulses. Of course, if I had, then you wouldn't have been born. Whitley and I both would have been denied one of the true joys in our lives."

The expression on Tressa's face had changed from sheer astonishment to sudden suspicion. "Is this leading up to something about Rob?"

"Not intentionally," her mother said, quite honestly. "I have decided to stop badgering you about the young man. You will have to make your own decisions about your future, at least insofar as this matter is concerned. I simply hope and pray—and beg of you, Tressa—that you don't rush headlong into something that you might regret. After all, this really is your first serious relationship."

Tressa's astonishment had returned. "Do you mean that,

Mother? That you're going to stop harping . . . I mean, badgering me about Rob?''

Julia nodded. "I'm going to do my best to stop, but I do want you to promise me that you will do a great deal of soul-searching before you do anything that you can't easily undo."

"I promise that," she said.

"You tend toward the impetuous." A wry smile crossed Julia's face. "I was going to say that it's a quality you inherited from your father, but then I was impetuous at your age."

For the first time since sitting down to supper, Tressa smiled, too. "Will you go a little easier on Dad? I don't want to say anything to upset you, but you know, don't you, that he cares so much for Anna? He's going through hell right now."

Her mother's tears returned. She squeezed her eyes tightly shut, trying to hold them back. "I know that, Tressa, and, yes, I promise to try. That's all I can do."

Tressa stood and slowly walked around the dining room table. She leaned down and hugged her mother. Julia lifted an arm up and returned the affection. A tear track glistened on her cheek. "Are you going out tonight?"

Tressa nodded. She saw the flicker of resentment in her mother's face and waited for some comment. None came. Then Tressa said, "But not with Rob. He's studying for exams. He's really very serious about his education. I thought I might go to the hospital or over to Dad's. I want to see if they've heard anything about Anna and how Mrs. Binder is doing."

Her mother was pleased with the news. "If you see Whitley, tell him for me—" Her words faltered.

"Tell him what?"

"Never mind."

Tressa's face fell. "You're chickening out, Mother."

But Julia Pynchon shook her head. "No, I'm not. I'll phone him later. It's something he should hear from me."

* * *

Whit detested hospitals. He gave them credit for doing some good, probably a lot of good, but, Christ, how he hated to walk into one of them. They were full of people at the mercy of other people—of staff who just really didn't seem to give too much of a damn. The doctors were at the top of his list. It wasn't that they made so much money. It's how they earned it. For doing what? Fifty or sixty bucks for walking into a patient's room, asking how they were feeling, and then moving on to the next. Sure, they had looked at charts and lab results and X rays, and they would be giving orders for treatment, but for that kind of money there needed to be a little more of the personal touch.

Then there were the nurses and orderlies. Many of them really cared about the people they treated, but who could tell it by the look on their faces or the way they acted. Most of them faced a long work shift, and the primary thought in their heads was getting through it with as little turmoil and inconvenience as possible.

Modern medicine, at least to Whit, seemed ultimately concerned with dollars and cents, as evidenced by the sad fact that the chief nurse in each area was called the "charge nurse," and her principal duty was to assure that each patient was properly billed for everything he or she received—a buck for a Tylenol . . . a sawbuck for a change of bandage. He could almost hear the cash registers ringing as he made his way toward the intensive care unit. Kathy had been moved there from the recovery room, and Gil was in the room with her.

That's what the woman at the information desk said. Of course, she had been wrong. Whit found a weary and frustrated Gil pacing in front of the doors to the ICU.

"How's it going?" he asked.

Gil appeared to have aged a decade since Whit last saw him just that morning. Shadows hung beneath his eyes, and he had a five o'clock shadow. His face was gray and drawn, his clothing rumpled and seemingly oversized, as if the man had worried away a good deal of body mass that day.

The sheriff just shook his head. "She's still unconscious."

"Have you gotten to see her?"

Gil shrugged. "They allow me inside for ten minutes or so every few hours."

"What's the doctor say?"

Some color returned to Gil's face, a flush produced by a sudden surge of anger. "The bastard! The last time I saw him was this morning when you saw him. The head nurse in there says he won't be back tonight."

"C'mon, Gil. Let's go down to the cafeteria. You need something to eat."

But Gil shook his head. "I have to stay here, Whit, in case something happens."

"You can tell them where you'll be. If you don't eat something, and maybe try to get a little rest, then you'll be in here, too . . . as a patient."

"No," the sheriff said, "I have to stay."

Whit sighed. "At least let me go down to the snack bar and bring something back up for you."

"No thanks. What about Anna?"

Whit shook his head. "Nothing, not a clue. None of the leads panned out. She's simply vanished."

The two men settled down on a cheap sofa located in the hall outside of the ICU. A small room itself, situated just outside the double doors, served as a waiting room for families with people in the unit, as it was called, but it generally remained rather crowded. Gil—and Whit, too—preferred the relative seclusion of the hallway.

"No information at all?" Gil asked, his eyes constantly glancing toward the unit's doors.

"Not a thing. I feel so damned helpless. So fuckin' useless. If there was just some direction to go—"

"Why would someone kidnap her?"

Whit shrugged. "Jesus, I don't know. Don't ask me to explain it, Gil, but I have this sense that she's still alive. I don't believe she's dead. I just don't believe it. I can feel her out there—in pain and misery. But she's alive."

"I understand it," Gil said. "I can feel the same thing. If something should go wrong in there—" He nodded toward the unit, "I would know it even before they came to tell me."

Whit leaned forward, gazing down at the cream-colored tile on the floor. "This is just the start of something, Gil. Something else is going to happen. There's more to this than we know. Something will break loose. It's got to."

Gil put a hand on his friend's shoulder. "We're all gonna make it. I've got faith."

Whit turned to look at his friend. "Faith, huh?"

Gil smiled.

"A gut feeling then. A hunch. Instinct."

Whit smiled. "Now *that* I can understand."

They both heard the footsteps coming down the hall. It was Tressa. She hugged them both, and all three settled back on the sofa.

"Any change?" she asked of Gil.

He shook his head.

She looked to Whit.

"Nothing on Anna either."

"What about the truck?" Gil asked, suddenly remembering it.

"I talked to the owner today. He was no help. Your people and the state boys are both looking for it. I checked with the lab late this afternoon. They turned up nothing on Anna's car, except the paint smears of course. They're still working on those."

"Can they match it to the missing truck?" Gil asked.

"If we can find it and provide them a sample."

Tressa remained quiet. She didn't know what to say.

"Where's Rob?" Whit asked.

"Studying," she said. "I just talked to him on the phone and told him I was coming here. He told me to tell you both that he was thinking of you."

"Who's Rob?" Gil asked.

"Tressa's heartthrob."

She blushed. "Daddy, don't be so crude."

Gil just nodded and glanced back toward the unit.

Whit checked his watch. "Well, I have to go. I have to pay a visit to the president of the college."

Gil looked back to Whit. "Are you still working that murder?"

"For the time being. We may have a break in that case at least."

Tressa stood, too. "I'll walk out with you."

Whit again tried to get Gil to go down with them for something to eat and again he refused.

"He looks exhausted," Tressa said once they were out of his hearing.

"He's going through hell."

"So are you, Daddy."

"It'll work out, Tressa. It has to."

"Mother's going to call you tonight. She's feeling guilty, I think—because of whatever she said last night."

"She should."

"Please, Daddy, give her a chance. I think she's really wanting to apologize."

"That'll be the day."

"I'm serious," Tressa said.

Whit stopped. "Well, I need to talk to her a minute, too, about Mrs. Weldon. I'll call her from here."

Tressa was suddenly concerned. "Maybe you should wait until she calls you."

Whit smiled. "No can do, sweetie. As I said, I need to talk to her about the murder. I won't mention anything else.

Listen, I don't know what your plans are tonight, but I have a favor to ask.''

"Anything," his daughter said.

"Would you head over to my house and just stay by the phone? I hate not being in touch."

"Do you think Anna might call?" Tressa was confused.

"No, but if she's been kidnapped, someone might call. Tony and I discussed it earlier, but it just didn't seem likely. Nonetheless, I would feel better if someone was there. Just lock the door, though, and don't answer it for anyone but me."

"Sure thing," she said, rising to leave.

"I'll tell your mother where you are when I talk to her."

"I have to stop at the store first, for some groceries. Mother had a short list. You know her lists."

Whit gave his daughter a hug. "Yeah, I've been at the top of one of them for years."


Anna snuggled as deeply as she could into the protection of the quilt. The window in the room in which she was chained had been left open a good eight inches. An old yellowed window shade was pulled down almost even with the opening. Throughout the evening she had watched as it became a portal for what seemed to her to have been every damned creepy crawly in southern West Virginia. With the coming of dusk, new ones—night things—were slipping inside to spend the night with her. Her captor didn't bother to leave on any lights. As much as she dreaded the approaching darkness, at least there would be no light to attract even more bugs.

Beyond the opening itself, Anna saw a maze of brown limbs flecked with dabs of green spring growth. The place she was being kept was in the woods—that much she knew. She had listened all afternoon for some evidence of other life beyond the walls of the old house. All she had heard was the chirping of birds, the buzzing of the various bees and wasps who flitted about, in and out the window. She had watched as a fat black spider crawled inside. It had given her the creeps. It ascended the wall once inside the room and had vanished into some high shadow as the sun had set.

With the sunset the room had started to cool. The warm nights of the past week or so were a thing of the past. On this night, it was going to become chilly . . . maybe not frost cold, but chilly enough to make Anna all the more uncomfortable. After all, she wore nothing but her bra and panties. At least the panties were dry now. And she wasn't tortured by those necessary bodily functions, not with the toilet seat available. The chains on her ankles were cold, though, and the cuffs around her wrists had tightened a little when she had used the portable toilet. But they weren't as uncomfortable as the caustic fiber of the hemp by which she had been bound earlier. She had even managed to consume the hamburger he had left and about half of the soft drink before she had spilled it.

A mosquito whined about her ear. She jerked her head to avoid it and then tried to wriggle deeper into the cocoon of the quilt. At the same time she tried to keep the short chain between her cuffed hands slack so that the metal bracelets wouldn't tighten up on her wrists. The maneuver was difficult, but at least it consumed the time.

Earlier in the evening she had found herself talking to the bugs, especially the little pesky yellow jacket that had darted about her bare feet. Her words to it had been the same words she would have spoken to the dark clandestine figure who had left after telling her that Kathy had died.

For a long time after he'd left, she had cried. Then, somehow, she had stopped believing him. He had told her the malicious lie to torture her. Kathy wasn't dead, and she wasn't dead either. Nor was she going to die. Somehow, some way, she was going to escape—by God!

* * *

The sudden sharp ringing of the phone startled Julia. She was sitting in the living room, engrossed in the PBS series "Nature." Sometimes she agreed with her former husband about the intrusive nature of the telephone. When the caller turned out to be Whit, she was even more surprised. For most of the evening, since her discussion with Tressa at dinner, she had been trying to reach him at his home. She had received no answer.

"I've been trying to call you," she told him.

"Why?" Whit asked. There were the remnants of his prior evening's anger in his voice.

"Because I owe you an apology, Whitley. My behavior last night was totally reprehensible."

"And crude, too," Whit said.

Julia couldn't help herself. She laughed. "Yes, it was. I am sorry. Have you had any success yet in finding Ms. Tyree?"

"Anna, Julia. Please call her Anna."

"Anna then," Julia said.

"No, not a bit. But we have had a break in the case of Mrs. Weldon. That's why I'm calling you."

Julia sat up in her chair. "What is it?" She used the remote control to mute the television's sound.

"Well, we've learned who she was seeing. Before I tell you this, Julia, you have to give me your word that you won't say a thing to anyone."

"Of course, Whitley."

"I mean it, Julia. I'm just telling you this to sound you out—to get your opinion."

"My opinion?" Julia said.

"You know the individual."

Julia frowned. "For heaven's sake, Whitley. Who is it?"

"Hardison."

Julia wasn't accustomed to hearing the man called by just his last name. It didn't immediately have any impact.

"Who?"

"The president of your college, Julia."

That's when it struck her, just as if she had been flattened by a trailer truck rolling down a long grade, its brakes burned out. "Absolutely not, Whitley. Why, that's preposterous."

"Not according to Eloise Weldon. She confided the information to someone."

"Whoever claims that—alleges that—is fabricating, Whitley. It can't be true. Hardison's married. His wife is a lovely woman. He wouldn't involve himself in something as sordid as an affair. Your source is clearly misleading you."

"My source, Julia, is Eloise Weldon's daughter. Several weeks ago, she told her daughter about the affair."

Julia found no words to respond.

"Are you there?" Whit asked.

"Uh . . . yes, I'm here. I'm simply speechless. It's simply so unlike the man—and unlike Eloise, too."

"None of us are what we seem, Julia."

"You've always said that, Whitley. I assume this goes a long way to proving your point."

That's when she heard the engine sound. Not that there was anything unusual about the sound of an engine. The street on which she and Tressa lived carried a lot of traffic. This sound, though, was somehow different. It seemed to come from the rear of the house, and certainly it wasn't the sound of Tressa's car. It was much too loud.

"That's strange," she said.

Whit didn't understand. "How do you mean?"

"Oh, I just heard something out back, as if a car just went through the old alley back there."

"Maybe it did," Whit said.

"That's odd."

But Whit had a question he wanted to ask. "You know Hardison, Julia. Is he capable of murder?"

"Of course not," she snapped. But then she said, "I wouldn't have thought him capable of this kind of tryst either."

"I'm on my way to interview him," he said. "Frankly, just given my brief encounter with him at the library the other morning, he didn't impress me as the type of man to kill, at least not in that fashion."

"Will you arrest him?" Julia asked.

"Not unless he confesses. There's no evidence. At this point, however, he is a suspect."

Julia's mind raced back over the grisly details from the murder scene. "But what about the purse, Whitley? I assumed that it was robbery."

"Actually," Whit said, "you assumed it was a case of mistaken identity. You thought you were supposed to be the victim."

"I felt guilty because I had asked Eloise to work in my place. I think my guilt manifested itself in that manner."

"As for the purse, if Hardison did commit the crime, he might have taken it along just to throw us off the track. Most of the thugs who would have pulled that kind of robbery wouldn't have risked taking so long to commit murder. I've never bought the robbery angle."

"You've shocked me, Whitley. You really have."

"Well, I'd better be off to Hardison's house. I tried to interview him earlier, but he was in Charleston this afternoon."

"Will you let me know what happens?" she asked.

"Yes, I'll call you as soon as I can."

"And really, Whitley, I do apologize—"

The line went dead.

"Damn him," she said, staring at the phone.

He had hung up on her. Click . . . just like that, while she was still talking.

He still infuriated her. She was about to hang up the phone, but something wasn't quite right. The phone line had sounded so dead. She tapped its button several times—no dial tone.

# THIRTEEN

GIL DICKERSON MUST have been dozing on the couch just outside of the hospital's intensive care unit. He didn't realize it, though, not until he came awake with a jolt as someone shook his shoulder. Both his eyes and his mind struggled to gain focus.

"God, where am I?" he mumbled.

"Wake up, Sheriff."

He looked up into the face of Kathy's doctor. Immediately he remembered where he was and why.

"What's happened?" he asked, sitting up, grimacing at the stiff pain of his injured knee.

"Mrs. Binder has regained consciousness. You can see her for a few minutes if you want."

Gil ignored the pain and pushed himself to his feet.

"Then," the doctor was saying, "I want you to go home and get some rest."

But Gil was limping toward the unit's wide double doors. "Is she going to be okay?"

"She's responsive, Sheriff. I think she's going to be fine."

Gil stopped at the doors. "She can talk?"

"Oh, I think so, but not right now. We still have a tube in her throat that makes speech rather difficult. She can respond. Don't force her though. She's still groggy and very confused."

He pushed open the doors. "I didn't think you were coming back tonight."

"The unit caught me before I left the hospital. It appeared to them that Mrs. Binder was coming out of it. So I decided to check on her before I left. They were right. Good people in our ICU."

Gil eased into the small cubicle. Her eyes were closed. "Kathy?"

He reached down and took her hand. It remained very cold. Bandages swathed her head, and a tube ran into her nose. Above and behind her, a large monitor mapped the beating of her heart. Each time Gil had been in the room, he had found himself unable to divert his eyes from the steady rhythm and measurement. It remained comfortably constant—always between eighty and ninety. He had found it encouraging, even if the ICU staff seemed indifferent.

"Kathy, can you hear me?"

Her eyelids fluttered and then opened. She didn't move her head. Instead, she just rolled her eyes toward him. Her mouth opened but then closed at once.

"Don't try to talk," he said, leaning down to kiss her cheek. "I just wanted you to know that I'm here."

She winked at him.

The doctor had come in behind him.

"She can respond to you by blinking her eyes, Sheriff."

Gil glanced back at her. This time, she blinked both eyes.

"Once means yes," the doctor said. "Two blinks means no."

"Can I ask her about the accident?"

The doctor nodded.

Kathy's face, though, became pinched.

"If you want to wait," he said.

She blinked . . . twice.

"Do you know who did this to you?"

Two blinks.

"You don't have any idea?"

Two blinks. Then she squeezed his hands very hard.

"What is it?" he asked.

The doctor moved closer to the bed as Kathy lifted her hand.

"She wants something, Doc." Gil was looking at the heart monitor. It was approaching one hundred.

"Is that it? Do you need something?" the doctor asked.

She blinked once.

"Can she write?" Gil asked.

"I'd rather not go that far with her just now." He leaned over her. "Please, Mrs. Binder, don't fatigue yourself just yet."

But she was still squeezing Gil's hand. Her lips started to move, and she managed to produce a hoarse whisper.

"I didn't understand," Gil said.

"Annnn . . ."

Her heartbeat was over a hundred. He leaned closer.

"Annnnaaa . . ."

The doctor was frowning. "You're exerting yourself, Mrs. Binder. I'm afraid I'm going to have to ask the sheriff to go home for the night. You've been given medication that will make you—"

"Annnnnnnaaa," she said, this time more clearly, almost gagging as she forced the word out.

Gil understood her. "She wants to know about the other woman that was in the car with her, Doctor. They're very close."

The doctor sighed. "Very well, but after that, Sheriff, please go on home. You need the rest as badly as she does."

He left.

Gil leaned over her. "She's missing, Kathy. Whoever did this kidnapped her."

Kathy closed her eyes.

"We'll find her. Whit will find her. You know how he is."

She didn't open her eyes for a few moments. When she did, they were full of tears. Gil pulled a tissue from a small box that sat on the stand by the bed and dabbed away at the drops of moisture that had rolled down the left side of her face.

"The doctor says you are going to be okay, Kathy. I don't know what I would have done if anything had happened to you."

She was still squeezing his hand, but this time the pressure was tender.

"I guess I'd better go and let you rest."

She blinked twice.

"Do you want me to stay for a little while?"

A single blink.

"Okay, until they kick me out." With his free hand, he caressed her cheek. The warmth was beginning to return to her body, but so, too, was the drowsiness. Her heart rate had dropped back into the eighties.

"When you're out of here," he was saying, "we've got some serious talking to do. It's time—"

He stopped and studied her face. She was asleep.

As soon as she had hung up the dead phone, Julia Pynchon hurried to the back of the house and peered through a kitchen window into the gathering darkness. The sun itself had dropped below the mountainous western horizon, but its afterglow still provided some illumination, enough for her to see the shape of a truck parked squarely in her backyard.

"What on earth!" she said, frowning at what might have been an apparition.

She opened her back door and squinted into the deepening shadows at the rear of her property. No doubt about it. An old truck had been parked in her yard.

After his ex-wife's phone had gone dead, Whit had tried to call her back. He had gotten a busy signal. Milbrook's phone system was notorious for its service, so he had thought little more about it. Besides, he was anxious to pay a visit to the president of Milbrook College. As far as he was concerned, that would put an end to the Weldon case for him. Tomorrow Tony would assign it to a state trooper. Whit's mind wasn't on the Weldon case. All he wanted to do was search for Anna—if only he knew where to begin.

Once on the campus of the college, it wasn't difficult to locate the presidential residence. The campus itself was small, just as the college was small. The home of the president occupied a beautifully landscaped half acre at the center of the campus.

Whit checked his watch just before he pulled into the circular driveway that led up to the house. It was 8:00 P.M. According to the president's secretary, whom he had phoned earlier in the day, Hardison had been due back in town about suppertime. He wanted an opportunity to confront the president unannounced—by ambush in fact.

The house itself was a stately two-story brick, its front decorated by white columns that reached from the first-floor portico all the way to the roof. A barrage of lights illuminated the parking area immediately in front of the portico. Whit parked his car and went to the front door. He rang the bell.

Hardison himself, still dressed in a suit and tie, opened the door. For a moment the college president didn't recognize Whit. When he did, there was a brief flash of fear, replaced by a practiced smile. "Investigator Pynchon, isn't it?"

"Yes, sir. I was hoping I might have a few moments of your time."

"About Mrs. Weldon, I assume."

"Yes, sir."

"Please . . . please come in. I just got back from Charleston."

Whit stepped into the brightly illuminated entryway. A sparkling chandelier hung over a wide hallway that stretched back to a set of wide stairs and then farther on back to what Whit could see was the kitchen. The aroma of food and coffee filled the house.

"Am I interrupting your dinner?" Whit asked.

"I was just having a cocktail prior to dinner," Hardison said. "Can I offer you anything?"

"Nothing, thanks."

A woman, not nearly so formally dressed, stepped out of the kitchen. She came forward to them, her curiosity obvious.

Hardison headed her off. "Gloria, this is Investigator Pynchon from the prosecuting attorney's office. He's investigating the murder."

He turned back to Whit. "My wife, Mr. Pynchon. Gloria Hardison."

She offered her hand, and Whit shook it.

"I can't tell you how upset my husband was by this," she said.

I can imagine, Whit thought, but he said, "A homicide, especially one as brutal as this, can be upsetting."

She was an attractive woman who looked to be in her middle forties. She was wearing a pale blue blouse and pants of the same color. In her manner she reminded Whit of Julia, but then that was understandable. Julia had always tried to pattern herself after women who occupied the more elite social strata of the college.

"Can I offer you something, Mr. Pynchon? A drink? Or perhaps coffee would be more appropriate?"

"No, thank you," Whit said. "I won't take much of your husband's time."

Hardison took the hint. "Let's go into my study."

He led Whit into a book-lined room just off the main entryway. It was dimly lit, filled with shadows, just the kind of study a college president might have. The desk itself was free of clutter, and a computer, its screen glowing, sat off to the side of the desk.

Hardison closed the door behind them and offered Whit a chair. He himself went around the desk and flipped off the computer. "I was making notes on my meeting this afternoon. Budgets can be boring things."

"I would imagine," Whit said, taking the seat. "I apologize for barging in without calling first. I phoned your office this afternoon, and they told me you would be home around suppertime."

The president of the college settled into the high-back chair. "Do you always work these hours?"

"Only when I have to," Whit said.

"So this must be rather urgent."

"I'm afraid so . . . Willie."

The use of the name brought a look of astonishment to Hardison's face. "What did you say?"

"I called you 'Willie.' Isn't that what she called you? Mrs. Weldon, I mean."

The surprise vanished, collapsing into an expression of utter despair. "Yes, Mr. Pynchon. That's what she called me. How did you find out?"

"I just did what I'm paid to do, sir."

"You must be very good at it. I had contemplated coming to you, talking to you about it. I suspected that you would discover the truth, but I never imagined it would happen so quickly. In fact, as I drove back from Charleston today, that's about all I could think about. That and the—" He stopped.

Whit kept quiet, waiting for the man to say something else. It was an interviewing tactic that worked almost every time. People being questioned couldn't stand the sound of silence. It made them want to say something else.

There were tears in Hardison's eyes when he started talking again. "Believe it or not," he said, his voice barely more than a whisper, "I really loved Mrs. Weldon, and she loved me."

"Why didn't you tell me?" Whit asked.

Hardison shrugged. "Your former wife didn't make you sound like a very understanding person. There was more to it than that, though. I was fearful that the relationship might become a matter of public knowledge."

"Or your wife's knowledge," Whit said.

"Yes, dammit. That, too. Does she have to know?"

"That remains to be seen."

"I love her, too, you know. I realize how vacuous that might sound."

"Vacuous?" Whit said. "I'm afraid my vocabulary is rather limited."

"Empty, Mr. Pynchon. Even silly. But it's true. I do love Gloria. It's just . . . I don't know. Perhaps I might as well just shut up, and let you ask the questions."

"You do know you're now our prime suspect?"

Hardison's anguish vanished. "A suspect! For God's sakes, Pynchon, I didn't . . . I mean, I couldn't have killed her. I loved her." He was still whispering.

"Nonetheless, I want to be sure you understand your rights."

Hardison's face whitened. "Mother of God, you're not arresting me, are you?"

"I'm just going to advise you of your rights."

"Isn't that what you do when you arrest people?"

Whit smiled. "Yes, sir, but it's also what we would do any time we interview a suspect."

The man's hands were trembling. From several feet away Whit could see them. It wasn't unusual. Nor was it pleasant for Whit. Fear was an emotion not easily watched, not unless you enjoyed the feeling of your own authority. For some cops it made their day. Not Whit.

"Let me get this over with," Whit said. "Then you can talk to me if you want. Or you can phone your attorney."

Hardison's trembling hand went to his face. "I feel sick."

"Just get hold of yourself, Hardison. Unless you confess to killing Eloise Weldon, I don't have evidence to arrest you."

Hardison's eyes went wide. "Confess? Of course I'm not going to confess."

"Fine, then just listen." Whit proceeded to give the man his Miranda warning. He had the card in his hand, but he didn't need it. Nonetheless, he always had it present and in sight. It prevented defense attorneys from spending an hour cross-examining as to whether he might have forgotten one or more of the necessary admonitions.

"Do you understand your rights?" Whit asked.

Hardison was slowly shaking his head. "I can't believe this is happening."

"Hardison, do you understand your rights?"

"Yes, of course."

"Do you wish to talk to me?"

"Do I have a choice?" he countered.

"Jesus, I just told you that you had a choice. You can remain silent."

Hardison stood. "Why should I do that? I didn't kill her. If I don't talk to you, it makes me look guilty."

"Or smart," Whit said.

"I did not kill the woman," he said, his eyes riveted to the door of the study. He settled back into the chair. "I'll talk to you."

"Where were you on Sunday night? From eight on?"

"Here," Hardison said. "Right here at this desk. I worked on a budget report all evening. I quit and went to bed—" He paused to think.

Again Whit himself remained silent.

"Oh, it was well after midnight."

"I assume that your wife can verify that."

Hardison closed his eyes. "So this is where she comes in?"

"Not necessarily," Whit said. "Was she here, too?"

"She went to church, Mr. Pynchon. She returned around 8:30 P.M. and went up to a room on the second floor that we have converted into a television room. She went to bed before I did. So, in truth, I doubt that she can verify my alibi. That's what you call it, isn't it?"

"Yes, sir. That's what we call it. Are you lying to me—just so I won't involve your wife?"

"No, I'm telling you the truth. The last time I saw my wife Sunday night was around eight-thirty—that is, until I went to bed, at which time she was sound asleep."

Whit pulled out a notebook and made some notes in it. "How long had you and Mrs. Weldon been involved?"

"Less than a year," he said.

"How much less?"

"Christ, I don't know. Seven months, I think."

"Did you know that she suspected she was pregnant?"

"What?" This time he didn't whisper. It came out loud and clear. The president immediately cringed at the volume of his own words.

"She thought she might be pregnant."

"But she told me that wasn't possible."

"Something made her think it was," Whit said.

Hardison slumped. "Was she?"

"No, sir."

The president's laugh was dry and humorless. "Do you know how many times I've criticized other men for not being able to keep their pants zipped? For years, I always thought I was above that sort of thing. Then, when I did become involved with Eloise, I rationalized it by thinking that we could control it—manage it. She was satisfied with our relationship. She knew I wasn't going to divorce my wife. And she told me she wouldn't become pregnant. I assumed she was using something or that she had already gone through the change of life. Isn't it odd, Mr. Pynchon? How things can be going along so smoothly, and then life suddenly decides to change the rules."

Whit shrugged. "It might be odd to you, Hardison. I see it every day."

"I guess you do."

"Did you kill her, Hardison?"

"Christ, Mr. Pynchon, what do you think?"

"I'm asking you."

"I'm not a killer. I'm not the type."

"Most killers aren't the type. Just like you said. You didn't think you were the type to cheat on your wife. You ended up doing it. I'm sure you had your reasons, but then so do most people who commit crimes, especially crimes that arise from the heat of the moment."

"I did not kill her."

Whit maintained what he hoped was a face devoid of expression. "You were with her Saturday night."

That accusation, too, caught Hardison by surprise, but his capacity to react was diminished. He just shook his head. "What don't you know?"

"I don't know who killed her."

"Yes, we were together Saturday night, but I repeat . . . I did not kill her."

"How did you two arrange your meetings?"

Hardison blushed. "Is that any of your business?"

Whit leaned forward. "Let's get something straight, friend. Anything relating to Eloise Weldon's life became my business when someone took that life. Now we can do this the easy way or—"

Hardison held up a hand to stop Whit. "I understand. You have me over the proverbial barrel."

Whit lost control over his emotions at that point. He got mad. "I'm not blackmailing you, Hardison. I don't need to.

If that's what you think, then perhaps we best just call Mrs. Hardison in here—"

"I'm sorry," the college president said. "We usually met in my office after she got off from work. Sometimes she could arrange vacation time when I had a trip and we . . . well, you probably get the picture."

"Oh, yeah, I get it, but I'm surprised your wife would buy the story that you had to work late on Saturday night."

"I told her it was for the meeting in Charleston. My wife is a trusting soul, I am very much ashamed to say."

"Based on your association with the victim, and in light of this situation, do you have any reason to suspect anyone of the crime?"

Hardison seemed taken aback by the question. "No, why should I?"

"Could she have been involved with someone else?"

Hardison's anger again flashed. "Of course not."

Whit cocked his head at the man. "You mean, she wasn't the type to do that sort of thing?"

Across the desk the man glared back at Whit. "That's a low blow, Mr. Pynchon."

"What about your wife, Hardison? Maybe she found out about the affair? That would certainly provide her with a motive."

The college president shot to his feet. "I resent your implication."

Whit stayed seated. "Get off your high horse, Hardison. She's got to be considered a suspect. I don't suspect her alibi is any better than yours. If it does turn out to be better, then you would be lying, right?"

"I've had just about enough of this. My wife couldn't kill anyone, certainly not in the fashion in which Ellie . . . Mrs. Weldon . . . was killed."

A knock sounded at the door. "Willard?" It was the voice of Mrs. Hardison.

The president's anger evaporated as he glanced at Whit. "Are you going to question her, too?"

"Not tonight."

"Come in," he shouted.

She opened the door. "Will you be much longer? I'm holding supper."

Hardison glanced at Whit, who shook his head.

"Not much longer, dear."

"Mr. Pynchon, would you care to join us? I've fixed more than enough."

Whit stood and looked back at the woman. The invitation was sincere. "I appreciate it, Mrs. Hardison, but I really must leave as soon as we finish."

"You would be more than welcome," she said.

Whit glanced back at Hardison and saw no welcome in his eyes. "No thanks," he said.

She excused herself and closed the door as she left.

Hardison remained on his feet. "I didn't kill Eloise. I know my wife well enough to tell you that she didn't either. If she had become aware of my indiscretion, I would know it."

"President Hardison, I don't want to offend you, but I have a job to do. It's not a pleasant job, but, as the saying goes, some S.O.B.'s gotta do it. You asked me a few minutes ago if I thought you killed Eloise. I don't think so. Nor do I think your wife did."

Hardison sagged in visible relief.

"But," Whit said quickly, "I've been wrong before."

"Not this time," Hardison said.

"Someone else will be assuming the investigation. I'll be certain to advise him of the delicacy of this situation. From there on it'll be up to that investigator."

"I thought you handled all of these kinds of things."

"Usually," Whit admitted. "But I have another matter that's going to require my full attention."

"Who will it be?"

"I can't tell you that right now. Tony Danton, the prosecutor, hasn't decided."

"Just as soon as you know, would you advise me?"

"Someone will advise you." Whit turned to leave. He stopped at the door to the study and turned around to the college official. "One last thing. Mrs. Weldon had told her daughter about her affair with you."

Hardison came quickly around the desk. "Oh, dear God."

"And Mrs. Weldon's son also knows. He appears to be something of a hothead. I just wanted you to know."

The man's face still hadn't recovered its color. This latest news seemed to knock the final wisp of wind from him. "Then there's little doubt the matter will become public knowledge."

"That depends," Whit said.

The man looked up. "On what?"

"On how quickly we can find the killer."

# FOURTEEN

THE NIGHT AIR carried with it a slight chill as Julia exited the rear door of her home and stepped into the yard. She moved with angry determination. Whatever fool had driven into her backyard had crushed the bed of tulips that lined the rear boundary adjacent to the old alleyway. Other than the occasional garbage truck that bounced through it, the alley had been all but abandoned for all of the years that Julia had lived at that address. At first the presence of the old truck had puzzled her, but quickly her initial confusion had mushroomed into a fury as she realized what damage the tires of the truck must have caused. Once she was within a few feet of the vehicle she could smell the odor of singed oil. In the cool evening she could even feel the heat coming from the battered old hood of the vehicle.

She marched up to the driver-side door and placed her hand on the door handle. When she tried to push in on the button, she realized it was locked. She peered into the window and could barely see the ripped bench seat inside. The cab was empty.

She glanced quickly into the truck's bed and was again startled. The tailgate had been dropped and a wide board extended from the bed to the ground.

"All right," she said aloud. "Who did this?" She was looking around the wide expanse of her backyard. She saw no one.

192

Julia then circled the truck, pausing to assess the damage to her tulip bed. The deep imprints of two tire tracks marred the cultivated plot of land. The stalks of tulips, some of which still remained in bloom, had been crushed into the soft earth.

"Bastards," she said, mumbling the word. As a rule, she didn't resort to such language, but on this occasion it seemed more than appropriate.

She completed her tour around the vehicle. Back at the front of the vehicle, she realized that she hadn't even both ered to check the license plate. So she returned to the rear of the truck. The plate itself was obscured by the board that cre ated a path from the bed to the ground. With her foot she shoved it off. It clattered to the ground, striking the bumper during its descent.

There was no license plate . . . just a holder where one had been.

"I'll be," she said, her indignation again muddled by the apparent enigma.

When she stood, her gaze was directed toward the house. A frown crossed her face. Every light on the second floor was ablaze. Always concerned with the increasing cost of her utilities, she made it a point of keeping lights off that weren't being used. She drilled the practice into Tressa, too, but sometimes the girl just forgot.

At least she had come home. Julia started for the house.

Whit didn't go directly home after leaving Hardison's. He stopped at the sheriff's department. The dispatcher was shak ing his head as Whit entered the control room. "We haven't found a thing, Mr. Pynchon."

"What about the truck?"

The dispatcher shook his head.

"Has the state crime lab called for me?" After regular courthouse hours, the lines into the seat of Raven County's government remained open. They rang in the control room.

"No, sir. No calls for you at all."

Whit sagged. He wanted to cry. He wanted to, but he didn't.

"Sheriff Dickerson's back in the kitchen."

Whit pulled himself together. "I figured he was still at the hospital."

"He came in a few minutes ago. I think he's fixing himself a bite to eat."

When Whit got back to the cramped kitchen facilities, Gil was standing at a long table with a shiny aluminum top. He was piling ham on a sandwich.

"How's Kathy?" Whit asked.

He knew the answer by the smile on his friend's face.

"She's conscious, Whit. The doctors think she's going to make it."

"Can she talk?"

The smile faded. "Not really, but she could answer questions by blinking her eyes. She doesn't know who it was. She didn't even know Anna was missing."

"Shit!" Whit slammed a hand down against the tabletop.

"I've got two full shifts of men out working on it. I phoned the state boys. Tony's apparently talked to the head man in Charleston. They're out in force. We haven't found a thing."

A rickety old chair had been shoved under the table. Whit pulled it out and slumped down into it. "I can't stand this helplessness, Gil. I wanna go out there and look, but where, gawdammit? Where?"

Gil didn't respond. He had no answer.

After a few moments of pained silence, Gil said, "Let me fix you something to eat."

Whit lifted his head, a meager smile on his face. "No thanks. I'm not hungry. I'll brave a cup of coffee."

Gil made an awkward turn on his bad leg and started for the industrial-size percolator.

"I'll get it," Whit said quickly. "You sit down and eat. You look worse than I do if that's possible."

The sheriff didn't argue. He dropped into a chair on the other side of the table and allowed his stiff leg to extend beneath it. "It's funny, Whit. It looks like Kathy's gonna make it, but Anna's still missing. It makes me feel somehow guilty."

"That's ridiculous," Whit said, returning with a Styrofoam cup full of the syrupy brew. "It just gives us one less thing to worry about."

"If we just had a clue . . . a direction—"

Whit was nodding. "That's what's so damned infuriating."

"I still think that stolen truck's gonna turn up. No way is the guy who did this, assuming it was just one guy, going to risk keeping it around too long. Our guys are checking every backwoods road in Raven County."

Whit shook his head. "He could have driven it over some mountainside in a thousand different spots. It might be months before we find it—if we ever find it."

"But what's the purpose? Why did he kidnap her?"

It was more just something to say than a question to which Gil expected an answer.

Nonetheless, Whit had one for him. "To get back at me."

Gil had taken his first bite of sandwich. He stopped chewing and said, in spite of a mouthful of ham, bread, and lettuce, "Why in the hell do you say that?"

"It's the only thing that makes sense. Maybe once Kathy can talk, she can tell us what they were doing up there."

Gil had swallowed the food. "I didn't get into that with her, Whit. The doctor was adamant—"

But Whit was waving his hand at his friend. "I know, Gil. I understand. It's a long shot anyway."

After a few sips of the aged coffee, Whit made a face and put the cup down. "Christ, that shit's awful."

"I'll have 'em make another pot," Gil said, starting to get up.

But Whit was on his feet before Gil could get his stiff leg out from under the table. "No need," he said to Gil. "Finish your dinner. I'm heading home. I need a drink. Wanna join me? I've got some bourbon."

Gil started to shake his head, but he suddenly looked up at his friend. "Why the hell not? Sure, I'll be along. Let me finish this and give the dispatcher some final instructions."

"I'll head on home. Let's see. You prefer bourbon and water if I recall."

Gil nodded as he worked on the sandwich.

"I'll have it waiting for you. I don't mean to rush, but Tressa's there. I asked her to stay by my phone. Just in case."

"See ya shortly," Gil said.

Once he was outside and in the garage area that provided a protected entrance to the jail, Whit slumped against a wall and fought back the tears. All day long he had believed that Anna was somehow still alive and well. Now, as the lonely night was securing its grip on the last few hours of the day, he was no longer certain. The intuition that had comforted him throughout the daylight hours was gone, replaced by a sense of foreboding and loss. He wasn't one to allow others to see his emotions. When a deputy's car pulled up in front of the courthouse, Whit wiped away the trace of moisture from his eyes and hurried out to his car.

The darkness defied description. Anna had never known it to be so dark. She had been on the floor, curled up in the quilt for what seemed like a whole night. At first she had expected her eyes to adjust to the darkness, but they hadn't. Either that, or the absence of light was so pervasive that there simply was no way to see. She couldn't even pick out the open window, but she could feel the cold air invading through it. She could hear things, too—the irritating chirping of crickets, the call of an owl that seemed to come close and then move away, even once the shuffling of some small animal outside.

Then there was what she didn't hear. No traffic sounds. No voices, even distant ones. No human sounds whatsoever . . . none at all.

No wind either. Earlier, just before sundown, she could see the brown leaves of an oak rustling. She had heard them, too. Some of the other trees had the beginnings of their spring foliage, and they rustled, too, though not as crisply as the dried oak leaves. The wind had vanished with the sunlight.

She tried to wiggle deeper into the thin protection of the quilt. The chains around her ankles were snug and cold, but otherwise they produced no physical discomfort. The handcuffs, though, continued to tighten each time she inadvertently tugged one hand against the other. The metal rims were now biting into her wrist, not yet very painfully but the constant chafing was rubbing her raw. She tried to remain still.

Even in the folds of the quilt she started to tremble. She didn't want to cry again. She had done enough of that, but she couldn't stop her mind from conjuring thoughts that brought tears to her eyes. First and foremost was the probability that she would never again see Whit. *Never. Christ, such a harsh and cruel word.*

So many things she would *never* do again.

She started to pray out loud. "God, I haven't done much of this, and it's maybe too late to start, but, please, I don't want to die. I—"

She laughed at her prayer. "I guess no one wants to. I mean, most people don't want to. Come to think of it, maybe some do."

She was silent for a moment. "Jesus, I'm talking to him as if he were right here."

To Anna, who somehow believed in a God but who had

never done much more than that, the urge to pray made her feel like such a coward. It made her think of her father, who had passed away several years before after a long siege with a bad heart. He had been such a brave man. He had known that one day very soon, maybe even that day, it would end for him. He had known that! He had lived with it every day for four years. When it had finally happened, on a rainy March night as he rested in a bed in a Kentucky hospital, he had been so peaceful and trusting.

"I know what's happening," he had said to her as she held his hand. "I'm not frightened. Just take care of your mother."

A few brief seconds later he was gone. A nurse, her hand on Anna's shoulder, had guided her out of the room. They had tried to revive him, as they had done several times before, but after a period of thirty minutes the doctor had come to her.

"He's gone," he had said.

She had known that for the full thirty minutes. She had been so sad—yet so proud of him, too.

She also thought of her mother, who had passed away nine months later. She, too, had accepted the fate that awaited her. In fact, Anna believed that her mother wanted it to happen. Her parents had been so happy together. It had been fitting that she join him . . . if there was some place for them to be joined.

*If . . .*

Their dignity made Anna ashamed for being so frightened, but, God help her, she couldn't help it. Death didn't scare nearly so much as dying—the process of dying.

That's the phrase the nurse had used when she had gone to be with her mother.

"Miss Tyree, your mother is in the process of dying."

She curled more tightly into herself and started to weep, as much at the memories as over her current dilemma.

That phrase, spoken so softly and tenderly by the nurse, had haunted her for years. The *process* of dying . . .

Was that her state? Anna's? Was she in the process of dying?

Back in the kitchen, Julia paused to listen before she called out her daughter's name. Tressa, bless her soul, wasn't the epitome of grace. When she was home, and upstairs, her movements were always telegraphed by her foot sounds. Her mother, though, heard no sounds. Well, that wasn't quite true. She heard the humming of a fan inside the refrigerator. She heard the dripping of a faucet at the kitchen sink.

She moved out into the hall and to the bottom of the steps. "Tressa? Are you home?"

Certainly it was time for her to be home—unless somehow she had managed to meet that man she was seeing.

"Tressa?"

Her daughter didn't answer. Julia headed up the steps, the first inkling of concern beginning to materialize inside her head.

At the top of the steps, she hesitated. "Tressa?"

By then she knew Tressa wasn't home, but someone had come up the steps and turned on the lights on the second floor. Someone had. Or had they? Julia Pynchon didn't like being intimidated. She remained greatly embarrassed by the scene she had created at the library on the morning she had found Eloise. It had been silly, acting as she had. It had been more than silly; it had been humiliating in the presence of Whitley and the president of the college.

Which took her mind back to Whit's phone call.

Even as she stood at the top of the steps, trying to remember if she had just been upstairs before Whit's phone call . . . if she just might have left the lights on and didn't recall, she shook her head at the thought that Eloise and Willard Hardison had been romantically involved. It staggered her sense of credulity.

She moved silently down the upstairs hall, peering first into her bedroom and then into Tressa's. The more she pondered the mystery of the lights, the more convinced she was that none of the lights upstairs had been on a few short minutes earlier.

And there was that truck parked in her backyard. She decided to call the police and was turning to go back down the steps when she remembered that the phone line had gone dead.

She stopped on the top steps. The events started to pull themselves together into a pattern which—

All of the lights in the house went off.

Whit found Tressa sprawled on the couch watching one of those music video stations that came in on the cable.

"Any calls?" he asked as he took off the corduroy jacket that had virtually become his trademark.

"All quiet, Daddy. Any news?" She pulled herself up and used the remote control to switch off the television.

Whit drooped into the worn recliner that had served him so well for years. "Nothing about Anna, but there's good news about Kathy. She regained consciousness, and she's going to be okay."

"That's good anyway," she said.

She stood and went to his chair where she settled down on the arm. Her hand went to his face. "I have this feeling that she's going to be fine, Daddy."

He looked up. "Kathy?"

"No, silly. Anna. It's just a feeling, but—"

"I had that feeling all day, too, hon. I don't have it anymore."

"You're a pessimist," she said.

"No, just a realist. If the bastard or bastards wanted something, why haven't they said?"

They both heard the sound of a car. Tressa started to go to the door.

"It's Gil," Whit said. "We're going to have a drink. You'd best head on home. To be honest, I didn't get to tell your mother that you were going to be at my house."

Tressa's face dropped. "Gosh, Daddy, she'll be furious."

"Actually, the phone line went dead while we were talking. The phone cooperative strikes again."

"I better try to call her," Tressa said.

Whit went to let Gil in while Tressa dialed the number.

"I was just going to make the drinks," Whit said to his friend.

Tressa was listening to the angry busy signal. "It still must be out of service. I'd better get home. Mother will think I told her a fib and went out with Rob."

She gave Whit a hug.

"Just have her call me," Whit said. "I'll vouch for your good behavior—at least tonight."

She hugged Gil on her way out. "Daddy told me about Kathy. I'm happy for you."

"Now if we can just find Anna," he said.

Whit had headed into the kitchen. Gil followed him. "She's a great kid, Whit. I don't know how two sourpusses like you and Julia produced such a pleasant offspring."

"Maybe she was the product of that one odd gene we all have," Whit said as he poured bourbon into two glasses.

"What odd gene? I don't have any odd genes."

Whit handed his friend the drink. "Of course you do. I read it in *Time*, I think. A recessive gene or something like that."

"You're the one with the regressive gene."

"Re-CES-sive, Gil."

They returned to the living room. Gil took the couch. It was easier on his leg. Whit claimed his recliner.

"I called the state police detachment before I left the jail," Gil said. "The lab phoned in some results to them."

Whit rocked forward in the recliner. "Why the hell didn't they call me?"

"They tried. You've been out running around all day. Anyway, they didn't get anything out of Anna's car that would help—other than the residue of brown paint."

"I already knew that. What about the paint?"

"They said they did get a good enough paint sample to match against the vehicle if we find it."

"Which really won't help a fuckin' bit," Whit said.

"Did you expect more?" Gil asked, trying to calm Whit.

"I had the right to hope, didn't I?"

Julia crept down the steps, trying to quiet the beating of her heart. A streetlight just across from her house provided enough illumination for her to see the steps. If she could just make it to the front door . . . if she could get that far and out of it, then she could run across the street to the Snyders. Or next door to the Hamiltons.

But then what if Tressa came back? She could maintain a constant vigil from either of those places. Head Tressa off before she came into the house. Better yet, maybe their phones were working. She could call the police.

Julia was at the bottom when the black figure, with a spherical head, stepped in front of her, blocking her way to the front door. She swung a clumsy fist at it, and her knuckles cracked against something slick and very hard.

No matter . . . she swung again. This time, a leathered hand wrapped itself around her wrist.

"What do you want?" she cried, trying to wrench free.

"You, Mrs. Pynchon." His voice was soft, hardly more than a whisper.

She kicked at him. He wrenched her arm behind her back. She wailed in pain.

"No use fighting." he whispered. "You are Julia Pynchon?"

She had stopped struggling. Every movement, no matter how small, sent flashes of pain from her elbow to her shoulder.

"Yessss!" she said, breathless from the pain. In spite of it, she could smell the musty aroma of the leather.

"Good. Wouldn't want to make another mistake."

She knew what he meant, and she knew that she had been right. Whit had been wrong. The man hadn't intended to kill Eloise Weldon. There was some small consolation in that.

As soon as her house came into view, Tressa knew that she was in deep shit, as she liked to say . . . but only to herself. All the lights were out. Her mother must have already gone to bed. She had done it once before when Tressa had been out on a date with Rob. Turned off all the lights and gone to bed. Just as now, even the porch light hadn't been left burning.

Tressa pulled to a stop along the curb in front of the house. Her mother's car was already in the driveway, and, since her mother usually left for work before Tressa left for school, she didn't want to block her. She would leave a note on the kitchen table telling her mother that she had been at Dad's the night before—that Dad was supposed to have told her that.

She hurried up the walk and was surprised to find the front door unlocked. She pushed it open and reached in to flip on the hall light. The switch clicked, but the light didn't come on.

"Dammit," she muttered, closing the door behind her. She moved over to the living room and reached inside for that light switch. It didn't work either. Maybe she hadn't gone to bed. Maybe something was wrong with the electricity.

"Mother!"

Her mother didn't answer.

"Mother! Are you here?"

Tressa moved back through the hall. It wasn't so dark that she couldn't see. Her hand touched the wall. It provided a guide as she entered the darker shadows back toward the kitchen.

"Are you here, Mother?"

A phone was located just inside the kitchen entryway. Tressa reached it and picked up the handset. It was dead. She hung it up.

Her concern had turned to agitation. What was going on? She moved back through the hall and started up the steps. The roar came from outside, loud and harsh, so sudden that it made her jump.

She clattered back down the steps and threw open the front door. A mammoth motorcycle thundered from the side of the house, its wheels spinning in the dew-damp grass as it hurtled for the street. The figure on the cycle wore clothing as black as the monstrous bike itself. He turned to glance back. That's when she saw the silver face guard.

What had been agitation blossomed into a full fear as she hurried back into the house. "Mother! Dammit, answer me."

She went back to the kitchen and peered out into the backyard. Even in the darkness she could see the outline of the truck.

# FIFTEEN

GIL FINISHED THE DRINK. "That's it for me," he said, favoring his leg as he rose from the couch. "I'd better go home and give this thing a little rest." He patted the injured knee.

Whit stood, too. "I think I'll have one more."

"Don't overdo it," Gil said. "It won't help things."

"Maybe it'll make me sleepy. I didn't get any rest last night, and I don't think I'll do any better tonight. Not without a little help."

"Try warm milk," Gil said as he moved toward the front door.

Whit made a face. "I hate milk, warm or otherwise."

Gil chuckled. " Somehow I suspected that."

The phone rang. Gil stopped at the door. Whit rushed to answer it.

Whatever was said to him was brief.

"Oh, sweet Jesus," he said into the mouthpiece. "I'm on my way."

Whit slammed down the phone.

"What's going on?" Gil asked.

Whit was already at the closet, yanking out his jacket. "That was the city police. Something's happened over at Julia's."

"What?" Gil said, trying to keep up with Whit as he headed out of the house.

205

"They didn't—or wouldn't—say. They just told me to get there pronto."

"I'll drive," Gil said.

"Like hell you will." Whit was already down the front steps, headed for his car.

With Whit squealing tires as they rounded corners, the two of them arrived at Julia's house within a few minutes. Police cars jammed the street. The flashing lights, though, weren't restricted to the front of the residence. As Whit pulled to a stop, with Gil in the seat beside him, he saw the flashing red lights at the rear, just red lights. No blue lights. That meant there was an ambulance back there.

"No," Whit was saying, over and over. "Dear God, no."

He was out of the car ahead of the handicapped sheriff, rushing toward the backyard of his former wife's house. A city officer threw himself in Whit's path before he reached the gathering of cops and members of the emergency medical team.

"You don't wanna go back there," the man was saying as he wrestled with the bulky investigator.

"Tressa?" Whit asked, momentarily giving up his struggle.

The cop frowned.

"My daughter, dammit! Has something happened to her?"

The man shook his head. "She's fine, Whit."

"Thank God."

"It's your ex-wife, man. You don't want to see her."

The sudden surge of happy relief evaporated. His struggle with the officer commenced again. "Julia? What's happened to her?"

"C'mon, Pynchon, trust me. You don't wanna go back there."

Gil had reached them. "You might as well let him go," he said to the city officer.

"Sheriff, I don't think—"

In that brief relaxation of tension, Whit broke free. He charged toward the scene of whatever it was they didn't want him to see. When he saw the old brown truck, brightly illuminated by the ambulance headlights and the other lights set up by the city police, he stopped.

Gil had hurried to catch him. "Jesus, Whit. It's the truck we've been looking for."

Several other officers were approaching Whit. He braced for them. "If anyone puts a hand on me, I'll break his face."

Coy Middleton, one of the city detectives, stepped forward. "It's your former wife, Whit. She's dead. She's been murdered."

"Julia?" Whit said, disbelieving what he had heard.

"Your daughter made the I.D."

"Tressa? You bastards! You let Tressa—"

"Gawdammit, Whit. Listen to me before you blow a gasket. Your daughter found her. She started screaming. A neighbor phoned us. We had them phone you before we even got to the scene."

"I wanna see her," Whit said.

"Your daughter? She's over at a neighbor's house. I'm securing your ex-wife's house for the investigation."

"No, dammit. I want to see Julia. Right-fucking-now."

"There's no need," Middleton said.

Gil was standing beside Whit. He nodded to Middleton. "He has a right, Coy."

"Whose side are you on?" the city cop said.

"His," the sheriff said, taking Whit by the arm. "Let's go."

Together, the two men moved toward the truck. Whit, sagging a little as they moved forward, used Gil for support.

"She's in the bed of the truck," Middleton said, moving up behind them.

"You're sure you wanna do this?" Gil whispered. "You do remember that I've been through this."

"I've got to, Gil."

"Give them some light in the bed," Middleton shouted.

Several police officers moved forward and directed the beams of their large flashlights into the rusting bed of the vehicle.

Gil peered over first. "Mother of God," he said, closing his eyes to the sight.

Whit looked.

His friend had a tight hand under his arm. He felt Whit's body flinch, but Whit didn't turn away.

"And my daughter saw this?" he asked, his tone icy.

Middleton was still behind them. "Like I told you, she found her. She had a flashlight. I don't know how much she saw. We got here moments before you and the sheriff. I'm really sorry, Pynchon."

Whit continued to gaze at the lifeless, mutilated form that had been his former wife. In the cool stillness of the late evening, with the lights still focused on the bloody display, wisps of steam rose from the warm, loosely coiled clump of intestines that had spilled from her cleaved midsection. The gaping wound ran from there all the way up to her throat. Whit absorbed the horror. He wanted to remember. He didn't want to forget—not ever. He had a reason.

Gil, not Whit, saw the piece of paper resting on her bared legs. "What's that?" he asked, moving around Whit for a closer look.

"A note," Middleton said. "We didn't touch it, but we did manage to read it. The letters are stenciled on there."

"A note?" Whit said, half listening.

"A note to you, Whit."

The investigator for the Raven County prosecutor's office continued to stare at the horror that had been inflicted on the mother of his only child. "What does it say?" he asked.

Middleton answered. "I may not get it word for word without climbing back up there to read."

"Just give me the basics," Whit said.

"It read, 'No mistake this time, Pynchon. I've got the Tyree woman, and she might be in the same shape. Life's a bitch, isn't it?' Something like that, Whit."

As if it required every last vestige of his physical strength, Whit took a deep breath and then wrenched his body away from the truck. Gil lurched after him, following his friend to a tree where Whit collapsed against it.

"She was right, Gil. Julia was right about the Weldon murder."

"This is crazy, Whit."

"Crazy? Yeah, it's crazy. It's revenge, Gil. It's the only theory that makes any sense when you consider Anna's kidnapping. It went back farther than that, though—all the way to Sunday night and the college library." Whit's head was spinning. He tried to shake it off.

"You couldn't have known."

Whit bent forward to take a series of deep breaths. Once he had the dizzy spell under control, he said, "Dammit, Gil! She knew! Julia somehow knew. I wouldn't listen."

Gil couldn't think of anything else to say.

Middleton came over to them. "Whit, your daughter's over there with the Hamiltons. She's taking it pretty hard."

"I'm on my way. Come with me, Gil."

Middleton walked with them to the back door of the neighbor's house. "We'll handle it here, Whit. And I promise you one thing, we'll do it right."

"You'd better," Whit said, the customary rancor absent from his voice. "Several more lives might depend on it."

* * *

God help her, but she was glad to hear that loud grumbling of the motorcycle. Her captor was coming back. She should have dreaded his return, but she didn't. The engine sounds grew louder. Anna managed to pull herself up and settle into the chair. In the effort the sharp grip of the cuffs tightened. By then, they were cutting into her skin. Maybe he would loosen them for her if she didn't give him a hard time. Over the past few hours, physical comfort had become a luxury for which she would do almost anything. Would she reach some point where she would do more than almost anything? Anna didn't want to think about it. All of her life she had thought of herself as a strong, courageous person. It had been self-delusion.

She heard the ponderous steps made by his black engineering boots as he mounted the porch. She heard the front door open, the sound of his feet as he stomped through the front room.

She held her breath as the door to the bedroom flew open.

"Still here," he said, his voice always the harsh whisper.

"I thought you weren't coming back."

"Sorry to see me?" he said, leaning against the frame of the door, his identity still concealed behind the shiny-faced helmet.

"I'm glad to see you. Could you loosen these?" She held up the set of metal bracelets.

"I warned you, didn't I?"

"Every time I move they get tighter. I tried—"

"The cops love 'em because of that. They get off seeing some poor jerk grind the skin off his wrists."

He stepped across the floor toward her and reached for her hand. "You try anything, and you're dead," he said after examining the cuffs.

"I won't. I promise."

He started to remove one of the sleek leather gloves but thought better of it. Instead, he stepped behind her and removed it. From the pocket of the black leather jeans he withdrew the key.

He stepped back around and took her arm. As he unlocked the left cuff, Anna's gaze settled upon a brownish moist stain on the thigh of his pants. At first she thought it was mud. Then she recognized it.

"Ohmigod," she said, seeing that the leather jacket was also marred by extensive splashes of the thickening gore. She averted her eyes.

He didn't understand her reaction. "What? What the fuck is wrong with you?"

"You're covered with blood."

He glanced down and chuckled. "Yeah, I guess I am."

He adjusted the left bracelet and moved to the right.

Anna kept her face turned. "Whose is it?"

"Not Pynchon's if that's what you're thinking."

"Who then?" she asked.

"His ex," he said, clicking the right bracelet shut.

She gasped and brought her hands to her face. In the process the cuffs started to tighten again."

"Fuck, lady. Lotta good I did." He lurched away. "See if I take the gawdamn time to help you again."

Anna was crying again. "You killed Julia Pynchon?"

Her captor was lowering the open window. "Gutted her."

"Dear God."

He was reaching inside the blood-covered jacket and withdrew a long stiletto. "Did it with this. Put it in down here." He placed the needle-sharp blade at a point just above his crotch.

Anna's eyes were closed. "Don't do this to me."

"And zip! All the way up to here." When he finished, the point of the blade was at his throat. "Didn't know it would be so messy."

"You're an animal," she said, her jaw clenched.

It didn't offend him. He just laughed. Behind the silver

visor, the sound was muffled and hollow. "It was time to let Pynchon know."

"Whatever Whit did to you . . . whatever it was, you probably deserved it."

"I've already told you," he snapped. "He didn't do a thing to me, not directly."

Anna almost asked him about Tressa, but she caught herself. Certainly the man probably knew about Whit's daughter, but she didn't want to remind him. Nor did she want to know if he planned to do something to Tressa.

Tears continued to roll out of her eyes. "If you hate him so much, why take it out on others?"

He shook his head. "You're a stupid bitch. I am taking it out on him. I wanna make him hurt. I wanna make him sweat. I want him to spend as many nights as possible lying awake, wondering what's gonna happen next—to who it's gonna happen."

"So you're going to kill more innocent people," she said.

"Innocent people? No, I'm not gonna kill any babies. They're the only innocent people I know."

"You're sick," she said.

He lunged for her. She reacted by falling off the chair away from him. As she hit the floor, her arms flew apart. The steel bracelets choked tight against her thin wrists. She didn't have time to scream. He was on her, the gleaming knife blade pushing against the skin of her throat.

Tressa's eyes were red and swollen, her lips trembling. "Did you see her, Daddy? Did you see what they did to her?"

Whit wrapped his arms around his daughter and pulled her to him. He hugged her, tears starting to roll down his own cheeks. "I saw, hon. I'm sorry you did, though."

He could feel the quiver rush through her body as she

started to bawl. She buried her face against his chest. They were alone in the living room of the Hamilton's home. The others—Gil and the Hamiltons—had slipped out to give Whit and his daughter the time alone.

"I'll get the bastard, Tressa. I know that won't do your mother any good, but—"

She thrust herself away from him. "I want you to get him. I want you to kill him. He butchered her, Daddy."

The malicious expression on Tressa's face shocked even Whit. Never before had he seen his daughter so full of hate and anger. She was entitled. He knew that. Nonetheless, for just an instant she shocked him, so much so that he quickly tried to pull her face back against his chest.

She resisted, thrusting herself away from him. "I saw the note, Daddy. He's doing it because of you, isn't he? Because of something you did to him?"

Whit slowly nodded.

"Who is it? Who hates you that much?" Her eyes had narrowed to angry slits. Her hands were clenched into fists.

Whit glanced behind him and saw a chair. He dropped into it, shaking his head as he went down. "I don't know, Tress. I guess there could be quite a few. You don't lock nice people up, and I've jailed my share of bad asses."

"He's killed Anna, too."

"We don't know that," Whit said quickly.

"You know he has! If he would do that—" Her voice trailed off. The fury seemed to drain away. "Mother made me so mad sometimes, but I loved her. I really did."

He motioned for his daughter to come sit on the arm of the chair. She obeyed. With his hand he reached up and began to massage the nape of her neck. "I guess I loved her, too."

There was a look of disbelief on Tressa's face when she looked down at him. "You loved her?"

"Not in the way that people do who should be married.

Not that way, Tressa. I did when I married her, but that was a long time ago. I don't think you ever stop loving someone. You just kinda change the way you love them. I can't explain it. If I didn't feel something for her, though, I wouldn't feel the way I do now.''

"Do you really think Anna's still alive?''

"Yes, I do. I don't think he's killed her yet. I don't even know why I think it's a male other than the circumstantial evidence. A woman would have a hard time doing the damage this person has done.''

"But you really, honest-to-God think Anna's alive. You're not just telling me that.''

He shook his head and reached to take her hand. "If he had already killed her, I think he would have let me know, probably in a rather terrible way. I think she's still alive, but we don't have very long to find her. I know one thing for certain. We need to get you out of sight until we do find him.''

"What about Mother?'' she asked. "The funeral, I mean. What about my exams? Not that they seem all that important now.''

"They're important,'' Whit said. "As for your mother, I don't know. I haven't even thought about that.''

"There are people to call, Daddy.''

Whit sighed. "I know.''

They heard a slight commotion just beyond the living-room's doorway. Tony Danton's head peered around the corner. "Can I come in?''

Tressa went to him, and he hugged her. Whit stayed in the chair. After the prosecutor released Tressa, he stood over Whit. "What can I say, old friend?''

Whit was still wiping away tears when his eyes met those of the prosecutor. "Nothing, Tony. I'm just glad you're here.''

"I'm heading on back outside to make certain no one

screws up the scene. I just wanted to let you know that I was here."

Whit pushed himself up. "I'll go too."

Tony stopped him. "You stay here. Tressa needs you."

Gil eased into the room behind the prosecutor. "We've found motorcycle tracks leading out of the backyard."

Whit frowned. "Motorcycle tracks?"

"He was riding one!" Tressa said.

All three of them—Gil, Whit, and Tony—looked at the young woman. "You saw him?" Whit said.

"Yes, he drove out of the backyard on this big black cycle. It roared like thunder."

"For god's sake," Whit cried, "did you see his face?"

She shook her head. "He was wearing one of those round helmets with the silvered faceplate. He was dressed in black leather and had on a wide silver belt."

Tony was turning to Gil. "Get that out to all the other agencies in the county. Pronto."

The sheriff was already on his way out of the living room as fast as his gimpy leg would allow.

"What else did you see?" Whit asked.

"Just that, Daddy."

"The license plate?"

"Christ, Daddy. It was dark, and he was almost flying out of the backyard."

"Try to picture it, dear. Sometimes you see more—"

"I didn't see it!" she snapped.

Whit didn't push. "It's okay. Just take it easy."

The Hamiltons were out in the hall. Whit went out to them. Oscar Hamilton offered his hand. "I'm sorry. Anything we can do, we'll be more than happy."

"You've done a lot already, and I appreciate it. I'd like for Tressa to stay here a little while longer if that's not too much of an intrusion."

Hamilton's wife, a formidable woman who carried her bulk

as if she were a linebacker, stepped forward. "She's more than welcome to stay the night."

"Thanks," Whit said, "but we'll make other arrangements. I just want to—well, you understand."

"Perfectly," Mrs. Hamilton said.

Tressa had overheard. "I'm going with you, Daddy."

He turned to her. "Just stay here for a short time, Tressa."

Tony was still in the living room. "I can handle things out there, Whit. Don't you think—"

"Dammit, Tony, I think we'd best get out there before some idiot drives over those cycle tracks."

Marsha Via had been more than happy to work an extra shift that night. She knew the sheriff needed the manpower in the field, and Marsha's sister had agreed to keep her daughter. As she wrote down the description of the helmeted biker, something clicked in her head.

"Large round helmet with a silver faceplate." Those had been the sheriff's words.

It was déjà vu . . . as if she had written those words down before.

"Uh . . . sheriff, hold on just a second." She released the mike key, trying to think.

*Dammit!* Where had she heard that description before?

"What is it?" he asked.

"Nothing. I thought it rang some kind of bell. I'll forward the description to the city units and the state police detachment."

"The city units are here," Gil said. "Just be sure it gets to the state's. Oh, and call it in to the chief down at Tipple Town and also to the college security boys. There might be a link to that killing at the college."

"Ten four." She thought the transmission was over.

Instead, Gil asked, "What kind of bell did you mean?"

She was still trying to remember. "I'm not sure. Gimme some time to think on it."

"Ten four."

"Round helmet. Silver mask." She repeated the description aloud several times.

Marsha had heard that general description before—very recently, too. She just couldn't remember when—or in what context.

Tony and Whit stood over the deep grooves that had been cut into the well-manicured lawn that surrounded his former wife's house. "Damn big cycle," Whit said.

"We can't be one hundred percent certain the rider was the killer."

"Yes, we can," Whit countered. "That explains that board laying behind the truck. He used it to get the cycle off the truck."

"You're too involved in this case to continue with the investigation," Tony suddenly said.

The comment caught Whit totally unprepared. He took a step or two back from his friend. "What the hell—"

"I mean it, Whit. Your emotions are going to cloud your judgment. You need to see to Tressa's safety and make the arrangements for Julia."

Whit's eyes sparked with outrage. "I intend to do those two things, Tony. I also intend to find the bastard who did this."

But the prosecutor was shaking his head. "I can't allow it, Whit. It's not how I do things."

Gil was coming up to join them.

Whit remained incensed. "For chrissakes, Tony, the bastard's still got Anna."

"Dammit, I know that."

Whit threw up his hands and prowled in a tight circle,

carefully avoiding the tracks. When he stopped, he was turned away from the prosecutor.

"What's going on here?" Gil asked.

Tony motioned for the sheriff to back off. He then went up behind Whit and put a hand on his shoulder. "C'mon, man, think about—"

Whit whirled and slapped the hand away. He reached into his pocket and pulled out a leather case. He jammed it down in Tony's shirt pocket. "There's your goddamn badge, friend. Now, you don't tell me what to do. I'm no longer your problem."

"Whit!"

His longtime friend and investigator was walking away, heading back toward the brown truck.

Gil moved beside Tony. "You must be outta your mind."

"I'm afraid he's out of his," Tony said.

The sheriff, though, wasn't buying it. "Christ, man, even in his state of mind he's a better investigator than anybody in the county."

"I plan to assign Monty Vickers to the case."

Vickers was a state trooper assigned to the local detachment. That news ignited Gil's temper. "Christ, Tony, let my department take it. I'll give it to Cardwell, and I'll stay right with him, just to keep him on the right track."

"Sorry, Gil, but your interest in the case is almost as personal as Whit's." Tony pulled the badge case from his pocket. "I go by the book, Gil. He knows that. Hell, he's the same damned way. He'll see the light."

"And you really think you can keep Whit out of this?"

"I'll do what I have to do."

Gil was shaking his head. "You cold bastard. You keep forgetting that this maniac has Anna."

"She's dead, Gil. You know it, and so do I. Sooner or later, he'll come to accept that, too."

The sheriff's eyes were on Whit, who had taken a position beside the truck, staring down into the bed.

"If that's the case . . . if it does turn out that sour, then you can kiss him good-bye. She's the only reason he's stayed."

Tony opened the badge case. The gold chunk of metal twinkled under the bright flashing lights from the nearby ambulance. "I think we've already said our good-byes."

# SIXTEEN

AS THE DEPUTY'S CRUISER pulled to a stop in front of Whit Pynchon's house, a gray glow, the first hint of the coming dawn, highlighted the double summit of Tabernacle Mountain. From the passenger side, Gil Dickerson eased his aching leg onto the sidewalk. Once it was free of the tight front seat, the rest of his body easily followed. His own vehicle was still parked in front of Whit's.

"You headin' home?" the young deputy who had chauffeured the sheriff asked.

He was leaning back into the car. "I'm going in to check on Whit."

"Not being nosy, Sheriff, but did Pynchon really quit last night?"

"For the time being," the sheriff said. He slammed the door shut.

The pre-dawn air still retained a chill as Gil limped his way toward the small front porch. There was a dampness, too, more than just from the dew. When dawn did come, Gil suspected that it would be gray and overcast. Maybe it would even rain, hopefully enough to make a little difference. He glanced into the sky and saw only a milky haze. No stars—certainly no moon. Fitting, he thought, as he painfully started up the short set of stairs that led to Pynchon's front door. His knee was giving him fits. He'd been on it far too long that night.

Gil doubted that Whit was asleep, but just in case he decided to ignore the doorbell and knocked lightly. The door opened almost at once. Whit stood there, still fully dressed in wrinkled clothes, needing a shave, smelling a little of booze.

"I see I didn't wake you."

Whit shook his head. "Tressa's asleep, though. Anna had some Benadryl she'd been taking for her allergies. I gave her a double dose, and it relaxed her enough to doze off."

"I won't come in then," Gil said. "I just—"

But Whit was stepping back, opening the door wider. "The hell you won't. You won't disturb her. She's back in the bedroom. I've just finished brewing some coffee, and I promise it won't be as bad as that stuff you serve at the jail."

Gil smiled. "At least you still have a sense of humor." He hobbled into the house.

"Your leg," Whit noted. "It must be bothering you."

"Throbbing like a bad tooth. Have you got any aspirin?"

"Doesn't everyone?" Whit said. "Grab a seat on the couch. I'll bring you coffee and an aspirin."

While Whit headed into the back of the house where the kitchen was located, Gil eased into the living room and literally fell down on the worn, comfortable sofa. He leaned back on one of the arms and lifted his injured leg onto the cushions. He could see where Whit had spent the night—in the battered old recliner across from him. Beside it, an ashtray was crammed full of cigarette butts. There was also an empty glass and a nearly empty bottle of bourbon.

"Here's the aspirin," Whit said. He also offered a small glass of water. "I'll be back with the coffee. You like yours black. Right?"

"And hot," Gil said.

Several minutes later they were both seated in the living room, both blowing over the lips of their mugs to cool the dark, fragrant fluid inside.

"Tony handled the scene pretty well," Gil finally said. "He sent one of my guys to Charleston with that note and some other odds and ends we found in the cab of the truck. The truck will be towed up to the lab later this morning. We took plaster casts of the motorcycle tracks. Damned good ones, too."

Whit only nodded.

"We also checked out Julia's house. It appears that the bastard cut the phone line on the outside. Somehow he then got inside and killed the power at the circuit box down in the basement. Julia must have been killed out in the yard, pretty near to the truck. He was a brazen bastard. The Hamiltons heard the motorcycle. They didn't think much of it since that street is pretty heavily traveled. Nobody else noticed anything out of the ordinary, not until Tressa found Julia."

"I must have been talking to her when the phone line was cut," Whit said. "I should have checked it out."

"Hell, Whit. The phone service goes down all the time."

Whit rubbed his eyes. "Yeah, that's what I told myself at the time."

"It was a reasonable assumption. You can't blame yourself for—"

Whit's eyes narrowed. "The hell I can't. You read that note."

"You're a cop, Whit. We all live with that kind of risk."

"But other people around us don't—or at least they shouldn't have to."

"What are you going to do?" Gil asked, coming to the point of inquiry that had brought him to Whit's home.

His friend shrugged. "Try to find Anna. I've been sitting here since we came back, going back through sixteen or seventeen years of cases . . . just in my mind. Trying to come up with some names of people who might wanna do this to me."

"That shouldn't have been too hard," Gil said.

Something similar to a smile momentarily appeared on Whit's face. "That's the problem. Too gawdamn many names."

The smile vanished quickly, though, and he continued. "Not really, though. A lot of them are dead, or too old to be reasonable suspects. Others are still in the can. To be honest, Gil, I really couldn't come up with a single name."

"It would have to be a real bad ass, Whit."

"I did have one idea. I'm glad you came by. Let me run it by you."

Gil adjusted his position on the couch. "Go ahead."

"Wonder if it has anything to do with the election you're involved in?"

The sheriff frowned. "What the hell do you mean?"

"Think about it, Gil. Whoever this son of a bitch is, he's managed to derail a lot of your support people. Kathy and Anna. Tony, too. I omit myself because you know how useless a politician I am."

"But why Julia for God's sakes?"

"Just to keep the pot boiling."

Gil shook his head. "You're reaching, Whit."

"Dammit, man. I've got to reach. There's nothing close at hand. Every damned suspect requires one long reach, and let's face it, Jake Brimm's probably capable of most anything. He hates my guts."

"You never have told me the full story about him—about the murder you think he committed."

Whit leaned forward. "Brimm arrested one of the town drunks, a harmless enough old bum who hadn't done anything worse than go to sleep in someone's front yard. He brought him to jail. Two guys had to carry the old man to the drunk tank. It was empty by the way. The next morning, when the day shift went to get him out, he was dead."

"What killed him?"

"He had three broken ribs, one of which had punctured

his lung. I think he was dead when Brimm and others dumped him in the tank. Brimm kicked the poor bastard to death when he found him laying in the yard. I know it just as sure as I'm sitting here, but—"

"You couldn't prove it," Gil said.

"I never really got the chance."

Gil still didn't buy the theory about Brimm's involvement in the present case. "Be that as it may, Jake Brimm doesn't ride a motorcycle."

"Hell, Gil. He could hire someone. You know some of those creeps that ride in those motorcycle gangs. They'd stir-fry their own kids if there was dope offered."

"I just can't see it."

"Any better ideas?" Whit asked.

The pain in Gil's knee was ebbing—perhaps because of the position it was in. The painkiller hadn't had time to take effect yet. He was looking at the bottle of bourbon when he next spoke. "How much of that stuff have you been drinking?"

Whit closed his eyes in frustration. "Not enough to affect my judgment. All I'm saying, Gil, is that it's one avenue to pursue. Right now, it's the only one to pursue."

"Tony's serious, Whit. He doesn't want you involved, not directly anyway. We talked after you left. He wants you to reconsider. Actually, he wants you to come in to the office this morning. He's going to pull most of the old files—go through them looking for a suspect. I tried to get him to let my department take charge of the investigation, but he nixed that. He's already talked to Monty Vickers. He's going to take it."

Whit shook his head. "Monty's a good state trooper. I'm a better investigator."

"That's what I told Tony, but he says he's got to go by the book."

Whit swallowed a sip of the coffee. "Fine, Gil. Let him. I'll do what I have to do."

"Which is, Whit?"

The former investigator leaned forward. "I'd like to talk to Kathy this morning, Gil. I'd like to know about the phone call that lured them up on the mountain. Maybe it'll help."

"I doubt that she'll be able to talk."

"Fine, then maybe we can ask her questions and let her respond however she can. I need to talk to her."

"Jesus, Whit. Tony isn't going to let you—"

"He can't stop me," Whit said, without even letting Gil finish.

"He can arrest you."

"For what?" Whit countered. "I sure as hell never could stop Anna from prying into our investigations. That's all I'm going to do now. I'm going to become a reporter of sorts."

"Working for who?"

"Free lance," Whit said. "A free-lance writer looking to uncover a story."

Gil had to smile. "You've got one set of balls."

"I've got to find Anna. What about it, Gil? Will you get me in to talk to Kathy?"

Gil nodded. "So long as she is medically up to it."

"I understand," Whit said.

But the sheriff had something else he wanted to say. "There's a good chance Anna isn't alive. You know that, don't you? Whoever this killer is, we do know he's bloody ruthless. He's killed twice already, both times with no compunctions whatsoever."

Whit's eyes turned misty. "I've got to find her, Gil. Dead or alive."

"What about the arrangements for Julia?"

"I called her sister. She lives in Parkersburg. I told her that I thought it would be more appropriate for her to handle things. She never has liked me, so she was very quick to agree. She's also agreed to take Tressa back with her after—well, following the services.''

"What about until then? I'm more than willing to assign some of my people to guard her.''

The moistness in Whit's eyes increased. "I was hoping you'd make that offer, Gil.''

Marsha Via was sleeping soundly when the phone rang. She cursed as she reached for it. "Yeah,'' she said.

"I tried to call you last night. You weren't home.''

It was Jake Brimm. "I worked second shift last night. In fact, I worked until three A.M.''

"What about the kid?''

"She spent the night with my sister and her husband. They got her off to school.''

Marsha remained flat on her back in the bed. Once the call was over, she just wanted to roll over and go back to dreamland. She wasn't used to working eighteen-hour shifts.

"Good. I'll come over.''

When Brimm said that, though, she rose up in the bed. "Not this morning, Jake. I'm exhausted.''

"You can sleep all day.''

"I gotta go in at noon today.''

"What gives?'' Jake asked. "I thought this was your day off.''

"Whit Pynchon's former wife was murdered last night. Anna Tyree is still missing. I guess somebody has it in for him. Anyway the entire department is working long hours.''

"Too bad it wasn't Pynchon,'' Brimm said. "I guess you will get comp time for all this work.''

"I don't mind.''

Brimm laughed. "Yeah, well, you're probably one of the few who don't. I'll be out in a few minutes.''

Her hands squeezed tight on the handset. "Dammit, Jake, I said not this morning.''

"You're gettin' kinda uppity, ain't ya?"

"I'm just tired. I need some sleep."

"I need somethin', too."

"So jack off or something." She hung up.

Jesus, she was really getting fed up with him. What worried her was the all too obvious probability that he would be her boss come January 1 of next year. What then? Would she be giving him blow jobs under his desk? She wasn't sleepy any longer, dammit! She threw back the covers and was just starting to pull herself out of bed when the phone rang again.

"Dammit to hell." She snatched it up. "I told you no. Not today."

"Marsha?"

*Dear God, it's not Jake.* Her mind raced. Had she said "Jake?" Used his name? She couldn't remember. She didn't think she had.

"I'm sorry, Sheriff. I thought it was one of those photography places. They've called twice this morning already." It sounded like a good lie.

The sheriff seemed to accept it. "They can be a pain. Listen, Marsha, I know how late you worked last night, and I know you're due back early this afternoon. I'm sorry to be bothering you."

"No bother," she said. "Any break yet?"

"None, I'm afraid. I have a kind of special assignment if you're interested."

"What is it?"

"Well, it's a rather out-of-the-ordinary request."

His tone baffled her. "Whatever is it?"

"Well, apparently someone's decided to conduct some type of personal campaign of revenge against Whit Pynchon. That appears to be the motive behind the death of Julia Pynchon, Anna Tyree's kidnapping, and even the death of the librarian this past Sunday."

"I heard the guys talking about it early this morning."

"I need someone to stay with Whit's daughter. She's almost eighteen, and she's a good kid. I know you have a daughter, so if you can't—"

But she wanted to. She wanted to do something to help. "My sister can take care of my daughter. Do you want me to stay with her at her place?"

"No . . . no. The services for her mother are scheduled for Friday, and she's going to stay in the area until then. Whit and I have talked, and we think it best to put her up in a motel. Only a handful of people will know."

"I'll do it," Marsha said.

"You'll get some relief help. By Whit when he can. By some other officers if need be. We just think it would be better if a female actually stayed with her as much as possible. She's pretty torn up."

"I'm sure she is," she said. "I'll take care of her."

"We want to keep this as quiet as possible, though. Don't tell anyone."

"I understand. When do I start?"

"Come in to the department a little before noon. We'll have the details worked out by then."

Gil had remained at Whit's. He was sleepy and exhausted, but his leg was feeling better. He hung up the phone and pulled himself to his feet. Whit was in the kitchen with Tressa. He joined them.

"She'll do it," he said.

Tressa, her face haggard and her eyes ragged from all the tears, was sitting at the table. "I don't want to stay in a motel, Daddy."

Whit was also seated at the table. He reached across and took her hand. "If I was following my gut instincts, I'd get you out of town now. Because of your mother, I know you want to stay, but you've got to be guarded."

"You can do it," she said.

"I've still got to try to find Anna."

Tressa fought back more tears. "We don't have many people left to turn to, do we, Daddy?"

He shook his head. "Not too many."

"It's like some crazy dream," she said. "It's so unreal."

"I want you to get dressed," Whit said. "Gil and I are going to see Kathy at ten-thirty. You can go with us if you want."

"When's Aunt Miriam due?"

"She said she'd be here around noon. She knows to contact the sheriff's department. She understands the precautions."

"I want to go with her to make the arrangements. I think you should go, too."

Whit and Gil traded expressions. "It should be up to you and Julia's family," Whit said.

"But you were family, too."

"Please, Tressa. Please understand."

She squeezed his hand. "I do. I want you to find Anna. I don't want anything to have happened to her."

Gil saw Whit's face and knew the tremendous effort he was exerting to control his emotions. In a lot of ways, it was almost as painful for Gil. Almost a year ago he had gone through the same kind of surreal experience following the murder of his wife. He knew the aching sense of loneliness that both Tressa and Whit were feeling, Tressa for her mother—Whit for Anna . . . for Julia, too, of course, but in a somewhat different fashion.

A sharp pain in Gil's knee reminded him that he didn't need to be standing. He took a seat beside Tressa. "I just talked to the department's female deputy. She'll stay with you at the motel. She's a fine young woman. You'll like her."

Tressa was nodding. "Just so long as I can go with Aunt Miriam to—"

"We'll work it out," Gil said. "You may have to go in a

police cruiser, but we'll see that you go. I don't want you to be frightened."

Her eyes snapped to him. "I'm not frightened, Gil. I'm mad . . . mad as hell."

Whit, who had used the brief interlude between his daughter and his friend to regain his own composure, responded with equal force. "Dammit, Tressa. You need to be frightened. I know Gil will take care of you if you'll let him. I also know that you're not above doing something rash. It's happened before."

"Can I call Rob?" she asked.

Whit sighed. "Do you have to?"

"He needs to know what happened . . . where he can find me."

"I don't want him finding you," Whit said.

"Daddy, don't do this to me. I need to see Rob."

"Who's Rob?" Gil asked.

"Rob Fernandez," Tressa said. "He came with me to the hospital. He's—"

Gil remembered. "Your boyfriend."

She blushed a little when she said, "Yes."

Gil looked to Whit, who shrugged and said, "I know my daughter. She'll contact him whether we want her to or not."

The sheriff threw up his hands. "A chip off the old block, huh?"

The knife wound wasn't deep. It wasn't even painful. It just itched, and Anna couldn't really scratch it, not without causing the cuffs to close up more tightly on her wrists. She had thought for certain that he was going to kill her. In that momentary explosion of anger, he had certainly intended to kill her. She, of course, had asked for it by goading him—calling him names, but it had been a spontaneous reaction on her part, just as his violent response had been.

The superficial cut extended from her throat to the crevice

between her breasts. He had inflicted it as punishment for her "attitude." That was the word he had used.

Then he had left her in the cloying darkness. She had been sitting in the chair when he left. The blood from the wound had gathered in the lower portion of her bra and had then started to trickle down her stomach. For a while it seemed as if it would never stop bleeding. She tried to wipe at it, but in the darkness she couldn't tell if it had done any good. Any serious use of her hands had tightened the grip of the cuffs.

She remembered she had become dizzy, probably not so much from loss of blood as from fear. Whatever the reason she had cautiously worked herself to the floor where she had wrapped herself in the quilt. At some point she had fallen asleep.

When she awoke, it was daylight . . . sort of. Through the closed window she saw the trees, but the green leaves were muted. It was cloudy . . . a dismal day. But what day? Anna tried to think. How many days had she been like this?

The attack had taken place when? Sunday night? No, she had been working so it had to be Monday night. The first night she had spent bound to the chair, unable to do anything . . . unable to even go to the bathroom. That had been Monday night. Yesterday he had given her some freedom. So that had been Tuesday, which made today Wednesday, of course. But had she missed a night somehow? Had she maybe slept through a whole day?

She remembered the blood on his leather uniform. After he had cut her, there had also been blood on the silver mask that concealed his face. He had wiped at it and only made the smear worse. That blood had been hers, not Julia Pynchon's.

Tressa was next. He had told her so. Damn him, she thought. She had to find some way to escape. She pushed herself up and onto her knees and crawled across the floor to the gigantic metal eyebolt that he had placed in the middle of the bedroom floor. With both hands kept very close together, she wrapped her fingers around it and pulled. It didn't budge. She started trying to turn it. No give that way either.

Strange that she didn't have to go to the bathroom. First thing every morning almost everyone had to go to the bathroom. But then she hadn't had anything but the small hamburger and half of a small soft drink the day before. Her body had used all of that nourishment. She eased back from the chunk of metal that protruded from the floor, far enough so that she could put the bare heel of her foot against it. She pushed until the pain stopped her.

She scanned the small bedroom, searching for something—anything—that might help her to escape.

# SEVENTEEN

MARSHA VIA WAS unlocking the door to her aging midsized Dodge when the white caddy wheeled into the driveway.

"Shit . . . shit . . . shit." She folded her arms and leaned back against the Dodge.

The caddy belonged to Jake Brimm, but he wasn't driving. His stepson, Jamey Christian, was behind the wheel. Brimm, the former sheriff, sat on the passenger side. They both exited the luxury vehicle.

"Glad I caught you," Brimm said.

Marsha was somewhat surprised to see the young boy. She didn't think the kid knew about her relationship with his father. If that was the case, at least Brimm wasn't likely to pull anything with the kid present.

"You know my son?"

She pretended she didn't. In fact, she hadn't actually met the boy. Brimm had shown her photos, though. She nodded to the short, somewhat chunky teenager.

"I told the kid here that you've been helping me."

"You're gonna get me in trouble, Jake. I wish you would keep some things to yourself." She meant it. If Dickerson found out that she was involved in the campaign, it meant her job. Besides, she had just about decided to switch camps.

"I keep a lotta things to myself," Brimm said, winking at Marsha with the eye that was out of his stepson's field of vision.

"I gotta get to work, Jake."

"I've been hearing things, Marsha . . . like maybe Whit Pynchon is history."

That she hadn't heard. It got her attention. "What do you mean?"

"I hear he told Danton where he could put his job."

"News to me," she said.

"That's the talk on the grapevine."

It almost slipped out—that she was going to be guarding Tressa Pynchon. She gave it a second thought and decided to keep it to herself. Last night, when the description had come in about the motorcyclist, she hadn't been able to remember where she had heard it before. On the other hand, she did know that Brimm's kid had a cycle.

The boy stood a few steps behind his father. He wore faded but expensive jeans, sliced at both knees. It was a current fad among the kids. He had a T-shirt with bold black letters reading "Shit Happens," and a solid green army jacket on top of it that did nothing to conceal the offensive slogan. His pudgy hands were dark with grease and dirt, and his round face had fallen victim to a bad case of acne, probably aggravated by his obvious lack of attention to personal hygiene. His eyes were small, set close together on either side of a rather fat but flat nose. He looked piggish.

"I don't really believe it," she said.

"See what you can find out. It's always nice to know about problems on the other side, especially when it involves that asshole Pynchon."

"I'll see what I can find out." She turned toward her car. "Now I gotta go."

A heavy hand on her shoulder wheeled her back around. "And I want those time sheets tonight." The smug smile had vanished from Brimm's face, replaced by a look of menace.

"I can't, Jake."

He slapped her. The blow hurt, but it also infuriated her. She flipped open the purse, and her hand dug for the small .32 she carried.

"Look out, Paw." Brimm was bringing back his hand to smack her again. He hadn't seen her move toward her gun, probably hadn't even expected it. When he heard his stepson's warning, he brought his knee up, knocking the purse from her hand.

"You bitch!"

"I'll have you arrested, Jake!"

He swung again, not so hard this time. She managed to fling her head back. His fingernails raked her cheek, but she avoided the impact.

"So help me God, Jake, I'll swear out warrants. I'll tell it all."

He backpedaled. "You do, woman, and you're dead."

The kid had started toward her, too, but he stopped as his stepfather held up a hand.

"Damn you," she shrieked, reaching down for her purse.

His own gun came from his hip pocket, a small .380mm in a holster especially designed to be carried in a pocket. It allowed him to fire the gun without extracting it from its leather case.

"Just don't do nothing silly," he said. "I'm sorry I lost my head."

She snapped the purse shut. "Just get the hell outta here, Jake."

"I said I was sorry."

He actually looked sorry. It shocked Marsha. "Jesus, Jake, you're not sheriff yet, and I am a goddamned deputy. You're crazy."

"I need those time sheets, woman. It's no big fuckin' deal. It ain't like I'm gonna blackmail Dickerson. If you wanna keep your job after I get elected, you best do what I say."

"Fuck you!" she screamed. "Fuck the job."

Brimm eased the gun back into his hip pocket. "You get them, woman. You do what I say or else."

She shook her head in disbelief. "You really are crazy."

The kid was leering at her as he and his father eased back toward the car.

"Gawdamn it!" he cried. "You best do it!"

The man was scaring the bejesus out of her. Maybe it was his eyes—the absolutely maniacal fury in them. He was like some unstable child being told by his mother that she wasn't going to buy him a toy. Well, almost like that, at least in his assumption that what he wanted was just something she absolutely had to do—like she had no choice in the matter whatsoever. Unlike the angry child, Jake Brimm, at that moment, appeared to be capable of almost any sort of coercion to get what he wanted.

"You're going crazy over nothing, Jake. It's bullshit. Those time sheets are bullshit. They're just chickenshit. The guys have got no bitch. Dickerson's doing it right." All the while that she was trying to talk sense to him, she was easing toward him. Marsha wanted to be rid of the man forever, but she didn't want him going away that crazy mad.

"That's not the fuckin' point, woman. I told you to do somethin' for me. I fuckin' expect you to do it."

The kid had opened the car door and was standing behind it, still leering at her.

"I'm not your slave," she shouted back, her own anger rising again.

"Like hell you're not." He lowered himself into the car.

"Jake!"

The door slammed, and the engine fired up. He slammed the caddy in reverse and threw dirt and gravel as he roared backward out of her drive.

"Jesus," she mumbled, her knees still trembling.

She hurried back into the house to straighten herself up.

* * *

Kathy's doctor hadn't objected at all to Whit visiting her in Gil's company. He had simply asked that no more than two people be in the small cubicle at any one time. That was the intensive care unit's policy in any event, so Whit had waited outside while Tressa and Gil went in first. Early that morning the tubes had been removed, and she was able to speak. The doctor, though, had cautioned them about tiring her.

As he sat on the couch just outside the unit, Whit found himself nodding off. The two nights without sleep were taking their toll. At some point he was going to have to try to grab a few hours. Otherwise, his mind was going to cease to function, at least in any productive sort of fashion.

Even Kathy's doctor had noticed it. Not just Whit's haggard appearance alone. The doctor had commented on the condition of all three. "You people need some rest. I'll prescribe something if you like. I know you're under a great deal of strain."

All three had declined. Whit feared that if he did slip into a deep drug-induced sleep, it would be hours—maybe even a full day—before he would be clearheaded enough to continue his search for Anna. The longer he waited, the heavier his eyelids became. He fought to stay awake as a bulky supply cart rolled by him.

Tressa must have exited the unit as the cart entered because she was suddenly standing in front of Whit. "You're falling asleep," she said.

He almost jumped to his feet. "No, I'm fine. How is she?"

"She's still pretty confused. The nurse said they were giving her something for the pain."

"Can she talk?"

Tressa nodded. "She just doesn't make much sense. They said for you to go on in."

Whit started for the double doors, but he stopped and turned. "You come, too."

"I can't, Daddy. Two people, that's all they will allow."

He was nodding. "I know. You can stay at the nurse's station. I don't want to leave you out here by yourself."

"I'll be fine," she said.

"No way. Come on."

"Oh, Daddy." She followed him inside. A nurse at the station started to rise in protest until Whit headed for her instead of Kathy's cubicle. He quickly explained, and she offered Tressa an unused chair.

Whit headed over to the cubicle.

Gil stood by the bed, holding the newspaper publisher's hand. To Whit, it appeared that she was asleep. "Has she told you anything?"

The sheriff shrugged. "She keeps nodding off."

"I know the feeling."

"She said something about the call—said a man wanted to tell her something about me."

Whit's body tensed. "About you?"

"That's what she said."

Whit leaned over her bed. "Kathy?"

Her eyes shot open. The pupils were large, almost unseeing. It startled Whit.

"That's how she is," Gil said. "The nurse said it was the medication."

"Can you hear me?" Whit asked, his mouth close to her ear.

"Yesh . . . I can hear you. Whit? Is that you?"

"Yes, Kathy. It's me."

"Anna? Ish she here, too?"

Whit glanced at Gil, who nodded.

"Yes, Kathy, she's outside. Can you tell me about the phone call you received?"

"Phone?" Her eyes rolled as she tried to focus on Whit. "Ish there a phone in here?"

"No, Kathy. I mean the phone call you got that prompted you to go to the mountain."

"Ohhh . . . that . . . that call."

Whit waited. She didn't say anything else.

"Can you tell me about it?"

She blinked. "Whatcha wanna know?"

"What did the caller say?"

"The caller?"

Whit looked again at Gil, who was shaking his head. "She's just too heavily medicated, Whit."

"I know what hesh asking," she said. "I know. I do know."

Whit leaned closer to her ear. "What did he say?"

"He said . . . he shaid . . . if I want Gil elected—" Her voice faltered. She closed her eyes and licked her lips. "Water? Can I have water?"

There was a pitcher on a table by the bed. Whit started to reach for it, but Gil said, "Let me check with the nurse."

He did, and she came to give Kathy water.

"Are you tiring her?" she asked, her voice laden with accusation.

"We're trying not to," Gil said, "but we need some information. It might save some lives."

The nurse placed an adjustable straw in a cup and poured only a small amount of water into it. She held it to Kathy's lips and allowed her a short sip.

"Ish that all?" Kathy asked when the nurse pulled the cup away.

"For now." She turned to Gil. "Five more minutes, then you must leave."

Gil nodded. He resumed the questioning. "What were you about to say, Kathy?"

She frowned.

"You said that the caller said that if you wanted me elected—"

"Ohhh. Yesh, if you wanted elected . . . if you wanted elected . . . I had to come to the mountain."

"You?" Whit asked.

She nodded. "Me."

"What about Anna?" Again, it was Whit.

"You said shesh outside."

Whit smiled. "She is. I mean, did the caller want Anna to come too?"

"He didn't menshion Anna."

The gentle smile on Whit's face turned to a frown. "But Anna wanted to go along?"

"Yesh, she wanted to go. I'm so shleepy . . . so shleepy . . . can I go to shleep?"

Whit eased away from the bed. Gil took her hand. When he saw that, Whit stepped from the cubicle. He motioned for Tressa, and together they exited the unit. Gil came out behind them.

"She dozed off," Gil said. "Damn, they must really have her dosed with something."

"This case has got something to do with this damned election," Whit said, his eyes heavy on Gil.

"I guess," the sheriff said, still perplexed.

"I'm gonna talk to Jake Brimm."

"Tony won't like that, Whit."

"I don't work for Tony. Remember?"

Gil was pacing the hallway. "Jesus, Whit, let's go see Tony. We can work this thing out. You can't go chasing around half-cocked—"

Whit put out a hand and halted his friend's nervous motion. "Just take Tressa to the motel. I'm trusting you to see that she isn't left alone."

It was Tressa's turn to protest. "I don't wanna go to a motel. Why can't someone guard me at your house?"

"Because I don't want the killer to know where you're at," Whit said.

"Rob wanted to see me this afternoon."

"Can't you just talk to him on the phone?"

Her face reddened. "Daddy! You promised! You said if I didn't try to pull anything I could—"

"Whoa! I know. That's what I said. Call him from the motel. You can tell him where you are, but warn him to be certain he isn't being followed if he does come to see you. Tell him that if he has any doubts at all, not to come. We're not playing games here."

"I know that, Daddy. I found Mother. Remember?"

"And tell Rob—"

Gil interrupted. "I'll talk to him after Tressa."

"Thanks," Whit said.

They started toward the elevator. Gil walked with Whit, Tressa a few steps ahead of them. "In this small of a town, there's no way to keep her location secret for more than a few hours."

"I know that," Whit said. "I just think it'll be easier to guard her at the motel. With all the coming and going, Julia's services and all, it just seems more practical."

Tressa was looking back at them. "To you maybe, but what about my clothes? What about Aunt Miriam?"

"We'll handle it," Whit said.

They stepped into the elevator. Whit was pleased to see that they had it all to themselves.

"Where can I find Brimm?" Whit asked.

"From what I hear, he spends most of his day out campaigning. You'd think I was hard to beat or something."

"If Brimm's involved in this, and I think the son of a bitch is, then you'll have no trouble whipping his no-good ass."

"It doesn't make sense, Whit."

The elevator stopped. Whit made Tressa stay inside until he and Gil checked out the lobby. Once they were outside and close to Gil's cruiser, Whit asked the sheriff, "What did you mean when you said it didn't make sense?"

A heavy breeze had started to blow. Thunder grumbled. Gil opened the back door for Tressa and closed it once she was inside. He ignored the wind as he looked across the roof of the car at his friend. "C'mon, Whit. You and I both know that I'm gonna get my ass creamed in this election. Especially now. Hell, until we get this thing worked out, I can't get out there and do any campaigning. The paper endorsement probably won't make it now. Why the hell would Brimm go to all this trouble? Like I said in there, I'm not that tough an opponent."

"I don't know shit about politics, Gil, but you just gave several good reasons why Brimm would do something like this—to distract you . . . to get the newspaper out of the race."

"Pretty silly reasons to commit murder, don't you think?"

"Brimm doesn't need a good reason."

"You say. Just you say. You didn't have a case against him."

"Let's get in the damned car."

"No, hold it a second! I'm serious. If this friggin' election is behind this, I'll bow the hell out now. I really don't give a damn about it anyway."

"It's more than the election," Whit said, opening the passenger door. He sat down in the car and closed the door.

Gil had no choice but to get inside, too. "What is it then?"

"I think Brimm also saw a way to get back at me."

"What happened was years ago, Whit."

"Brimm's the type that doesn't forget."


State Trooper Monty Vickers sat on one side of Tony's desk. Tony sat on the other. The desk itself was cluttered with stacks of files.

"Damn, these things are dusty, Mr. Danton."

Tony pulled his attention away from a thick file on a five-year-old homicide. "They go back more than ten years."

"Is that how long Whit's been with you?"

"No, he's been here fifteen or sixteen, but the older files are in storage."

"Think he'll come back, sir?"

Tony shrugged. "Who the hell knows?"

"You think he's gonna continue to muck around in the case?"

"Just as sure as the damned sun is gonna come up tomorrow," the prosecutor said.

"Do we try to stop him?"

Tony checked another file, then tossed that old homicide into the pile of impossibles. "That bastard died of cancer in prison. Scratch him. What did you just ask?"

"Do we try to stop him? Pynchon, I mean."

Tony stared out the window at the murky day. "We'll just play it by ear. If he starts messing things up, then we'll do what we have to do."

"What makes you so sure that it's an old case of Whit's? I mean, why do you think it's that sort of revenge?"

"Because, Vickers, it takes one sick son of a bitch to do what this guy is doing. He's committing assault . . . hell, murder . . . with the deadliest weapon of all . . . revenge. It's gotta be a consequence of some former case we've prosecuted here."

"So you might be a target, too," the trooper said.

Tony pulled his eyes away from the window and looked at the state cop. "The thought's crossed my mind."

The phone rang. Tony picked it up. "Danton here."

His swarthy olive-colored face brightened. "Great! Have you got a match?"

The pleased expression faded. "How damned long will that take?"

Vickers wished he could hear the other side of the conversation.

"That's a good idea," Tony was saying. "If there's anything this office can do, let me know."

"A break?" Vickers asked as Tony hung up.

"Damn right. Finally. Your lab people found a print on that note."

"Kinda hard to bring them up off paper, sir."

"They managed." Tony stood and went to the window. "Christ, I wish it would go ahead and rain."

The wind had started to blow, but the clouds remained stingy with the water they held. Little more than a fine mist dampened the panes.

"Can they put a name on it?"

Tony shook his head. "They're sending it to the FBI."

"Christ, that'll take forever."

"According to the lab guy, he's made contact with the FBI. He explained the situation, and they promised top priority."

Vickers chuckled. "Which doesn't mean shit."

"It must in this case. They wanted an image faxed to them. Apparently that will help narrow the field. In the meantime, your boss—the superintendent—has ordered a helicopter to fly the print to Washington."

"Jesus, somebody must know somebody."

Tony wasn't listening.

"Mr. Danton?"

"I'd sure as hell like to let Whit know the good news."

The muted sound of distant thunder only made Anna's thirst even more unbearable. She imagined standing in a torrent of rain, her mouth open to collect the cool drops. Her weary mind, drifting somewhere between coherency and dreamland, milked the image. She sighed, almost sexually, as she conjured the downpour, feeling it cascade over her body, washing away the dirt and sweat and other things that made her feel so corrupt. Her thirst had become the most recent discomfort in the series of adversities that began with the horrifying ride down Tabernacle Mountain. On top of that, her stomach had been growling all morning. She was hungry, too.

She no longer fantasized about escape. That's all it was, she had decided. Just a fantasy, a hope without potential. The bastard had her. She hadn't been able to even turn the huge bolt that held her prisoner in the center of the room. Nor was there anything in the room to help her.

She lay on the floor, curled into a fetal position. Her mouth made saliva in an instinctive effort to quench her thirst. It only made things worse, speeding along her dehydration.

The thunder lessened as it moved away from Raven County. It had been nothing more than a tease, a promise broken. Anna's mind receded, pulling into itself, trying to escape the circumstances of the body in which it was held captive.

# EIGHTEEN

THE MILBROOK MOTEL had been operating on the western side of town for about as long as anyone could remember. It looked about as old as it was. Its rooms were clean and spacious, like old motel rooms used to be, but the exterior needed a paint job. The owner, though, didn't do enough business to make a face-lift feasible. The room numbers themselves had been painted on each door, and they were as faded as the rest of the paint. Marsha squinted at them as she guided her car through the narrow parking area. She had brought her personal car to the motel rather than a cruiser. That had been the instructions left with the dispatcher by the sheriff. It hadn't even rained enough to get her windshield good and wet. The pump on her windshield washer had burned out a few months ago. She hadn't found the extra money to get it fixed. So when she turned on the wipers, the dampness smeared across the glass.

"Damn," she muttered, about to turn around and find the main office when one of the doors opened. She saw Gil Dickerson step out and wave at her. By that time a little beyond the room, she braked and eased the car backward so that she could pull into a space close to the door.

Before exiting the car, she took a quick look in the rearview mirror and grimaced. How was she going to explain the bruise and scratches on her face to the sheriff? The guys back at the station had really given her a hard time when she had blamed it on a closet door.

As she exited the vehicle, she kept the battered side of her face away from the sheriff and hurried into the room. Had she been paying attention, she would have noticed the long white Cadillac pulling into the entrance to the motel lot.

The sheriff wasn't an especially happy man when she entered Room 103 at the Milbrook Motel.

"Christ, Marsha, I thought you were going to be here a little after noon."

She was turned away from him, taking off the raincoat she had put on at the jail just in case. "Sorry, Sheriff, I was detained."

Tressa was in Room 102, an adjoining room. That had been Gil's idea, and the owner of the motel, not at all averse to currying favor with the county sheriff, had been more than happy to cooperate. At least it would give Tressa, as well as those who might be guarding her, some degree of privacy. The door between the two rooms was slightly ajar.

"I want to get to the hospital. Visiting hours at ICU are restricted, and—"

As Marsha turned, Gil saw her face. "Christ Almighty, what happened to you?"

"It's nothing," she said, brushing by him to go back to the lavatory at the rear of the room.

"Nothing! You've got a bruise the size of a baseball, not to mention the scratches."

"I walked into my closet door."

Gil was following her. He caught her and turned her around so he could examine the injuries more closely. "Closet door, my ass, Marsha. Somebody did that to you. Those scratches—"

"Please, Sheriff, let it go."

Gil was shaking his head. "I can't do that, Marsha. If

you've got some sort of problem, especially of that nature, I need to know about it. I can't risk Tressa's safety—''

"It's over," she said. "I swear it."

"Are you going to press charges?"

She tried to smile. "Against a door?"

Gil blinked. "C'mon, Marsha, don't play games."

"It's personal, Sheriff."

"A boyfriend?" he asked.

"Just a door . . . like I said before."

Tressa eased into the room. She didn't know Marsha Via, but even she reacted to the dark, ugly swelling on the woman's face.

Gil motioned for her to come into the room. "Marsha, this is Tressa Pynchon. Tressa, Deputy Marsha Via."

Tressa gawked at the bruise. "What happened?"

"A door," Marsha said.

Tressa looked at Gil, who shrugged. "I don't believe it either."

Marsha went to a chair and settled down in it. "I see you managed to get two rooms." She was pulling a comb from her purse, and both Gil and Tressa noticed her hand shaking.

Gil turned to the daughter of his friend. "How about going in the other room a minute?"

She nodded that she understood and quickly hurried from the room. Gil heard her turn the television on. He sat down on the bed across from Marsha. "I just can't let this drop, Marsha. I need to know what happened."

The deputy, her eyes starting to fill, looked up at him. "Please, sir, don't make me tell you."

"It can't be that bad."

She started to bawl.

"Christ, what is it?"

She tried to stop the tears, but she couldn't. Gil stood and went to her, kneeling in front of her. "Get a grip on yourself, Marsha."

She had her face buried in her hands. Gil put a gentle hand under her forehead and lifted. She didn't resist.

"I'm no monster," he said. "I've had a few troubles in my life, too."

She sobbed a few more times and then began searching in her purse. Gil pulled a handkerchief from his hip pocket. "Use this. It's clean."

She wiped away the tears and took a deep breath. "I think I should resign, sir."

"Resign? Marsha, for God's sakes what's going on?"

"I've been involved in Jake Brimm's campaign. I've been feeding him information—or at least he's been wanting me to. I really haven't given him anything."

A sudden, icy realization formed in Gil's stomach. "Brimm! He did this to you?"

She nodded.

"That son of a bitch!"

"I got involved with him before you even became sheriff. After that, after I got to know you, I decided I just couldn't help him any longer. He came to my house today, just as I was leaving to come here."

Gil rose to his feet and started to pace the room. "What was he wanting from you?"

"Time sheets," she said, starting to sob again.

Gil stopped pacing. "Time sheets?"

"Yes, sir."

"Why?"

She blew her nose into his handkerchief. "He says you're abusing the overtime law. I told him that you weren't. Sheriff Early had been, but you weren't. I told him that, and I tried to stall him. He went crazy, Sheriff. He scared me."

"Christ, Marsha, those time sheets are public records. Hell, all he had to do was ask me for them."

His answer seemed to stun her. "Public records? Our time sheets?"

"Hell, yes. That's no big deal. I can't see him making such a big to-do about that."

She shook her head. "It wasn't that so much. At least I don't think so. I told him no, and that's why he flew mad. Just because I wouldn't do what he wanted."

"Have you been romantically involved with him?"

The question made her laugh. "I've been having an affair with him. There hasn't been a damned thing romantic about it, not for a long time. He promised me a better job, Sheriff . . . more money. I'm so ashamed."

Gil went to the bed and sat down. "Now, Marsha, I have a serious question to ask. Be honest with me. It's crucial."

"I have been honest with you, sir."

"This goes beyond the election. Do you think Brimm might be implicated in these murders—in the kidnapping of Anna Tyree?"

Her eyes widened. "Jesus, Sheriff, I don't think so. I mean he never said anything to me that might—" She stopped to think.

"From what you said, he sounds like a pretty violent man."

"I think he's capable of it," she said.

Brimm had backed the Cadillac into a parking space on the other side of the motel's lot. He was a good hundred feet down from the room into which Marsha had vanished. He was alone in the vehicle. If only he had been alone when he had gone to Marsha's—

The kid, though, had been with him. That had been a mistake. Not that Jamey had been frightened by his father's display of anger. He'd seen the temper all too often. In a way the boy had enjoyed it, seeing the fury directed at someone other than him.

"You shoulda taken that gun away from her, Paw."

Brimm had kept silent, though, still seething at the woman.

Didn't she understand? He could do so gawdamn much for her.

"You shoulda kept the gun," the boy repeated.

"Shaddup!"

The boy had. Brimm had dropped him off at their house and had then driven to the courthouse just to see if Marsha's car was there. It had been, and she had been getting into it. That's when Brimm had decided to follow her.

And where did she fuckin' go? To a gawdamn motel room! There was a nigger in the woodpile. That's what his own father had always said when things didn't look so good.

He reached into the ashtray and withdrew a half smoked cigar. Lighting it, he settled back to wait. Something was going on in that room. He didn't know what, but he wasn't leaving until he goddamn well found out.

Tressa remained in her room watching an afternoon soap. Marsha Via sat in a chair, her eyes still red from her bout of crying. Gil held the phone. He was talking with the dispatcher at the jail.

"Have you heard from Pynchon?" he asked.

"Not a word," the dispatcher, a young male deputy, said. "He's a popular man this afternoon."

"Whadaya mean?"

"Mr. Danton called here a few minutes ago, looking for Pynchon. He also asked if you were here."

"Danton?"

"Yes, sir. Then a woman called. She said she was his ex-wife's sister. She was looking for Pynchon, too. She's at the college."

Gil, though, was debating with himself. Should he tell Danton about Brimm? No, he decided, Whit needed to know first. He owed his friend that much.

"If Pynchon contacts you," Gil said, "have him call his daughter. He'll know where to reach her."

"You want me to forward your call over to the prosecutor's office? Mr. Danton said for you to get in touch with him as soon as you could."

"I'll call him in a few minutes. I'm tied up right now."

Gil hung up. "Can you handle things here if I take off?"

Marsha looked up. "You mean you trust me to do this? After what I told you?"

"About the only harm you did was to yourself, Marsha. I'm not going to fire you. If Brimm isn't involved in this, and if he does get elected, then you and I both will be looking for jobs."

"Will there be a unit stationed outside?" she asked.

Gil frowned. "I've been thinking about that. From what you told me, I'm not sure I should trust any of the other people, not right now anyway. I don't know who's on Brimm's side and who isn't. I don't think any of them would be involved in the murder, but they might not be above letting something slip to Brimm."

"I can handle it by myself," she said, seeing the wisdom in what he said.

"You are armed?" Gil asked.

Marsha picked up her purse and withdrew the small .32 caliber automatic. "I have this."

He took it and looked at it. "Not much firepower."

"I'm pretty good with it."

Gil pulled his own weapon from its holster. It was a .357 with a three-inch barrel. He handed it to her. "Can you handle this?"

She took it. "It's kinda heavy, but sure . . . I can handle it."

"Keep it. I'll take this." He dropped the smaller automatic in his pants pocket. "Keep the door locked, and don't let anyone in but Whit or me."

She nodded that she understood. "I'm really sorry about all this, Sheriff."

"Let's just get through this, Marsha. Don't let me down."

"Never again," she said.

Gil called Tressa. She eased open the door that joined the rooms.

"I'm going to try to find Whit. Marsha's going to stay with you."

The female deputy still held the revolver in her hand. "You'll be safe with me. I promise."

Brimm was stubbing out the cigar when the door to 103 opened. Gil Dickerson stepped out of the room and headed down the sidewalk.

"Motherfuck!" Brimm said aloud. "That gawdamn, two-timing, shit-faced cunt."

It was all he could do to contain himself while the present sheriff of Raven County got into the black Oldsmobile that was parked all the way down at the end of the lot. Brimm recognized the vehicle now, but it had been parked so far away from the room that he hadn't even noticed it.

"That gawdamned bitch," he said, his temper continuing to build.

In Brimm's mind not only had she been double-crossing him in the election, she was also fucking Dickerson. Why the hell else had they met at a motel room? He reached over and opened the glove compartment, pulling the small .380mm from its shadowy recesses.

Brimm didn't even bother to duck as the dark black Olds rolled right in front of him. Dickerson never looked his way. *The crippled bastard. Looking so fuckin' satisfied with himself.* As soon as the car had pulled out onto the highway going back toward Milbrook, Brimm swung open the door of the Cadillac. Exiting the car, he pulled the gun out of the modified holster and tossed the leather aside. He headed across the parking lot, the small black gun jammed in his jacket pocket.

* * *

Jake Brimm lived in a sprawling brick rancher in Pleasant Valley, an upscale subdivision in north Milbrook. The house looked as expensive as the others that decorated the rolling hills of the subdivision, but there was no doubt that it belonged to Jake Brimm. An oversized sign was staked in the front of the house. On a white background with a red border the massive blue letters read, quite simply, "Brimm for Sheriff." The driveway was filled by a beige recreation vehicle that seemed almost as long as the house itself.

Whit pulled his vehicle to a stop at the bumper of the luxury camper. The overcast was beginning to break up. Patches of blue sky were visible to the west. The much-needed rain had never materialized. It had been that way through much of the spring. Sometimes there had even been rain, but not enough to offset the deficiency created by the dry winter.

As he climbed out of the car, he saw no sign of activity around the house, but he could hear the sound of a hammer on metal coming from the rear of the home. He moved toward the sound. It came from a garage that had been hidden from view by the bulk of the RV. At the rear of the vehicle Whit found himself staring into a single garage door that was open. Inside, the meaty figure of a young man was bent over a black motorcycle. The vision brought Whit to a dead stop.

The boy glanced up. Whit's presence startled him. "Who the shit are you?"

"That yours?" Whit asked.

"Yeah. What's it to you?"

Whit eased into the garage. The kid had stood up. He had a mallet in his hand, clutched as if he just might use it.

"Take it easy. I was looking for Jake Brimm."

"He ain't here."

"Are you his son?"

Again, the kid said, "What's it to you?"

When he had first confronted the corpulent teenager, his first reaction had been to pull out his badge case. Then he remembered. He no longer carried a badge case.

"I wanted to talk to your father about the election."

The grip on the hammer eased. "Well, mister, like I said, he ain't here right now."

Whit had moved closer to the cycle. "Nice bike. I used to ride them when I was your age. In those days, they looked a lot different." Whit was looking at the deep treads on the tires, wondering if they matched those left in Julia's yard.

"Paw bought me this 'un."

"You always bang on it with a hammer?"

The boy shrugged. "I had a little spill the other day and put a dent in the rear fender. I was just trying to work it out."

"You get hurt?" Whit asked.

"Naw . . . wasn't anything big."

"Got any idea when your dad's coming back?"

The boy shook his head. "He's out politicking. Sometimes he don't get back till after dark. Makes my old lady really mad."

"Is she here? Your mother?"

The suspicion was reborn in the boy's dark eyes. "She's gone to the grocery store. What's your name, mister?"

"I'll try to catch your dad some other time." Whit kept his eyes on the boy as he backed out of the garage.

"You some kinda cop?"

Whit shook his head. "Nope."

"Don't you want me to tell my old man you was here?"

Whit had reached the rear corner of the RV. "You can if you want. Tell him Pynchon was looking for him."

"Pyn-what?"

"Pynchon." Whit made a gesture with his fingers. "As if to pinch someone—or to put the pinch on someone."

The boy frowned. "I heard that name before."

"You're probably going to hear it again."

\* \* \*

Tony Danton made a face as the sudden sunlight spilled into his office. "So much for the damned rainstorm," he said to himself. He was continuing to search through old cases. His hands were gritty with dust and dirt. Monty Vick ers had gone to lunch, after which he was going to try to locate Whit. Tony wanted to talk to his old friend. If Whit wouldn't be too pigheaded about it, they could work something out— some way for him to remain involved in the case.

His secretary appeared in the doorway. "There are some people to see you."

He looked up, irritated by the interruption. "I told you I didn't want to be disturbed."

She closed her eyes to underscore her patience with his mood. "Yes, you did, but I thought you might want to make an exception. Willard Hardison, the president of the college, is here with Julia Pynchon's sister. She's rather angry since she can't seem to locate Whit."

Tony's expression changed. "I know how she feels. Send them back."

The woman marched into Tony's office first. Her appearance gave him a sudden attack of chill bumps. She was a little heavier than her sister, but at first glance she looked so much like Julia Pynchon that Tony thought he was seeing her reincarnation.

"I hope *you* can help me," she said, her emphasis indicating that she hadn't been pleased with the efforts of others to do so.

Tony just stared.

Willard Hardison followed her inside. "I reacted the same way," he said. "They do bear an uncanny resemblance."

"Were you twins?" Tony asked.

"Of course not," the woman said. "I'm a year younger than my sister."

The college president had used the right word. It was uncanny. Tony shook off the shock. "I'm afraid I can't help you, uh . . ." He didn't know her name.

"Woolford . . . Miriam Woolford."

"Mrs. Woolford."

"Miss Woolford. I've never married. Just why can't you help me? Mr. Pynchon indicated last night that I would be able to contact him by way of the sheriff's department."

"I'm trying to find him, too," Tony said.

"Doesn't he work here, Mr. Danton?"

"Well, he did—and, yes, I assume he still does, but he's working on the case, and—"

"What about Tressa?"

"We're looking for her, too, Miss Woolford. I gather Whit has placed her somewhere discreet . . . for her own safety."

"And he didn't tell you?" She didn't believe him.

"No, ma'am. He didn't."

Hardison seemed uncomfortable in the office. "Mr. Danton, Miss Woolford came to the college because she didn't know where else to go. She went to Mrs. Pynchon's home, but it was cordoned off."

"We haven't finished our work at the scene," Tony said.

The woman glared at Tony. "You do understand that I am here to bury my sister. It seems to me that the family of a victim is entitled to a much greater degree of sympathy and cooperation."

"You have our sympathy," Tony countered. "And you can make yourself at home here until I can locate Whit and Tressa."

She stood. "President Hardison has already offered me the hospitality of his home. You may reach me there when you find Mr. Pynchon. I always warned my sister that she would come to grief because of that man. I'm sorry to have been right."

Tony started to reply but saw no sense in it.

She was on her way out the door. Hardison remained

seated. "I need to speak with Mr. Danton," he told her. "I'll be out in a few moments."

She vanished.

Hardison shrugged. "I can understand her frustration."

"She bears a striking resemblance to her sister, both in appearance and attitude."

"Mr. Danton, Julia Pynchon was a fine person."

"I don't need any lectures from you about Julia," Tony said. "I suspect I knew her much longer than you did. About what did you want to speak to me?"

The president twisted in his chair. "Given the events that have transpired, well, I assume I want to know if I remain a suspect in the death of Eloise Weldon."

"Your lover?" Tony asked, not at all reticent about embarrassing the man.

Hardison's eyes flared. "Yes, Mr. Danton, my lover."

Tony's phone rang. "Excuse me for a moment, President Hardison," Tony said, glad to be able to leave the man hanging for a few minutes.

His secretary told him that an official from the FBI lab was on the phone for him. "Put him through," he said.

The prosecutor covered the mouthpiece. "You're no longer a suspect, Hardison. Not for murder anyway."

"What precisely does that mean?"

Tony smiled. "Nothing. It means nothing. Now, please excuse me. I have an important call."

The man blinked and pushed himself to his feet. "You can reach Miss Woolford at my house." He wheeled and fled the office.

Tony returned his attention to the phone. "Tony Danton here."

"Are you the prosecuting attorney?" a female voice asked.

"Yes, ma'am."

She identified herself as an official with the print division of the FBI laboratory. "We have a tentative match on that print we received."

"Already?" Tony asked.

"Thanks to the computers and compact discs, it doesn't take long. We have identified enough points of similarity to say, at least unofficially, that the print is that of a 26-year-old male by the name of Thomas Kirby, Jr."

"Thomas Kirby, Jr." Tony repeated the name as he wrote it down. "It means nothing to me. Do you have anything else on him?"

"Yes, sir. One of the reasons that we were able to so quickly isolate a match is that Kirby is wanted. In fact, he's pretty high on our list. He's from Washington state. Tacoma to be precise. He's wanted in connection with the double homicide of his mother and father."

"His mother and father?"

"Actually, sir, he was adopted. He has a rather extensive juvenile record in Tacoma and was a member of a violent motorcycle gang. The Tacoma Police Department is faxing his record to us."

"Do they have a photograph?"

"Yes, sir."

"I need it . . . as soon as possible."

"Will do, Mr. Danton."

"Is Kirby his real name?"

"Yes, sir. His adoptive parents' name is Cruise."

"Any other information?"

"Not yet, sir. As soon as we have it, we'll get it down to you. You do have a fax machine?"

"The local state police detachment does. Fax it there."

# NINETEEN

CONFESSION WAS INDEED good for the soul. Marsha Via could feel her guilt fading away as she sat in the worn chair. Maybe Jake Brimm would be elected sheriff, and, yes, maybe she'd even lose her job. So what? At least she didn't feel like a treasonous slut any longer.

Tressa Pynchon had returned to her adjoining room, but the sound of the television no longer seeped through the small crack in the door that connected 103 to 102. Marsha rose and eased toward the door. She inched it open. Whit Pynchon's daughter lay on the bed, her face buried in the pillow.

*Poor thing.*

Marsha remembered the death of her own mother not so many years before. That had been different, though. Her mother had suffered for a long time with cancer. Her death had been a release from the suffering. While Marsha still missed her, she found consolation in the knowledge that the incredible pain finally had ended. The deputy couldn't even imagine the horror of coming home to find your mother butchered, gutted by some unknown killer.

She stepped into Tressa's room. "Can I get you anything?"

The girl lifted her head, and Marsha saw the tears.

"No thanks. If Rob—he's a friend—"

"The sheriff told me about Rob."

"If he comes, just let me know so I can straighten myself up before he sees me."

Marsha smiled. "Sure, hon. You oughta try to get some rest now."

"Do you know Anna Tyree?"

Marsha shrugged. "I've heard of her. I think I've seen her around the courthouse."

"You know she's missing, too?"

Marsha nodded.

"If you hear anything about her, let me know?"

"I will. Why don't you try to sleep?"

"I can't," Tressa said. "Besides, my aunt's also supposed to get in touch with me. She's due in town this afternoon so we can take care of Mother's . . . well, the services."

"I know about that, too."

That's when they both heard the knocking on the door.

Tressa sat up. "I bet that's Rob. Tell him to give me a few minutes."

"I will," Marsha said. She hurried back into the other room to answer the door.

Whit found a pay phone just a couple of blocks from Brimm's residence. He phoned the sheriff's department and asked for Gil. The dispatcher told him that the sheriff was on his way to the courthouse.

"This is Pynchon. Tell him to wait on me. I'll be there in five minutes."

"Oh, Mr. Pynchon. I have a couple of messages for you. A woman by the name of Woolford has been trying to reach you."

Christ, Whit had forgotten all about Julia's sister. "Where is she now?"

The dispatcher gave him a phone number. "Where is that?" Whit asked.

"The home of the president of Milbrook College."

Just great, Whit thought. But he said, "You said there were a couple of calls. Who's the other one from?"

"Mr. Danton. He wants to talk to you, and he says it's urgent."

A message from Tony? That struck Whit as more than just odd. "Is he in his office?"

"He was when he called."

Whit checked his watch. "Call over and tell him that I'm on my way there. I'll get in touch with the lady after I get there."

The pounding became more insistent as Marsha approached the door. "I'm coming," she shouted, a little angry over the unnecessary persistence exhibited by the impatient visitor.

When she reached the door, she didn't open it. Instead, she peered through the small security hole that was located at eye level.

The person on the other side of the door was Jake Brimm. Her heart rate increased at the sight of him. "What do *you* want?" she shouted.

"Open the gawdamn door."

Christ, he must have followed her here. How else would he have known where to find her so quickly? If that was the case, then he had also seen the sheriff leave.

"I'm working, Jake. Please leave."

"Sure you are, you fuckin' whore!"

"Jake—"

Something exploded against the door. He had just kicked it. She stumbled back from it. "Dammit, Jake! Don't make me arrest you!"

Tressa was peeking into the room. "Who is it?"

"Trouble," Marsha said. "Go in your room and close the door. Then phone the sheriff's department."

"Is it the killer?"

"No. I mean, I don't know. Just do as I say," Marsha said. She was fumbling in her purse, trying to find the small handgun.

"Open this door!" Jake was shouting.

Marsha dumped the contents of the purse onto the bed. The gun wasn't there.

He crashed against the door a second time. He was trying to break it down. That's when Marsha remembered that Gil had taken her gun, leaving behind the larger caliber weapon that he carried.

It rested on the dresser.

"I'm warning you, Jake." She started for the gun.

The doors on each of the units of the motel had been built in a different time. In the backwoods of West Virginia, a motel owner found it hard to justify the exorbitant cost of new metal doors. In the long history of the Milbrook Motel, nothing had ever happened to make him think that he needed them.

The door itself held. It was the aging frame that finally yielded to Jake Brimm's assault. It splintered an inch above the door catch. The door flew open as Marsha's hand reached out for the gun.

"Gawdamn you!" Brimm bawled, his momentum carrying him straight toward her.

They collided just as her fingers touched the wooden pistol grips. She careened back into the room, leaving the gun twirling on the slick finish of the chest. Brimm didn't go down to the floor with her. Instead, he picked the .357 up from the tabletop.

"You two-timin' bitch."

Marsha was on the floor, crawling back from him. "It's not what you think, Jake."

"You fuckin' two-timing bitch." He started toward her, the gun held down at his side.

She backed into the bathroom area, her eyes wide open

with fear. "You best listen to me, Jake. I'm here working. You're interfering. You're obstructing an officer."

Brimm hadn't even noticed that the door to the adjoining room was slightly ajar. He moved up to a position adjacent to it, the gun still held loosely in his right hand. "I oughta kill you," he said. "I had plans for you. I was gonna make it right for you."

Marsha cursed herself as she started to cry. She was a cop, dammit! Not a sniveling helpless female. "Don't do something you can't undo. Get out of here, *now*!"

"Not yet." Rage colored his face crimson. "You know I'm gonna win this election, and you best believe—"

The door to the adjoining room rocketed open. It caught his right side. The .357 came loose and fell to the floor as Jake catapulted sideways.

Marsha made a lunge for the gun as Jake crashed into a nightstand. Tressa stood in the now open door, her face frozen by terror.

This time Marsha actually managed to get the gun in hand. Brimm, though, had recovered quickly. He was on his hands and knees, charging back toward her. Her index finger found the trigger just as he reached her. She didn't mean to squeeze, not right at that moment anyway, but his coarse hands were all over, trying to pin her to the floor.

In the closed confines of the small room, the discharge of the .357 nearly ruptured all of their eardrums. The bullet itself struck the wall and then ricocheted harmlessly into the mattress.

"Get back in your room!" Marsha shouted.

Tressa held her hands over her aching ears.

The female deputy still had the gun in hand, and Brimm continued to attempt to bring her under control.

*"Out!"* Marsha cried to Tressa.

Tressa obeyed, hurrying back again to the phone. She picked it up, trying to remember what number to dial. The door between the rooms slammed shut behind her, making such a noise that she yelped. She dialed "O" for operator.

His breath, reeking of coffee and cigar smoke, smothered her face. His weight kept her tight against the floor. She still had control of the gun, but his fingers were working on her fingers, trying to break her grip.

"Damn you," she said through clenched teeth.

"Let go of the gawdamn gun," he bellowed.

"Like hell, I will."

He pulled her hand closer so he could improve his own grip on the weapon.

Neither of them saw the figure coming in through the open front door.

"So help me," Brimm was saying, his spittle dampening Marsha's face. "You're gonna regret this. I'm—"

But his eyes went wide, then locked on her. Blood spewed from his head. It flooded out of his dark hair and dripped into her face. His fingers maintained a grip on hers, but they were no longer prying. They were squeezing . . . squeezing—

She tried to resist the pressure on her finger, but—

Tressa waited to be connected to the sheriff's department. "For god's sake, hurry," she cried.

"It's ringing," the operator said, her own voice unperturbed by the panic of the caller.

The second explosion wasn't so loud, not with the door to the adjoining room closed, but even the operator heard it. "What was that?"

"A gunshot," Tressa said.

"Raven County Sheriff's Department."

"Go ahead," the operator said.

The sheriff's department answered just as the door to room 103 opened.

* * *

Whit parked his car in the courthouse lot and was entering the garage area that led into the Raven County Jail when Gil, accompanied by another officer, rushed out. He nearly collided with Whit.

"What's happening?" Whit asked.

"Quick," Gil said. "Come with us. We've got trouble at the motel."

Whit's heart hitched. "Tressa?"

"She just called, but she didn't get to tell us anything." They were running as they talked, heading for Gil's cruiser.

"Oh sweet Jesus."

"The motel owner called, too. He says he heard gunshots. You drive." Gil tossed Whit the keys.

"I'll take my car," the other deputy said.

Whit was peeling out from the curb as Gil reached over to hit the light and sirens. A delivery truck jammed on its brakes as the sheriff's cruiser wheeled out in traffic just in front of him.

"Just watch it," Gil said.

Whit had the accelerator to the floorboard. "Oh, Christ, Gil, if anything's happened to Tressa—"

The sheriff's car, followed by the second vehicle, sped down Milbrook's main street. With the siren blasting, most of the traffic got out of their way. When a car didn't, Whit wheeled around it.

"Watch the traffic light up here," Gil cautioned.

Whit slowed just a little, just enough to be sure that he wasn't going to plow into the side of a car coming through the intersection. Luckily they had the green light.

The sheriff held on, bracing himself with his hands and his good leg.

"What did Tressa say?" Whit asked.

"She just identified herself and said they needed help. That was it. The dispatcher didn't know what she was talking about, but I was standing right there. The second call came before I could even get out of the control room.''

"Please, God," Whit said, "let her be all right.''

They reached the motel, and Whit wheeled the car into the parking lot. "Watch yourself," Gil said. "We don't know what we've got.''

But Whit wasn't listening. Brakes squealed as the cruiser screeched to a stop in front of room 103.

"Dammit, Whit." Gil reached out to stop his friend from jumping out of the car, but he wasn't fast enough. Whit had opened the door just as soon as he'd turned into the parking lot.

Gil hurried to get out of the cruiser.

By that time Whit had reached the open door. His .357 with the two-inch barrel was drawn. He stopped, bracing himself, and then stepped inside. A man was sprawled face down on the bloody carpet.

"Who is it?" The question came from Gil. He stood behind Whit.

Whit bent down, grimacing at the circle of blood that surrounded the man's head. He peered at the face. "Damn, Gil, it's Jake Brimm.''

At that instant the door that connected the two rooms swung open. Whit lifted his weapon. Behind him he heard Gil scream, "Police! Freeze!''

The young man had his hands up.

Whit was frowning. "Rob?''

"Yes, sir. Tressa's in here. She's fine.''

Whit had Tressa in his arms. He couldn't hug her tightly enough. Gil sat on the bed, examining the tire iron. "You sure put his lights out," he was saying.

Rob, still apparently shaken by it all, sat beside Gil on the bed. "I didn't know what the hell to do. I came in. I saw this guy on top of the woman. I saw the gun in both their hands, so I ran back and got the tire iron from the car. I just tried to kind of tap him.''

Gil shook his head. ''You tapped him all right.''

''Will he live?'' the kid asked.

The sheriff smiled. ''Yeah, the doc says he'll live.''

Rob shivered. ''Jesus, he was losing so much blood. I thought maybe he was bleeding to death. I was going to call an ambulance when you all arrived.''

''Head wounds can fool you,'' Whit said, still clutching his trembling daughter.

The bathroom door opened, and Marsha Via stepped out. She was toweling her hair dry. ''You can say that again.''

Gil waited for her to come fully into the room. ''How did he find you?''

She collapsed into a chair. ''He followed me from the jail, I guess. When he saw you leave, well, he just lost control then.''

Tressa looked up at her father. ''So he's not the killer?''

''I don't know,'' Whit said. ''I mean, maybe he put his son up to it. The kid's got a motorcycle. I want to match the cast we took from your mother's yard with the tires of the kid's bike.''

''His son?'' Gil said, surprised by Whit's statement.

''After what Kathy told us at the hospital, I went to Brimm's. He wasn't there, of course, but I found his kid working on a cycle in the garage—a large, black cycle.''

''That's his stepson,'' Marsha offered. ''Brimm told me the kid got a ticket a few weeks back for riding without a helmet.''

Whit eased his grip on his daughter. ''I would like to get a look at that helmet. We've got enough probable cause to get a search warrant—''

''Forget it,'' a voice said.

Whit turned just as Tony Danton entered the room through the connecting door.

"What's that mean?" Whit said, glaring at his former employer.

"It means that Jake Brimm's son isn't the prime suspect."

Whit was frowning. "C'mon, Tony, if he isn't, then who is?"

The prosecutor leaned down to Tressa. "Hiya, Sugar. You okay?"

She smiled. "Yeah, Tony. Still shaking but I'm okay."

Whit wasn't all right. "You're jackin' us around, Tony. What's going on?"

Tony ignored his old friend and former employee. He turned to face Gil and the young man seated on the bed. "I don't think we've met," he said, looking down at Rob Fernandez.

Gil made the introduction. "Rob here put out Brimm's lights with this." He was holding up the tire iron.

Tony took it and tested its weight in his hands. "So much for Brimm's political aspirations. I'd say you just cinched the election, Gil."

Whit was easing away from Tressa. "Dammit, Tony, will you talk to me?"

The prosecutor wheeled. "You? Why should I talk to you? You have no official standing. I need to talk to Gil, though."

He turned back to the sheriff. "Let's step outside."

Whit's arm shot out to latch onto Tony's shoulder. "Just a gawdamn minute."

The prosecutor was smiling. In his hand he had Whit's badge case. "Of course, if you were to take this back, then you might be privy to the information I have."

Whit's eyes narrowed. "You're full of tricks, aren't you?"

"Not tricks, Whit, but I do have some new information."

"Do I get to handle the case?" Whit asked.

The smile on the prosecutor's face faded. "As the old song goes, Whit, with a little help from your friends?"

"What do you mean?"

"I mean, are you willing to just be a part of it?"

Whit looked to Gil, who was nodding, indicating that he should answer yes.

Tressa was still beside him. "Please, Daddy, do it Tony's way?"

He reached out and snatched the badge case. "Fine, but I do wanna get a search warrant for Brimm's house and garage."

"As I said, Whit, Brimm isn't my prime suspect."

"His kid then," Whit said.

Tony was shaking his head.

"Then just who is?" Whit asked.

"Thomas Kirby, Jr."

Whit's brow knitted. "Never heard of him."

"You're about to," Tony said. "But first—"

The prosecutor turned to Tressa. "Your aunt is in town. She wants to talk to you."

Tressa was looking to her father. "I need to see her. We need to work things out about Mother."

Whit nodded. "I know. Maybe Deputy Via could go with you."

Marsha was quick to say, "I'll do anything you need me to do."

"I'll go along, too," Rob said.

Tony gave Tressa the number where her aunt could be reached, and Rob offered the use of his car. She placed the call and was told that her aunt had just left for the Milbrook Funeral Home.

"Go meet her there," Whit said. "Just be careful."

She had her arm inside Rob's. "Don't worry, Daddy. I'll be fine. I'm well protected."

"Seems like a nice kid," Tony said as soon as they were out the door.

Whit was staring out the room's window, watching Rob

Fernandez open the door for Marsha Via and his daughter. "I hope so, Tony."

"Who's this new suspect?" Gil asked.

"The lab guys managed the impossible and lifted a clear print from that stenciled note. Through the miracle of modern communications, we've already gotten a tentative match. The print belongs to a Thomas Kirby, Jr. He's wanted out in Washington state for the murders of his adopted mother and father."

"So what's he doing here?" Whit asked.

"Does the name Thomas Kirby mean anything to you?"

Whit thought about it, then shook his head. "Not a thing."

"How about Buster Kirby?"

Whit's face was blank for an instant, but then his eyebrows arched. "Buster Kirby? The one I killed?"

"Thomas Kirby, Sr.," Tony said. "The main file is somewhere in the storage room, but there was enough info in the master card index to refresh my memory."

"Somebody fill me in," Gil said.

Tony did the honors. "About fifteen years ago, not long after Whit joined my office, Buster Kirby pulled an armed robbery at a service station. The clerk didn't exactly cooperate with Kirby, so he emptied a .12 gauge load in the guy's face."

Gil grimaced.

"Believe it or not, the fella lived. Back then, our mug book wasn't nearly as thick as it is now, and Kirby had had some priors. So, as soon as the clerk was able, he picked Kirby out of a group of mug shots."

Whit jumped into the explanation at that point. "I took a couple of the state boys with me to arrest Kirby, assuming we could find him, of course. He lived in the northern part of the county in an old farmhouse. As soon as we got in view of his place, he cut down on us. It was some firefight."

"One of the state boys was pretty badly injured," Tony said, "but eventually they flushed him out of the house."

"The hell we did. He had us pinned down. We didn't even return much fire. For one thing, we didn't know if there was anyone else in the house. We just waited him out. I figured after dark he would try to make a break into the woods behind his house, so I took a couple of guys and circled around back. Sure enough, just before midnight, he slipped out. We waited for him to get well clear of the house and then ordered him to drop his weapon. He started blasting away."

"So you shot him," Gil said.

"Actually, no," Whit answered. "In the darkness he didn't know where the hell we were. He emptied his shotgun at us. As he was trying to reload, we rushed him and took him alive."

"So what happened?" the sheriff asked.

"One of the state cops searched him while I checked inside the house. I found his wife and a kid. Best I remember, the kid was around ten. We got them outside. By that time, Kirby was cuffed and in the back of one of the state police cruisers. I'm standing there talking to his wife when all of a sudden bullets start to fly again."

"An accomplice," Gil said.

But Whit was shaking his head. "They hadn't searched Kirby well enough. He must have had a small handgun stuck in his boot. To make matters worse, they had cuffed his hands in front rather than behind. He was shooting at us from inside the damned car. The first bullet he fired got his wife. Somebody pulled the kid out of the way, and I fired into the cruiser. The bullet hit him right in the nose."

"Jesus," Gil said. "So this is his kid, come back for revenge."

"Seems likely," Tony said. "I gather he was adopted not long after that by a couple who lived somewhere in southern West Virginia. They later moved to Washington state. Too bad the kid took after his old man. He became a member of some dope-head motorcycle gang. One night he roars home on his cycle and uses a motorcycle sprocket chain on his adopted father. He disembowels his mother. Then he vanishes.''

"So how do we go about finding him?" Gil asked.

Whit had been thinking about that. "He left here when he was ten. The only place he probably really remembers is that house. I say we start looking at that house. Trouble is, guys, I can't remember where the hell it was."

# TWENTY

ANNA COULDN'T GET WARM. The chills racked her body even as she buried herself more deeply in the quilt. Her tongue felt swollen and fuzzy. She tried to suck some saliva from the inside of her mouth, but she had none. Her stomach growled. The hunger was bad; the thirst was worse. In some deep corner in her mind she knew that dehydration could come on very quickly. How long had it been since she had had anything to drink? There was the small cup of soft drink the day before, most of which she had spilled.

*Twenty-four hours . . .*

*No . . . thirty-six . . . more than that . . .*

She really couldn't remember. How long had she been here? A day? Two days? It all was just a muddle now.

She started to cry, but there were no tears.

The chills struck again. She pulled the bedclothing more tightly around her.

Maybe he wasn't coming back?

*Maybe that's how he's going to kill me . . . let me die of starvation . . . no, dehydration will get me first.*

"Please," she said aloud, though even she hardly understood the word. It sounded more like "plesh," her tongue was so swollen.

She dared to peek her head out from the bedclothes. It remained daylight. Bright sunlight streamed in the closed window. The room itself was stuffy, but Anna smelled the

274

stuffiness more than she felt it. To her, the small bedroom was more like a refrigerator. Her eyes, now having some trouble focusing, settled on the white wax cup that lay overturned just beyond her reach.

*Or is it? Maybe I can stretch and get it? Maybe there's just a little left, some melted water from the ice? Anything.*

She emerged from the bedspread as if she were some pale moth sliding from its chrysalis. Her arms, trembling from the cold and still clamped together by the cuffs, reached toward the cup. Her fingers came up two inches short. If only she didn't have on the cuffs—

Suddenly she started to laugh. A vision had bounced into her mind, a vision of her hands sliding out of the metal bindings. Skeletal hands. Fingers reduced to white bone. She would escape one way or the other. He couldn't keep her like this forever. God would see to that. He would take her first.

The disoriented sense of humor abandoned her. She shook off the morbid residue and used her knees to work her body a smidgen closer to the cup. The chain around her ankle started to chafe. She reached again, oblivious to the evertightening grip of the handcuffs. Her wrists were already black-and-blue beneath the circular metal restraints. In a few places they were bloody, worn down to raw tissue.

She ignored the pain and stretched . . . streeeettched . . .

The middle finger of the left hand touched the cup bottom. It moved, its opening turning to her.

Several small drops of water rolled out onto the old hardwood floor.

"Nooo!" she shrieked, jerking against her restraints.

They punished her for even so timid a rebellion. The searing pain milked the final few drops of fluids from her tear glands.

* * *

Rob eased his car into the spacious parking area behind the Milbrook Funeral Home. Tressa stared at it, her lower lip trembling.

"I don't want to do this," she said.

Marsha, seated in the back, reached over and touched her shoulder. "No one wants to do it. You're doing it for your mother."

Rob took her hand and squeezed. "Play tough. You can do it."

She looked around at him. "Will you go in with me?"

He stiffened. "I can't, Tressa."

Her eyes widened. "You can't?"

"I mean, it's just not my place. Perhaps Deputy—" He didn't know the woman's name.

"Via," she said from the backseat, "but just call me Marsha. I should go with you, Tressa, just in case."

A woman stuck her head out the funeral home's back door. "That's my aunt," Tressa said.

Rob patted her hand. "Go on in. You'll be fine."

Tressa took a deep breath. "I don't know what to expect."

"Don't look at me," Rob said. "I've never done this before."

"There's not that much to it," Marsha said. "My mother passed away a few years ago. You'll select a casket, discuss what your mother will wear, who will handle the services, the money arrangements, that sort of thing."

A man in a black suit, evidently summoned by her aunt, who had now vanished, exited the rear of the building and came toward the car. Tressa opened the door and got out. "I'm Tressa Pynchon," she said.

The man extended a dry, very white hand. "Frank Sayles, Miss Pynchon. You have our sympathy. Your mother's sister is inside with President Hardison of the college. We've been trying to contact you. President Hardison's wife called to say that she thought you were on the way. We waited."

Marsha was pulling herself from the backseat.

"This is Marsha Via," Tressa said. "Can she come in with me?"

"A friend of the family?" the funeral director asked.

Tressa nodded. "Yes, she is."

"That's fine," Sayles said. He was glancing down into the car. "Uh, is this Mr. Pynchon?"

Tressa shook her head. "No, he's a friend, too."

"Will Mr. Pynchon be—"

Marsha was shaking her head. "He didn't think it would be appropriate."

"I see," the man said. "We'll just step inside."

Tressa glanced back at Rob. He smiled at her and gave her a thumbs-up. "I'll wait out here."

Whit and Tony brushed away dust-filled cobwebs as they made their way toward the rear of the damp storage area to which the prosecutor relegated his oldest files.

"Everything in here is over ten years old," Tony was saying as he eyed the stacks of cardboard boxes.

Whit swatted at a small black spider that dangled in front of his face. "It smells like a graveyard."

"That's mildew," Tony said.

"Mildew, my ass. It's rot, pure and simple. Are these things organized in any way?"

Tony sneezed. "Hell, I can't remember. I think we wrote dates on the boxes, but it's been so long. Most of the stuff nowadays we store on microfilm. I'm surprised you can't remember where the house is."

"It's been fifteen years."

"Christ, you killed a man there."

The truce between the two men had remained somewhat tentative. At that statement, Whit wheeled. "It's not like I had any damned choice."

"I know that," Tony said. "I'd just think you would remember."

They had reached the deepest recesses of the storage room. The only illumination came from a single 100-watt bulb that dangled from a cord behind them. As a result their own bodies cast dancing shadows on the boxes.

Whit squinted at the discolored stack of cardboard. "I remember the house. I just can't remember the damned turnoff. I wasn't even driving."

"Who was?" Tony asked. "Maybe he's still around."

Whit thought about it for a moment. "Sam Crookman, I think."

"Hell, he retired from the state police five years ago."

"Like I said, Tony, it's been a long time. I'm not even sure there will be any information in the file to help us. What's the date?"

Tony held a small slip of paper so that the light could hit it. He read the date of the offense out loud. That much information, at least, had been kept on a card in a master index file.

"Step back and let some light in here."

The handwritten dates on the end of the boxes were faded, some of them virtually obliterated by a coating of thick gray-green mildew. "This stack's only two years off," Whit said, moving down to examine another.

"Even if we find the place, it seems like a wild-goose chase," Tony said.

"I thought of that. Gil's people are making calls to all the motels in the area, just in case the bastard checked into one of them when he came to town. You got a handkerchief?"

Tony frowned. "Where's yours?"

"I don't carry one, dammit."

Tony pulled it out and gave it to Whit. He used it to wipe mildew from a box and then squinted down at the date. "Now we're in the right year," he declared as he hauled the box out of the stack.

He carried it under the light and set it down. "I hope it hasn't dry-rotted." He flipped it open. Silverfish scurried for the deeper recesses of the box.

Whit ignored them and started thumbing through the tabs on the files. "Hell, they're labeled by file numbers!"

Tony pulled up the card. "The number is—" He read off a series of numbers and letters.

Whit closed his eyes. "This could take all goddamn afternoon."

"You guys back there?" a voice called out.

"Yo!" Tony shouted.

Trooper Monty Vickers walked into the glow of the light. "Your secretary said you were over here. She also said you had a suspect."

Whit glanced up. "How long have you been stationed at this detachment, Monty?"

"Six years. Why?"

"Not long enough," Whit said, continuing to thumb through the files.

"What's going on?" the trooper asked.

Tony explained, then said, "Why don't you and I grab another box from that year and start through it?"

Vickers cast a dubious glance toward the stained stack at the rear of the room. "Kinda messy, aren't they?"

"You're dressed for it," Whit said, without even looking up. "Your uniform's the same color as the mildew."

"Damn, Whit, don't get testy with me. If I'd wasted some son of a bitch, I'd sure as hell remember where it happened."

Tony saw Whit start to rise. He put a restraining hand on his shoulder. "Just grab that top box, Monty. The one right over there."

* * *

Marsha Via and Tressa exited the funeral home precisely thirty minutes after they had gone inside. Rob sat on the front of his car, enjoying the warm afternoon sunlight.

Tressa was wiping tears from her eyes. "Daddy should have been here," she was saying to the deputy.

Rob eased off the hood. "How'd it go?"

"Very well," Marsha said. "They selected a lovely casket."

But Tressa's crying intensified. "How do I know what sorts of insurance Mother had? Aunt Miriam looked at me like I was stupid or something."

"At least Mr. Hardison knew about the state insurance," Marsha said. "That will cover the arrangements with some to spare."

"It's like some nightmare. I can't believe this is happening. They haven't even received Mother back from—"

"They will," Marsha said.

Rob, though, was frowning. "What was she saying?"

Marsha shook her head so Tressa wouldn't see.

But it was Tressa who answered his question. "They sent her to Charleston for an autopsy. She isn't back yet."

Marsha was opening the door. "I'll get in first."

Rob held the door as the deputy climbed into the back of the powder-blue compact. Tressa got into the front seat. She continued to wipe at her tears as Rob pulled away from the funeral home. "Where to now?"

"Maybe you'd better take me back to the motel so I can get my car," Marsha said. "Tressa's going to go to her house and find something for her mother to wear."

"Her blue dress," Tressa said. "If my aunt doesn't like it, she can go to hell."

"I'll be glad to run you over there," Rob said, glancing back at the female deputy. "It's kind of out of the way to go back to the motel. We could go back to the motel after Tressa picks out the clothes."

"Tressa was afraid that she might be tying you up."

Rob looked at Tressa. "You know better. I'm sticking with you like glue."

The young girl sagged with relief. "I'm glad," she said. "For some reason I dread going to the house. I haven't been back there since—" Her voice broke.

"You won't have to be there long," Marsha said.

"I can't get that image out of my mind," Tressa said, struggling against the tears. "That bastard riding out of the backyard on that hellish motorcycle, all dressed in black, with that grotesque helmet. He looked like something out of a space movie—some kind of monstrous spaceman."

Marsha's brow knitted. "Spaceman?"

"That's what he looked like," Tressa said.

Rob braked for a red light.

"Spaceman," Marsha mused. "I remember!"

Both Tressa and Rob looked back at her.

"I remember now. When I got a description of the guy, it rang a bell. Now I know why. Some old woman called in a few days ago and said she saw a spaceman in her yard."

"Where?" Tressa asked.

"Somewhere way out in the country. I thought it was one of those kook calls so—" She stopped in midsentence, her mind switching gears. "Rob, before we go to Tressa's house, stop at the courthouse. I wanna see if the note I made on the complaint is still on the blotter. Maybe there's a connection."

"The blotter?" Rob said.

"The desk blotter. You know, one of those desk pads the banks give away with blank sheets that you tear off. I'm usually the one who tears off the old ones, and I haven't torn this one off yet. The woman gave me directions to her home and her name."

"Here it is," Tony said, brandishing a thin folder.

"Not much to it," Whit said, reaching for it.

Tony handed it to him. "That's because you short-circuited the trial procedure."

"Very funny," Whit said, opening it.

The standard police report rested on top of the other papers. Whit's trained eyes scanned for the address of the subject—in this case, the address of Thomas Kirby, Sr., alias Buster Kirby.

"Shit. It's a post office box."

He flipped to the next sheet. It was his typed report on the incident. He started reading it. "Ah, here we go."

"So where is it?" Tony asked.

Whit was shaking his head. "Damn, I'm still not sure. According to what I wrote, you leave Milbrook on State Route 39 and drive until you reach State Route 212."

"That's the Eades Creek Road," Vickers said.

"You drive for three miles on Eades Creed Road and turn left at a red garage. That puts you on a private right-of-way that goes back a mile or so."

"No wonder you're confused," Vickers said.

"Why?" Whit asked.

"Not long after I came, they relocated the Eades Creek Road so they could dredge the creek. Eades Creek, remember?"

Whit snapped his fingers. "Of course. So the turnoff and the red garage is on the abandoned portion of the road . . . the old Eades Creek Road."

Vickers was shrugging. "I'd say from those directions that it would have to be. They dredged and straightened about six miles of the road because of the flooding in the northern section of the county."

"Do you know how to get on the old portion?" Whit asked.

"Uh, yeah. It's been awhile, but I think you have to go about two miles below where your directions leave off. I think they built a bridge over Eades Creek just so the folks who live on the old section of the road could get out. We don't seem to get many calls out that way."

"Let's go," Whit said.

"Whoa!" Tony said. "Let's think this thing out for a few minutes. I think more than two guys oughta go up there."

"I'll get Gil," Whit said. "He can call in some of his day-shift officers. We'll have enough."

Tony shook his head. "Damn, Whit, think about it. What if he's there with Anna? If so, you're going to end up with a hostage situation worse than the one before."

Whit nodded. "I know that, but there is no way to approach that house without being seen. I remember that much. He's got a wide killing ground on all sides."

"What's the terrain like?" Vickers asked.

"It's a typical hollow, Monty. The house sets at the very end, assuming it's still standing. The road comes up to the front door, and it's surrounded on the other three sides by forest."

"What if we wait until after dark?"

"Then we'll be blind," Whit said. "No way we can use flashlights, and we'd have to park way down the road and move up on foot. I don't think it matters. Either way he's going to see us."

Vickers pondered the dilemma. "It's kinda late today, but we could get a helicopter by tomorrow, maybe do a fly over."

"No way," Whit said. "I'm not waiting for tomorrow."

He turned to Tony. "I think the best bet is for me to go up by myself. One guy might get in close enough without being seen."

"That's crazy, Whit."

But Vickers was nodding his approval. "Not a bad idea. We could try to head up there now while there's still light. Keep in the woods. We could easily cover a mile by nightfall."

Whit was looking at the trooper. "What's this 'we' shit?"

"It's still my case, Whit. Besides, this is the kinda stuff I used to do in Vietnam. I was a real ace on night recon."

"I still don't like it," Tony said. "He might see you or see your car parked there."

"What's the alternative?" Whit snapped. "We've gotta go up there. You know it, and I know it. If we take an army up there, he can kill Anna—if he hasn't already—and make a break into the woods. Besides, maybe he isn't even there."

"As for transportation," Vickers said, "we can use some-one's private car and go out of uniform. They could drop us off just into the hollow and then haul ass outta there."

Tony looked to Whit. "You don't object to Vickers go-ing?"

"Like he said, it's still his case. I don't give a damn, just so long as we get our asses into gear."

"If Thomas Kirby, Jr., is up there, and if you do end up in trouble, what then?" Tony asked.

"I'll take a flare," Vickers said. "We could have some guys stationed somewhere outta sight somewhere above the mouth of the hollow on the old road. They see the flare, they come in like ghostbusters."

Whit managed a smile. "I like the way he thinks."

Tony remained undecided. "I dunno about this."

"What have we got to lose?" Whit asked.

Tony had an answer. "You've got Anna to lose. I've got a good state cop and you, who, I hesitate to add, is one of my best friends."

Whit bowed his head slightly. "I appreciate that, Tony. However, I think it gives us the best shot at getting Anna, assuming she's even there."

"Okay, go for it," Tony said. "You can use my car. Gil can drive you."

Rob cursed a car that screeched to a stop in front of him. Two cars ahead someone had stopped to back into a parking place. "I shoulda stayed off Main Street," he said to Tressa and Marsha. "Sometimes traffic in this town is as bad as getting around in some big city."

"It's because all the businesses are on this one street," Marsha said from the backseat.

"I'm gonna take a back street," he said, still stopped, waiting for the car ahead to wiggle into a tight parking space.

"You're through the worst," Marsha said.

But Rob was shaking his head. "I hate this kind of traffic."

The car ahead of him started to move. Rob gunned his engine and turned right at the first intersection they passed.

"Now you have to get across traffic to get to the courthouse," Marsha said, not pleasantly.

He was speeding down the street, not even bothering to turn left onto the residential streets that ran parallel to Main.

"Where are you going?" Tressa asked.

"I know what I'm doing." He was gazing straight ahead.

Marsha leaned forward. "For god's sake, Rob, we don't have time for this."

He slowed the car down. "Sorry, I just have a thing about traffic. I'll turn here and head back toward the courthouse."

Tressa glanced back at Marsha. "He can go around Orchard Drive and be right at the courthouse."

The deputy settled back. "Yeah, I guess he can."

They had driven so far away from the center of town that houses along the fringe of Milbrook were sparse, separated by spacious wooded lots.

"I like it out this way," Rob said.

Tressa didn't answer. Her thoughts had returned to the issue of her mother's funeral attire, specifically what jewelry she should get.

"If you take a right up ahead," Marsha was saying, "it'll be easier to get on the jail side of the courthouse. It's a little longer distance-wise, but you'll save time.'"

Rob accepted the advice. The narrow road led through an area that was being developed as a subdivision. The trees already had been bulldozed, and the developers were preparing to cut roads into the various building sites.

"I bet these places are going to cost an arm and leg," Marsha said, gazing out at the narrow strip of cleared land on her side of the vehicle.

Rob slowed the car down as he approached a portion of the street that was covered with a hump of mud. "Looks like a mess," he said. "The bulldozers did it crossing the road."

Tressa's thoughts remained on her mother. The deputy leaned to her left to get a better view of the street ahead. "It's not too bad."

But Rob stopped the car.

Tressa glanced at him. He was reaching under the seat.

"Now what's wrong?" Marsha said.

His hand came up with a compact black object.

# TWENTY-ONE

GIL AND MONTY VICKERS were over at the jail gathering their forces. Tony and Whit had stayed at the prosecutor's office where Whit was pacing the hall. He didn't like the wait. "C'mon, Tony, Gil can go ahead and take Vickers and me to the drop point. You can round up our backup people while we're making our way up the hollow."

Tony was shaking his head. "I still have my doubts about this, and I want to know that everything is in place before we move."

"We're losing time."

"A few more minutes won't matter."

"You don't know that," Whit said flatly.

"You're letting your emotions overrule your common sense, Whit. Think about it for—"

Vickers, accompanied by another trooper, entered the lobby. They saw Whit and Tony and headed down the hall toward them.

"We've got a faxed photo of the suspect," Vickers said, offering Tony a sheet of paper. "Pauley here ran it over from the detachment."

The prosecutor snatched it. Whit tried to peer over his shoulder.

"The quality's terrible," Tony said.

Whit, though, was studying the murky reproduction through squinted eyes. "He's familiar."

"Not to me," Tony said.

Whit pulled the paper from the lawyer's hands and held it as far away from his face as he could. "That damned beard covers half his face, but I know this guy from somewhere."

The photograph was little more than a smudged, very dark caricature of a person's face. The most pronounced aspect of the reproduction was the massive beard. It grew high on the cheeks. A bushy mustache obliterated the mouth. The face itself was haloed by long hair.

"His hair may not be that dark," Vickers said. "It just shows up that way in black and white."

"Is that the best we can get?" Tony asked.

Vickers looked to Pauley, the other trooper. "Did you all ask for them to send it again?"

"No, sir," Pauley said. "That's about as good as any of them are. 'Course we haven't gotten that many."

Whit studied the face. The eyes, that's what he seemed to recognize. He tried to reconstruct the image in his mind with a lighter color hair.

"We've got everyone rounded up," Vickers said. "Gil's ready to take us to the mouth of the hollow."

But Whit really wasn't listening. He continued to shake his head as he gazed at the face. "So help me God, I know this person from somewhere. How old did you say he was?"

"Twenty-seven," Vickers said.

"He looks older."

"It's the beard," said the other trooper. "Maybe he don't even have a beard now."

Whit's mind went to work again, this time visualizing the face without hair.

At that moment Gil came into the prosecutor's office. "Anybody know him?" he asked. "I looked at it over in the jail, and he looked sorta familiar."

"Same here," Whit said. He carried the sheet of paper into his office and placed it on the desk. The others crowded in behind him. Picking up two file folders, Whit placed one over the lower half of the face just below the nose. The other folder he placed over the forehead just below the hairline.

The face that glared back at him brought on a swift case of anxious nausea. "Ohmigod, Gil."

The sheriff frowned as he tried to put a name to the face. "Do you know him?"

"Hell, yes! You do, too," Whit said.

"I asked why you stopped," Marsha said.

Rob didn't answer. He jerked around, the dark object clutched in his hand.

Tressa thought she knew what it was, but she wasn't sure. Well, she was certain. She knew exactly what he had pulled from beneath the seat, but it seemed so out of place, so alien that it defied comprehension.

Tressa started to say something, but she didn't get the chance. Her ears were ringing and throbbing from the discharge of the small handgun.

Tony was on his tiptoes, looking over Whit's broad shoulder at the miserable fax reproduction. "So, who the hell is it?"

Gil's mouth dropped as he realized what Whit already knew. "Jesus, it's that kid Tressa's been seeing."

Whit was turning to Tony. "His name's Rob Fernandez. I mean that's what he calls himself. He was with Tressa and that female deputy at the motel. You saw him, Tony."

"I really didn't look at him that closely, but I can't remember him looking anything like that."

"Take off the beard and the long hair," Gil said.

Whit had slumped back on the desk. "And lighten the hair. It's him by God."

"Marsha should still be with them," Gil said.

Whit's hand snapped up the phone. "Maybe they're still at the funeral home."

Tony's hand went to his forehead. "Jesus, if that's who it is, we stood right there in front of him and talked about Thomas Kirby, Jr. He knows we're probably on to him—or will be soon."

"What's this 'we' stuff?" Gil said. "You did all the talking about Kirby."

Whit was talking to someone at the funeral home. He ended the conversation by slamming the phone down. "They left fifteen minutes or so ago in the kid's car."

"You killed my mother!" Tressa flailed at him with her hands, her nails. She should have been trying to get out the door of the car, but she wasn't. She was coming across the seat at him, punching and scratching and screaming.

Marsha Via sat in the backseat, her head driven back against the top of the seat, her dead eyes gazing upward at the roof of the car. The small caliber bullet had made a tiny ragged hole just above her left eye. It remained inside her lifeless brain.

Rob, caught beneath the steering wheel, tried to fend off her fury. He still had the gun in his hand, but he wasn't ready to kill Tressa—not just yet.

"You bastard," she shrieked, trying to reach his face with her fingers.

The compact automatic occupied his right hand, the one closest to her. He was trying to hold off her unexpected attack with his left. One of her nails reached his cheek. He felt the searing pain as it opened up the skin.

"Damn you, Tressa. I'll kill you now." He tried to display the gun, to brandish it at her, but she just kept coming at him, her fingers now talons that ripped at him.

He clenched his left fist and jabbed at her. His knuckles made rigid contact with her neck. He heard her gasp and cough as the blow pushed her back to her side of the seat. Trying to take advantage of the break in the assault, he shifted the .25 caliber automatic to his left hand. Before the transfer was complete, she was back at him, her nails digging for his eyes.

Now, though, his right hand was free. He reached through the furious windmill of her arms and managed to get his fingers on her throat. Her assault didn't let up, but his reach was much longer than hers. As a result her blows fell against his upper arm and shoulder.

He was panting now, winded by his efforts. "So help me, bitch, I'll kill you here and now."

He managed to adjust the gun in his left hand so that he could pull back the small hammer. With his right holding her at bay, he aimed it at her forehead. The keen click of the automatic's hammer froze Tressa. She stared at the small black opening in the barrel.

"Just get your hands away from me," Rob said.

Her fingernails were dug into the material of his shirt just below his shoulder. Tears streaked her face, and her jaws were trembling with fury.

*"Do it!"* he shrieked.

She dropped her hands into the seat.

"Scoot over as close to the door as you can get, but don't even think about opening it."

Tressa didn't move.

"Gawdammit, I told you to get over there."

"You . . . you—" She couldn't think of a bad enough word. She settled for "bastard" again.

His own chin quivered. His eyes flared in anger. "You call me that again, and I'll empty this gun in your face."

"I thought I loved you. I should have listened to Mother."

The car smelled of gunpowder. As Tressa moved away from him, she glanced back at Marsha Via. The sight produced another surge of anger, but he saw it coming and jabbed the gun at her face. "Don't do it. You know I'll kill you."

"You're going to anyhow," she said. "Have you killed Anna?"

He shook his head. "If you behave, I'm gonna take you to see her."

"Why?" she asked. "Just tell me why."

"Your father killed my father and mother."

"I don't believe that."

She could see his insanity now. It twisted his face into someone she really didn't recognize. His eyes were open wide, his pupils a little dilated, but he held the gun firmly.

When he spoke, it was through clenched teeth. "I don't give a shit what you believe. I was there."

"But my mother, Anna, the woman back there, the woman at the library, they didn't have anything to do with it."

"The first woman at the library was a mistake. You told me your mother was supposed to work Sunday night. That was your fault, bitch. You killed her."

"You're out of your mind, Rob."

"I'm not Rob."

"Oh yeah, I forgot. Just who the hell are you?"

"Thomas Kirby . . . Thomas Kirby, Jr. That's who I am. Your fuckin' father didn't even remember my father. I saw him back there at the motel when that shyster mentioned my father. Your bastard of a father didn't even remember him for chrissakes! How many people has your fuckin' father killed?"

"And you did all of this just to get back at him?"

"I wanna make him hurt. I want him to hurt like I've hurt."

"You're crazy."

She saw the fist coming at her, but there wasn't anything she could do. She tried to get her arm up to block the blow, but it came too quickly. His knuckles caught her just below her left ear.

Anna slipped between moments of agonizing reality and long hazy journeys into delightful fantasy. She had no control over it. If she had, she would have abandoned reality forever. It hurt too much. Her fingers were cold and tingly. The handcuffs cut deeply into her wrists. Blood streaked her arms and hands. She couldn't see the skin beneath the tight metal bands, but she imagined that the skin was gone—that the metal was chafing against exposed white bone. The misery made her try to freeze her hands and wrists against any movement, which in turn produced a tense twitching that brought back the torment.

Her dry tongue filled her mouth. The sensation gagged her. When she gagged, she coughed. The coughing drew the swollen lump of her tongue toward the back of her mouth, and she gagged some more.

Perhaps the worst thing about her periods of coherency was the realization that she had a long way to go before she died—a long, miserable, torturous time. She wanted to go to sleep, to drift away, hopefully forever. Over the past few hours she had tried to force her consciousness deep into the peaceful recesses of her head. It didn't work. The blessed relief possessed its own schedule. Maybe it was a matter of relaxation. Or maybe it happened when the physical agony reached some threshold of intolerance.

Whatever caused it, she smiled. She was sinking yet floating, drifting over and under, escaping the pain and the gagging and the coughing.

*Thank you, God . . . please take me, God . . . don't let me go back . . . don't—*

And then the discomfort simply was no more. She walked with Whit along a flat, white beach, hand in hand. A warm summer breeze caressed their faces. They had the wide beach to themselves. He was smiling, sort of bouncing as he walked, happier than she had ever seen him before. It was true. He became a different person at the beach. High grass-covered dunes flanked them on the right; on the left the blue-green ocean, alive with gentle swells that only whispered as they rolled onto the beach. Nothing existed beyond the dunes and the sea. She pulled him toward the dunes, toward a sandy, soft, and sensual cradle that she knew she would find among them, a place where they could curl against each other. There, they would hear the murmuring of the timid surf, the music of the seabirds, the slamming of a door—

Her eyes opened.

*The slamming of a door!*

The loud noise had wrenched her away from Whit, away from the beach, back to the place to which she never wanted to return.

"No!" she wailed aloud. Her will struggled against the return, but there other new noises that overwhelmed her and yanked her back to reality. Something crashed on the floor in the other room. That voice, the one that had always been just a harsh whisper . . . it was loud now, full-bodied, angry and insistent.

"Don't fight me, dammit!" He was talking to someone. He wasn't alone.

A heavy bulk slammed against the door that led into her prison. Anna made the mistake of trying to move. The searing pain bit into her wrists. Both hands started to burn. A scream followed her sharp intake of breath—her own scream, she realized, just as the door to her room burst open.

They planned to complete the initial debarkation quickly. At that point, the exercise was the most vulnerable, the most visible. Gil was driving an old and appropriately rusty Ford truck that belonged to one of his deputies. It blended well into the culture of the hollows, which was why they decided on it rather than Tony's new Lincoln. Monty Vickers and Whit were crowded into the front seat with Gil. Their gear, what little they planned to carry, was loaded into the bed of the truck. All three wore plain clothes—Gil, a denim jacket, a plaid shirt and jeans, while the trooper and Whit wore camouflage fatigues. In other places in the nation the two passengers might have looked a bit out of place. Not in mining country. The camouflage jackets had become a symbol of the growing militancy and activism of the United Mine Workers.

Though almost four o'clock, the sun still remained high. A good four hours of daylight remained, more than enough time for Whit and Vickers to hike along the edge of the hollow for a mile or so to their destination.

The road itself was narrow. On either side deep ditches made it almost impossible for two cars to pass at the same time. The foot of a wooded mountain cramped the road to their left. On the other side a guardrail and a short bank separated them from Eades Creek. During a normal spring, water from the surrounding mountains raged through its altered channel, but not this year. A narrow trickle snaked its way through the barren rock of the exposed creek bed.

"I hope to God we don't meet anybody," Vickers said.

Gil shrugged. "If we do, just throw up your hand and wave. We look right at home here."

"How far to the turnoff up the hollow?" Whit asked.

"According to the Department of Highway guys, we should get there any minute."

The mountain started to slip back from the road as the valley flared out. Whit moaned as several mobile homes came into view.

"Shit," Vickers said, "nobody mentioned them."

Gil slowed the truck and pointed. "There's the turnoff up to the Kirby place."

"With house trailers on either side," Whit said.

No one was in sight, but they were obviously occupied. Cars were parked in the barren front yards. Laundry hung behind one of them.

"What now?" Vickers asked.

Whit answered. "Turn around, Gil. Drive back around the curve. You can let us out there. We'll circle the ridge and stay pretty high up. I doubt anyone will see us."

Gil eased the car on up the road and actually pulled into the dirt road that led into the hollow. A door to one of the trailers opened.

The sheriff slammed the truck in reverse as a small boy came bounding out into the yard. He was waving.

"C'mon," Vickers urged. "Let's get outta here."

But Whit had another idea. "Stop a second, Gil."

Gil looked at Whit as if he had lost his mind. "We don't really wanna chat with the neighbors, do we?"

Whit was motioning for the small boy.

Vickers rubbed his forehead. "Is this a good idea, Whit?"

The kid approached the passenger side of the car, and Whit rolled down his window. "Hiya, kid."

"Howdy, mister. Lookin' for som'un?"

"Naw, not really. Just wondering where this side road leads."

The boy didn't even blink when he said, "Up the holler."

The kid was probably around six or seven. He wore a T-shirt and ragged jeans. Tennis shoes, looking like hand-me-downs three times removed, adorned his small feet. His face and hands, though, were clean, and his hear neatly trimmed.

Whit smiled. "Anybody live up there?"

"Sure, mister. The Manns, they live up there."

"The Manns?"

"You lookin' for 'em? I ain't seen 'em for a day or two."

"How many are there?" Whit asked.

The boy frowned. "How many what?"

"How many Manns? Up the hollow?"

"Just Mr. Mann and his wife. They're kinda old."

"That's all?" Whit asked, feeling a slight sinking feeling. "Nobody else?"

The boy was shaking his head. "No, sir."

"Shit," Vickers said.

Gil sighed.

The kid had paused, but he spoke again. " 'Cept for that guy on his motorcycle. He's been up to see 'em."

"Has he been up there today?" Whit asked.

The kid shrugged. "Don't know for sure. I just got in from school."

He shoved Tressa into the room. She fell on top of Anna. Her hands were bound behind her by a short length of rope. Her legs remained free. She tried to get to her feet, but he shoved her back down and quickly grabbed her ankles. With her feet in the air and her arms tied behind her, she was helpless. He wrapped a second piece of rope tightly around her ankles and then knelt to tie it to the huge eyebolt that protruded through the center of the floor.

As he did, Tressa glanced at Anna. "Are you all right?" Anna nodded.

"He killed Mother," she said.

Anna tried to speak, but her bloated tongue got in the way. Her words came out garbled and incoherent.

"What have you done to her?" Tressa cried.

"Just shut up, bitch."

"Go to hell," Tressa countered.

He jerked on the rope, causing Tressa to yelp in pain. "You stay down there. Don't even move."

"Bastard!"

He backhanded her. The force of the blow sent her head back against the floor, and for a moment she was stunned. By the time she regained her senses, he was in the front room.

Anna, tears streaming down her face, ignored the pain as she brought her cuffed hands up to touch Tressa's face. The young girl was starting to cry, too.

"That's Rob," Tressa said through her tears. "I mean, he's not Rob. That's just who he said he was."

Anna again tried to say something, but it was no use.

Tressa saw the streaked discoloration in Anna's hands. She saw, too, the dark circles around her friend's eyes, the sunken appearance. "Oh, Anna, what's he done to you?"

He stuck his head in the door. "Shut the fuck up!"

"You're gonna kill us, aren't you?" Tressa said.

He smiled, but it wasn't the same kind of smile that she had fallen in love with. This one was evil and mocking. It gave her chill bumps.

"I'm gonna go out on the front porch and wait for your dear old daddy. He'll be coming, and when I hear him, I'm gonna torch this place and slip off into the woods. Isn't that a good idea?"

"Bastard." This time, she muttered the word.

He heard it anyway. "Thass okay, bitch. You'll be saying worse than that when you burn alive."

# TWENTY-TWO

"LET'S GET OUR WATCHES synchronized," Vickers said.

"You and Gil handle that," Whit said, opening the truck door. "I don't wear one. I'll start getting the gear out of the back of the truck."

Gil had completed his turn around and had driven back around the curve. They were out of sight of the mobile homes.

"In exactly one hour, I'll bring in the other units. We'll go on up beyond those mobile homes and wait."

"What if the guy comes back after that? One of those folks might say something to him if they see a squad of police cars go by."

Whit had been listening as he checked the firearms they were going to be carrying. He came back to the open door. "I've been thinking about that. There are three mobile homes. Maybe when you return, you should send men into each one of them—put the lid on those people until after this is over."

Gil nodded. "Yeah, we can do that."

"There's something else," Whit said. "That kid—Rob, Kirby, whoever the hell he is. He was there when Tony came to the motel. He knows most of what we know. In other words, he knows we're onto him."

Vickers looked confused. "We talked about that earlier. What's the point?"

"He's probably desperate to accomplish whatever it is that he ultimately hopes to accomplish."

"Which is?" Gil asked.

"Kill Tressa . . . Anna, if he hasn't already done so. Kill me. I mean to say, I think he's desperate, but I don't think he's going to run. Let's get into the woods before he drives right by us."

Whit handed Vickers the high-powered rifle. "You take this. I want the shotgun."

Vickers accepted it as he exited the truck. "Fine by me. Those damn scatter guns bruise the hell outta my shoulder."

"I hope we don't have to shoot," Whit said.

They each donned a set of binoculars and strapped canteens on their belts.

"One hour," Gil said. "If you get there early, don't make a move until we're in place."

Whit had the flare gun in his hand and was studying the rugged terrain. "You think you all will be able to see this thing in the daylight?"

Gil shook his head. "Not worth a damn. Just fire off a shot from that blunderbuss, Whit. We'll hear that."

"But take the flare gun," Vickers said. "I think it'll be visible. It kicks out a lotta smoke in the daytime."

"Watch out for snakes," Gil said. "If you see one, try not to shoot it."

Vickers shivered. "God, I hate 'em."

The two woman could do nothing to comfort each other. Anna continued to seesaw between spells of lucidity and bouts of rambling fantasy. During the latter episodes, she talked to Tressa as if she were Whit. In other circumstances her comments would have been embarrassing to the younger woman, but nearly all of what Anna said was so garbled that Tressa couldn't understand it.

She could hear Rob, or whoever he was, moving about in

the front room. Several times he passed in front of the door, but he hadn't returned to the bedroom.

"Can you hear me?" Tressa whispered.

Anna's eyes rolled up at her. "Whit?" Her father's name was barely audible, hardly more than a muffled whisper.

"Listen for a minute, Anna. It's me . . . it's Tressa. We need to try to do something. If I turn around, can you try to untie my hands?"

Anna's only response was to tremble.

"Please, Anna! Try to understand me."

Tressa managed to work herself around to a point where she had a good view of Anna's hands. The grim sight crushed her plan. Both hands were discolored, the fingers inflated and ugly. Dried blood stained the upper side of her hands and had trickled down her arms.

"Your hands, Anna . . . can you move them? You need to try to get some blood circulating."

She sensed him before she actually saw him. He stood in the doorway, dressed completely in shiny black leather. A wide metal belt circled his waist. The hideous black helmet with its shiny faceplate was clamped under one arm. In the other he held a small Styrofoam cup.

"How could you?" she asked in a tone so civil that she even surprised herself. "I thought you felt something for me. How could you be so cold-blooded?"

No emotion colored his face. "I saw him kill my father. They killed my mother, too."

"Your father was a criminal."

His blue eyes narrowed. "Like father, like son."

"You sound proud of that."

He stepped into the room. "Your friend needs water," he said.

"She can't drink it without help."

He placed the cup of water on the floor and pulled something metallic from the pocket of the leather jacket. "I found these in that cunt cop's pocketbook. Sit up."

They were handcuffs. When Tressa saw them, she managed to work herself to a sitting position. He moved behind her. Anna was muttering.

His gentle touch was gone as he undid the knot in the ropes that bound Tressa's hands. "You try anything cute, and you'll regret it. I can make you hurt bad."

"You can't hurt me any worse than you already have," she said.

He jerked her arms up behind her back. The pain knifed into her shoulders, and she cried out.

"See, bitch. I can still hurt you. I can make you whimper if I want."

"Tesha!" Her name came from Anna.

"Be still," Tressa said, breathless from his demonstration. "We've got water for you."

He continued to work with the knot until her hands were free. She rubbed the red welts that circled her wrists, but her relief was only momentary. Quickly he was in front of her, clamping the metal cuffs on her wrists.

"Tresha?" Anna said something else, but Tressa couldn't understand her.

Tressa's attention was on the knot of rope affixed to the eyebolt. If he left her as she was, she could use her hands to loosen the knot.

"What are you going to do now?" she asked, hoping to keep his mind occupied, so he wouldn't think about the knot through the eyebolt.

"Take a little trip down the road."

The pace of her heart quickened. "How come you're giving her water?"

He checked the cuffs and was evidently satisfied. He stood. "I may need her to move. Don't let her drink it all at one time."

She stared up at him, waiting for him to leave.

He didn't. Instead he said, "Go ahead—give her a couple of sips."

Dammit, thought Tressa.

She reached down and retrieved the cup. It wasn't even half full. "Is this all?" she asked.

"I don't want her getting sick."

Tressa turned to Anna. "Can you sit up? Here's some water."

Anna licked her lips as she tried to comply with Tressa's wish, but the best that she could do was to lift herself up on her elbows. The tautness of the cuffs brought tears to her eyes.

"Look at her hands!" Tressa cried. "They're turning black."

"That's her fault," their captor said. "Same thing'll happen to you if you're not careful. I know a lot about handcuffs."

"I bet you do," Tressa said.

She managed to tip a little water into Anna's mouth. It strangled her, and she started to cough.

"I warned you," he said. "Just a few drops at a time."

"You're making me nervous," Tressa said, wanting more than anything for him to leave them alone.

He just grinned at her. "Tough shit, bitch."

How could one person be so different? As she allowed a few more drops to fall into Anna's mouth, she couldn't help but remember him as he had been. Sweet and tender, never cross, never pushy. Even when they made out, he was the one who showed the restraint. She should have suspected something then.

"That's enough," he said. His foot shot forward to kick the cup from Tressa's hand. The water spilled all over Anna, who started to bawl.

"Get outta here," Tressa shrieked.

"You'd like that, wouldn't ya, bitch . . . so you could lean down and untie the rope. You think I'm dumb? A dummy couldn't have pulled this off."

He reached down and grasped the short metal chain that connected the cuffs. He was close, his face within inches of Tressa. She spit. The gob of saliva hit his right cheek.

The blow to her cheekbone came from her blind side. It knocked her over on top of Anna.

"I really dreaded killing you," he said, his eyes full of hate and anger. "I did, Tressa. I really did. Now, I'm looking forward to it. I'm not even sure I wanna wait for your fuckin' father to see it."


"Listen," Whit whispered.

He and Vickers had navigated maybe a half mile of their trek. A little more than a hundred yards below and off to their right, the narrow dirt road snaked its way up the hollow. The going was slower than they anticipated. It wasn't just a simple slope. High up on the ridge they encountered long stretches of rocky cliff. They worked their way along the bottom of them, dodging gargantuan boulders and treacherous rock formations.

Vickers stopped. "Whaddaya hear?"

"An engine."

The trooper heard it, too. "A chain saw?"

"No," Whit said, "it's a cycle."

"Coming up or down?"

The spring foliage remained somewhat spotty, but there was enough growth to obstruct their view of the road. "He's coming down," Whit said.

Vickers unslung the rifle. "If he's alone, maybe I can get a shot."

Whit snatched the weapon. "Jesus, Monty, what if you miss? Listen, if he's actually living up here, then maybe

Tressa, Anna, and the deputy are still at the house. We can get them out while he's gone."

"What if they're not up there?" Vickers asked.

Whit shrugged. "In that case, if you happen to kill him, we may never find them."

The engine noise increased quickly. They saw the dust before they actually saw him. When they did catch sight of their quarry, it was only momentary glimpses between the bright new green leaves of the deciduous forest.

"He's got the helmet on," Whit said, "just like Tressa described him."

Vickers was checking his watch. "Jesus, it's almost been an hour. He might run right into our guys."

"I hope they have sense enough to grab him," Whit said. "Let's get a move on. It can't be much further."

"Tressa?" She spoke the name of Whit's daughter with remarkable clarity.

"You feel better already?"

Anna nodded. "My mouth anyway. My belly's cramping, though, I feel like I'm going to be sick. My hands, they're numb and cold all at the same time."

"It's Rob, Anna. He's the killer."

"Rob?" The name didn't at once strike any chord of memory.

"Rob, Anna! Rob Fernandez. The boy I was seeing."

Anna grimaced and closed her eyes. "I'm sorry, Tressa."

"He killed my mother."

"I know, hon. He told me. I think he told me. My mind's so fuzzy."

"Mother's impression was right. She hadn't even met him, but she didn't like him."

"Why?" Anna asked. She started to cough before Tressa could answer.

"Oh, Anna, it's all my fault. He killed a woman deputy, too."

Anna sucked in air, trying to get her breath. "But why?" she asked again.

"Daddy killed his father. His mother, too. Or at least that's what he says."

"When?"

Tressa shook her head. "I don't know. A long time ago, I think, when he was little. He said he saw it."

"How's Kathy?" Anna asked.

A small smile appeared on Tressa's face. "She's going to be okay."

Anna sagged in relief.

"I wonder where he went," Tressa said.

"He'll be back," Anna said.

This time Vickers heard him first. "He's coming back this way."

They had seen the small house as they had crossed a rocky ridge that ran vertically up the slope. Whit recognized the powder blue car parked behind a new pick-up truck. It convinced him that the hostages were probably in the house. The house disappeared from sight, though, as they moved down the ridge. The trees had thinned somewhat, and the road itself was in plain view.

Whit heard the bike, too. The machine was flying. "Maybe he saw the backup units."

For the second time Vickers was readying his weapon. "Let me try to take him, Whit."

"Christ, Monty, it's a good hundred yards."

"I think I can do it."

"What if you miss?"

"As loud as that damned cycle is, he may not even hear the shot."

Vickers had a point. The whining roar of the engine was

getting closer. "Decide quick, Whit. If he has got them in that house, and he gets back inside—"

"Okay, take him."

Vickers dropped to his knees and positioned the barrel of the rifle against a tall birch tree. Whit didn't even bother with his shotgun. The range was much too great.

"Here he comes," Whit said.

Vickers had the stock of the weapon pressed tightly against his face. Whit could hear him breathing. "Take it easy," he said.

The bike came into view. Its driver huddled very low, his chest pressed down almost on top of the wide handle bars. Dust shot out from the rear, creating the impression that the machine was propelled by some loud rocket engine.

"If you don't think you can make the shot, Monty, give—"

The rifle cracked.

"—it up." Whit finished saying, his eyes locked on the flying mass of black.

Just as the bullet reached the cycle, the front wheel hit a small pothole. It launched the machine a few feet into the air. The slug struck just below the driver's chest, smack dab in the middle of the gas tank.

The cycle went one way, its driver the other.

"Jesus," Whit cried, "let's get down there."

"Where is he?" Vickers asked, looking up over the barrel.

"He was thrown into the brush on this side. I think you missed him and hit the bike."

The motorcycle itself had careened into the woods and was on its side, white smoke rising up as the gas spilled on the hot manifold.

The two men crashed down the side of the mountain. The road remained in sight until they were within twenty-five feet of it. At that point the density of the forest increased.

"How do you know I didn't hit him?" Vickers was asking.

Whit was in front, pushing his way through the increasingly tangled thicket that grew along the road. "I don't know for sure. If you didn't, maybe the son of a bitch broke his neck in the fall."

Just before he broke through to the dirt road, Whit jerked back the handle of the pump and slammed a shell into the breech of the gun. The motorcycle rested on the other side of the road. White smoke continued to boil up from it, and the stench of gasoline drifted through the still air.

With the gun in front of him, Whit moved quickly up the road, his eyes scanning the brush. Vickers was behind him, his rifle held at the ready.

"I bet he's headed into the woods," Vickers said.

Whit didn't think so. "I'd say he's headed right up the road . . . right back to the house. I wish to hell that you'd hit him."

"I would have if he hadn't hit that hole right when I squeezed the shot off."

"He might be up there waiting to ambush us."

Whit was already moving up the road. "Let's just hope he's as good a shot as you."

"Dammit, Whit, I tried." Vickers pulled the flare gun from inside his belt. "I'll give the signal."

"Save it," Whit said.

"C'mon, Whit, I'm in no mood to play cowboy. I'm calling in the backup."

"They'll be here," Whit said. "Just as soon as they see the smoke and hear the explosion."

"What smoke? What explosion?"

Whit pointed back down toward the motorcycle. The billowing smoke had been replaced by a blazing fire that was spreading quickly in the dry tinder.

"Christ," the trooper cried, making a move toward the budding conflagration.

Whit reached and grabbed him. "Some other time, Monty. The gas tank on that cycle could go at any minute."

"Oh, shit. Let's go."

They were still in sight of the fire when the small gas tank blew.

—*warumph*—

They both dropped down to the dusty surface of the road as scraps of hot metal showered down upon them.

"Jesus," Vickers cried, brushing a small searing sliver from the back of his hand.

Whit glanced back over his shoulder. Bits of burning plastic and stuffing from the cycle's seat dropped into the dry woods on the other side of the road. Flames leaped up almost at once from the spots where they landed. A small mushroom cloud of dark smoke rolled high into the sky.


"That was a gunshot," Gil said.

He stood at the front of his cruiser with Tony. Eight other police vehicles were parked in a line behind it. All of the officers, a combined force of troopers and deputies, were out of their car.

Bill Conners came up from his vehicle. "That wasn't no shotgun. I thought he was gonna fire a shotgun."

Gil looked to the prosecutor. "Let's move. It's close enough for me."

A deeper blast, more like a sharp rumble, punctuated his words.

"Look!" someone cried.

Gil turned and saw a trooper pointing upward. He followed the officer's finger and saw the ball of black smoke lifting above the ridge. "Uh-ohhh. That looks like big trouble."

In the wake of the initial dark smudge, a column of white smoke lifted into the deep blue of the afternoon sky. "A fire," another officer cried.

A moment of stunned silence swept across the gathering.

It was Tony who shattered it. "Somebody radio back and tell them we've probably got a forest fire."

Gil was shaking his head. "Those mountains will go up like the Fourth of July."

"We'd better move," Tony said, hurrying back to the door of the car.

Gil, hopping in deference to the stiffness in his knee, piled in behind the steering wheel. "I hope that fire hasn't cut us off." He hit the car's ignition.

"Maybe our suspect set it on purpose."

Gil's tires screamed as he pulled onto the narrow highway and headed toward the turnoff that would take them up the hollow. "If so, Tony, he just might have committed suicide."

"I smell smoke," Tressa said.

Anna sniffed. "Me, too."

At that instant Thomas Kirby, Jr., alias Rob Fernandez, bounded through the front door of the cabin and straight into the bedroom. His outfit wasn't so shiny anymore. In fact, it was covered with dust.

"Your gawdamn father's on the way, bitch. He's gonna die, bitch. And so are you, roasted alive, just like I said."

"What's that smoke?" Tressa asked.

Thomas Kirby cackled as he spoke. "A forest fire. Your smart-ass daddy set the damned woods on fire. So he's gonna be the one to kill you, not me."

He continued laughing wildly. "I think it's neat. I couldn't have worked it out better."

"You're crazy," Tressa shrieked.

Anna was looking out the window. She could see the clouds of smoke rolling by the house. Already she could feel it stinging her eyes. She started to try to say something to him, but when she looked away from the window, he was heading back into the front room.

He vanished from sight for a few moments. When he reappeared in the doorway, he carried a small shotgun. "You girls get down. I wouldn't want you shot. That'd be too easy."

He disappeared again. Moments later, they heard the loud, flat blast of the gun, followed by that maniacal cackling.

# TWENTY-THREE

THE LOAD OF BUCKSHOT delivered by the shotgun exploded in the dust of the road two yards in front of Monty Vickers, spraying him with sand and ricocheting pellets. He dived into the dust, trying to rub away the sting from his cheeks.

Whit dropped beside him. "Are you all right?"

"Christ, he almost got my eyes."

The sound of the shotgun had almost been lost in the mounting roar of the fire as it sucked in the air that was its fuel. Whit looked back at the increasing intensity of the blaze. "We won't be getting any help from that direction. You go to the left. I'll take the right."

Vickers continued to rub his face. It was dirty, streaked with a combination of dirt and sweat. "The fire's coming this way, Whit. It's gonna overrun us and the house. Those cars in the driveway will blow us all to Kingdom Come if their gas tanks go."

"On the other hand," Whit said, "they may be our way outta here."

"C'mon, Pynchon, get fuckin' real."

"So what do you wanna do, Vickers? Just lay here and get scorched? We stand a better chance in the open area near the house."

"If the bastard doesn't shoot us!" The trooper was yelling now, trying to be heard against the constant sound of the fire.

"Just stay low. Let's go."

Vickers glanced behind him. The fire's vanguard, a dancing flicker of a brushfire, was within ten yards of them. "Mother of God," he said, scrambling up the road on his hands and feet.

A second explosion of dust kicked up beside Whit, who was several yards ahead of the trooper, moving toward the cover of the old well near the front of the yard. With his own shotgun, and still on the move, Whit unloaded a barrage of his double-ought and then jacked another shell into the chamber. He fired it, too. Both times his weapon had been pointed into the air. He didn't want to take a chance on hitting any hostages that might be in the house.

Vickers was moving toward the other side of the yard and the two vehicles that occupied the short drive leading up to a side entry into the house.

Whit shouted at him, but the trooper couldn't hear him. The air rushing into the fire was deafening, something like the sound of a jet engine. They were so close to the blaze that the smoke wasn't a problem. It billowed above the flames and settled to the ground far beyond the small frame house. Whit pumped another shell into the gun and discharged it into the air.

Vickers heard that. He glanced at Whit. The kid in the house must have heard it, too. The small pellets from his weapon slammed into the wooden structure that surrounded the well. Whit ducked beneath, maintaining his eye contact with Vickers. He motioned for the trooper to move around to the back of the house.

Vickers mouthed the word, "What?"

"Around back!" Whit shouted, motioning.

The trooper nodded. He didn't start to move, though. Instead, he lifted his rifle and aimed it at the house.

"Nooo!" Whit cried.

The sharp crack of the rifle, so different from the flat concussion of the shotguns, was easily heard above the fire's sound.

Whit stood, waving his arms, shaking his head. Vickers, though, was aiming. He fired a second time. Whit was just about to break across the yard for the trooper when he saw Vickers jerk, then drop to the ground. He rolled one way, then the other, his left arm clutching his right shoulder. Whit couldn't see any blood against the dark green of the trooper's uniform, but there was no doubt that the trooper had been hit.

The blaze was filling the valley with a windy heat. Sweat rolled down Whit's face, stinging his eyes. The seething inferno was already warming his back.

The well, he thought.

"Well water," he said aloud. It would cool him, cool his clothing.

He glanced at Vickers who had stopped rolling and had managed to pull himself against one of the vehicles. His chin was slumped down on his chest, but Whit could see his hands moving. He was alive.

Whit then turned his attention to the ancient structure of the well. It might have been here when he came to arrest Thomas Kirby, Sr. It probably was; he just hadn't noticed. A rope, attached to the handle, descended into it. Whit eased a hand to the wooden handle and tried to turn it. It wouldn't budge.

"Dammit," he said aloud.

A shotgun blast from the house drove him back down to the ground. The rope reaching down into the well was fouled somehow. He waited for a few moments, then reached for the handle again. Still, he couldn't budge it.

He dared to lift his head above the short wall to peer down inside.

"Jessusss!" He reeled back away, appalled by the odor and the sight—the stench of death, the bloated darkening face of a corpse, the rotting body entangled in the well's rope.

"We can't make it!" Gil shouted.

"Dammit, man, we've got to get through," Tony countered.

The two men were at the front of the column of police cruisers. The smoke was worse on that side of the fire. Through the blinding haze, some twenty yards ahead of them, they could see the blazing skeleton of a once-towering pine obstructing the narrow dirt road.

"There's no way."

"A copter," Tony said. "The state police have a copter."

But Gil was shaking his head. "The turbulence around that fire would bring it down."

"Christ Almighty, Gil, we've gotta do something."

"Yeah, what we've got to do is get ourselves outta this hollow before the fire gets behind us."

"Dammit, Gil—" The prosecutor reached over to place a hand on the steering wheel.

Gil lifted it away. "C'mon, Tony, I'm as worried as you, but Whit's a big boy. He's got Vickers with him. I've got a little faith in both of them."

Tony just nodded.

Gil picked up his mike and keyed it. "Let's start backing outta here. Get a move on it."

Ashes were cascading down on the hood of Gil's cruiser as he waited for the vehicles behind him to move. "I know how you feel, Tony. It's the sense of helplessness. The forest rangers are sending a copter in to get an aerial view of the fire. Maybe there's enough of a clearing around the house to set down. I'll check with them."

"I know it's probably a waste of time," the lawyer said. "I mean because of the turbulence, but if we could just see what was going on up there."

Gil was watching the ash as it formed a thick layer on the hood. "I know what's going on. They're going through the worst kind of hell this side of dying."

As much as he needed water from the well, Whit didn't take a second look inside. He suspected the body was that of the old woman who had lived here. The old man was probably inside, too, down in the bottom. The Manns, according to the kid who lived down at the mouth of the hollow. He looked over to Vickers. The trooper was trying to crawl, his right arm dangling uselessly on the ground.

"Stay put!" Whit screamed.

Vickers couldn't hear him. Given the look in his eyes, the trooper was in shock. Whit had no choice. He had to try to get across the open killing ground to Vickers. The fire seemed intent on doing whatever it could to frustrate Whit. Besides the obvious, the probability that it would toast all of them, the damned blaze didn't even have the decency to drop its smoke on them. Whit could have used it for cover.

He slid three more shells into the cartridge chamber of the shotgun, inhaled deeply of the hot air, and made a break for the trooper. He expected to feel the scalding touch of buck-shot.

But inside the house Thomas Kirby, Jr., was saying good-bye to the two women.

"Are you going to kill us now?" Tressa asked. A rope attached to the short link of chain between the handcuffs was also secured to the leg of the bed. Since the rope on her ankles was still tied tautly to the eyebolt, she couldn't even move. Every time she tried, the handcuffs compressed against her wrists.

He chuckled. "Not much need. The fire'll do it for me, hon. I'm gonna sneak out the back door, kill your son of a bitchin' old man, and then get away into the woods. I just wanted you to know what's going to happen since you won't have a very good view.''

Anna's eyes burned from the fumes gathering in the house, but the few sips of water she had received had helped her tongue. ''You'll never get away.''

''She talks!'' Kirby said, smiling broadly. He knelt down beside her. ''You know, I never figured on getting away either. That was fine by me. Thanks to that fire Tressa's old man started, I think I can manage it. The other cop's probably dead. Even if I don't get Pynchon, he won't chase after me. He'll try to save you two. In just a few minutes that'll be impossible, once the fire manages to circle around behind the house. Oh, and I'll be out there in the woods just to make sure, well ahead of the fire of course. So I get a free ticket out of here if I can run fast enough, and I've always been able to run.''

He stood.

Tressa tried to kick at him. The vain effort made the cuffs on her wrist click one notch tighter. She whimpered in pain.

''Don't worry,'' he said, smiling. ''It won't last much longer. You'll probably suffocate before the flames get to you.''

Then he was gone. They heard the back door open and then slam shut.

Whit pulled the trooper back to the cover of Kirby's car. ''C'mon, Monty, you gotta stay under cover.'' Whit could see the blood now. It glistened on the dark green fabric of Vickers's uniform. The blast from the shotgun had ravaged the trooper's shoulder.

''The fire,'' Vickers said. ''The cars. They'll blow up.''

Whit looked at the approaching flames. The fire itself was spreading up the mountain slopes as quickly as it was coming toward them at the head of the hollow. "We've got a few minutes yet," he said.

The ash was starting to fall on them. It reminded Whit of a hot, black snow. Some of the particles still glowed with live sparks. "Stay down," Whit said. "I'm gonna try to draw his fire . . . find out which window he's at."

Whit slowly raised his eyes above the rear of the blue car. That's when he saw the head that was visible in the backseat of Kirby's car. Its hair glistened with coagulating blood. It took his breath away until he realized that it wasn't Tressa. Nor was it Anna.

The female deputy then . . . Via. She was dead.

Thomas Kirby, Jr., was a killing machine. It boggled Whit's mind. It also created a cold, gnawing tumor of fear in his gut. What were the chances that Anna and Tressa were even alive? Slim to none, he decided, and braced himself for it. He lifted his head even higher. If both of them were gone, then it didn't give Whit much reason to care.

He saw nothing in the windows of the small house. A movement on the roof, though, caught his attention. A small flicker! A fire! One of the larger pieces of ash had caught the old tar roofing on fire.

"Jesus," he said.

He was leaning against the trunk of the car, frozen by the sight of the fire. The car itself shifted a little. It was enough of a warning. Whit looked to his left just in time to see Kirby come up with the small shotgun in his hand. The boy's eyes reflected the fire behind Whit. It made them sparkle with madness.

Whit rolled off to the side of the car just as the gun exploded. Most of the blast missed him, but several spheres of lead buried themselves in Whit's upper arm. The pain was fierce as he dropped into the rough gravel of the driveway. He still possessed the presence of mind, though, to look at once for Kirby. But he was nowhere to be seen. Where the hell had he gone?

There was a second blast. Whit was prepared to accept it . . . and whatever followed, but he felt nothing. Somehow he still clutched his own twelve-gauge pump. He managed to roll away from the car and looked under it, intending to fire the shotgun at Kirby's feet if he saw them.

No feet, none at all, but he did see Vickers slumped fully on the ground, his face ravaged by that second blast, the one that Whit had expected to receive.

"Damn you!" Whit shouted. He sprung to his feet, his furious gaze scanning the hellish landscape for the silhouette of the killer. He had vanished again.

Whit made a break for the front door of the house.

Anna's coughing became constant. Her body, already weakened by dehydration, couldn't tolerate the smoke that was filling the small house. The helplessness infuriated Tressa. She struggled against her bonds and clenched her teeth against the pain. Somehow, by some way, she was going to get loose. She had to get loose.

"Tressa!"

The voice shocked her. She looked toward the door.

"Daddy!"

He rushed to her. "Thank God, you're alive. And Anna, too. Oh, thank God."

Then he saw the cuffs. "Oh, Jesus, we've gotta get you two loose. The house's burning."

"The ropes, Daddy. Just cut the ropes. We can manage to walk out with the handcuffs on."

Whit, though, was struggling with the rope that was knotted through the eyebolt. Tressa's constant tension had pulled it tight. Above him he could hear the crackling of the flames as fire filled the house's small attic. Smoke poured down from the surface of the ceiling. His eyes started to water.

"Dammit to hell!" he shouted, his own frustration making the task even more difficult.

Finally, as if he'd found the key to some mystical puzzle, the knot came loose. He moved up his daughter's form until he reached the small rope that held her to the leg of the bed. He didn't bother with the knot. He simply lifted the bed and pulled the knot off.

"Get Anna," Tressa said. "I can do the rest."

Anna hadn't said a word. She continued to cough, but she was also smiling at him. He managed to smile back and said, "I thought I'd never see you again."

Then he realized that she was bound to the eyebolt by a chain and lock. "Damn . . . damn . . . damn." His eyes frantically scanned the room, looking for something—anything—to break the chain.

Seeing nothing, he bolted for the front room. He returned seconds later with a metal poker that had been sitting beside the small fireplace. He inserted the tip of the poker in the lock and wrenched. The long shaft of metal started to bend. Above them, a section of the ceiling broke loose. Fire and ash billowed into the room. Tressa screamed. Whit kept wrenching, putting the full weight of his body behind it. The poker bent even more, but finally something broke. It turned out to be a link of the chain. Whit dropped to his knees beside Anna and gathered her into his arms.

Even with her hands painfully cuffed, Tressa had managed to get to her feet.

"Out the front," Whit cried.

She ran. Whit followed at a much slower pace with Anna cradled in his arms. The heat in the house was intense. As they stumbled out the front door, it wasn't much cooler. The inferno surrounded them. The clearing in which the house stood had become the eye of some blistering hurricane. The roar was deafening. Hot wind lashed at them. Tressa, unable to use her hands to balance herself, stumbled down the steps.

When she got to her feet, she started to turn, looking for some place to which they could escape.

Whit, still carrying Anna, eased down the steps. He passed her and headed toward the side of the house. Tressa looked at him, her face full of helpless fear.

"Over this way!" Whit shouted. He was nodding to his left, away from the cars parked in the driveway.

The truck that was parked in front of Kirby's car was already starting to suffer from the heat of the house fire. The paint on its hood and right front fender was bubbling and peeling.

Whit saw it. "Hurry! That looks like a root cellar over there." Anna continued to cough. She buried her face against Whit's chest. If she had to die, she wanted to be as close to him as possible.

As she rounded the corner of the house, Tressa saw the old wooden door resting flat on the ground. It was located about fifteen feet from the house.

"Open it!" Whit shouted.

She bent over and wrenched it open. Cool musty air rushed out at her.

"Jump in," Whit ordered.

At other times, Tressa would have worried about the spiders and worms that surely must inhabit the dank darkness below her. This time, though, the terror on the outside was far more fearful. She dropped into the hole. It was about four feet deep and was still cool. Beneath her feet, she felt round objects that collapsed into mush beneath her weight. She didn't care. In the heat of the fire storm's eye, it felt as if she had dropped into a refreshing pool of water.

Whit dropped to his knees and lowered Anna into the pit. He jumped in then, wedging himself into the cramped space that was left. He pulled the door closed over them.

The savage roar of the fire lessened as the comparatively cool darkness engulfed them.

"Will we live?" Tressa said.

"If we don't suffocate," Whit said. "The fire is consuming so much oxygen."

Anna's coughing eased. In the blackness of the hole, Whit couldn't see her, but he felt her hand reach up and touch his face. "What took you so long?" she whispered, her voice hoarse and very weak.

Before he could answer, fiery light flooded their sanctuary. It momentarily blinded Whit. He didn't see Kirby at first. He just heard him.

"Out!" the kid was shouting.

Then Whit's eyes adjusted. He was able to see the kid, standing above them, holding the wooden door. The shotgun was pointed right in at them.

"Out! Out! Out!" he was shrieking.

Kirby's face was blackened by soot. His hair had been scorched. Strips of skin dangled from his roasted face.

Whit's immediate instinct was to reach for his weapon. But he didn't have it. Somewhere he'd lost it or left it.

Behind Kirby, Whit could see the holocaust—flames streaming skyward, giving the smoke the color of blood. "If we're gonna die, kid, it's gonna be in here."

Thomas Kirby lifted the shotgun to his shoulder. Whit closed his eyes. The explosion was earth-shattering. The walls of the pit actually moved, but, other than the concussion, Whit felt nothing else. He jerked open his eyes just in time to see Kirby engulfed in a surging wall of flames. The kid shrieked and let go of the root cellar door. It smacked shut. Something hammered down on top of it—the kid himself, Whit figured. He reached up and grabbed the inside handle and held it tight. A second explosion, this one even worse than the first, caused dirt to sift down from the sides of the pit.

Both Anna and Tressa were pressed against Whit.

"What is it, Daddy?"

The metal handle on the interior of the homemade door was becoming scorching hot. Whit, though, refused to release it. "The cars," Whit said. "The gas tanks in the cars. They exploded."

# EPILOGUE

THE FIREFIGHTERS HAD just started to map their offensive against the blaze when the rain came. The boiling clouds of smoke had concealed the threatening sky, and they hadn't really expected rain anyway. There was a fifty-fifty chance in the forecast, but then it had been in the forecast a lot lately. Other than a few sprinkles, it had never materialized.

The first drops started falling around six-thirty that evening. Within ten minutes a steady moderate rain began. It was the kind of rain that nourished the soil rather than the usual spring deluges that washed down the mountainsides in great muddy gouts. The firefighters had cheered.

Gil and Tony had gone up at once in the chopper. The land was still hot, steaming now instead of smoking, but the fires were dying down. Curved wiper blades kept the rain off the front of the cockpit as the pilot guided the machine up the ravaged hollow. The other two men were silent. They were as glad as the rangers and firefighters that the rain had come, but both of them figured it was too little and too late.

"If this keeps up," the pilot said, trying to make conversation, "the boys won't have anything to do. It's nice to see God cooperate once in a while."

Gil was peering ahead. Dusk was still about an hour away, but under the thick clouds, aided and abetted by the steam and smoke, it was already almost dark. "There's the house," Gil cried. "What's left of it anyway."

The chopper pilot descended, clutching the stick as he encountered the rising turbulence created by the superheated ground. "Hang on."

They dropped toward the square foundation that represented the remains of the house.

"We've got bodies," the pilot said. "One at nine o'clock and another at two o'clock."

Both Gil and Tony had to consciously visualize the face of a clock in order to pinpoint them. Even then, they weren't certain that the formless lumps of charcoal were actually bodies.

"How can you tell?" Tony asked.

"Spent a lotta years doing this over Nam," the pilot said. "Take my word for it, they're bodies."

The copter hovered.

"Look," Gil cried, "that one's moving."

The pilot adjusted his horizontal attitude so they all could see. The dark mass was moving, rolling actually.

"Christ," Tony said. "There's some kind of door under the body. It's opening!"

The pilot dared to drop the copter a little lower. "Jesus," he muttered as the blackened corpse came to rest.

The charred door flopped back on the ground. Whit Pynchon emerged from the hole. He waved and held out his hands to cup the rain. Two other heads appeared.

"Two women," the pilot said.

"Great!" Gil clapped. "It's Tressa and Anna."

They waited for more survivors to emerge. None did.

## ABOUT THE AUTHOR

Dave Pedneau is a former reporter, columnist, and magistrate court judge. His novels include A.P.B., D.O.A., and B.O.L.O., all published by Ballantine. He lives in southern West Virginia with his wife and daughter.

*Follow*
*Whit Pynchon and Annie Tyson-Tyree*
*on the trail of murder*
*in these novels by*
# DAVE PEDNEAU.

## A.P.B.

A serial killer is loose. The victims: wives of local cops. This one gets personal for Pynchon, and dangerous for Tyson-Tyree.

## D.O.A.

A double shooting of a young girl and her pregnant mother send Pynchon and Tyson-Tyree off to find out what the victims knew that turned out to be so deadly.

## B.O.L.O.

Hard drugs, mass slaughter—this is a bad one. A killer who never misses lures Annie into his gunsights. And this time Whit can't help her.